DATE			

Hidden Pictures

Novels by Meg Wolitzer

♦

SLEEPWALKING

HIDDEN PICTURES

♦

Hidden Pictures

〓〓 ⋘ ✦ ⋙ 〓〓

Meg Wolitzer

Houghton Mifflin Company ✦ Boston ✦ 1986

Library of Congress Cataloging in Publication Data

Wolitzer, Meg.
Hidden pictures.

I. Title.
PS3573.0'564H5   1986   813'.54   85-31695
ISBN 0-395-36002-1

Printed in the United States of America

Q 10 9 8 7 6 5 4 3 2 1

For Nancy Davis
Gary Glickman
and in memory of
Julia Reynolds Cameron

It may be said that natural selection is daily and hourly scrutinising, throughout the world, every variation, even the slightest; rejecting that which is bad, preserving and adding up all that is good; silently and insensibly working, whenever and wherever opportunity offers . . . We see nothing of these slow changes of progress, until the hand of time has marked the long lapse of ages, and then so imperfect is our view . . . that we only see that the forms of life are now different from what they formerly were.

—Charles Darwin, *On the Origin of Species*

PART ONE

Find the
Hidden Pictures

There were twenty objects hidden in the tree. There was a hat, a glove, a soup spoon, a diamond ring, and a snow boot, among others. All of them were folded in among the branches and the trunk, pretending to be part of that tree. Laura could draw these pictures perfectly. It was her talent, this rendering and concealing. She had started working on them when her marriage began to fall apart, and they calmed and distracted her. She usually opened with a few lines of text, such as: "Mrs. Brown came home one day to find that all of the things in her house had blown away. Can you help Mrs. Brown find her missing objects? There are twenty of them altogether."

Laura had been doing illustrations for *Jumping Bean* magazine for over a year, and now she had been given her own page each month. She also did other assignments for the magazine: illustrations for stories and poems, and once, for the special Halloween issue, she had been given the cover. Still, it was the hidden pictures page that she loved best and spent the most time on.

You had to know exactly what objects to look for in order to find them. You had to be pointed in the right direction in order to see.

It was a perfect conceit for her life. She was twenty-six years old and lost. Perhaps something was hidden, but she didn't know where to look, or even what to look for. No one had supplied her with an itemized list. No one had said: *There are twenty objects in this tree. Find them and you will live a happier life.*

David would be moving out on Friday. He had found an apartment down in the Village, on Horatio Street. It was a trial separation, they agreed, and it didn't necessarily mean that it would be forever. All the same, there was an air of permanence to it, especially on moving day. He wanted half the furniture, and one household was cleanly divided into two. David got the dining room table, the frayed kilim rug, the desk from the study, cartons of random objects, and a few framed prints depicting scenes of life in Holland. On the afternoon of the move, two men came and silently hauled everything off while Laura stood watching.

"Can I get you something to drink?" she asked the men in a tiny voice, but they didn't seem to hear. They just went about their business, slowly dismantling her life.

Laura and David had gotten married right after she had finished college. He was given a pediatrics residency at St. Vincent's in New York, and they moved to a huge, drafty apartment on Central Park West. In the beginning, she would watch David and try to figure him out. He was dark and lanky and liked to walk around the apartment naked. Without clothing he seemed tribal, sexual, territorial. He would pad through the rooms eating an orange, splitting apart the sections with his thumbs, looking lost in thought. He seemed to her brilliant and incomprehensible. Sometimes she thought she had married him for these qualities alone. She had assumed they would be enough, would carry her through.

It was several months into the marriage before she could admit that she was unhappy. One afternoon, sitting in her friend Carolyn's tiny apartment, she simply said, "I don't like my life."

She and Carolyn were smoking. It was something they did on occasion, clandestinely, like schoolgirls.

Carolyn looked at her for a moment. She took a drag on her cigarette, and then said, "You're serious?"

"Yes," said Laura.

"Explain," said Carolyn.

"I can't," Laura said. "There's no story to tell. Nothing concrete." She paused. "Don't you ever feel absent?" she asked.

"Absent when?" asked Carolyn.

"Like when you're in bed with someone, maybe," said Laura.

Carolyn leaned back in her chair and shook her head. "No," she said. "That's usually when I'm most there. Someone's touching me, and I feel like I exist. I don't know," she said. "I'm different from you. Maybe I'm more desperate. I need people more. You always seem so solid to me, Laura, like a clam or something. I, on the other hand, am always flying off into a million pieces."

"But you always survive," said Laura.

"Everybody survives," Carolyn said. "That isn't the point. I mean, why get married if all you want to do is survive? There has to be something more to it. I want marriage to be a big Ferris wheel or something. I want to get into great fights with my husband, the kind where you throw pots of soup at each other. You know, *passion*."

Carolyn talked of passion as though it were some vague, intangible force that everyone felt and no one could describe, except in the most extreme terms, the terms of people playing charades. Was that really passion — two lovers flinging soup?

Laura and David were very careful not to get in each other's way. Even their clothes hung apart in the closet, separated by a wooden divider that David had built. Sometimes Laura had the

5

urge to pull open the closet door dramatically and say to David, "Look inside. What a metaphor. Just look." She imagined him glancing up from *Gray's Anatomy*, blinking at her, and not getting it. But why *should* he get it, after all? It would have been an odd thing to point out.

It had always seemed to her that David liked her silences and what he perceived as her shyness. It had been a pattern they had established from the start. When they began seeing each other she had been only a college sophomore, a shy girl who studied art and hoped to become an illustrator of children's books. She was inexperienced in all ways, but this seemed to please David.

They had originally met at a Connecticut College mixer in the spring of 1966. Laura was standing with a few friends by the giant punch bowl when David came over and ladled out some punch for himself. Then he turned and lifted his glass to her, and her friends discreetly scattered. Later that night she walked around campus with him, the overhead lights turning everything green and luminous. She felt as though they were walking through the halls of an aquarium.

They talked about school at first. He was in medical school at Yale, and he told her about anatomy class, and how in his first year the stench had made him run from the room, but then he grew used to it, like everyone else. She listened closely, nodding, trying to imagine the specifics of his life. He asked very few questions about her, but she didn't mind.

They began to see each other every weekend. They would sit on stools in coffeeshops, or else they would stay in David's blue Plymouth and kiss for hours. They made love for the first time in that car, parked deep in the woods of New London. It was raining, and the car had a damp, enclosed feeling to it, like a coatroom in an elementary school. Laura imagined heaps of galoshes around her, and the warm, exerted breath of children. David stroked her hair and told her to relax, but still she held on to him as though she were drowning. She willed it to be over, and when it was she lay against him, feeling the downpour of rain shake the car.

The afternoon had been a disaster, but they never referred to it. They continued to make love on occasion, and always it was the same. She liked being with David at all other times. She showed him the ideas she had for children's books, and he was a good critic. They went to the Yale Art Gallery and looked at Flemish paintings; David had little pockets of information about almost everything: art, science, the nature of romantic love.

"Read Plato's *Symposium*," he advised her, for it had been his favorite book when he was an undergraduate at City College. He explained that he had liked the idea of all those men sitting around and talking about love. After that book all he had had time to read were medical texts and complicated graphs. He seemed wistful for the atmosphere of ancient Greece, for some territory he couldn't quite imagine.

In the fall of her senior year he asked Laura to marry him. They were sitting and studying on a hill in West Haven one afternoon, eating the sandwiches that Laura had brought. David finished and wiped his mouth. He folded the piece of wax paper into a perfect miniature sailboat, and then he looked at her for a long time. She remembered how bright his eyes were, and yet how dark. He was Italian; sometimes this fact thrilled her. *I have an Italian lover*, she would think. Even his name resonated: *David Giovanni*. It made her think of Italy: of warm stone, and bread, and cathedrals.

David's hair was blowing a little, and the day was full of wind and leaves and cars somewhere below in the traffic loop. She sat up straighter, feeling her vertebrae separate, a light release along her spine. The moment seemed extended and important.

"Well," he finally said, "do you think you'd want to get married this summer?"

She said yes right away, and she thought how good this was, how memorable: eating sandwiches on a hill in the wind, having

7

a handsome man in a turtleneck sweater ask you to marry him. Then David did the oddest thing. Without asking, without even letting her know he was going to, he reached out and unfastened the seed-pearl buttons of her blouse. She opened her mouth to object, but he said, "Shhh," and she was silent. He hooked his fingers through the straps of her bra and lowered that as well. Soon she was sitting there half-naked and he was smiling, looking at her.

"Lovely," he said.

The whole thing had taken ten seconds. *Lovely*, he had said, and this was a word he had used before when looking at her breasts. Maybe it was the universal word to be said at moments like this; it seemed respectful, admiring. A word you would use when examining a tiny, fragile teacup in an antique store. But here he was, opening her blouse out in the open air. She was annoyed and had the impulse to push him away, to cover herself up. But he had just proposed to her, and she had said yes, so now she said nothing.

Laura became pregnant their first year of marriage. She woke up with morning sickness every day, and David stood over her as she vomited into the toilet, and he stroked her hair back from her damp forehead. When she was through, he gave her small shards of ice to suck, and he knelt down on the aqua tile floor with her.

Eventually the sickness passed, and instead Laura felt light as a balloon when she woke up each day. She floated through the apartment reading a worn edition of Dr. Spock. She underlined certain passages as though the book were an art history text from college. In her sixth month, Laura was approached by strange women on the street who stopped her and placed their hands flat against her stomach. Pregnant women, it seemed, were public domain, like statues in parks.

In the intense heat of an August morning Laura gave birth to a boy. He weighed over seven pounds and had tufts of blond hair and sharp, almost fierce features. She examined him closely when he was handed to her, and she wanted to isolate this moment, to keep it apart from anything else that might happen in her life. The room was airless and everything looked so *pink*: the walls, the new baby, the bit of sky she could see out the window. Her parents called long distance to say what flight they would be taking from Iowa the next day.

They named the baby Ian. It was a name that Laura had once read in a novel; Ian had been the brother of the heroine, the sensitive young man who always looked shyly downward before speaking.

In the following weeks, Laura thought only of Ian. She hardly slept, and she sleepwalked down the hall when she heard him cry in the night. She sat with him in his room and made up little songs at four in the morning. "You are a little cupcake," she sang, "and your frosting's blazing white. You have a little candle that gives off a blazing light." Then she was embarrassed that David might have heard her, but usually he was fast asleep at these times, or else out on call.

David was out on call every third night that year. He would come home and go to bed early in the morning, just when the birds were screeching and Laura was waking up. They began to slip out of synchrony. Ian was her constant companion now.

When David had an evening off he would come sit next to Laura in the living room, and they would watch TV. She would be on the couch knitting, occasionally glancing up at the screen. Images of Vietnam rolled by.

"Tell me things," David said one night.

Laura continued to knit and did not look up. She held the little blue web of wool between her hands, moving along the rows at an expert pace. The copper needles were as smooth and graceful as chopsticks.

"What kinds of things?" she asked finally.

"Oh, I don't know," he said. "Like what you did today, for instance."

9

"What do you think I did?" she asked. "I changed diapers. I nursed Ian. I cleaned the kitchen. I worked on the illustrations for 'The Puffin Family on Magic Island.' "

But that wasn't what he wanted to hear, she suspected. He wanted her to tell him about the spirituality of motherhood, those quiet, epiphanous moments spent leaning over the crib and looking into the temporary blueness of your baby's eyes. But of course it wasn't like that most of the time. David wasn't there for so much of it; he was out tending to other people's children. Lately she had begun to feel like a single parent. When David was away all night she imagined that she lived alone with Ian, that it was just the two of them in the apartment together. Ian had been conceived immaculately; he had been born on a spotless white bed, sprung painlessly from some clear fountain inside her. This was a pleasing image, and she found herself returning to it again and again.

Laura took Ian for long walks, and she often stopped at her favorite Italian grocery store on Amsterdam Avenue. The store was called Portelli's, and David liked it when she brought home a lump of fresh mozzarella in water, or some mortadella, or provolone. The woman who ran the shop was young and beautiful. Her hair was pulled back off her face, swept cleanly up from her neck and coiled at the top of her head. Her skin seemed polished, as though she rubbed it with imported oil. It reminded Laura of women on the beach — women with a dark gleam to their skin. Some women had it all year; she saw them on the street occasionally, and thought it must be a secret society: Women of the Gleam. They walked with confidence, their skin glowing, their shoulders back. They knew something that she did not.

The woman in the store was in this society. She wore a white cotton apron that she wiped her knife clean on. Laura liked it when the store was empty and she and the woman could have a moment to talk, to be young women together, one buying, one selling.

Laura pointed to the provolone in the slanted glass case, and the woman bent forward to bring it out. She used tongs, and wrapped the cheese in paper, as though it were a wonderful birthday gift. Laura could see the exposed nape of her neck, the wisps of hair that had sprung free. She imagined leaning across the counter and saying to the woman: *Tell me your secret, how you can live so simply and beautifully. Tell me how to do the same.*

This had become the highlight of her week: standing in the cool, smelly shop, watching a young woman wipe a knife off on her apron.

At night, David would touch Laura in small, hopeful ways, trying to bring her around. When they made love, she would sometimes open her eyes and watch as the numbers rolled on the digital clock. Nights were broken up by awkward lovemaking and by Ian's cries. He would need someone to go rock him back to sleep, and David and Laura debated whose turn it was. Laura never actually minded tending to Ian when he woke up crying; it was the principle that mattered.

"I did it last night," David would say.

"You weren't here last night," she would answer. "Remember? You were at work. I did it last night."

"You don't have to be snide," he would say.

They would whisper fiercely to each other, and finally one of them would give in and stagger from the bed, muttering all the way down the hall.

In the early morning Laura would watch as David did fifty pushups. There was such fury to them, his torso and head locked into position. His hands seemed riveted to the floor. Laura watched from the bed as his body rose and fell. She didn't know how to reclaim him anymore, and she realized that she had lost the desire.

After David left for work, she would get up and start her day. Sometimes she would take Ian for a walk in the park. She smiled at the other young women, all of them bonded by their status as mothers, all of them wheeling pastel strollers up and down the shaded paths.

She would probably live apart from David, she knew. She no longer had any idea of what made people happy together. She thought of her parents, who spent their evenings eating seedless grapes and listening to the radio. They sat on the porch of their house in Ames, Iowa, looking out over the spread of land, and for them it was enough.

One afternoon she asked David if they could go for a walk. It was May, and the air smelled of fresh manure and flowers, and the ground was springy. Ian was strapped in a red sling on David's back, and people smiled at the sight of this appealing young family. For a long time they just walked.

"This is terrible," Laura said, gesturing largely; she might have been referring to the trees, the park, the world.

But David nodded. "I know," he said.

"I never know if I'm making it up or not," she said. "Sometimes I worry that I'm just spoiled and I only *think* we're unhappy. We have a terrific baby, right? We have good jobs. It should be enough."

"It's not," David said. This was the first time he had really wanted to talk about the marriage, and she suddenly was frightened. She had no idea of what he would say. "It's a waste," he went on. "Living like this."

"What do you mean?" she asked.

"I feel that you have no understanding of my life," he said. "You get to stay home all day, and I go out and watch kids die. Did you even know that I'm doing a special oncology unit now? You never ask about my work. These kids are all dying; their hair is falling out, they're eight years old. They all look like old men. Their parents weep in my office, tell me they can't go on living. Then I come home at night to *this*. To being silent all the time."

His voice was urgent, the way it occasionally sounded when she stood brushing her hair and he wanted her to come to bed. She stood looking at him in the bright sunlight now and couldn't think of a single response. Should she embrace him, come forward and hug him hard? No gesture seemed spontaneous. She desperately wanted to go home, to unstrap Ian from David's back and rock him in her arms by the living room window. She wanted to make up a new song to sing to him.

"I need to go home," she said.

"Well, fine," David said, "but it's typical, Laura."

"What do you mean?" she asked.

"You're so cold," he said, and then he repeated it.

Nobody had ever accused her of being cold in her life. She had always been told that she was too nice, too bland and unassuming. Just a privileged girl from the Midwest, nothing more.

"You never want to touch me, for one thing," David went on. "It's like a chore for you. I thought you would come around, but it's gotten worse. You're like this princess nobody can touch."

"That's not true," said Laura, and she felt herself about to cry. She looked away from him, over toward the trees and the pond. The park was blurring now. In a few seconds she was in tears. As if in sympathy with her, Ian flailed his arms in the air and began to cry too. Only David stood there silently, looking down. He shut his eyes.

"I didn't mean for this to happen," he said. "I'm sorry." The three of them were like the planets of a little orbit. "Forgive me?" he asked, and at last she nodded, and they slowly headed home.

Something had shifted during that walk. They were kinder to each other, it seemed, but it was a kindness brought on by resignation.

One evening Laura wandered into the bathroom and found David sitting on the closed toilet, rolling a joint. This surprised her; she didn't even know there was any in the house. They had smoked together only once, before they were married. She had fallen asleep from it that time.

David looked up. "I had a long day," he said. "You're welcome to join me."

She shook her head. "You don't have to do that in the bathroom," she said. "You still live here, you know. You can come into the bedroom if you want."

"No," he said. "I like it here." He licked the edge of the rolling paper, lightly sealed it.

"All right," she said flatly. "I'm going to bed. Please shut off all the lights when you're done."

David waited until he heard her footsteps retreat down the hall. He lit a match and took a few hits off the joint. It reminded him of being in medical school again and sitting around a couple of times with some friends from his class. Altogether, he had gotten stoned only about a dozen times in his life. Mostly he had been too conscientious about studying. He would walk across the campus at Yale and see the undergraduates with their long hair, the petitions that they thrust in his direction, the odor of pot smoke that clung to their clothes. He had taken part in several marches against the war, but usually he had to leave early, to return to his carrel at the library, or his room downtown on Dwight Street, where all his study notes were. He often hurried past groups of protesters, embarrassed not to be among them, guilty about it because he sympathized with their cause — he deeply cared about it. But there were 206 bones in the human body, and each one had a name, and he needed to know them all.

David had a very low tolerance to drugs, and he found himself getting stoned easily now. He leaned back against the toilet and sniffed the air. It smelled of the pear-scented soap that Laura bought at a bath store downtown. He liked it.

He looked around the room. Everything seemed newer than usual, and easier to look at. The empty bathtub had a few plastic toys heaped inside it: the requisite duck and boat, and a big sponge in the shape of a clown's head. The toys were innocuous, but they reminded him of the hospital. The pediatrics ward was filled with such toys. He didn't want to think about sick children right now, with their life-support systems and their Close-and-Play phonographs. He had spent the morning giving oxygen to a five-year-old girl, cupping a mask over her face, and in the background a woman's crackling voice sang a song about a little teapot, short and stout.

"It's her favorite record," the girl's mother had said. "Please let her listen, Dr. Giovanni. She's been through so much; it keeps her calm."

David closed his eyes now, breathed in the sweet odor of smoke and pears. He felt high, but he didn't feel that paranoia that sometimes accompanied getting stoned, or that awful need to run out to a convenience store and buy armloads of pointless food. He felt only fluid now. *I want this fluidity forever*, David decided. *I want it when I'm by myself, and when I'm with a woman.*

There was a nurse at work who had large doe eyes, and he was almost positive that she looked at him with desire. He imagined taking her into a supply closet and making love to her. There among the folded wheelchairs — a stack of them gleaming in the dark room — they would pull off their white clothes and feel loose and easy and fluid. She would know what to do; she would not have to be coaxed, like Laura.

Laura was pretty and yet rigid. David would watch as she stood to dress for an evening out; she would put in her earrings, or cock her head to the side as she spritzed on perfume from an atomizer. She was so good, so capable. She bought pear-scented soap when something plain and utilitarian would have done. Everything she did, every moment, had a sort of restraint to it. Every small act was like a Japanese tea ceremony.

She handled Ian so wonderfully, too; she knew how to stop his crying in the middle of the night. Many mothers were not as perceptive as she was. When David was at the hospital, feeling necks for swollen glands, or looking like a miner into the tender darkness of children's throats, he often thought of Ian. It was an inevitable association.

You could always hear crying on the pediatrics ward, and it was in startling contrast to the cheerful decor — beanbag chairs, large, bright posters on the wall. There was Snoopy, snout up, doing a crazy dance, little curved lines in the air to indicate that his feet were moving frantically with joy.

If Ian were ever to get very sick, David would not be able to tolerate it. Every parent felt that way. You spent all your energy trying to make the world safe — strapping children into car seats, hiding poisons on the highest shelf, making sharp edges blunt. But there were other things, subtler things, that you couldn't protect children from. David and Laura were so unhappy together, and Ian was going to be wedged in the middle of their misery. But he would survive it; they all would.

The joint had burned down to a tiny stub, singeing his fingers. He shook it into the sink and ran water over his hands. Then he stood up and looked around the small room, suddenly anxious to leave. Everything was dazzlingly *aqua* — the tiles, the walls, the shower curtain. He wanted to climb into bed and have Laura there with him, warm and talkative. He only wanted intimacy — hipbones lightly bumping as husband and wife arranged themselves for sleep.

David would look at her sometimes as she slept, and he would run through a checklist in his mind. *Is she lovely?* he would ask. Yes. *Do you desire her?* Yes. *Do you understand her?* Not really. *Does she understand you?* Probably not.

He thought back to the early days of their marriage. He had been so hopeful then; he had imagined years of standing behind Laura as she worked on her children's drawings. He would rub her smooth neck, massage her temples. Late at night they would lean against each other, sleepy from the separate efforts of their days. *Tell me things*, they would whisper. *Did you miss me?*

He had liked the idea of Laura working at home. It was a relief to think that someone would be in the apartment all the time, watering the coleus, keeping the rooms continuously inhabited.

When David was eight, his mother had taken a job at the Big and Tall Ladies dress factory in Manhattan. She had gotten up at the same time as David and his father and his sister, Celeste. They would leave the apartment in one cluster and ride the elevator down together. It was one of their few family activities.

Out on the street, last-minute instructions were uttered: who would take the dog for a walk in the afternoon, who would start dinner. Sometimes, as he sat in school, David would picture the empty rooms of the apartment. He would take a tour of them in his mind, travel through the railroad flat, thinking: *Empty, empty, empty.* After school he and Celeste would fix themselves a snack, or punch each other, or something. Eventually their parents returned and everything went back to normal, but it was that first moment of stillness that David hated. In the evenings he would stay close by his parents. He would stand behind his mother in the tiny kitchen and pick off the bright threads that she had collected on her dress that day at work.

But now Laura would be home all day; she even wanted to be. She stayed inside drawing pictures of little farm animals, and David went off to save the lives of children. This was how he liked to refer to his work, self-mockingly. There he was at the hospital, reaching his hands into the armholes of incubators, touching the perfect skin of infants who weren't ready for this world.

"I'm lonely," Laura announced one afternoon when he came home. David put down his things and gathered her up in his arms, consoling her. It was the same gesture he had made that morning to a mother whose little boy had choked to death on a button. He wanted to console all the women he knew, and he wasn't sure why. He kissed Laura and he rocked her back and forth, and soon they were sprawled out on the corduroy couch, and he was easing them into lovemaking. She still held her body straight and tense, as though she would be graded for posture. Some women took longer than others to understand the odd vocabulary of sex, he told himself for a long time. One day Laura would simply unfold, open up to him like a science problem that must be looked at a thousand ways before making sense. Eventually the answer reveals itself in the most simple manner, and you stand there blinking in wonder.

But Laura had remained static, and they ended up living like monks of a silent order. They devoted too much time to small rituals, to anything but talk. Once Laura stayed in the living room watching the Jerry Lewis Telethon all night. Another time, David slept at the hospital even though he wasn't on call. The bed there had begun to feel safer to him, more familiar. He liked the stiff hospital linen, the way it was tucked in hard at the edges.

As the marriage wound itself down, they said less to each other but looked at each other more. Each stood in doorways, watching with some private bewilderment or grief. David stood in the doorway of the study in the early morning, watching Laura work at the drafting table. The light was still blue from dawn, and she stood over the slanted table in her flowered nightgown, squinting at an illustration. Her hands were dotted with ink.

And she had stood for a long time in the bathroom doorway at night, watching him roll a joint. Just the other day she had come in, unannounced, as he lay in the cloudy water of a bath. He sent her a silent message, *This is your last chance to save it all*, as though one person could possibly do the work of two. But he was willing her to do just that, to come forward and climb into the water, lifting her skirts around her.

CHAPTER TWO

She was distracting herself with anything she could find. The other day it was movies: a double feature at the Thalia, both of which she had seen before and had not particularly liked, but it wasn't the quality that mattered. She just wanted to be away from the empty apartment now. David had taken Ian for the day, had zipped him into a snowsuit and whisked him off.

"Make sure he's warm enough," Laura called as they left, and immediately wanted to retract it. David was a pediatrician, after all; he knew about keeping children warm.

Today Laura was going to art galleries. Carolyn was taking her, and they walked along Fifty-seventh Street in the snow. Laura had been an art major in college, and she and Carolyn used to love spending the day like this, but today she felt grim. She could barely focus on all those oversized canvases spread thickly with paint.

Finally Carolyn took her into a photographic gallery. Laura would love this show, Carolyn assured her. The photographer was named Julia Price. She was famous for her simple black and white portraits and her still lifes. There was something forlorn about her work, Laura thought, but still it was quite beautiful. She walked around the gallery looking closely at each photograph, reading all the tags.

"Francesca at Home, Wellfleet 1965," one read. "Mollusk Hunting, Sag Harbor 1968," read another. Finally, in a corner, Laura found a self-portrait of Julia Price. It was such a surprise, right after a series of still lifes: wooden spoons, eyeglasses of the dead. There was the photographer in a loose sweater, sitting in some empty room. Her face was made up of hollows. She looked as though she had just been startled awake from an afternoon sleep. She was stark, impressive, and for some reason Laura could not stop looking. She was drawn in by the dark hair, the long, elegant wrists.

"Are you ready?" Carolyn asked, coming up behind her.

"I can't believe anyone looks like that," Laura said. She wanted to place her hand flat against the surface of the photograph, the face. The tag read "Self-Portrait on an Aimless Sunday, 1969."

The gallery was closing for the day, and a tall young man walked around on the varnished floor, dimming lights. "Let's get some coffee," Carolyn said, and they went outside into the snow.

They sat together at a noisy diner nearby, and it reminded Laura of their college days. The air in the diner was filled with smoke and smells from the grill. Dark men called out to each other in what Laura first assumed must be Greek, but which turned out to be only shorthand phrases for orders. "Sal no dress!" the men called, and Laura and Carolyn had to lean close across the booth to hear each other talk.

She envied Carolyn's lightweight life. Carolyn spent her days at a desk in an office, but at night she went out with men, and sometimes took them home, sometimes didn't. She lived in a studio apartment in the Village, and her diaphragm could often be sighted in unusual places when Laura came to visit: on the kitchen counter among the copper pots and mixing bowls, or on a window ledge, with the cat.

"Are you doing okay these days?" Carolyn asked. "Does the magazine keep you busy?"

"Yeah," Laura said. "Sometimes. This month I'm illustrating a story called 'Alfred and the New Babysitter.' Have you seen it?"

"I was the one who pulled it out of the slush pile," said Carolyn. "It was written by a sixty-three-year-old woman in Houston. It's the first thing she ever wrote."

Carolyn had helped Laura find a job at *Jumping Bean*. The magazine was run entirely by men and women in their twenties. It called itself "a children's magazine devoted to nonsexist, nonracist art, stories, and fun," and was printed on heavy, glossy paper, and smelled deeply of ink. It had been in existence for only three years but had already won several awards for excellence. This year, the *New York Times Magazine* was doing an article on the rise of creativity among children, and was featuring *Jumping Bean* in the piece.

Carolyn worked in the editorial department, sifting through unsolicited manuscripts all day. Sometimes Laura would stop by the office to drop off a drawing, and there would be Carolyn in a corner, surrounded by an avalanche of manila envelopes.

"You have it easy," Carolyn would tell her, and Laura knew that it was true. All morning she sat on her stool in front of a drawing table and hid objects in trees, in farmyards, in oceans. The hidden pictures page was considered one of the best features of the magazine. Laura received more mail from children than anyone else did.

She did not do the drawings for the money; she would have taken the job no matter what the pay. When she was very young, her parents had sold one of their farms to set up a trust fund for her, and now she drew heavily from it each month. Between that and what David gave for child support, she did fine. It embarrassed her, this access to money, and so she almost never talked about it. She had no great ambitions for spending it, either; she just wanted to be able to cook good things for dinner, and buy nice clothes for Ian and toys for him from F. A. O. Schwarz. Maybe in a few months she would take Ian on a vacation somewhere. She could sit by the water with her little boy in her arms. This image suddenly depressed her greatly. She imagined herself sitting on a folding chair on a beach for the rest of her life, baking like clay.

"I know it's only been a few months," said Carolyn, "but I do know some terrific men. I could have a party."

"No," said Laura quickly. "I don't want that."

"Sorry," said Carolyn. "I'm just trying to help. I'm not sure what you want."

"I'm not either," Laura admitted. But how awful to think this — that without her marriage, she was lost. Still, she did not want to be with David anymore. She looked out the window of the diner, and saw that the snow was getting heavy, and the sky was darkening. "I've got to get home," she said. "David's bringing Ian back."

They paid the check and stood out on the street for a second, pulling on gloves and hats.

"I'll call you soon," said Carolyn. "I'll keep dragging you to art shows. Maybe even a screening of something, if I can get tickets." The two women embraced lightly and separated.

When Laura got home, she started dinner and paced around the apartment, absently touching objects on tabletops. David did not appear with Ian at the time he had promised, and she had fleeting images of him kidnapping Ian, disappearing with him to another part of the world. Laura would go insane with grief. Her life would be spent trying to locate her son.

At nine o'clock David carried Ian into the apartment, singing. "We had a great day," David said. "We did a million things. We saw a silly man in a hat, remember, kiddo?"

"Yeah," said Ian, and David lowered him to the floor. Ian

grabbed Laura by the leg, wrapping himself around her. She loved the urgency of his tug.

"Hi, sweetie pie," she said, bending down to kiss the top of his head.

David crouched down too, and soon the three of them were on the floor in the bright kitchen, giving the illusion of a family. There were cooking smells infusing the air, and Laura had turned on WQXR. A violin concerto, a simmering pot of soup, the big kitchen windows steamed up with heat. Sometimes she wondered if she should ask David to stay; it seemed to be what he wanted to hear.

But he was standing up, brushing dust from the knees of his pants. "I'll call tomorrow," he said, and then he was gone. She watched from the window, waited a minute until she saw him slip out into the dark.

David zipped his jacket up to his chin and hurried down the steps to the subway. This was always the saddest time for him, this moment of leaving the old apartment and heading for the new one. He disliked living alone; he wanted a lover there with him, and he wanted a child sliding into bed with them both in the morning. It would be a big bed with the covers falling off, a noisy, bumpy bed like a hayride.

He found himself alone now much more than he had imagined. He often bought frozen food for dinner, or things in cans. Once he bought something just because it was called Hungry Man's Dinner. It had seemed very appropriate.

The new apartment was in a good location. He liked walking through the narrow, bending streets of the West Village; it was like being in Italy. David let himself in and was overwhelmed by the smell of latex paint. He had just finished painting the last room. It had actually been relaxing to stand on a ladder and run a wet roller along the walls. Now all of the work was finished, and the apartment had a resolute finality to it. Plants hung in windows, and the three prints of Holland were hung over the couch at eye level.

David went into the kitchen and opened the freezer. He took out a box of Mrs. Paul's fish sticks and broke six of them off from the solid block. *Oh, Mrs. Paul*, he thought, *let me come live with you*.

He stood there for a moment, feeling ridiculous. *I don't want to do this much longer*, he thought. *I want to be married again*. He wanted a woman to come into the room, take one look at him, and tell him to leave the kitchen, to go amuse himself for a while. She would leave the sad fish sticks to thaw on the counter, and in five minutes she would have whipped up some elaborate Szechuan dish.

"Please," David said aloud, and then he lit the oven for his frozen dinner.

There came a point, after four months of separation, when everything became easier. David had begun to date again: two nurses, and then a radiologist named Susan. He would pick her up after work in her office down the hall. There she would be, standing in front of a wall of light, peering at a set of x-rays.

"Just a minute," she would say to him, and she would continue to squint at the blue shadow of someone's doom.

He didn't want Laura to know he was seeing anyone, and yet he desperately wanted her to figure it out. He had no idea whether or not she would be upset by the news. He lay in bed with Susan sometimes, his hands folded behind his head, and tried to figure out what Laura's response would be. *Fine*, she might say. *I'm glad you're happy*. Or else she might turn away from him and press her face into her hands. *It's hard for me to hear this right now*, she would say. *I've been very lonely*.

"The thing about my clerkship in neurology was that they treated me like a second-class citizen," Susan was saying. "I mean, they acted like I didn't count at all."

He lay close against Susan and listened to her for a while. She was talkative, unlike Laura, who used to make love with him and then lie next to him looking away. At first he had thought that Laura must be muted by a passion she couldn't articulate, but later he realized he was wrong.

These days Laura slept in the very center of the bed and often scissored her arms and legs as she lay there, like the man in the Leonardo drawing. She was at the center of her own small universe. The other pillow had been put back in the linen closet, buried under piles of towels and sheets.

When Laura thought of David now, it was with a sort of wistful, uncomplicated fondness. It was hard to explain to Carolyn or anyone else why they had decided to separate. No one was able to understand it fully; in this way, their separation bonded them, made them co-conspirators.

Every morning Laura got up and drew pictures for a while in the study, and then when Ian woke up she would make breakfast. He was a quiet little boy, and he spoke only when he really felt like it.

Sitting at the table across from her, he asked, "Can I have Froot Loops every day if I want?"

"Yes, I guess so," she would say absently.

After breakfast she would take him to the park, or if it was cold outside or raining they would stay in and put on puppet shows. After a while Ian would need a nap, and Laura would sit by the living room window, looking out at the park. Being alone felt pure to her. She wondered if you could ever feel that way if you lived with somebody; she doubted it. When you lived alone, you didn't have to turn yourself over to anybody else. You could keep yourself clean, like a cat.

This is what I am good for, she would think. Hiding objects in a tree. Taking care of a small blond boy. Setting the table again and again. It was a life that felt almost rural at times. It reminded her, in a way, of growing up in Iowa. She thought about that earlier life, tried to fit it in. She had been a shy girl, the type who blushed at anything. Her father owned several farms, and sometimes he took Laura, his only child, out on the back of a big red tractor, and in the strong sun they would drive up and down the rows of corn. Laura could feel the machine pulsing warm beneath her, and she was so suffused with happiness that she barely knew what to do with herself. It was a childhood full of soft fabrics and good, sturdy breakfasts.

When she went East to college, she was the only one in her school to leave the state. Other girls married local boys, raised livestock, lived three miles from their parents. Laura was taking a radical step away from her family, and she was the subject of much talk in town. No one could understand why she wanted to go. If she needed to go to a good school, they said, why not Grinnell? She barely understood the impulse herself. She had scored high on her college boards, and Eastern colleges had sent full-color catalogues to her house. She had sat in bed every night reading the catalogues as though they were romance magazines. She looked at pictures of girls carrying books and walking under stone archways. It had appealed to her in some instinctive way, and so she applied.

"I just hope you know what you're doing," her mother had said uneasily as she helped Laura pack at the end of August. The suitcase was full of hand-knit sweaters and mufflers. Laura's three aunts, Maude, Dinah, and Corinne, had stayed up late at night that summer, knitting acres of bright wool for her. In the background, the radio softly broadcast the voice of the prairie.

Four years later, when Laura married David, her parents were deeply relieved. At least she would be taken care of, they thought, and they never questioned her choice. Her separation from David was such a shock now. She had told them over the telephone, and they had been so upset that they had to hang up and call her back. They begged her to come home to Iowa for a while with Ian. She pictured herself sleeping once again in the narrow, chaste bed of her childhood, and the thought of it made her cringe.

"Isn't there any chance of a reconciliation?" her mother asked once. "Can't you at least have dinner with David, try to work it out? Whatever it is, it can't be *that* bad, Laura. Can't you even try?"

She explained to her mother that she saw David all the time now, when he came to pick up and deliver Ian. She had even had dinner with him the week before. She had invited him spontaneously, and he had accepted. Laura was apprehensive that whole day. She had walked in circles around the apartment, compulsively straightening up. There wasn't much to do, since she hadn't yet replaced the things that David had taken. The apartment often felt like a gymnasium, with wide open spaces for Ian to play in.

She went into Ian's room. He was sitting in the middle of the floor, surrounded by toy cars. "Guess what, sweetie," she said. "Daddy is going to have dinner here tonight. You can wait up to say hi to him before you go to sleep."

Ian didn't look up, and she wondered if he had heard her. After a while he said, "Is he going to live here again?"

"Well, no," Laura said, and the question threw her.

"Oh," said Ian. He bent his head to examine the wheels of a tin hot rod. She could see the even part in his hair, the clean scalp showing through. He had already been fed and was scrubbed and ready for sleep, wearing a pair of yellow Dr. Denton's.

"Did you know that I could eat you up?" Laura said then, reaching down and pretending to bite his arm. This was the sort of thing you spontaneously said to your child, and if he laughed, wonderful. If he didn't, you felt like a jerk.

Tonight Ian just sat there spinning the wheels of his tiny car. He didn't say a word or even pull away.

"Well," said Laura, "I guess I'll go in and start dinner. Daddy will be here soon, and you guys can spend a little time together, okay?"

Ian nodded, and Laura left the room. Nothing was working. She was so tense that she felt like telling David not to come.

But the dinner surprised her; it was relaxed, and conversation was easy. She wasn't even sure why she had invited him, but now, as he stretched his legs out at the kitchen table, she realized that she just wanted company. She felt as though they were two old friends sitting down to eat.

"Sorry that we have to eat in the kitchen," Laura said, "but since you took away the dining room table, I haven't gotten around to buying a new one yet."

"That wasn't meant to make me feel guilty?" David asked lightly.

"No," she said. "Not at all."

"Good," he said, smiling. "I'm glad."

She ladled tomato soup into his bowl, then her own. He murmured compliments, and then there was a moment of quiet.

"How have you been?" David asked.

"Okay," said Laura. "Getting better. I've been working all the time, and seeing Carolyn, and Rachel. I'm also learning how to do things like fix leaks in the apartment. I'm becoming like you."

"I hope not," he said. He paused. "How are things in general, though?" he asked. "Like day to day? I mean," he said, "are you seeing anyone?"

"No," she said. She finished her soup and looked away.

As David watched Laura across the table, he wondered why it was that whenever anything intimate got discussed, she removed herself. It was almost a programmed response, and it amazed him.

"You think I'm obsessed by sex," he went on, "but I'm not. I just want to know what makes you happy. I've never known."

She looked at him again, and now she was smiling a little. "I guess I don't know, either," she said apologetically. "You don't *think* about being happy. You either are or you aren't."

"I disagree," said David. "It's more complicated than that."

He felt a great unburdening then. We were always wrong for each other, he thought. The failure was inevitable; it was just a question of time. We were both young and hopeful and looking to extend ourselves, but it wasn't enough. Some element was missing, some connective tissue that bound people for life.

Laura was eating a piece of bread now, and her lips shone with butter. He wanted to kiss her, but it would have been wildly inappropriate. Instead, he just leaned back in his chair and looked at her. We'll both find someone else, he thought. We will re-arrange until it feels right and good. We will each attend the other's wedding, sitting discreetly in the last row of the chapel, and we will wish each other well.

CHAPTER THREE

Laura sat for Julia Price on a Friday afternoon in January. She would always remember all the facts about that first day: how it was snowing lightly out, and how Julia had come to the door holding a cigarette and asked Laura to leave her wet boots on the mat. Laura, stooping down to pull off the boots, took a fleeting look around the front hall. There was almost nothing there — just a single folding chair and a bare coatrack. Julia had already begun to walk ahead, saying "Follow me" and leaving a thin line of smoke behind her. The air smelled of tobacco; it was as strong as gunpowder.

For weeks afterward, Laura would mumble things about coincidence, about fate. "What are the chances," she would say to Julia, "that I should see your show, think you're a wonderful photographer, and then a few weeks later be sent to you?"

But Julia did not find it extraordinary. "Well," she said, "I do a lot of work for the *Times Magazine*, and my show has been pretty well reviewed. It's not so odd."

Laura usually hated having her photograph taken. She tended

to look dull in pictures; her blond hair and light skin made every shot seem overexposed. She kept remembering an image of herself from adolescence, standing in the sun with five other students, posing awkwardly for the French Club, the First Aid Club, the Lida Rose Girls' Choir.

The night before the photo session with Julia Price, Laura had gone through her closet trying to find the right outfit. She finally chose a beige skirt, a cream blouse, a silk scarf. There was an odd excitement involved with having your picture taken professionally, she realized. The *Times* article about children's creativity would be running in six weeks. Her photograph would not be large, but still she wanted to look good. She felt as though she were choosing an outfit for a high school date.

Julia Price did not disappoint her. She took her time picking angles to shoot from. She changed rolls of film, and as she worked Laura began to talk shyly about herself, and Julia responded with questions.

"When you lived in Iowa," Julia asked, "did you ever go out to the Amana Colony? I've always wanted to photograph them, but I thought they might confiscate my camera."

"I went there a few times with my friends," Laura said. "Somebody's mother would drive us. The people looked like they were from a time warp—all those bonnets and beards."

"*Bonnets and Beards*," Julia said, smiling. "It sounds like the title of a book about life among the Amanas. You'll have to write and illustrate it someday."

Laura blushed, pleased. She wanted the session to last a long time. Julia paid attention even as she moved about the studio, directing Laura to walls covered with white sheets, to chairs, windowsills. Finally Laura was sitting on the sill and Julia was very close to her, leaning against the glass too. She felt as though she were looking at the self-portrait of Julia; it all flooded back to her—the afternoon at the art gallery, and the way she had stood there for so long, just looking.

Now she wanted to unstrap the camera from around Julia's

31

neck and place it with a gentle thud onto the windowsill. She wanted to ask Julia if they could have a real talk. No more pictures. Just two women talking like intimates.

But then Julia was done, and Laura was silent. "I'll have the contact sheets ready in three days," Julia said. "If you want, you can come by and look at them, or else I can just drop them in the mail."

"I'll come by," Laura said. "No problem." She didn't want to leave just yet. Julia was so interesting; she had probably traveled widely. It was easy to imagine Julia Price standing out on an African veldt, wearing khaki hunter's clothing, a camera strapped around her neck. Everywhere Julia went, she would still be smoking those French cigarettes.

"Goodbye now," Julia said at the door, and Laura looked at her for one last second before turning away. Everything about Julia was startling: the white skin, the deep-set eyes, the dark hair that scalloped into a widow's peak in front. Laura walked a few blocks when she left the studio. She was in downtown Manhattan, a part of the city she was unfamiliar with. It had begun to snow harder now. The street was like a little snowstorm paperweight; everything had been shaken up and was slowly landing.

That night she cooked a special dinner: baby asparagus and steak au poivre, which she cut up into tiny bits for Ian. She was in a high mood and even agreed to read *Goodnight Moon* aloud three times before Ian went to sleep.

Laura stayed up until midnight, watching old reruns of police shows on television. The cops busted a junior high drug ring on the first show, and went undercover as women on the second show. Finally she shut off all the lights in the apartment and went to bed, but it was extremely difficult to fall asleep. Lying there in the center of the bed, she kept thinking about the photo session and the way Julia Price's camera kept clicking so fast, jarring her with its buzzing *zzzz* sound.

On Monday morning Laura returned to the studio. She and

Julia sat in the white room on folding chairs and went through several contact sheets. "That one," Laura said, pointing to the shot she liked best, and Julia circled the frame with a red oil pencil.

"I like that one best myself," said Julia. "You look sunny in it. Appealing."

It surprised Laura that Julia would like anything that could be described in that way. *I am sunny*, she thought, *and Julia Price is a thunderbolt.*

Julia looked as though she had gotten very little sleep the night before. She was wearing a creased gray blouse, and her eyes were tired. Maybe she had stayed up all night making love, and in the morning had just come out front to meet Laura. Maybe some anonymous man was still sprawled on a bed in the back, behind the white curving wall.

"These are wonderful," she told Julia. "I usually look much worse in pictures. But you've made me look better; I look more interesting here than I think I really am."

Julia cocked her head. "You look pretty much the way you do in person," she said.

"Well, I'm pleased," said Laura.

Then there was an extended moment of silence. Julia's work was finished; there was nothing more to be said. But she was making no move to stand up and usher Laura out. Instead Julia continued to sit there, the contact sheets balanced on her knee.

"Look," Laura said quickly, "if you're ever free, maybe we could have dinner or something."

Julia looked surprised, then smiled slightly. "Yes," she said. "I'd like that."

They continued to look at each other, and Laura felt her face get warm. She felt as though she had been caught in an embarrassing act. She stood up then and said that she would call. All she wanted to do, suddenly, was leave. She felt that she had made some terrible faux pas that she didn't really understand.

Standing at the curb of whatever unfamiliar street she was on — Vestry, or Laight, names that sounded made up — Laura ran through the events in her mind. First she was positive that Julia Price had no intention of having dinner with her. Maybe everyone who sat for Julia Price asked her to dinner, and Julia always said yes, and never went.

On the other hand, maybe Julia really did want to have dinner with her. *I'm not too boring*, Laura thought. Julia had seemed interested in some of the things she said. There was that conversation about the Amanas, and then about the magazine. Laura thought she had been fairly eloquent; she had made a pretty decent impression.

Then she thought, *Why does it matter so much? Why do I care so deeply?* And she really couldn't answer that.

There were many distractions over the next couple of weeks, but still she continued to think about Julia. One night Carolyn had a dinner party, and six people crowded into her tiny apartment and ate with plates on their laps. Laura found herself sitting on the low futon couch next to a bearded man named Tom. They bumped elbows occasionally as they ate, and apologized. Tom told her that he taught English as a second language. ESL, he called it. She realized that there was a good chance that he had been invited to the party expressly for her. Carolyn was sitting close to a man named Craig, her arm around him, and the other couple, Polly and Art, were holding hands as they talked about the recent birth of their daughter. They had used the Le Boyer method: dim lights, Chopin, warm water. Laura and Tom were obligated to focus on each other.

Tom was a widower, he told her over the course of conversation. Laura was shocked. He was only thirty and his wife was dead. She had been killed by a drunk driver on the Massachusetts Turnpike, he said, and he looked down at his lap as he spoke. "This is one of my first evenings out," he explained to Laura.

She wanted to say, *Well, I think you're doing fine*, but she

34

didn't. She just sat there next to him, feeling his sadness and not knowing what to say. They sat close together by necessity, trying to resume a normal conversation. She felt his sleeve brush against her bare arm.

At some point during the evening Laura went into the kitchen, where Carolyn was bending down to the oven, sliding out a second tray of lasagna. "They're really plowing through this," Carolyn said. "I'm not going to have any leftovers." She stood up, and her face was flushed from the heat of the oven. "Are you having an okay time?" she asked.

"It's great," Laura said, "although I suspect that you invited Tom for me."

"You figured it out," said Carolyn. "Is it such a crime? He's lonely, and I thought you might like him. He has that sort of academic look, like David."

"It's okay," said Laura, "but I told you before, I'm not interested in meeting anyone."

"All right, forget it," said Carolyn. "But don't you ever get lonely?"

"I've been busy," said Laura. "Ian needs me all the time, and I'm doing some last-minute drawings for the title page." She paused. "Have you seen Julia Price's photographs yet?" she asked.

"Yeah, they look great," said Carolyn. "I was meaning to tell you. You look really classy."

"I'm thinking of inviting her to dinner," Laura said casually. "She was so interesting."

Carolyn took off her oven mitts. "What did you find to talk about with her?" she asked.

"A lot of things," said Laura. "I was nervous at first, but she was great."

"I'm glad it worked out well," said Carolyn. "The piece will be great publicity. When Larry Graves went to have his picture taken the other day—you know, with his hand puppets and all—he said she was cold. And I was also talking about the photo spread with somebody in the art department, and they said that Julia Price was supposed to be a lesbian. But people are always saying things."

Laura didn't know how to respond to this, and so they began to talk about something else. She helped Carolyn carry more food and wine into the living room, and then she sat down again. At the end of the evening she stood in the doorway, saying goodnight to Tom. She wished him luck with his teaching, and they shook hands warmly. But still she was anxious to leave; she had left Ian with Mindy the babysitter, and she didn't want to keep the girl out too late.

In the cab heading uptown, Laura tried to figure out whether or not to arrange a dinner with Julia Price, and when. It had been nineteen days since she had gone to look at the contact sheets. That seemed to be a reasonable amount of time; she didn't want to appear too eager.

Laura summoned up an image of Julia Price. She *was* odd, but in a good way. Maybe she really was a lesbian. It didn't seem impossible. Perhaps the imagined man behind the curved wall in the studio that morning had really been a woman. Laura had not known any lesbians before, at least none that she was aware of. At college there had been a large, jockish girl in her dormitory named Claire Mudd; people speculated about her, but then she had gone off and married a boy from Princeton.

Laura thought of Julia in some deadlock in a loft, wrapping herself into the elegant arms of another artist: a figurative painter, perhaps, smelling of turpentine. A young girl with a braid that you might feel compelled to bring up to your mouth and taste the ends of. Julia and Tatiana: two bodies climbing all over each other while in the background Billie Holiday rasped out a song about desire.

Julia the photographer, then, taking pictures of the young girl, her braid freed from its helix. There would be that whirring sound, all through the night, like locusts — the breathing sound of cameras, the insect sound, the predatory sound.

Julia Price, Laura thought, your work is frightening. Not frightening like Diane Arbus. You don't see tragedy in every human face, a twisted, broken body under every suit of clothing. You don't go out of your way to find the worst people on every street: the woman with the artificial eyebrows, the man with the eyes of the cow next on line in the slaughterhouse, the boy whose clenched hands and face read death, death, death. Julia Price, she thought, you frighten me in the voluptuousness of every still.

Laura imagined going back to Julia's studio and being photographed a second time. It would be different now. She would lean against the white sheets, thinking, This is a chamber where there is no gravity. This is not a wall with a sheet stapled to it. It is Julia Price's bed, shot like an avant-garde film, shot from above, and when Julia comes to stand next to me, holding a light meter in her hand like the Statue of Liberty, she is really lying in the bed with me. It is bright in the room because it is late morning. We have slept together and are just now drowsing awake.

Laura was horrified with herself, but these thoughts kept coming back. This must be what she wanted, what this fixation was about. She considered it, then rejected it, but still it kept her awake at night.

Two weeks later Laura was finally sitting in a dark Mexican restaurant with Julia, having dinner together for the first time. Conversation was halting. Laura kept dipping crumbs of tortilla chips into a pool of hot sauce. Her throat burned, and her drinking glass was empty. She choked on the sauce then, and Julia gave her her water.

"Here," Julia said, pushing the glass across the table. Laura gasped for air, drank up.

"God," Laura said when she was through. "I'm sorry. That spice just hit me all at once."

Julia Price smiled, a half-smile, really. She and Laura looked at each other seriously then; Laura felt her stomach drop. Something was happening here, she was sure of it. This was not ordinary at all. She didn't know what to say to Julia. She felt caught. She was sitting and looking at Julia without blinking, and Julia was looking back.

Laura thought: *If I look away now, we could let it go. I could break this off here, we can get the check and leave, and I might run into her again sometime, and we will chat.*

Instead, she said, "I think you're very attractive," and she had absolutely no idea of where she had found the voice for that, where the sudden valor came from. Inside her, she supposed, there was a brave swordswoman riding a horse, threshing her way through the trees and out into the open air. Whacking at branches and determined to chase whatever she wanted.

"I didn't know you were interested in women," Julia said quietly.

The moment was protracting. It was time to take responsibility for it. "I haven't been," Laura said. "Not before. It's just now. This is very compelling to me, that's all." She brought her napkin up to her mouth, held it there for a few seconds. She didn't know what she was doing.

Julia smiled, cryptic. "So that's that," she said.

Laura was frozen in position. In the restaurant, it was someone's birthday, and four mariachis in big hats came and stood by the man's table and sang a rousing version of "Happy Birthday" in Spanish. Laura could barely breathe.

"Let's leave," Julia said. They paid the check and walked outside. On the cold street, Julia said, "This is very flattering. It makes me speechless, though."

Laura shoved her hands into the deep pockets of her coat. For the first time in her life, she had pursued something without really thinking about the consequences. It had been a terrible mistake. She would have to nod and duck her head and go back uptown to Ian, and never get over the colossal embarrassment of the evening. She had read Julia wrong, and it was awful.

But then Julia took Laura's arms, slid them from her pockets.

She held Laura's hands in her cold ones as they stood together. "Do you want to come up?" Julia asked, and all Laura could do was nod and be led around the corner and into the big freight elevator like a child.

In bed Laura thought of how she and Julia had just walked through the street with their arms barely touching, but now their bodies were flush. Julia's hair was falling into Laura's face, a wave of brown and gray. Her apartment—in the back, through the studio and the darkroom—was just as Laura had imagined it to be. All white, all clean, no visible idiosyncrasies. That in itself, she realized later, was the most blatant idiosyncrasy. Julia's bed was no more than a thin pallet, and she and Julia began to step out of their clothing together, like two friends in a department store dressing room. Julia looked up once in a while, smiling a little. She unstrapped her wristwatch, and that was when Laura felt the absolute seriousness of this, the irrevocability. Oh God, oh God, what was she doing? The babysitter would be pacing the living room floor, prowling into the pantry, looking for a bag of M&M's.

"This isn't a death sentence," Julia said then. "We don't have to do this."

"But I want to," Laura said. "Very much."

"So do I," said Julia, and then she stepped across a small pile of clothing and came into Laura's arms. Laura was wearing only her shirt now, a last measure of protection. Julia had nothing on, and Laura felt the coolness of her skin, a temperature that seemed right for amphibians. They kissed, and their embrace was loose at first, tentative.

Julia moved her mouth away, then pressed her face to Laura's forehead, leaving a damp baby-kiss behind, the aftermath of a bubble blown through a wand. Laura's heart moved urgently inside her shirt. Julia's fingers unbuttoned her and a hand slipped inside, like a letter going into an envelope. Her other hand was bracing Laura's hip.

Oh God, Laura thought, but this time it was from surprise, not fear. She was aroused by this hesitant kiss, by the slightest pressure of the palm of a hand. Julia was older, and Laura felt like a teenager coming into a first, startling contact with the erotic life, smashing into it head-on. She felt first fifteen, then eight, then three. She was completely in the thrall of this serious woman, this woman who had the body of a French boy. This was what everyone smirked about, this was the source of global scandal.

She and Julia rolled on that soft, thin wafer of a bed, and Laura was thown into a new gear that she had never before had the chance to test. Julia was pressed against her and they stared at each other once again as they had in the restaurant. This time the lighting was even lower. Julia was all grace and an octave of guttural sounds.

They held each other in an extended embrace, and Laura could feel the vertebrae in Julia's back. Julia was like an elegant baby dinosaur, the key to an era so unimaginable. She was all darkness, all strong bones and a sensitive eye that picked up every nuance of light or shade.

Laura had to leave, finally. Ian was at home with the babysitter. Perhaps he would wake up in his sleep, wonder where his mother was. She could barely bring herself to get dressed again; the clothing she had been wearing seemed so irrelevant. She stepped back into it, and thought it hung differently on her now. She and Julia walked through the darkroom and stood together for a moment. The room smelled of chemicals, and there was one small red light burning in the corner. The sound of running water came from somewhere in the wall. They embraced once again in the darkroom. Julia's body was deep red from the light, like a piece of exquisite neon, an advertisement for herself.

CHAPTER FOUR

Everything pointed toward obsession: the constant phone calls she made, the dreams that woke her, the way she had started doodling Julia's name and profile all over sheets and sheets of good sketch paper, like a schoolgirl in love.

She tried to reconstruct every moment that had passed between them, in an effort to see how this had possibly happened. She thought of Julia, pictured her lighting a chain of cigarettes and finally a bayberry candle, placing it on the floor by the bed.

At forty, Julia Price had been involved with women for twenty-four years. "Come on, even in high school?" Laura had asked once, incredulous. "No boyfriends?" It was unthinkable — such a great-looking woman with long arms and legs, dark hair, pale skin. "Weren't you prom queen?" Laura asked. "Weren't you the yearbook editor? Weren't you the lead in *Our Town?*"

"No, no," Julia had said, laughing. "I wasn't any of those things. I never wanted to be."

She had lived, instead, a secret life, taking the train from her parents' Scarsdale home into Manhattan so she could meet an older woman named Yvonne and sit in an unheated apartment fooling around and looking through a first edition of *Nightwood*. Then Julia would let herself be held, sitting in Yvonne's oversized rocking chair. The chair moved forward and back, standing still but all the while tilting Julia further away from adolescence.

"That was what I was doing in high school," Julia said.

"It must be biological, then," Laura said. There was no boxiness to Julia, no gym whistle hidden on a lanyard under a blouse. Laura could not let go of the ideas that had found their way into her mind years before.

After she and Julia became lovers, she began to think of women as airy, open, manageable. She thought about walking alone with Julia in a quiet forest, discussing what vegetables they would be steaming that night for dinner.

"Do you know that this is completely new for me?" she would say, and Julia would smile and tell her, "No kidding." It seemed to amuse Julia deeply.

"I never felt this way with David," Laura said one day as they lay in bed. "I never even came close. This is a whole different world."

"A *Whole Different World*," said Julia in a loud voice. "*The Story of Lesbianism in America*, by Laura Giovanni."

She made up titles like this all the time; it was something she liked to do. Laura would babble on and on, and Julia would occasionally add some wry comment. Laura had never wanted to talk so much in her life. She had certainly never wanted to talk so much about sexuality before.

One afternoon she went to the nearby branch of the New York Public Library. She went into the children's room first and took out a few Curious George books that she thought Ian would like, and something by Maurice Sendak, and then she went into the adult nonfiction section and found the aisle where all the books about homosexuality were shelved. Most of the books were old, had been published decades earlier, and had long passages in them which made her want to die.

"Many Lesbians seem to possess certain traits usually seen only in men," read one book, called *Sexual Inversion in Perspective*. "But the presence," it went on, "of a dominant, aggressive personality and a strong, developed musculature, often accompanied by a loud, coarse sense of humor, only mask a pathetically underdeveloped woman hiding underneath. It is possible, through extended psychoanalysis with a gifted clinician, to release the woman, and give her a normal life."

The book was published in 1951, and was edited by three people named Schultz, Lasker, and Urdwell. She wondered who they were; she said their names aloud like a litany. She imagined them with pinched faces, gray suits, dark nylon socks with an inch of white leg showing between the sock and the cuff of the pant leg. She would locate Drs. Schultz, Lasker, and Urdwell and become their patient. Laura imagined herself lying down on a couch while the three psychiatrists scribbled in three separate notepads. She was beyond hope, they would concur. She was inverted; her reflection would appear right side up in every teaspoon.

Laura sat on the floor between shelves and tried to think of herself in this context, but it didn't make sense. It all seemed absurd. She had barely talked about sex with anyone in her life.

"Don't question everything so much," Julia would say.

David used to initiate conversations about sex, but they always embarrassed Laura. He had wanted to know what it was like for her, what it felt like to be female. She had stuttered out answers, tried to change the subject. She would tell him yes, sex did take a lot of getting used to, and no, she hadn't seen a lot of naked men in her life.

David's body had been so different from all of the bodies she had seen while growing up: girls with tiny pinches of breasts, narrow hips, girls she had worshipped, been best friends with, loved very deeply without ever thinking anything of it, never questioning its appropriateness.

She thought about Julia now, and immediately wanted to purge herself of these thoughts. She would desperately look for a man to focus on. All she could summon up were advertising icons — long-jawed men with cleft chins and stern expressions. The Marlboro Man, squinting out from a billboard prairie. She tried to imagine sleeping with the Marlboro Man, lying with him out among the sagebrush by a campfire. He was as male as could be, with a slightly skunky smell to him. She forced herself to dwell on the Marlboro Man and on handsome screen actors.

She went to see *East of Eden*, and while Ian slept through the show, his head resting sweetly on her arm, she hoped that something sharply *male* in the movie might interest her and she could relax about her feelings for Julia. She could let the relationship dwindle out, and it would become just an interesting quirk in her history, a brief lapse.

"Have you ever had dreams about women?" Laura asked Rachel one day over the telephone. Dreams were safe territory — one had no control over one's dreams. They were odd, unpredictable little night-movies. You could dream about someone you hadn't seen in years, someone who had never meant anything to you — a friend of your mother's, or a boy who had been in your class in first grade and whose name you barely remembered. All you remembered was the plastic lunchbox he carried, or the way he slicked his hair back with water, or that he broke his tooth in the playground.

"Erotic dreams?" asked Rachel. "Is that what you mean?" She seemed flattered to be asked. In college Rachel had lived in the library, and while Laura had spent her time with David, and Carolyn had dated different men from Wesleyan and Dartmouth, Rachel had been a scholar only, a medievalist studying the Visigoths. She had won almost every academic prize, had been the only one of the three women to be elected to Phi Beta Kappa.

"I don't have that kind of inner life," Rachel said. "You and Carolyn do, but not me. I don't have erotic dreams."

Rachel was now a graduate student at Columbia. She carried a heavy knapsack with her to class each day, and had a slightly myopic look and a vagueness that made one think she was levitating. She was writing a thesis on the Black Plague.

Inner life. Laura liked the term; it was so safe, so airtight. Rachel did not know that this inner life had bloomed, had spread outward into the atmosphere. Laura lived it, breathed it. She could not get away from it.

It seemed so unlikely to her that she was having a love affair with a woman. But then, it had always seemed unlikely that she would ever possibly be involved with a man. Loving a man, she had learned in childhood from a pink pamphlet, was different from anything else. With a man there was strange breathing into necks, ears, and some kind of plunging, then release. None of the gentle hand-holding and sleekness that she associated with girls. Laura had forgotten that early female appeal, dropped it from memory when she met David. But there it was, so many years later, in the form of Julia Price, whose long, pale arms set a camera on a tripod and tipped Laura into something she barely understood.

"There is nothing," Julia often said, "to understand. It just *is.* You're making it more complicated than it needs to be."

But Laura didn't know how to go about it any other way. Julia expected her to be nonchalant, to simply slip into this life as though it were a piece of loose clothing. Laura was paranoid that someone would find out. She began to avoid Carolyn, and she was evasive when she saw David. Those first months, she spent all her time with Ian and Julia. She would bundle Ian up and bring him to Julia's loft. She would set him down on the couch with a huge pile of toys, and later, when he was napping, she would go into the back with Julia, behind the wall. Laura could feel only the pressure of Julia's hands, the thrum of her own heart. She understood the concept of longing; it wasn't abstract anymore.

What do I do with all of this? she would wonder. All this newness, the heavy vapor that swept her up so cleanly every time she even touched Julia's sleeve. She tried to talk about it again and again, but Julia never really wanted to listen.

"You're getting repetitive, you know," Julia would say. "Let's go do something else."

Then Laura would feel embarrassed, but this never lasted long. She would watch Julia stretching out over the diagonal of the bed, and she would be engaged in the sight, as though watching a movie. Julia was an enigma in every way. She rarely ate; she seemed to exist only on air and coffee and the fumes from photographic chemicals.

"Eat this, you're becoming anorexic," Laura would say, dropping a bag of groceries onto Julia's counter, and Julia always ate what she gave her. Julia appeared so forceful, but Laura thought that in some way she was quite passive. She went through life mildly, and interesting things seemed to happen all around her. She had had a score of lovers. Laura was never sure where she had met them or how anything had been effected, but she stopped asking. Julia was elliptical by nature, and somehow this was exciting.

Once Julia talked at length about someone she had slept with decades earlier in Tangier. Julia was not quite eighteen then. This was a time when Tangier still had its share of writers and artists, young aspiring types searching the streets for a glimpse of Hemingway. Julia had gone to Morocco, she explained, just to get a tan.

"What do you mean?" Laura asked. "You're kidding, right? Weren't there closer places where you could have done that?"

"I guess so," said Julia, "but I never did anything easily then. I was deathly pale all year. You could see the veins everywhere in my body. I was almost transparent. My parents were worried, so they sent me off to whatever warm climate I wanted. This was the one I chose."

Julia met Elizabeth in a café. She had looked across the room full of dark men drinking and playing strange games with coins and cards, and there was Elizabeth, waiflike, writing on pale blue airmail stationery and painstakingly drinking a glass of bitters. Elizabeth was about the same age as Julia, and was also American. She lived with her parents in a wealthy section of the city; her father was a diplomat. At the age of seventeen, she had already lived in Africa, Brazil, and New Zealand.

"I am so godawful bored," she said to Julia that first day. "Can you save me?"

So Julia, a year older and by this time sexually knowledgeable, seduced a willing Elizabeth in the bedroom of the house where Julia was living for the summer. The Resnais family, who were boarding her, thought it lovely that their brooding young guest had a friend.

"Ah bon!" they said to the two girls, and Julia repeated these words to Elizabeth as they lay in each other's arms moments later. The bedroom door had a lock on it. Julia would push the bolt through its slot and she and Elizabeth would laugh at the high drama they were carrying out daily.

They began to write half-jocular love letters to each other, and had them delivered by local boys who begged in the street. A nine-year-old dressed only in white drawstring pants would hand Julia a letter. She would press a coin into his hand and he would run away.

"Dear Julia," one letter read. "Meet me at the Casbah at moonlight tonight, and I will show you everything you need to learn. You are the light of my existence, the saving grace of my summer. I drink Angostura bitters today and think of you. I am clipping my nails into a small pile now (see enclosed). I don't want to risk scratching you and leaving a mark . . .

"In September, when I go off to Sarah Lawrence, will you

come and visit me? I'm sure there are other girls there who are in love. Until this evening at the movies, when we can hold hands in the dark, I will think only of you. Remember — Rita Hayworth in *Gilda* at 7:30. As M. and Mme. Resnais always say, 'Ah bon,' pour toujours. Je t'aime. Elizabeth."

This episode had a somewhat tragic, if typical, ending. Elizabeth, in a moment of carelessness, left one of Julia's similar although more artful letters on her bureau top. Elizabeth's mother, the diplomat's wife, found the letter and wept.

"It's only a *joke*, mother," Elizabeth tried, but the mother looked at her child and knew that it was not. Elizabeth had grown up amazingly over the past several weeks. She was vain now, and studied herself in the mirror for hours. She smirked a lot. She was sensual. She sat wrapped in a towel on the terrace, clipping her nails and admiring her hands. The girl was sleeping with someone, another girl — that strange one from New York City.

The following morning, mother and daughter left Tangier. Elizabeth managed a final note to Julia, saying she was being forced to go to Dakar against her will, that her mother was watching her every move, and that she was going to have to see a psychoanalyst in Bronxville in the fall.

For Julia, it had all been play, wholehearted roughhousing. Back in New York there was art school waiting, and the woman Yvonne, who talked constantly about the experimental filmmaker Maya Deren and had a variety of interesting friends. In Yvonne's apartment there were dinner parties; one man often came wearing eyeshadow. Julia never knew what any of these people did for money. They were all "in the arts" in one way or another, but it certainly wasn't very lucrative for them. There was talk about the imminent opening of a play at a theater lab. The man in the eyeshadow had the lead. It was called *Hand Me Some Raisins*, and when Julia went to see it the theater was nearly empty. She had felt so sad for these people — how hard they tried, and how little reward there was. They were men and women who lived on the edge at all times. They were always borrowing money from Yvonne, who seemed poor herself.

Julia was the kid in this crowd, the tender one they treated gently. Julia hadn't understood anything in the play; she had tried hard, but it had seemed so pointless to her. Two men stood onstage arguing with each other. Finally the old, crusty curtain fell, and Julia clapped her hands as though she had loved every moment, but it had depressed her deeply. She stopped seeing Yvonne, and spent more hours in the darkroom at Cooper Union, where she was a student. She became an excellent photographer, a natural. At twenty-one Julia Price's name was known. People paid surprising amounts of money for her prints.

The years after that were nebulous to Laura. She did not know whom Julia had lived with, what she thought about, or what she did up until the time when they became involved.

"Do you have some dark secret?" Laura asked. "Some really terrible story in your life?"

Julia shook her head. "Of course not," she said.

But Laura told her everything, even when Julia didn't solicit the information. She wanted to tell her about her marriage to David, and about her love for Ian. Since she and Julia had begun seeing each other, Laura feared that she had been putting Ian aside. It wasn't any concrete sort of negligence — she still fed him well and took him to the park and read him stories — but she was vague when she was with him. "Ma, look at my knee," he would say, and she would be lost in thought, would hear his voice as if from the end of a tunnel, and would finally turn to him, flustered. She was heady with her feelings for Julia. She wanted to be a lover; she feared that being entrenched in motherhood would take that away.

"I'm becoming slack," she said to Julia. "Ian's going to want to live with David one of these days."

"Maybe you really want that," Julia said. "Couldn't that be possible?"

Julia had no deep love for children, but she was always very tolerant of Ian, let him fool with her cameras when Laura brought him over. He would play on the floor at their feet as Laura and Julia held hands.

Sometimes Laura would sit alone in the studio while Julia went off to develop some film, and she would be overcome with terror. *What am I doing?* she would ask herself. *Stop now. Stop this immediately.* She imagined her mother and father finding out — sitting at the kitchen table and reading a confessional letter from Laura. Her father would sit and stare at this piece of paper that was covered with lines about his daughter being involved with a woman. His only daughter. Laura's mother would rest her head on her arms and cry bitterly, just like the diplomat's wife. But in the deepest sense, neither of them would truly be able to understand, or picture what the love between women could possibly entail. They would have a vague image of two women hugging, perhaps, but then the scene would fade without resolution.

There was no pressing need to tell them; they had already been through enough grief with the separation, and she knew this would be much worse. One afternoon, a month after she had started seeing Julia, Laura decided to tell Carolyn. She needed to voice it already, just to hear how it sounded. She met Carolyn downtown for an early supper.

"I have something big to tell you," Laura said as they slid into a booth.

"Is it bad?" Carolyn asked. "I'm not prepared for bad news. I never am."

"No," said Laura, "it's not bad at all." In the darkness of the restaurant she told her that she and Julia were lovers. She watched Carolyn carefully as she spoke. Carolyn's face didn't change at all, and Laura couldn't tell what she thought.

"I have to hand it to you," Carolyn finally said, leaning back against the seat. "You were always the one who *did* things. Usually in a quiet way, though. I mean, there we were in college, all of us talking about men all the time, and then you quietly slip out and marry one. And now this. It's incredible." She shook her head.

There was an awkward pause, and then a waitress appeared out of nowhere, murmuring that the salad bar came with the entrees and they could help themselves. Laura and Carolyn stood and walked obediently to the salad bar. Laura clutched a small wooden bowl and leaned over a plastic partition, randomly scooping up shredded lettuce, a nest of sprouts. Then she was done, but still Carolyn stood on the other side. Laura couldn't see her face, only her hands. What was she thinking? Would they just stand there forever? Laura wondered.

Finally Carolyn was through, and they carried their bowls back to the table, not saying anything. "Look," Carolyn said after they had been sitting and eating for a minute. "I don't know how I'm supposed to respond to this."

"Forget it," said Laura. "Please forget it."

"I can't forget it," said Carolyn. "You're my friend; I want to know what's going on with you. But I have to be honest, don't I? It *is* a shock to me."

"Yes," said Laura. She didn't want to continue this conversation, but it was too late.

"Well then, tell me about Julia," said Carolyn. "Tell me how it happened, at least. I'm not horrified, Laura, just surprised. I can't hide that. But I really do want to know what you're feeling. I've been wondering about you lately, the way you've been so secretive."

Reluctantly, Laura spoke about Julia. She drank wine as she talked, and soon she became less hesitant. Wine always did that to her. She described Julia's face, her loft, that first dinner they had had. She was going on for too long, she suddenly realized, and so she stopped.

Carolyn seemed transfixed. She shook her head again. With

her full face and placid smile, she looked like a Buddha. "I think you ought to go easy," she said. "Just make sure that you know what you're getting into."

"I know exactly what I'm getting into," said Laura.

"It could be a way to get back at David," said Carolyn. "Subconsciously. And David would probably think you were doing it just to spite him."

"That's what you think, too, right?" said Laura.

"Well," said Carolyn, and she looked down. "I'm not sure what I think yet. I *am* overcome, and maybe a little bit by jealousy, I'll admit. I'm not thrilled with my life these days. Editorial bureaucracy can get really boring. I think Craig isn't right for me, and I miss Nicholas, but he's in love with someone else. It sounds like a soap opera, I know that." She looked up, leaned forward across the table. "I just don't want to see you hurtling into something you aren't sure of," she said.

"I am sure," said Laura.

"You can't be," said Carolyn. "There hasn't been time. Give it time. Then come back and tell me you're sure."

"I don't need to report to you," said Laura. "I don't want your approval."

"I'm sorry," said Carolyn. "Just be careful, Laura. It sounds like you're okay, but I worry about you."

"I know," said Laura. She felt all the tension of the evening, the way it was distilling, settling in.

"Let's not do this," said Carolyn. "Let's not be like this with each other, okay?"

Laura agreed, but when they hugged goodbye, there was a withholding to Carolyn's embrace. *I have become one of the dangerous,* Laura realized. *I am someone to watch out for.*

Something was being scrambled; she felt as though she were on an iceberg, floating away from everyone. She wanted to be leaner, tighter. Not more masculine, just more compressed. She wanted to travel light. She looked around the street at women carrying purses—all those appendages weighing them down. Leather sacks filled with Max Factor, sunglasses, old gum wrappers. She began to wear clothing with pockets instead. She dropped her wallet and keys deep into the pocket of her pants and ventured out onto Central Park West.

In the spring she would sometimes cook dinner on the roof of Julia's building. They would set up a hibachi, then sit in the wind and eat together. One night Julia brought a tape deck out onto the roof, and they listened to Edith Piaf singing "La Vie en Rose."

"This is just so we can feel like we're in Paris," Julia said. "I can pretend I'm Atget, taking a break from my work."

It occurred to Laura that beneath the dark clothes, the coolness, Julia was something of a romantic. It thrilled her to know this. She looked across at Julia, watched her try to light a cigarette in the wind. It must be a moment like this, she thought, that would make someone want to take a picture. In another moment the pose would be lost. Julia would lean back in her chair, change expressions. Much of the time she was less accessible, and Laura would start to panic. Where did people go when they got that absent look in their eyes? Whenever Laura saw it coming on, she would try to distract Julia out of it. She would offer herself up like a sacrifice. She would lean into Julia's neck, kiss her until Julia finally was forced to pay attention. In that way, Laura knew, lovers were like children, climbing all over the parent until they got what they wanted. Eventually, everyone succumbed. Julia would dip her head down, would grab Laura by the shoulders, and say, "All right, already." Then they would make love, propelled mainly by impatience. That middle place was no good. Laura could not hang all over Julia for too long, because Julia was irritable.

Every moment between them had to turn into something important; Laura worked toward this. She made sure that when Julia

53

came over, the apartment looked just right. She put a bowl of oranges in a little oblong of light on the coffee table, so that it might look poetic. Julia and Laura could sit on the couch with the light-dappled oranges before them, and Laura could only hope that Julia was thinking, *What a lovely moment. Two women sitting here looking at a still life. This moment is pure and unbroken.*

Julia never commented on anything; she merely expected things to be a certain way, and that was all. Such a love was ineffable, Laura thought, and suddenly she was embarrassed by the bowl of oranges and dumped them back in the refrigerator.

"So, are you seeing anyone?" David casually asked one day when he came to deliver Ian. Laura felt stunningly guilty. David had asked her that question only once before, and she had truthfully been able to tell him no. But now she felt the answer was apparent. She walked down the hall with him. Ian ran ahead into his bedroom, clutching a big green crayon in his fist. He seemed happy, manic from his day with his father. Laura and David sat together in the living room.

"Well, yes, I am seeing someone," she said at last. "Are you?"

"Sort of," said David. "I just knew you were involved, the way you seem every time I talk to you. It's like you want to get off the phone. Like you have somebody to meet. And you even look different."

"Less wifely," Laura offered.

"I suppose that's part of it." He lowered his eyes. "I really miss being married," he said. "I didn't think I would. I start to think about the way you used to be awake sometimes when I'd come home from the hospital. How we'd have coffee together at five in the morning."

She felt a sudden pull toward those early days. She thought about sitting in the pitch-dark kitchen with David, leaning against him, yawning. She let him embrace her now, lovingly, chastely. His body was the same as she had remembered, but it felt so odd compared with Julia's. David played racquetball at the Yale Club, and he had the hard arms and chest of an athlete.

"Let's go to bed," he whispered, and he touched her neck, her shoulders.

She pulled away. "No," she said. She thought about his fervor, and his cheek sandpapering her body, and she wanted no part of this. She shifted away from him on the couch.

"You're very hard to read," he said.

He looked so handsome, with his Indian shirt opened low, and those dark eyebrows that made him appear slightly Mephistophelean even in the gentlest of moments. He shook his head, absently rubbed his thighs.

"So tell me about him," he said. "Are you in love?"

"David," she said, "it's sort of complicated." He was watching her carefully as she spoke. "I don't know whether I'm in love," she said. "Sometimes I think I am, I'm sure I am, but then I don't know." She stopped, looked out the window. "I'll just say it," she said. "It's a woman."

"What?" David said. "What?"

"A woman," Laura said, and she felt embarrassed repeating it. She thought she might begin to laugh hysterically.

"Jesus," he said, and he shook his head back and forth.

"I didn't know if I should tell you," Laura said. This was just a throwaway, a sentence designed to fill up the space. They sat and looked at each other, endlessly.

"What am I supposed to do with this information?" he asked. "Am I supposed to be really thrilled about it — to say, 'Oh, I'm so glad my wife is liberated enough to become a lesbian'?" He ran his hands through his hair.

"I'm sorry I told you," she said. "I don't want to have a scene."

"Well, you should have thought about that first," said David. He stood up abruptly. "I'm not going to sit here and listen to this," he said. "I have better things to do. Tell Ian goodbye." He started putting his jacket back on, shrugging hard into the sleeves.

"What are you so *angry* about?" she asked as she followed him to the door. "We're not married anymore. We've been separated for ten whole months, David."

He stood facing her in the hallway. "You obviously don't understand anything outside yourself," he said. "You can't even imagine what it might be like to be me for one minute. You never had any empathy. You really have this anger toward men, Laura. Maybe it's time to get yourself a therapist. You can afford it."

It was the only moment that she ever remembered wanting to slap him. "Get out of here," she said.

He opened the door and backed out, his hands in the air. "Oh, so tough," he said. "It's your new tough attitude, I guess, to go with your new tough lifestyle."

Laura slammed the heavy door. The wind chimes in the hallway swung wildly; glass pieces clattered together. She stood leaning against the door for a minute, unsure of what to do, and then Ian came into view, standing at the other end of the hall, looking at her quizzically.

"It's all right, sweetie," she said. "Daddy and I just needed to say some things to each other, and we got angry. But it's okay now." She walked over to him and began to talk in a low, comforting voice. He showed her his drawing of a spaceship, and she praised it to the heavens. Her head ached; all she wanted now was sleep. She wanted to be lying on Julia's white mattress, close to the ground.

Being with Julia was the only thing that calmed her these days. She felt the schism between what she did and what she could talk about. "How do you do it?" she asked Julia. "Haven't people been giving you a hard time for years, telling you it's a phase?"

"No," said Julia. "I just don't spend time with those people. I don't have any use for them."

In Julia's universe, you just went through your life looking interesting and unapproachable, and people left you alone unless you didn't want them to.

One afternoon Julia, Laura, and Ian were taking a walk downtown. It was a bright April day, and Laura suddenly saw David coming toward them. He was all the way down the street, but she knew it was him. His face was tilted up toward the sky as he walked, getting a little sun.

She started to warn Julia that this was David, that she wanted to avoid him, but it was too late. Ian was shouting, "Daddy! Daddy! Daddy!" David was now looking right at Laura.

"Hi there," he said when he was a few feet away. "I thought that was you." He bent down and hugged Ian. "Hey, kiddo," he said. "Isn't this a surprise."

"Julia lets me click her camera," Ian said.

David shielded his eyes in the sun. "Hi," he said to Julia. "I'm David Giovanni."

"Julia Price," she said.

They didn't shake hands. Laura kept watching everyone, trying to keep her anxiety down. Julia looked so beautiful at that moment, with her hair pulled loosely back and her camera hanging like exotic jewelry around her neck. David just stood there. Ian jumped up and down, singing to himself about Julia's camera.

"We really have to go," Julia said. She ducked her head, stood awkwardly. Laura felt a swell of pride, as though she had somehow invented Julia. When Julia was in the company of men, Laura often felt as though her beauty was there with a caveat attached to it. *None of this is for you*, it seemed to say. *There is no way to get through.* A thick wall of glass curved around Julia Price, and she posed delicately inside it. But Laura could somehow plunge through the surface, as though she had laser-beam properties, and brush the hair from those dark eyes. None of it was for men, and some of it, she knew, was for her alone.

"Was that completely horrible for you?" Laura asked when they were alone again around the block.

"I get uncomfortable very easily," said Julia. "Usually I make a quick exit. Like at the opening of a show I once had. There were all these people standing around and looking at the photographs, eating little bits of cheese and saying things about my work, and I just stood there feeling uncomfortable. So I left. I was with Roberta at the time, and she knew what was going on. She went into the back and grabbed my coat, and we snuck out the delivery door."

Roberta. It was a new name, but Laura didn't ask anything. Still she wanted to know facts, to understand Julia's life. One day Julia let her sit in the studio while she photographed a mime. He was dressed in whiteface and a black leotard, and he positioned himself all over the room, inside imaginary cages, or climbing imaginary stairs.

"Isn't that enough?" he asked after two hours. "I'd love to just get stoned or something."

"I guess I have all I need," Julia said, and she put her equipment away. They smoked hashish from the mime's redwood pipe, and when he finally left, after some funny, directionless conversation, Julia and Laura were still quite high. They sat on the floor, their faces close. Laura could smell the deep smoke in Julia's hair.

"He was nice and all," said Julia, "but I just hate mimes." Laura laughed and kissed her. She felt as though they were two gentle animals courting, hesitantly bumping and backing away. Then they were serious, breathing everything in and being fueled by the charge of words and movements.

Julia was a mix of chemicals and hashish and good shampoo. She had lived, she had done so much; Laura wanted some of it to rub off. She wanted to pull it out like a splinter — have Julia yelp, change her in some way, but then have her be grateful, need Laura there.

She feared that Julia didn't need her. "I don't want to be your teacher," Julia said one night, completely without a context. "It's fun at first, but then it doesn't interest me anymore. I think you can hold your own by now."

"I don't think of you as a teacher," Laura said. "I have my own life."

"Then live it," Julia said softly. "Don't let this whole thing make you feel like there's nothing else. What about your friends? What about your kid? Sometimes I get the feeling that you think I can teach you to be a gifted lover of womankind, or that I can make everything acceptable to you, since no one else you know will accept it."

Laura couldn't speak; her throat tightened. "Are you ending things?" she finally asked.

"No," said Julia. "That wasn't my intention. It's just that you seem so lost all the time. You need to move forward. This is the twentieth century. We can't just loll around in bed together all day, as fun as it may be. I don't mean to sound callous. It's perfectly understandable, this feeling you have of all of this being so *risqué.*"

"It doesn't seem so risqué anymore," said Laura. "I've gotten over that."

"Well, it's not the way you come across," said Julia. "And you have to understand that my patience for this is not very high. None of it is at all scary for me, the way it is for you. It's just my *life*. It's confirmed in me, Laura. Every time we go to bed together, I don't stop and think, 'Jesus, what would X think?' I find it endearing sometimes, but I really can't sympathize."

Laura turned her head away and began to cry.

"Please don't do that," Julia said. "Look at me."

She took Laura in her arms and held her against the hollow of her chest. It occurred to Laura that Julia was completely right, completely on the mark. Why, though, did she have to be so *bloodless* about it all? Laura didn't think that Julia would ever break, or if she did, it would be in a very different way. She would fall apart without tears or the clouding of features. She would pace her studio and take strange photographs of plants for a few days. She would tie her hair back very severely in a knot.

She would not eat. She would not wash. She would become even more odd and earthy and, in some way, more desirable.

Julia took a series of photographs of Laura late one night. Ian had fallen asleep on Julia's couch. His crayons were scattered on the floor like pickup sticks. Julia held one in her hand and examined it.

"Burnt Sienna," she read. "I love those names."

Laura smiled, thought of Italy, and a fire destroying a town. Paintings lapped at by flames, canvases curling like parchment. Burnt Sienna.

It was very still in the room, and then Ian coughed in his sleep, rolled over on his side so they could see his face. "He really is a good-looking little boy," Julia said, and she began to take a few photographs of him. Then she turned. "Would you take off your blouse?" she asked Laura. "I don't want to be prurient about it; I've just wanted to do a series like this for a while."

Laura unbuttoned her shirt and sat on the floor. Soon she was back on that windowsill where her photograph had originally been taken. This time the lights of the city were behind her in the dark glass, the lights from other people's windows, where they sat and ate dinner or watched "Hawaii Five-O" or balanced their checkbooks—whatever it was that people did in their lives. She had forgotten how other people lived. She didn't feel conventional any longer, and she had lost a sense of what was proper, what was decorous.

Julia's camera kept on going, and Laura let herself be languorous, or playful, or shy. In a few frames she held her face in her hands. Finally she made her way back to the center of the room, back to the glazed wood floor, and she sat with her head thrown back, self-conscious but liking it. She felt like a dog with its snout tipped out a car window.

"Wonderful!" Julia said. "Don't move!"

Laura froze in place. When she finally changed position seconds later, quickly sitting up so that it made her dizzy, she saw that Ian was awake. He was not even three years old, but he was staring at her almost profoundly. His light eyes were open, cleared of sleep. Laura felt a chill then, as though this were a moment he would remember as a man, or perhaps only remember the fringes of, and wonder if it had been a dream. It would be a moment that would come back to him if he were in psycho-analysis at age thirty. She was forming his history for him, and at that moment she had no idea what sort of history it was going to be.

CHAPTER FIVE

They got back from the beach at three and threw their damp things onto a chair. A rain of sand hit the rug. "Oh, just leave it," Julia said, and in one stroke she pulled back the summer quilt from the bed. "I just want to lie down," she said. "I used to lie here and read *Little Women* until my mother told me I had to shut off the light. Then I would read by flashlight. I stopped at nothing."

Now the sun pressed in hard through the beveled windows of Julia's old room. Her mother had died two years earlier and the house in Sag Harbor belonged to Julia, an only child. She and Laura and Ian went out to the beach on an occasional weekend, and Laura had begun to feel comfortable there. She knew where all the small essentials were: the special knife Julia used for cleaning fish, the electrical tape. She had memorized the house, and now she was trying to memorize Julia.

On the white cast-iron bed, Laura unhooked Julia's bathing suit and ran her hand over the spot where the clasp had bitten into her shoulder. *When I am old, will I remember that dent?* Laura wondered. *Is it the sort of fact that will stay with me forever?*

That day at the beach they were hot and uneasy and still they chose to lie together, the outlines of their sunburns slowly appearing like a Polaroid image. Laura pressed her face to Julia's shoulder and told her that she smelled like the shore. Seagulls, wind, tar, the works.

"And especially cocoa butter, I hope," said Julia. "I love that smell."

Yes, Laura told her, that too. The deep, edible smell of suntan lotion. They lay there in the small, warm room, drifting off into sleep. Down the hall, Ian was playing with a set of alphabet blocks. Laura could hear the heavy clunking of wooden pieces, and it lulled her.

The telephone rang then, made them both jump. It was an old phone with a jarring ring. "Wait a sec," Julia said, and she climbed over Laura and went to answer it in the hall. Laura listened. "Why are you calling here?" Julia was saying. "I didn't know you had this number." Then, "No. I don't think so. Not now. I'm sorry, I just can't." There was a long pause. "Are you going to be all right?" Julia asked. "You're sure? Okay then. Yes. Yes. Good." She hung up and came back into the room.

"What was that about?" Laura asked, even though she knew Julia never liked questions like this.

"Just someone I used to know," said Julia. "Nothing worth reporting."

"Oh," Laura said, and she didn't ask anything more.

Julia was not faithful to her. She had never promised she would be, and they had never talked about it, but still it troubled Laura. After the summer ended and Julia closed up the house and went back to the city, the secrecy seemed to increase. Women left cryptic messages on Julia's answering machine, which Laura would hear when Julia played back the tape. "Hello, this is Gabrielle," one said. "I'm calling to find out what happened with Grace."

63

And another one just said, "Julia, it's me." And then the hum of a dial tone.

Laura began to panic. She knew that she couldn't say anything; Julia would just move further out of reach if she did. Laura stayed home more, reading stories to Ian and watching television. She would sit on the couch with Ian on her lap, and she would fantasize about calling Julia up, even late at night. "Hi," she would say easily. "Are you busy?"

And Julia might sigh and say yes, she was working, but Laura could come over for a little while. One hour would expand into several, and finally the light would come in the windows of Julia's loft, where she and Laura would be lying fast asleep.

There were many opportunities to have big conversations about the relationship, but Laura always missed them. It was like jumping in during a skip-rope game; you had to pose yourself there on the sidelines, waiting, and you had to know exactly when to move.

One afternoon Laura sat in Julia's studio while Julia went through a sheaf of proofs. She was peering through a magnifying glass, and she lifted the glass to her face so her eye was like a small, dark globe. Laura just sat and watched.

"Something wrong?" Julia asked.

Laura waited. "No," she finally said. "Nothing." Again, she had missed her chance, not that she even knew exactly what she would say.

In the end, it really didn't matter. Julia brought it up on her own time, with very little trouble. They were having coffee in a bar downtown one Sunday afternoon. Ian was with David for the whole weekend. It was late in the day, and out on the street men and women carried their fat copies of the New York Times and buttoned their coats up to their chins.

Laura and Julia sat in the quiet bar talking about trivial things: Julia's work schedule for the week, Laura's deadline for her next drawing.

"Look," Julia said, "I have to say something to you."

Laura's heart lurched; she felt as though she already knew Julia's words.

"I don't think we've been particularly happy these days," Julia said. "I really don't have enough time to give you what you want." Her voiced wafted off, caught some small breeze and was carried along. "I feel your neediness," she said, "and it frightens me." At the other end of the room, a waitress mopped the oak bar with a rag. No one was listening to this; there were no witnesses.

Julia pressed her hands to the steaming cup in front of her, and was quiet. Her face became abstracted in that moment— mapped with lines, like a Cubist woman. The angles split apart; she looked as though she had been drawn with a compass and a protractor.

"Well, fine," Laura said, and she knew she sounded like David, her voice hardening around the words. She felt desperate. Of course it wasn't working, but she wanted to force it anyway, to sit and jam all the wrong pieces together, make them interlock somehow. She and Julia had always forced themselves together —the light and the dark, two parallel tracks. Wanting it to work so much, Laura had thought, *I will make any necessary changes for this woman.* Going outside the natural order required that. Two women together had to create their own order. That fluidity of young college girls holding hands in public—that was something new. It was a generational difference.

With Ian in the equation, the balance was thrown off. She saw herself captured by a camera; there she would be, holding the hand of a woman, and also holding the hand of her son. The three of them would make an ungainly crew as they crossed the street together.

"I have to leave," Laura said. "I'm too upset now. I don't want to talk about it."

"I'm not saying we can't ever see each other," Julia continued. "You're not even listening."

"I can't, *okay?*" Laura said, and then she fled.

65

She rode the subway home with the numbness of a junkie. She leaned against the seat, feeling other people watch her. Her face looked spooked, she knew. Children would be frightened; her own son would be frightened if he saw her now.

She put her face down into her hands and wept openly. Her shoulders moved up and down and she let herself cry all the way to Eighty-first Street. The train trembled through the dark tunnel, and everybody in the car was now studiously not looking at her. Finally a tall Muslim who was selling sticks of incense came and stood before her.

"Can I help you, miss?" he asked, and his face was serious. He really believed that she could be helped. Perhaps he believed that she had lost her faith.

"No," she said, shaking her head. "No." She stood up quickly; it was almost Eighty-sixth Street. When the train stopped, she ran through the doors and all the way up the stairs into daylight.

"Where's Julia?" Ian began to ask. "I want to go to her house." He would come into the kitchen while Laura was cooking dinner, or into the study while she was working on a drawing. He would stand in doorways and ask the question, and then he would wait for her to answer.

The first time he asked, Laura didn't look up right away. She was working, sitting at her drawing table with a Rapidograph in her hand, and she moved quickly and jerked a line across the page. "Shit," she said under her breath. Ian was still standing there, waiting. "We'll see Julia soon," Laura said. "Right now, isn't it time for a certain someone to be getting ready for bed?"

The second time he asked about Julia, she was more prepared. She told him that Julia was very busy, but they would see her someday soon. Meanwhile, she said, they would have a lot of fun without her. Laura tried to think of examples — a trip to the petting zoo, the Ice Capades — but she faltered.

"Oh," said Ian. It was his stock response to everything these days. She looked at him and she knew then that all of his earliest memories would be of loss. His father had come and gone, and now so had Julia, who had never particularly loved Ian to begin with.

Laura began waking up early in the morning, at the same hour as the birds. In one of David's medical books she had once read something about early-morning wakening being a symptom of clinical depression. She would lie in her bed now feeling a heaviness as the sun rose. She got up and drew the shades all the way down.

Oh Julia, she would think, *what are you doing now?* Are you sitting under the white light at your worktable, cutting up prints with a special pair of scissors? Is there some woman hovering in the background, wearing your black and gold Japanese bathrobe, waiting for you to pay attention to her?

No woman would be stupid enough to overstay her welcome in Julia's loft. Julia would light a cigarette and absently finger some negatives, and the woman would know that her time was up, at least for the day. Julia would withdraw into herself; those same eyes that had been so focused the night before would now be dull, directed elsewhere. You could shake Julia Price like a rag doll, but she would not respond the way you wanted her to. She chose what to do with her body; she chose when to be intense and sexual. When she didn't want to be that way, she was just an underfed, ethereal woman in gray angora, nothing more.

Laura could elaborate about the mystique of Julia, but sometimes it was hard for her to understand what Julia had seen in her. She had always tried to ask, somewhat coyly, but Julia had never come right out and told her.

"I mean, I'm not a great beauty," Laura said once. "I know I'm pretty in that way that lots of women are. *Perky*; that's what some man called me once. And I wasn't even sexual when you first met me. I was so tense. What did you like about me?" she asked. "I need to know."

67

"Your *aura*," Julia said, rolling her eyes. "Stop asking me so many questions. I feel like I'm on 'Jeopardy!' Just come over here and sit down already."

Laura was rendered silent by this slick, elusive woman whose hipbones jutted out, whose long wrists often held twenty bracelets. When Julia took them off, they clattered to the floor. Some of them rolled away like little hoops. Laura wondered often what Julia wanted from her, what she felt, and she could not figure it out. Julia liked things to be muted, oblique.

Sometimes Julia would offer a light comment, an appraisal. "Your hair is gold," Julia would say. "Like down. It's wonderful."

She touched the back of Laura's neck, where indeed the hair there was down, just a patch of peach fuzz like the one Ian had had as an infant. Was that enough to make Julia want her — the randomness of appearance, the soft hair on her neck, her long torso and rounded shoulders? Laura wasn't responsible for any of this; it was all genetics, a passive part of her, something she was not particularly proud of or embarrassed about. It didn't seem to be enough to draw Julia to her.

It was only now, with Julia gone, that Laura began to understand why Julia had wanted her. Julia liked sleeping with women she thought of as mainstream: young, earnest girls, or women who had been married and had babies. It was like breaking and entering into the closed world of the family, the world of convention. All the divorced women Julia slept with probably had big, bright kitchens well stocked with dishes and salad spinners and pastry tubes. They lived in real houses or apartments, not just white rooms. Julia kept her own life empty and filled it with other people's clutter. And then finally, when that clutter had begun to become her own as well, she backed away, claiming no responsibility.

At least this was how Laura postulated it. Her theory made it easier, somehow, to have been left. To be left, and left by a woman, was a double shame. *I can't even make it in the lesbian world*, she thought. *I am not desirable enough. I am not lovable enough.*

The one generous act she had done was to give birth to Ian. She would watch him as he played with his cars or talked to himself, and she would think, *My little boy, my sunbeam. My constant companion.* At three he meant more to her than anyone ever had. He had nothing to do with this new side of her life, the side that had turned up so inexplicably.

One day, when David took Ian for the weekend, Laura didn't know what to do with herself. She wanted to call Carolyn or Rachel, but it had been a long time since she had seen either of them, and it would be awkward. She could call Gretchen, she thought, boring but kind Gretchen, who worked as a copy editor at *Jumping Bean* and who was always available for dinner, it seemed. Laura realized that she herself was available these days—she had very few plans lined up. She had let her group of friends from college lapse, and she felt sorry about that. David had taken up all of her time and thoughts, and so had Ian, and then Julia.

Laura sat in the living room and looked at the photographs of herself and Ian that Julia had taken. Laura had framed them in silver, and they were lined up across the coffee table. She looked at a shot of Ian in a red snowsuit, standing by the gate in Gramercy Park. The picture was almost a year old. She had ceased to have any sense of the passage of time; Ian was once tiny and pink, and now he raced around the park with a kite, talking about Big Bird and his toys and a crane he had seen wrecking a building.

Take inventory, Laura told herself. *Take stock of your life, and then you won't feel so depressed. You'll realize that you have an embarrassment of riches all around you.*

In a desperate moment she sat down and made an actual list. "Good job," she wrote. "Good apartment. A beautiful child." Then she stopped, unable to think of anything else.

She wanted to get up and call Julia, but didn't. Julia would say, "Just a minute," and would muffle the receiver with her hand, and speak to some woman who was there with her in the room. Maybe it would be the mythical Tatiana, the young braided artist. She might be home on vacation from the Rhode Island School of Design, where she was still doing her figurative drawings, focusing mainly on the figures of women, and getting away with it, because all painters were obsessed with women's forms. It was allowed. The eye did not discriminate, did not say what was appropriate.

In the world of art, women could look unabashedly at other women's bodies. In college Laura had stood for hours in the slide room of the art library, taking notes on *Odalisque*. And in childhood, skinny-dipping in black, freezing lakes, stepping out onto the rocks, grasping hands for balance, Laura and her best friend, Annie Carrington, would be naked and cold and shrieking like birds. Back at the house, they would compare flat, hairless bodies. Soon they would develop, and all of the clean symmetry would be gone, but for now, as they wrapped themselves in thick towels that felt like fleece, their narrow bodies hummed with possibility.

Laura had barely looked at anyone's body since childhood. In college she and her roommate Charlotte had politely averted their eyes while getting undressed. But she had loved to look at Julia; she had sat and stared at her for hours, trying to make up for lost time.

"If you want to look at women," Julia had once said, "you should go to the Q.E.D. sometime. It might normalize it for you. I mean, you're *allowed* to look at women there. It's encouraged."

The Q.E.D. was a notorious women's bar that had been in existence since the 1950s, hidden away on a side street in Chelsea. Laura had walked past it once with Julia during the daytime. All she saw was a wooden door with a diamond-shaped window cut into it. There was a red curtain hanging behind the glass, and she could not see inside. There was no sign. It was all very plain, very subtle. You had to know about the bar through a friend; it wasn't even listed in the telephone book.

She decided, now that she had nothing to do, that she would go to the Q.E.D. She would actually go inside, have a drink. She thought about it all afternoon, and then in the evening, after she had eaten dinner alone and finished reading a Margaret Drabble novel, Laura put on her coat and headed downtown.

She had the cab pull up at the corner of Ninth Avenue because she didn't want the driver to know where she was going. She imagined him turning around and leering knowingly as she stepped onto the curb. There were a few women standing outside the bar. They were smoking and leaning against the building. They were young; one of them seemed to be a teenager. They all looked as if they knew each other. Laura gave them a grim smile, a tight line that she hoped would look friendly but would not encourage conversation. Then she thought: *They're not even interested in conversation. Don't flatter yourself. They're young and casual, and you're somebody's mother. You're a nervous wreck. They can see it in your eyes.*

She entered the bar and gave another smile to the bouncer, a black woman with a puffball Afro. The woman sat on a high red stool, collecting money in a Tiparillo box. Laura paid the three dollars admission and had her hand stamped with a tiny lavender women's symbol. What if it never washed off? she thought. What if she had to wear it like an incriminating tattoo for the rest of her life? The room was very dark, and a dance floor pulsed from several yards away.

She looked around at the women sitting at small tables, drinking, grabbing up handfuls of pretzels from little wicker baskets. She could not, for some reason, focus on any particular face. Her vision jumped from woman to woman — those dark forms casually standing and talking, or sitting, or dancing. It was the dancing that threw her. A slow song was on now, and the dancers were pressed together, barely moving. One woman had her hand flat on another's back, slowly arcing it like a windshield wiper.

Laura remembered the night that she and Julia had danced to Benny Goodman in Julia's loft. It was like being in their own white ballroom together — the smooth floor was perfect for such dancing. Julia led, and it had seemed natural that she would. Laura let herself be ushered around the room, all the while smiling, eyes closed. When the record ended, they had sat down together right on the floor, a place they went back to so many times, and Laura felt warm and happy. Just from dancing. Julia ran a finger slowly across Laura's forehead.

"You're sweating," Julia said.

"No, I'm glowing," said Laura.

Now she stood alone in the Q.E.D. and she felt incredibly old. All the women looked like smug college kids. Some of them reminded Laura of herself in college; they just dressed differently. They wore jeans and Indian-print blouses. They wore sneakers and suspenders and Oberlin T-shirts. The bar was very warm, and everyone had taken off sweaters and jackets. Laura was the only one who still stood there all bundled up in her camel hair coat. She felt like a mother coming to pick up her kid at a high school party, standing and waiting patiently in the door.

Two women brushed past her then, and one of them stopped, as if in afterthought, and asked Laura if she had a light. Laura was so startled that it took her a moment to respond. She felt as if she were just being woken up in class and made to answer an obscure question about Peru. She was about to say no, she didn't smoke, but then she remembered Julia's lighter. She still had it; she had carried one of Julia's many lighters in her coat pocket for months last year. She reached into her pockets now, and her left hand found the smooth cylinder. Her fingers wrapped around it, drew it out. She felt triumphant in that small moment.

"Here," she said, and she held it up to the woman's cigarette. There was a scrape of friction, and then a little flame shot up. The woman leaned forward, connected with the light. In that instant, Laura got a good look at her. The woman's hair was cut razor-close, like an army boy's, but her face was beautiful and quite female. No one would ever mistake her for a man.

"Thanks," the woman said, drawing back. Smoke coiled out, and the woman retreated, her arm around her friend's shoulder.

Laura watched them walk away, their bodies connected at the shoulders and hips. They were lovers, and were probably in love. Julia had been open about being a lesbian, but she had never been open about being Laura's lover.

The music switched then to some early Motown, and a group of women bombarded the dance floor. Everyone was jumping and dancing to the Temptations. In the daylight, most of these women went back to their ordinary lives, fell deeply in love and kept it a secret, turned it into a private joke. Only here the joke was shared. A woman in the corner was stroking another woman's hair, twisting it between her hands as though wringing out water.

Finally Laura pushed her way back to the front and out the door. The bouncer murmured something, but she didn't hear. She stood out on the quiet street again and leaned against the building, her hands deep in her pockets. She held on to Julia's lighter tightly.

She would have to go home now and let herself into the empty apartment. She would walk around folding Ian's scattered cloth-ing and looking at the pictures that Julia had taken. She would stand in the middle of the cavernous living room, feeling as though everything had dropped from her, everything she had once had: a husband, a family, an appropriate life — all of it gone, irretrievable.

She stood in the street and waited for a cab. When one finally came, she sat in the back and closed her eyes as the cab traveled uptown. When she got home, she rummaged in the depths of the medicine cabinet and found an old vial of David's sleeping pills. She swallowed one blue pill with a glass of cloudy city water, and soon fell asleep.

In the morning, everything was calm. When she pulled the

curtain open she could see a red kite lifting over the trees in the park. It made her think of Ian. He would be home in a few hours, back in the living room with his toys scattered around him—chunky Tonka trucks whizzing across the rug and into the darkness under the sofa.

She went to the bathroom to wash, and saw that the stamp from last night was indeed still there on the back of her hand: a tiny, perfect hieroglyph.

CHAPTER SIX

I t was time to choose a nursery school for Ian. David and Laura visited several progressive ones; at the Calder School they sat on miniature chairs and watched as the children played games in circles. There was much running and jumping going on, and the classroom smelled distinctly of paste. David sat with his knees almost touching his chest. Some of the women were looking at him and smiling sympathetically. He adjusted his tie and tried to focus on all the children, who were first skipping, then galloping, then hopping, according to the teacher's whims.

His chair was a few inches from Laura's. She leaned toward him and whispered once in a while, and everyone naturally assumed they were married. He wanted to transmit a secret message to these women, to tell them to look at his hand, see that he wore no wedding band. All the young mothers at this open house had a hip, casual look to them. Even the teacher looked as though she went to foreign films on weekends.

"I like this place," he whispered to Laura, and she nodded.

They agreed, later that day, that they would enroll Ian at the Calder School in January, if he was accepted. The application procedure was complicated; Ian actually needed recommendations. Who could they ask, David wondered — Mindy the babysitter? There was no question in David's mind that Ian would be accepted everywhere. Ian was intelligent in a quiet, persuasive way. People liked him at once.

One day, when David was carrying Ian piggyback, Ian leaned over and said in his ear, "Someday, Daddy, when you're old, I'll carry *you* like this."

"That's probably true, kiddo," David had answered, and suddenly Ian felt very heavy.

When he was with his son he always tried to gauge how Ian felt. David had done some research on divorce and how it affects children. He asked Ian careful questions, trying to find out if he was happy. Ian always sounded fine, but it was so hard to tell. Children kept things to themselves. Sometimes children were ill for days and days before they would say a word.

David spent time with Ian every weekend, but each time they saw each other, Ian threw himself into David's arms as though it had been years. David loved the way that hard little body was flung at him like a football. He opened his arms and caught his son against him, wrapped him around his chest, taking the blow fully.

He had painted Ian's bedroom wall in his apartment with a big rainbow. Ian would jump on the bed and try to touch all the colors, naming each one. David and Ian would be boys together. They ate SpaghettiOs right from the can. They went for long walks in the Village and talked about cars. David took Ian to the hospital and gave him a grand tour. He let Ian bop his knee with a reflex hammer. He felt dizzyingly young himself when they were together. He had rarely felt this way when he and Laura were married.

The week before, he had found out that Laura and her woman lover had broken up; Laura had told him so over the telephone when he had asked how things were going. "I don't want to start another fight," he had said. "I'm asking you without any malice." He felt bad about his earlier behavior that day in her apartment, and he wanted to make it up to her, somehow. He didn't want to take back any of the things he had said; it was just that his tone had been so harsh, and Ian had heard the whole thing.

He had asked Ian a few questions about the woman Julia. *Do you like her?* he asked. *Does she have good food at her apartment? Do you get to sleep there sometimes?*

Then one day Ian told him that they hadn't been to Julia's in a long time, and David had come right out and asked Laura about it, trying to learn the truth.

"It's over," she had said. "I don't want to talk about it with you, David. Please don't ask me."

David felt relieved. That part of her life had come and gone. It happened to women sometimes, he knew. They slipped in and out of lesbian relationships, and then it was as though nothing had ever happened. He wondered if Ian would even remember this phase in Laura's life, if he would grow up and speculate about it.

Every time David was with Ian now, combing that fine blond hair after a bath, he would think about Laura's own blondness and how it bonded mother and son. David was the solitary dark one, the one with hair all over his arms and legs. As an adolescent he had felt self-conscious about the sudden crop of hair on his body, but later on, when he had sex with a tough girl from St. Catherine's in Brooklyn, she had told him that she loved the hair on him, that it gave her something to hold on to.

His wife and son were blessed with a blond sleekness that very few people had. They both had the bodies of seraphim, that golden skin and slippery hair. When David made love to Laura that first time in his car in the woods, he had thought to himself, *What a pleasing sight we make. What contrast.* He loved the contrast that was implicit in lovemaking.

Women approached him all the time now at work; he was a

minor celebrity in the hallways. He had given a lecture recently on vegetarian diets for children, and was becoming known as an alternative-care physician, a new-age practitioner. It wasn't exactly accurate, but he didn't protest.

In January he met Vanessa, a social worker who worked in the clinic of the hospital. He had seen her a few times in the elevator, and had made a few inquiries to find out who she was. She was almost as tall as he, and was willowy-thin, with long red hair. She looked like a woman from one of those pre-Raphaelite paintings that Laura had loved. She looked like Burne-Jones's Ophelia, with her hair spread out all around her.

They had their first conversation at an administrative meeting. The hospital staff was crowded into a large conference room, listening to endless details and electing new officers for committees. Everyone was drinking coffee, trying to stay alert. During the break, David stood at a folding table, stirring a packet of sugar into his cup, when Vanessa was suddenly beside him, pouring coffee for herself. He smiled and introduced himself.

"Oh, I know who you are," she said. "I've seen you."

"Well, I know who you are, too," he said, and they both smiled, pleased with themselves.

He suddenly remembered that he had first met Laura while standing at a table pouring out punch for himself, and this seemed like a good sign. Maybe all the important relationships he would have with women would begin while standing and pouring some liquid. They would share libations, as the ancient Greeks had done.

They talked superficially, complained about how boring the meeting was, and later, when it was time to leave, they went out for dinner. He was due back at the hospital at eight, but there was a good hour and a half free now. He felt his chest expand as they rode down in the elevator.

Over dinner at a Thai restaurant a few blocks away, he began to tell her about his marriage and his separation. He wished he could tell her everything.

"Any children?" she asked.

"One," he said. "His name is Ian." He extracted a photograph from his wallet of Ian at a petting zoo, hugging a lamb.

Vanessa held the picture up to the light over their table. Ian's image turned translucent. "He's beautiful," she said in a hushed voice, and David knew that she meant it, that she was not just saying a platitude. He wanted to cry out, *Let's go to bed together! Let's go see my kid!*

"I love children," Vanessa was saying. "I used to do some developmental psych, back in my fledgling days. I loved having kids in the office. Now I see whole families, and I rarely get to see the kids alone. Some of these families are so troubled, I just wish I could take the children home with me."

"I know what you mean," said David. "I often feel that way, too."

As they ate and spoke, David became more excited. Here was the first woman he could really talk to in a long time. She didn't shy away from the subject of other people's children, the way so many women seemed to these days. Susan, the radiologist, had had zero enthusiasm for kids. She had never wanted her own. She was so efficient, with her diaphragm and her inexhaustible supply of Ortho-Gynol cream. The relationship had never really taken off, and they had stopped seeing each other; it was quite mutual.

But Vanessa was different. She didn't start to look bored when he talked about his son, and she didn't try to steer the conversation elsewhere, either. She asked a lot of questions about Ian, and David spoke freely.

"I have unlimited visitation rights," said David. "But it's never enough. We try and spend weekends together, but I'm at work so much now. Next year should be easier."

There was such a closeness to that first dinner; it left David with a good feeling throughout the night. As he pumped a kid's stomach at two in the morning, he was still thinking about Vanessa. "Steady now," David said, and he held the little boy's hand. He wished then that Vanessa were watching him; he wanted to perform for her.

David pursued Vanessa over the next few weeks. Sometimes she seemed to be pursuing him, and this excited David more than her fine skin, her hair, her narrow eyes. He would walk by her office; most times she wasn't in, but the door would be open. On her desk was an array of little objects: statuettes with sayings on the bottom, coffee mugs, an orange juice can with a sprig of flowers in it, even though it was winter.

David went to bed with her the third week after they met, and soon she was there all the time in his apartment, his bed. She did calisthenics every morning in a tight purple leotard. She left her hair loose, a long red wave moving with her as she did her sit-ups and leg stretches. She also did yoga; her favorite exercise was called "Salute to the Sun." When she was done she came back to bed, unwashed. She drew back the cover and lay on top of David, letting him feel every one of her bones, every bit of dampness. Her leotard looked almost black. Her sweat was sweet to him; it had an odor like broth cooking.

"I'd like to meet Ian," Vanessa said one morning. They were both standing in the bathroom, getting ready for work. She was shaving her legs — one leg up on the closed toilet — and he was drying himself off after his shower. The bathroom was still steamy and fragrant.

"I'd like you to meet him, too," said David. He was uplifted by the thought but also apprehensive. Poor Ian, and his ever-increasing cast of characters. David wanted to make sure that Vanessa was someone who would stay in his life, someone who wouldn't disappear.

David told Vanessa about Laura's affair. He said it lightly one afternoon. "My wife went through a lesbian phase recently," he said.

Vanessa just sat there contemplating this. "You mean, she wasn't a lesbian when you were married?" she said.

80

"Not to my knowledge," he said. "Not to hers, either." He immediately felt embarrassed and wanted to talk about something else. He felt as though Laura's behavior was some reflection on him.

But Vanessa was fine about it. "Well," she said, "it's a pattern we're seeing more of lately. Wives on the rebound from marriages. Picking up young men in bars, or having lesbian relationships. Something they would never have dreamed of doing before. It's a way to cope with their new freedom, and make sure that it doesn't turn into loneliness. Of course," she added, "the impulse could be quite real, quite necessary, but mostly I think it's just another way to reach out and not feel so alone in the world."

Yes, yes, he thought, that was it. It was hard being *anybody* alone in New York, man or woman. When you were alone, you began to think that you would always be that way, that you would end up dying alone in a single-room-occupancy hotel. You lapsed into bouts of existential thought. You got out your old copy of *L'Étranger* and you grew extremely depressed.

Laura was alone all the time now. Every time he called to speak to Ian, she was there. She always said she was busy, that she was working on a drawing, or cooking dinner, or reading, but he could recognize a pitch of loneliness in her voice.

"I know you're still kind of angry at me," he would say, "because of how I reacted that day, but I just want you to know that I'm concerned about you, Laura. I think you should get out more."

"I get out as much as I'd like," she said. "I'm fine, David, believe me."

But somehow he couldn't; she seemed overly eager to prove that she was thriving. When he saw her during his visits to pick up or deposit Ian, she looked so pale, humorless. She still hadn't bought any new furniture for the apartment, and it wasn't that she didn't have the money. The place looked depressing now.

He remembered how cold the rooms got in winter. The heat, when it came, clattered through the pipes in the early morning. David used to wake up and think a train was about to run him down.

He thought of Laura, wrapping herself in a blanket in that cold apartment. And Ian, shivering in his youth bed. He had one final urge to go back there, to try and set things right, but then that passed, and he knew that he would never want to live there again.

He was with Vanessa now, and she provided his heat and light. She made his apartment feel more populated. She left her makeup case out on the counter of his bathroom, and he would sometimes examine it—all the bewildering tiny pots of color and gloss, and some viscous substance that he couldn't identify. Vanessa loved cosmetics. She liked anything you could put on your face and later wash off. She used egg masks, natural kohl, lipsticks in berry flavors.

He couldn't help comparing the two women. Laura seemed to need so little to get through the day, but she was never truly happy. Vanessa, on the other hand, needed so much, all those millions of accessories, yet she seemed to be quite content.

Once he came up behind Vanessa when she was "putting on her face," as she called it. He stood and watched her in the mirror, saw the careful way she applied brown eyeshadow with a tiny brush and dark red lip gloss with her fingers.

She was beautiful, and she had easily allowed herself to be included in his life. He thought then that even she must know something about being alone, that no one was immune to it. She needed him; he was good company. He put his arms around her neck, and she smiled slightly in the mirror, and continued to color herself in.

CHAPTER SEVEN

On his first day of school, Ian clung to Laura's leg and would not let go. His urgency first touched and then embarrassed her; he was getting too old for this, she thought. She stood in the center of the classroom and gently tried to pry him off. Finally the teacher came over and lured Ian away with the promise of magic markers. Soon he was off in a corner, drawing happily.

"He'll be fine," the teacher assured her, and her voice was kind but dismissive.

Before Laura left, she stood for a moment in the doorway, watching another kid approach Ian hesitantly. Socialization started so early. Was this the root of courtship, the way the boys and girls played together, or punched each other softly?

For a few minutes she wandered the gleaming halls of the school. In every classroom, these things were taking place; it was just that the ages changed. At the end of the hallway was a classroom full of serious sixth graders, all of them wearing plastic eye goggles and melting things over Bunsen burners.

She felt slightly jealous of these children; she wanted to be one of them again. In sixth grade Laura had loved school more than any other year. Her teacher, Miss Bannister, taught school as though it were a game. Once she stood with an apple perched on her head, acting out the William Tell story. She was glamorous, and very generous with her time. The classroom was full of animals: cell-block tiers of guinea pigs and gerbils and parakeets, and a window with four fishtanks bubbling in it. The class was known as Miss Bannister's Menagerie, and when the end of the year came, several of the children cried and had to be pulled from the classroom. The teacher would not be back in the fall. She was moving East, she announced on the last day of school.

Years later, when Laura went off to college, she had a recurrent fantasy of searching for Miss Bannister, tracking her down to a fashionable apartment in Manhattan and ringing her doorbell. The two women would sit outside on the terrace, sipping mai tais and becoming the best of friends.

The love you felt for a teacher was always cumbersome. You could never talk about it; you just had to sit there every day listening and swooning. Everyone Laura had ever really loved was a teacher to her in some way. Certainly David had been, at first. He would take her up to the laboratory at Yale and show her slides under a microscope. He explained things so well all the time — the action of DNA and RNA, the names of different trees, the rules of basketball. He had a careful, didactic voice that she trusted fully. And Julia had been a teacher as well, without really enjoying this role.

Laura continued to walk down the hall. She went by the gymnasium and peered through the portholes on the double doors. A film was droning away, with an ancient soundtrack. The projector sputtered out words, the voice of some narrator, probably long dead. On the screen an Eskimo woman slipped under a fur blanket, her breasts darkly bare for a moment. The children in the audience whooped.

84

She knew the film; it was *Nanook of the North*. She had seen it herself in school, two decades earlier. She wondered if she too had laughed in embarrassment during that moment in the film. She wondered whether Ian would laugh. He had already seen his mother naked many times, and once he had accidentally seen Julia on her way into the shower. Laura had never made a big deal over things like that. Sometimes when she got dressed in the morning, Ian would come into the room and sit on the edge of her bed, watching with only a vague interest.

These days her morning rituals were carried out without much pleasure or thought. She felt herself switch into an automatic gear. She would feed Ian and walk him to school, and then she would return to the apartment to work. When she was done, she would sit in the living room and listen to music until it was time to pick Ian up. On weekends she would sit in her study with her old terrycloth bathrobe on.

One Sunday afternoon Ian came into the room and said, "Ma, are you ever going to get dressed again?"

She realized then that she had been wearing her bathrobe for twenty-four hours, had even slept in it. She hadn't gone outside, and she had forgotten to shower. She was suddenly embarrassed.

"You're right, sweetie," she said. "I'll get dressed now and we'll go for a walk."

She took Ian to the Museum of Natural History, a place he loved. They had been there many times, and he had one favorite display. He raced right past the arching skeletons of dinosaurs and the windows crowded with tomahawks and feather head-dresses, and led her into the wing that featured life-sized dioramas of prehistoric life. Ian pressed against the braided rope and stared at the scene inside.

"Cavemen," he whispered to himself.

Inside the window a caveman was bringing home an animal for supper, some sort of furry, dead thing slung over his shoulder. The cavewoman was waiting back at home, building a fire. She knelt just inside the cave, and her arms were piled high with wood. There was a genderless cave-child sitting out in the dirt, playing a game with small rocks. It was like any family anywhere in the world.

Ian seemed fascinated. Out of all the displays, this was the one he went back to again and again. Was it the idea of prehistoric life that thrilled him, she wondered, or was it just a family that he wanted? She watched him in the dark shadow-light of the museum and tried to figure it out. He was staring at the scene, transfixed, and his mouth was dropped slightly open. He held on to the rope and strained to see into that other life.

She worried that Ian would grow up deprived. There was no way to tell; he was a placid boy who liked to keep things to himself. In that respect they were very much alike. In other ways, she felt so separate from him. She would remember, *He's a boy*, and this would throw her off.

One afternoon Ian brought home a drawing he had done in school. It was a picture of a house, with tall, broccoli-like trees on either side. Inside the house, a man with a hat on smoked a pipe, and a woman sat at a table, eating what appeared to be spaghetti. A little boy sat on the floor, playing with a dog.

They had no house like that, they had no dog, and Laura and David were legally separated. But this was Ian's vision, and his teacher had deemed it perfectly normal. It left Laura unsettled, though. Where was Ian getting his imagery? She always expected him to bring home angry, dark drawings of a house divided, but he never did.

After nursery school let out, Laura would sometimes take Ian to the park. He would play in the sandbox and she would sit with the other mothers on a bench nearby. The mothers sat close together, talking about their children. They never knew one another's names, and yet they spoke as if they were intimate.

"Our kids play well together," the thin woman said to Laura one afternoon.

Laura watched as Ian and the thin woman's daughter poured sand into each other's buckets. "It's nice," she said.

The thin woman shifted on the bench and sighed. "She's got learning problems, my little girl," she said. "They already diagnosed it."

"I'm sorry," said Laura.

"Well, she still has a good time," said the woman.

They sat and watched. In a few minutes the elegant woman showed up and sat down on the other side of Laura. She arranged her elaborate scarves and purse. "Hello again," she said. "Been here long?"

"Just a few minutes," said Laura. The elegant woman's son had just stepped into the sandbox very timidly. One leg was out, one leg in. He looked toward his mother for encouragement, and she nodded for him to go ahead.

"I hate how he's so scared," the elegant woman said. "I used to be like that as a girl, always cringing, and I hoped that my kids wouldn't end up that way, too. His father's so loud and fearless, and Benjamin is so timid about everything."

"Don't worry," Laura said. "Look at him." Benjamin had finally climbed into the sandbox and was sitting between Ian and the thin woman's girl. They were all sifting sand into big red pails.

"I worry about Ian, too," Laura said after a while. "His father and I are separated. I worry that he's missing something."

"It will all be fine," the thin woman said. "We may not get through our lives, but they will. They'll do just fine."

In the sandbox, the children looked like businessmen making a deal. Sand got passed from hand to hand, poured and filtered through fingers. At the end of the afternoon, the women collected their children and left in the dimming light, saying they would see one another soon. Laura held Ian's hand as they walked home. "Did you have fun?" she always asked, and always he considered the question very carefully before saying yes.

In April of that year, Laura turned twenty-eight. She spent her birthday quietly. Julia did not call. Laura and Ian had a big pancake breakfast and then went out for a long walk down Columbus Avenue. They sang songs as they walked, and she taught him the words to "Go Tell Aunt Rhody." Even now, the song still made her sad. In kindergarten she had wept over the old gray goose, who died in a mill pond, standing on her head. But Ian seemed to like the song, and his voice was sure. When they got home Laura did some sketches, and Ian played with his See-and-Spin toy. He pulled hard on the string. "HOW DOES A COW SOUND?" asked a phantom male voice.

"Moo," said Ian, and a moment later a cow sound corroborated. Ian kept pulling the string, working his way through an entire barnyard.

"Remember when we went to Iowa last time to see Grandma and Grandpa?" she asked. Ian nodded. "We'll go there again soon," she said. "You can play with Hector the dog again; it'll be fun. Maybe this summer. You can sleep in my old room."

That afternoon, as expected, her parents called from Iowa, and each of them spoke to her from a different extension in the house. "Is it still cold in the city?" her father asked.

"No, it's pretty nice out," Laura answered.

"Well, we've got almost a foot of snow," her mother said. "You should see your father riding on his new snowplow. He looks a sight."

The conversation halted then, and her father coughed. "We wanted to ask you, Laura," he said, "seeing that it's been so long now." He paused. "Well, we wondered if you and David might be considering getting back together again."

"I've read about that happening," her mother said.

Laura didn't know what to say. Even now, after all this time, they still thought she would live with David again. "No," she said softly. "I doubt it very much."

She put Ian on the phone after a while, and he talked in non sequiturs about school, and a squirrel he had seen in the park, and what had happened on "Sesame Street" the day before. Laura's parents listened attentively, holding on to every word.

When he was through, Laura got back on to say goodbye. "Well, happy birthday again," her mother said. "We've sent you a check in the mail, and you ought to be getting it soon. We didn't know what to get you this year, what you like anymore."

It was a moment that made Laura want to give in to the easy comfort of her parents' voices: her father's slight rasp and her mother's hesitation before each word. Laura had heard these voices her whole life, across kitchen tables, through screen doors. They had said different things to her: *Come down for supper, dear,* or *What a beautiful dress.* Mild words, always. Her parents were the mildest people in the world. There they were out on their farm, eating seedless grapes in the evening, listening to the radio. They were a permanent fixture on the farm, and Laura liked that. Throughout everything, she could always invoke the image of her parents, William and Cecile, and they were always right there on the same porch, at twilight.

Later that evening she had dinner with Carolyn and Rachel. The three women went to a Japanese restaurant and sat on straw mats. They held lacquered soup bowls in their hands. The lighting was low, and they drank thimbles of plum wine. Laura felt her face grow warm as she drank.

"Well," she said, looking at her watch, "I'm officially twenty-eight."

"It's a good age," said Rachel. "I liked turning twenty-eight. Thirty is going to be the hard one."

"I can't think that far ahead," said Laura. "I have no idea where I'll be in two years." She imagined herself still in the apartment with Ian, still making the same simple dinners for him: baked chicken, sweet potatoes, Bosco. Still thinking about Julia Price every so often, and feeling that slight disorientation that always accompanied thoughts of Julia.

"I know that I don't want to be alone," Laura said.

"You and Ian could stay at my apartment if you want," offered Carolyn. "I get depressed on my birthday, too."

"I don't mean now," said Laura. "I mean in two years. I don't think I could bear to be alone."

"What about a lover?" Carolyn asked, and her voice was careful. *Lover* was such a neutral, ambiguous word. But somehow it was appropriate here. Whenever Laura imagined having a lover now, she couldn't give the person a body, or distinct features. She just imagined that same feeling she had had with Julia, being held in those long arms, and then that desire to *talk* about it to someone, wanting to broadcast it. To say: *I have never been touched like this before. Let me tell you what it's like.* The desire to explicate, to imbue with vocabulary.

"I don't know," said Laura. "It doesn't just happen that way. You don't just *find* a lover."

The Japanese waitress slipped into the room then, removing plates. The women were silent. "Yes you do," said Carolyn, when the waitress was gone. "That's how you met Julia, isn't it? It isn't any different between women. Don't these things just sort of *happen*? I mean, isn't it the way people meet each other?"

"I don't even remember anymore," said Laura.

There was a moment of birthday desperation then, and she wondered how any of them would get through their lives. It seemed that there were so many women alone in New York, women standing on line in supermarkets buying cold pasta salad and diet soda. It was the added element of choice that made being alone acceptable, even desirable. This other kind of loneliness was something else; it was the thing her parents worried about for her. It was the kind of thing she worried about for Ian as well—hoping that when she left him at school each day, he would not be ignored by other kids and abandoned in a remote corner with the fishtank and the hamster cage.

At the end of dinner, the waitress came back and silently presented Laura with a plate of red bean ice cream that had a single candle burning in the center. Rachel and Carolyn sang to her in unsteady voices.

"Make a wish," the waitress said, bending down, the sleeve of her kimono lightly brushing Laura's cheek. Instantly Laura remembered Julia in her kimono on a Sunday morning, Julia embracing her with the black and gold wings of that kimono. Laura closed her eyes on the vision now, and made a wish.

CHAPTER EIGHT

T here's a woman at school," Rachel said, "who I think you should meet."

Laura knew what that meant.

"She's nice," Rachel added. "She's writing a thesis on Colette."

Laura said she didn't feel like meeting anyone, but later in the week, when Rachel invited her to a women's poetry reading at Columbia, she agreed to go. It was understood that this woman, Fern Bergman, would be there. The more Laura thought about it, the more she realized that meeting Fern Bergman would be a good experiment. She could find out whether Julia had been a fluke, a flash in the pan.

Mindy the babysitter was unavailable, so Laura put Ian in his stroller and took him along with her. The poetry reading was held in a large, bright classroom. Laura was late, and when she got there, someone was already reading. She crept quietly into the room, maneuvering the stroller between chairs. The audience was made up mostly of women, and a few men. Laura spotted

Rachel in a corner, sitting next to a thin, dark woman who must, Laura thought, be Fern Bergman.

Laura took a seat by the window. She hoisted Ian out of his stroller and up onto her lap. He was falling asleep already, and his thumb was hooked in his mouth.

The poet finished, and there was polite applause. Then another poet stood at the front of the room. Her name, she announced, was June Wolf, and she would be reading from a work in progress. She flipped through some loose pages and began to read:

> "I am a river
> I come forth with great rushing water.
> Do not be afraid to dip your foot in.
> O the water may be cold and rough,
> But the bottom offers sweet rest and shade
> Down among the rocks and coral
> Down among the silver flickering fish.
> I am a river
> I am a woman who lives in Brooklyn.
> Here are the keys to my apartment."

Laura snickered, and then Ian woke up and began to cry. He struggled to get off Laura's lap. Every head in the room now turned toward her. The poet was tentatively beginning a new poem, but her voice faltered. This was Laura's cue to move, to get out. She held Ian in her arms and managed to push the stroller forward with her elbows. Soon she was in the hall, and someone closed the door behind her.

When the reading was over, Rachel and Fern found Laura, and they all went out for coffee. Ian was asleep once again.

"What a cute kid," Fern Bergman said.

"Thank you," said Laura. She glanced quickly at Fern; the woman had straight black hair parted severely in the middle. Her face was undistinguished, her features somehow blurry. She spoke in a tight, nervous voice.

"I might have a kid someday," said Fern. "If I ever finish my thesis."

"Oh, you'll finish," Rachel said. "Just get through comps and you'll be fine."

They sat at a table at the back of the West End Café. Laura periodically glanced down at Ian, who was sleeping through it all. Laura listened to Fern talk and watched her carefully. *I can never love Fern Bergman*, she thought, and it gave her a small moment of triumph to know this. The fact that she could not love Fern Bergman, that she was not in the least attracted to her, was significant. Laura took a deep breath and leaned back in her chair, relaxing finally.

"The whole department is sexist," Fern was saying. "I tell you, it's everywhere."

"I don't know," said Rachel. "My experience has been pretty good here. I've been treated well."

"You're in a different department," said Fern. "Try comp lit, and then you'll be singing a different tune."

Laura felt blissfully removed from the world of academics. "I'm an illustrator," she said when Fern asked her what she did, and the title had a real cachet to it.

"It's so nice to meet someone who's not a graduate student," said Fern. "Everyone I know lives in these pigeonhole apartments and spends their lives in the library. But you live in the real world. I mean, you have a *kid*. That's amazing."

Rachel looked pleased, and Laura realized that she must think the set-up was working. Rachel moved back an inch from the table, as though to give Laura and Fern more room.

Somehow the subject of women came up, and Fern talked openly about the first lover she had ever had, back at Brandeis. "We were supposed to be studying the Talmud for this religion class," said Fern, "but things ended up getting sexual. You know. These days, I don't really care whether or not I meet the woman of my dreams. I just want to finish my thesis. Just a couple of months more, and then I can breathe again. Then I can be out there again."

Out there was a term that Laura didn't understand. She supposed that she herself was *out there*, but she felt so enclosed by the trappings of her life — by her drawings, her apartment, her sleeping son. *Out there* was somewhere else.

"I need to get my little boy home to bed," Laura finally said. Rachel looked more disappointed than Fern.

"Nice to meet you," Fern Bergman said, shaking Laura's hand.

"You too," said Laura, buoyed up again from the desire she did not feel.

David and Vanessa went away for the weekend to an inn in Vermont. Every morning a small carving board with homemade bread and butter was left outside their door.

"Oh, look," Vanessa exclaimed each morning, surprised all over again. It made David want to say to her, *What are you so surprised about? They do that every day. Don't be a child.* Then he felt guilty for just having these thoughts. Why shouldn't Vanessa be surprised and touched by someone else's small gesture? Perhaps he could learn a lesson from this.

At night they had dinner in the small dining room, surrounded by crystal and heavy silver and the soft light from the fireplace.

"Let's not go back to the city," Vanessa said. "Let's just hide out here forever. We could get jobs as lumberjacks."

David smiled and held her hand across the table. His earlier annoyance with her had disappeared, and was replaced by a real benevolence. He thought then that he would do anything for her. He wasn't even sure what this meant, exactly — this desire to do *anything* for someone. It was the only way he could think of to understand the different things you might feel for a woman. It wasn't something you could quantify; you could only say, *She is someone I would do anything for,* or *She is someone I would do certain things for.*

Vanessa was demanding, but he realized that this was a trait he liked; Laura had been anything but demanding.

"I really wish we could spend more time together," Vanessa would say, and David would be startled.

"Of course," he would answer. "We'll make a point of it."

He brought Ian to meet Vanessa for the first time on a Saturday morning. He felt extraordinarily tense as they walked to her apartment. Ian's hand was locked in David's, and he was chattering away about something he had seen on television. David needed a drink of water; he needed something to soothe him, something clear and cold and simple. This must be what it is like to be a child, he thought, and to wake up parched in the middle of the night. Thrown out of a dream, the throat like sand.

"How far is it?" Ian demanded.

"Just around the corner," David said.

When they got to Vanessa's, David immediately went into the kitchen and drank three glasses of water from the tap while Vanessa and Ian stood there waiting.

"Well," he said, when he had finally had enough, "now I can introduce you properly. Vanessa, this is my extra-terrific son Ian, and Ian, this is my special friend Vanessa." It was a sort of idiotic thing to have said, he knew, but he was beyond the point of caring.

Vanessa was helping Ian out of his ski parka, that tiny red suit with mittens attached by clips. "Here," Vanessa was saying. "I'll just hang this up in the closet for you, Ian, then we can go see what toys there are for you to play with."

Toys. David had forgotten to bring some of Ian's toys over to the apartment. Ian would fling open the bedroom door and find nothing there for him. They would have to improvise; David imagined himself desperately knotting two towels together into the crude shape of a doll. "Here's Raggedy Andy," David would say, thrusting the thing at Ian and praying for the willing suspension of disbelief.

But Vanessa had taken care of everything. When the bedroom door was flung open, David found himself staring into a warehouse of toys. A train set was laid out in a huge loop on the rug. A few large stuffed animals were slung across the bed, and a Nerf basketball hoop had been attached to the wall. Here and there were random, unfamiliar toys.

"Wow," Ian said, standing still in the doorway. He looked up at David. "Can I play with them, Dad?" he asked in a reverent voice.

"You'll have to ask Vanessa," said David. "I think they belong to her."

"Of course you can play with them," Vanessa said. "And when you come back here you can play with them again. They will always be here for you."

David thought that she must have gone out to Toys-R-Us one day while he was at work, and spent a fortune. He was overwhelmed by this gesture, the way Vanessa had been overwhelmed by the bread and butter that had waited outside their door. The world was made up of small gestures. They were all linked together in a kind of enzyme chain, and somehow they made up a whole life.

David and Vanessa stood in the doorway for a few minutes and watched Ian playing. He went over to the train first and sat in the middle of the loop. He looked like a little pasha, dazed and indulged as the train clattered along its course, bells ringing, engine wheezing. It was all there to entertain him, and he knew it. David looked at the expression on Ian's face: the happy smugness of a little boy, eyes half closed like a cat in a patch of sun.

When David looked at Vanessa now he was shocked to see the same expression there as well; Vanessa had scored a coup. Ian would love her forever. He would want to come back here again and again, back to this cream-colored bedroom with all these bright new toys. The room had taken on a new tenor; it was usually so clean and light, with Vanessa's white bedspread and wicker furniture. This was the bed where they made love all the time, this surface as long and grand as a runway, and now it was covered with stuffed animals. The room smelled different now, too; it had the odor of new toys, of polyurethane and cardboard. Ian sat in the middle, inhaling it all.

That night, as they ate pizza in the living room, Ian sat in Vanessa's lap, playing with her scarf.

"What a charmer already at three and a half," she was saying. "Just think what you'll be like when you're your daddy's age."

"I have a cow," said Ian. "It could wear a scarf if it wanted to."

"Nothing like a good non sequitur," David said to Vanessa.

He took Ian back to his apartment a little later. He didn't want to have Ian see him sleeping with another woman. As they left Vanessa's, he felt sad saying goodnight.

"You are wonderful," he whispered into her hair.

David carried Ian most of the way home; he positioned him so that he could feel Ian's warm breath against his neck. It was a landmark day, and he would come to refer to it as the Day of Toys. It was the day he was absolutely certain that Vanessa loved him. She would not have promised that Ian could return again and again if she had not seen this as lasting for a long time. A dishonest woman might do that and then break up with the father a week later, leaving the poor little child to fantasize for the rest of his life about the wonderful array of toys he was once allowed to touch. They would grow more elaborate in his mind until every night the kid lay in his youth bed imagining gigantic walk-in dollhouses with faucets that ran cherry soda, and life-sized stuffed animals that could talk when you pulled a string. All of this gone because of a lover's change of heart.

You couldn't do that to children; it was as simple as that. Occasionally David thought of Laura and Julia, and wondered if Ian had felt abandoned.

"Julia had cameras," Ian would say, "and a chair you could spin in, and a room that was white."

Was there wistfulness in his voice, or was that a subtler emotion that evolved later in life? David wasn't sure. It was touching to imagine a three-year-old feeling wistful. He often imbued his son with the emotions that he himself felt.

Don't long for anything that once happened, he wanted to say to Ian. *Your mother and I weren't happy together. Your mother and Julia weren't happy together. Be glad that things move forward all the time.*

Children might not be able to understand the past, or nostalgia, but David was certain that they could understand progress. They were so keyed into the idea of forward motion; they were proud of themselves when they were finally toilet-trained, or learned to walk.

Ian had just staggered up from the bedroom floor one day and walked zigzag across the room for the first time. Laura and David had called out to him, their arms open, but Ian had let out a single laugh and continued to walk right past them and out into the hall, where of course he fell. They watched as he picked himself up slowly and then continued to walk farther. It was pure progress, David had thought, and there would be no turning back.

CHAPTER NINE

When spring came and the days turned warm, Laura opened all of the windows in the apartment and let the air blow through. Ian sat on the floor in the living room, and the wind lifted his blond hair up all around his head, as though he were playing on the deck of a ship. Laura put children's records on the phonograph, and Ian danced around the open area to the music. She envied his ability to move loose-jointed like that, his lack of self-consciousness. She liked to watch him as he moved, as he figured out the different things his arms and legs could do.

In May Laura decided it was time to buy some new furniture. Not too many things — just a big, soft chair for now, and a dining room table.

She had passed Knock Wood a few times when she went to visit Carolyn in the Village. The furniture in the window of the store was very beautiful — handmade, heavy oak pieces that were notched and glowing. The store itself was large and sunny; Laura had often peered through the window but had never gone in.

She wandered into the store late one afternoon. There were only a couple of other customers there; two old women were testing out a bench. Carpenters were at work in the back room; she could see a man wielding a saw and could smell cedar shavings.

There weren't many finished items around, since most of them were built to order. Laura envisioned a very long, oval table for the dining room. She pictured a table with heavy legs, with no seams in the middle, no parts that folded out. A table where people would sit down to eat after spending the day hunting or fishing or inventing something.

"Can I help you?" a young man asked.

She said yes and began to describe what she wanted.

"We have a wonderful tablemaker," he said. "Do you want to come see some finished tables?"

She followed him into the workroom. A radio was playing some blues, and a few men were at work. "Come," the salesman said, and he led her through yet another door. In the very back, behind the workroom, was a smaller room. When they entered, there was a blur of wood chips flying into the air.

"Hey, Jane!" the salesman called over the whir of a saw, and in a moment the noise and precipitation stopped. Everything floated to the ground; a woman stood facing them.

"Sorry," she said. "I didn't hear you come in."

Her face was flushed from working. She cocked the saw against her hip and smiled. Laura blushed and immediately felt idiotic. It was only a smile, nothing more. She was too responsive; she was a sensitive plant, curling up at the slightest provocation.

The salesman explained what Laura was interested in, and then disappeared. Laura looked around. The room was crowded with tables: three or four in various stages of completion. She was so distracted by this woman that she could barely focus on anything. She could see only a plateau of wood, both pale and dark. The woman reeled off a list of prices and styles, and Laura didn't understand a word she said.

She was the kind of woman Julia would have pointed out on the street, whispering, "See, that's one over there. I can just tell." She was small, with blond hair cut blunt and a single bright earring in one ear. There was a thick silver band on her wrist. Her eyes were surprisingly blue. Once again Laura was drawn in; she felt a familiar elevator-drop of arousal.

Laura blindly ordered a table, agreed to anything. She didn't know what size she wanted, or what type of wood. Anything was fine: cherry, oak, walnut, a whole forest sprouting up in her dining room. She ended up spending much more money than she wanted to. The woman had Laura sit down for a minute while she filled out an order form, and Laura watched as she propped a clipboard on her knee and began to write.

Laura looked wildly around the room for something that would calm her, some object she could fix on. The woman put the clipboard down then and looked at her. "Can I ask you something?" she said.

Laura nodded. "Sure," she said nervously.

"Do you really want a handmade table?" the woman asked. "I mean, they're very expensive, and I put a lot of time into them. Maybe you just want something from a regular place. You could go over to Workbench; I hear they're having a sale."

"No," Laura said, mortified. "I'm sorry; I was thinking about something else. Your tables are beautiful. Really. I do want one."

"Okay," the woman said, and she continued to write.

She was boyish, almost handsome, Laura thought. *Handsome* gave images of strong features, good lines. It reached beyond the boundaries of gender.

"What's your name?" the woman asked, and Laura was startled.

"Laura Giovanni," she answered, and immediately realized that this was not a personal question; the woman needed to fill in her name on the order form. Laura gave her address and her telephone number, and she felt disappointed.

But then the woman put down her clipboard and said, "I'm Jane Bloom."

Laura wanted to laugh. She was out of her element here; she didn't know what she was doing or what she felt. At that moment all she really wanted to do was keep this woman there, detain her a little longer. It was the same type of feeling she had initially felt with Julia.

"Have you been building furniture for a long time?" she asked. *What a boring question!* she thought, but it was the best she could come up with.

"I've done a lot of things," said Jane. "Soldering. Stained glass, too, but it was bad to breathe in all that lead. But I like this best."

"Oh," said Laura. All words had flown away from her.

Jane began talking naturally, telling Laura how stained glass had ultimately seemed so useless to her. Building tables, she said, was different. She liked the thought of people sitting around a table, and kids spilling milk on it at dinner.

Laura thought of Ian; she imagined him growing up and doing his homework on the dining room table that Jane had built. She imagined herself coming in with a plate of Twinkies and a glass of milk, placing them gently down next to his loose-leaf binder. The tabletop would be speckled with paper reinforcements.

"Well, my kid would certainly spill milk on your table," Laura said, and in an odd way it was a seduction line. She spoke as though it had another meaning, as though "milk" and "table" were code words.

"Ah, you have kids," Jane said.

"One," said Laura.

There was a momentary lull. Jane would think she was married. She would think Laura was peculiar, flirting with her but not really knowing what she was doing. "Look," Laura said, "would you like to have a drink with me?"

Jane paused. "Sure," she said. "You mean today?"

Laura's voice lifted. "Today, or whenever," she said. "I mean, I am free today, if you could make it."

Jane looked at the clock. "I get off in an hour," she said. "Then I have to wash up. I could meet you in an hour and a quarter. Would that be all right? Just come to the entrance of the store."

"Fine," said Laura. "I have some errands to run anyway." She wondered where these words were coming from. She tried to invent at least one errand — didn't she need *anything* for the house, some orange juice, or light bulbs, or thread? She left the store and walked out into the street.

In Washington Square Park Laura sat on a bench and listened to the litany of drug dealers who were strolling along the paths. "Smoke, smoke, smoke," they said in soft voices. Laura leaned back against the slats of the bench. She wondered again what she was doing. She had no idea of what she could get from a woman. She couldn't imagine ever living with one. Everyone would know, and she was too old to have a roommate. But who, actually, was *everyone*? There seemed to be an anonymous group of judges out there in the world, arbiters of taste and morality. "It's what *everyone* is wearing," her mother would say when she took Laura shopping in Des Moines, and held a pleated skirt against Laura's waist. *Everyone will know.* It was stupid to give your life to these faceless people; they probably weren't even paying attention. They were flying off to Paris, selecting the fashions that would become the hit of the Midwest, or telling someone else how to live. No one was looking, at least not closely.

At six-fifteen Laura met Jane at the entrance of the store, and they walked around the corner to a small bar on West Fourth Street. Laura drank her usual single glass of white wine, and Jane had two beers. Laura supposed that it was up to her to carry the conversation. What would this woman be interested in talking about? It almost didn't matter. Anything would be preferable to silence.

Laura finally spoke without thinking. "I know this is very intrusive," she said, "but are you gay?" She knew at once that it was a ridiculous thing to have asked, but she needed to know. She took a long drink of wine.

Jane smiled. "Well, that's being blunt," she said. "But don't worry." She leaned back. "I've been gay my entire conscious life," she said. "And you?"

"Just this year," said Laura, "and now I don't know what I am."

"So you trusted me," asked Jane, "because of my one earring?"

Laura was confused. "What do you mean?" she asked.

"Well," Jane said, "some people think it's a statement to the world."

Laura did not know anything about signals or symbols or dress codes. Her own love for Julia Price had felt unique, sexual, wrapped up in the ideas of comfort and danger. She had never once thought of it as a political choice. She vaguely knew that there were women who did, women who had very little to do with men, but she could not really understand it.

They sat across from each other in the dark bar, and Laura listened as Jane told her about her last girlfriend, a woman named Franny. One afternoon Jane and Franny had decided to pierce their ears, so they had gone to a Woolworth's in Queens and had one lobe pierced each, and split a pair of starter posts.

"You sure you want only one hole?" the saleswoman kept saying. "I've never done one hole only, except to some of those fairies who come in here."

But they had insisted, and the saleswoman had shrugged, and swabbed Jane's earlobe with alcohol. A lot of lesbians wore single earrings, Jane explained to Laura. In Paris in the 1920s, pinkie rings had been the vogue.

"So what's *your* story?" Jane suddenly asked.

It still unhinged Laura to have to talk about anything, and yet if she didn't, she would be perceived as coy. She stammered a few disjointed things about Julia, and their breakup, and her confusion. She explained that she still saw her time with Julia as an isolated event and could not draw any conclusions based on it. Jane didn't press for details.

Laura was flirting; there was no question about that. She heard herself speak, and her voice had a slightly manic quality to it. "I'm in transition," Laura said. "That's the only way I can describe my life right now."

"I like that," said Jane. "*Transition*. It's so ambiguous."

"I try to be ambiguous," said Laura.

"I noticed," Jane said.

There was a long silence.

"So, did you think I was gay when I came into the store?" asked Laura. "Did I look it?"

Jane shook her head slowly, smiling. "I really didn't think about it," she said. "I was working. I do think about other things, you know."

"Like what?" said Laura, and she knew this was a flippant question, a silly line, and she was pleased with herself. She realized that she didn't feel terrified here. It wasn't like her first dinner with Julia. There was an element of sweetness with Jane that was new to Laura.

"Well," said Jane, leaning her head in her hand, "like money. I think about money a lot. How I don't have any."

"What else?" asked Laura.

"Food," said Jane. "And sleep. I love to sleep, and never have enough time. I'm always being woken up by my stupid alarm clock at ridiculously early hours."

"Me too," said Laura. "I have to get my little boy ready for school every morning. He watches cartoons at dawn, and I'm usually half asleep."

"But it must be terrific to actually be a mother," said Jane. "You have all that power."

"It doesn't feel like power," said Laura. "It feels like *something*, but not power." She ripped her napkin into little shreds. "Have you ever wanted to have children?" she asked.

"Yes," said Jane. "I used to fantasize about it, but I could never imagine raising a child alone. It seemed too hard. I need people around me. Not so much because I need distractions all the time, but because I just like knowing they're there. They can even be in the next room; they don't have to be in my presence all the time. It's just the idea of it that I like." She paused. "It's really been a long time since I thought about having kids. It just sort of stopped being an issue. I never made enough money, and the thought of being a single-mother lesbian food-stamp recipient sort of depressed me. You know those women you see in Seven-Elevens — the ones holding a baby over their shoulder, and buying Slim Jims and a pack of beer? Those mothers who look like they're sixteen?"

Laura nodded.

"That's my biggest fear," said Jane. "Becoming like that." She took a long drink. "I see mothers a lot and I feel sorry for them. They look so tired, a lot of them. Not you," she said. "You look wide awake."

Neither of them said anything for a while. Then Laura said, "I am. I love being a mother. It's the only thing that I do naturally. I guess it's biological. It's the only thing that I don't question, that I don't have any regrets about."

Jane nodded. "That's good," she said. "I have this friend Danielle who says that she wants engraved on her tombstone the words: I REGRET EVERYTHING."

Laura laughed. She wanted to hold Jane's hand, but instead she wrapped both hands around her wineglass; she worried for a moment that she might snap off the stem.

"Women are great," said Jane.

It was a disembodied remark, Laura thought. In a comic strip it would be the kind of remark left to a thought-bubble, and not actually uttered aloud. But Jane had not seemed self-conscious saying it. Who, though, was Jane referring to? Was it her friend Danielle who inspired the remark, or was it possibly Laura? Or was it just a remark about *generic* women?

"I agree," said Laura, uncertainly.

She did agree; she had always felt strongly about women. There had been fierce loyalties to friends ever since she was very young. She had been preoccupied by girls in a way she had never been by boys. Boys and men were always in the background; she grew up with a line of farmhands calling things out to her as she stood in the road waiting for the school bus every morning. The farm was filled with men; everywhere she went there was a young, muscular man hovering in the background. They smelled uniformly of manure and industrial soap. They built swings for her in the barn, and one of them made her a doll out of cornhusks. She let them do these things for her, never took any of it seriously.

It was the girls she thought about. There was a great distance between houses, and Laura had to be driven most everywhere, except to visit her friend Annie Carrington, who lived at the next farm, and to whose house Laura would race even in thunderstorms, pushing her way through the high corn to get there. Annie would be standing on the back porch of her frame house, waving Laura on. Annie was just a tiny stick figure to her at that distance, but the thought of her always led Laura forward: Annie in her yellow house, wearing a yellow dress bordered by tiny blue flowers.

Is that what you meant? Laura wanted to ask Jane. That old feeling for women from way back? *Women are great*, Jane had said, and Laura had been surprised to hear her say this. She could not have imagined Julia saying anything like that. She wondered if Julia really liked women, in her heart of hearts.

It was getting late, and Jane was glancing at her watch. "I've got to get on the subway," she said. "It's a long ride."

They exchanged telephone numbers, writing them down on damp cocktail napkins, and Jane said she would call. The table would not be ready for another six weeks. They would see each other before then, Jane promised. On the street, Laura grasped Jane's hand and held it for a fleeting second. It was like touching a piece of art in a museum—she did it so no one would see, she did it just for the sensation of doing it, and then she ran away.

Laura walked uptown for a while. She felt a little bit drunk and happy. Jane had been so easy to talk to, finally. Laura was reminded again of Annie Carrington. She and Annie had had a very quiet friendship. They never worked themselves up into a frenzy about anything. They would sit in the Carringtons' barn for a whole afternoon while it poured outside. The rain would slide off the roof, and the place would be damp and warm, and when they left, their dresses would be stuck all over with little splinters of straw. They played long rounds of Geography, thinking up places they weren't sure really existed: Zanzibar, Mallorca, the Isle of Wight. Neither of them had ever left the Midwest, even though their families were wealthy. Iowa was God's country, Annie's father proclaimed over dinner; he didn't need to go anywhere else. The high point of the year was the 4-H festival at the fairgrounds. Both families went. The fathers were not really friends, but on that one day, both men would stand in the sun together and talk, waving their soft hats to stay cool.

"Bill, did you order that feed from Callahan's?" Annie's father would ask.

"No, his prices were too high last year," Laura's father would answer. "I've switched dealers."

It was male talk; Laura and Annie would stand impatiently nearby, waiting for it to finish. Yet somehow it was also exciting; their fathers lived in a serious, adult world that they themselves knew nothing about. The men would take care of everything and keep the crops thriving. All Annie and Laura had to do was talk about school. As long as they kept their grades high, no one ever bothered them.

Annie's parents were even more passive than Laura's. Her mother would occasionally come into the doorway of the barn and say in her flat voice, "Have you girls done your earth science homework?"

"Hours ago," Annie would answer, and her mother would nod, satisfied, and leave them alone. She would return only with a reward: two plates of pie she had baked. There were no responsibilities; childhood stretched itself out endlessly, like the fields between their houses.

At night in bed the two girls would send telepathic messages to each other. "Think about me at ten o'clock," Laura would say right before she went home for dinner. That night, as they lay in their separate beds, they would try to bridge the distance between them. Laura would close her eyes and think of Annie, picture her face, long and serious, and her blond hair pulled back with a red ceramic barrette.

One day it was Annie who ran across the field. Laura was eating breakfast and reading *Cherry Ames, Flight Nurse* when she looked up and saw Annie coming. "What's Annie up to, do you suppose?" Laura's mother asked.

Her father squinted, looked out the window. "You girls might as well be Siamese twins, you're together so much," he said. In a minute Annie was banging on the screen door.

"I have to tell you something terrible," she said, breathing hard.

"What is it?" Laura asked. "What is it?" Her parents looked on, alarmed.

"We're moving to Idaho!" Annie said, and then she began to cry. They embraced as though she had just announced a death. Laura held her, that narrow eleven-year-old girl whom she spent all her time with. What would they do without each other? Who would move into the house across the field? Probably two old people, farmers right out of *American Gothic*, a husband and wife who would take pot shots at Laura with a rifle if she tried to run through their property. She and Annie would never see each other again. They would never sit in the barn together eating rhubarb pie and allowing themselves a kind of extended dreaminess, the rain and the warmth suspending them in time in that gigantic, cathedral-high room.

One inevitable day the moving vans came and Mrs. Carrington directed the men in and out of the house. Annie and Laura wept and clung and had to be separated by the hands of Annie's father, who was gentle but passionless about the whole thing.

"Come on, girls, it's not the end of the world," he said. "There's always the American postal service. You know how to read and write; that's what you go to school for, after all. Annie, don't cry like that. We have a long car ride ahead of us."

On that hot afternoon Laura stood alone in the road and watched as the Carrington family drove off for the last time. *I thought Iowa was God's country!* she wanted to scream at Annie's father. But she just stood and looked at Annie and her brother, Tyler, who were pressed to the back window of the gunmetal Oldsmobile, cartons piled all around them, blocking the exits. Those tall, quiet parents of hers were taking her away, and there was not a thing Laura could do about it. She had no claim over Annie — she was not a parent, she was just a friend, and friends were routinely separated; it was a fact of life, Laura's mother had said. But Laura wept open-mouthed in the road, leaned against the Carringtons' empty, tilting mailbox until her parents came to find her and bring her home.

Several weeks passed after Laura met Jane, and Jane did not call. Laura spent her time working on drawings, playing with Ian. Every afternoon they watched "Sesame Street" together; it was a ritual that she loved. He would lie on the couch with his head in her lap, and she would stroke his hair. He knew all of the songs, and sang along. Once in a while he became so excited by the music that he had to leap around the room, but he always returned to her before the end of the show.

One night the telephone rang and it was Julia. She was a few blocks away at a dinner party, she said, and she thought she might stop by, if that was all right.

"Of course," Laura said.

It was pouring outside, and when Julia came over she stood in the hallway for a moment and shook the water from her hair. They sat in the living room, and Laura served tea. She was glad that Ian was fast asleep; she didn't want him to see Julia and to run around shrieking, "Julia's back! Julia's back!" It would be embarrassing; Julia would try to smile and would look away. "I'm not really back, you know," she would feel obliged to say after Ian had been returned to his bed. "I *know* that," Laura would say, humiliated. "You don't have to tell me."

But instead they just sat together on the couch, keeping a civil distance. Laura realized that she no longer had the desire to be with Julia; it had somehow lapsed without her missing it. She also didn't have the desire to cook for Julia anymore, to show her how well she could take care of her. Julia advocated autonomy — told Laura that she would not be her teacher or the mainstay of her life — yet on her own, Julia Price became a half-life, an underexposed photograph, a last trace of hair and eyes showing up against a dark background.

Laura thought about the time she had made love with Julia on that couch, how Julia's sweater had crackled with static as she pulled it over her head. Julia always withheld when she made love, always gave the impression that there was something else to her, some part she would not relinquish.

"I thought I would see how you were getting along," said Julia. "I'm going to London for a few months. Leaving on Thursday." She finished a cigarette and tamped it out in a saucer.

"I'm doing fine," Laura said. "I'm seeing someone," she added, and she couldn't look Julia in the eyes. It wasn't even completely true. She looked down in her lap, suddenly embarrassed. When she looked up, Julia was still watching her.

"That's good," Julia said. "I'm glad."

Julia's smoke had laced through the air, and Laura felt trapped by it, by Julia. "Look, you'll forgive me," she said finally. "I need to get to sleep. I've got to get up with Ian at seven."

Julia pulled her shoulder bag around her and stood up. In the doorway she said, "I'm glad you're doing well, Laura. I'll send you a postcard of the Royal Family."

After she left, Laura realized that Julia hadn't even asked her anything about the person she was seeing; she hadn't even been interested in the gender. Did Julia think Laura was seeing a woman, or a man? Maybe she didn't even care.

I'm seeing someone—she had actually said that. Now that she had told Julia this, she needed even more desperately to make it true. She was moral; she had gotten that much from her parents. She kept wondering why Jane didn't call, as she had said she would. Had Laura been too forward, inviting her for a drink? Had she been too gauche asking if Jane was gay? Laura considered making the call herself, but then decided it would be too embarrassing. She couldn't chase this woman. She would have to wait it out.

When six weeks had gone by, Laura decided that Jane would not call. There was the summer to start thinking about. Carolyn wanted to know if she was interested in renting a house with her out at the beach for a week or two. David wanted to take Ian away on a short vacation, and there were arrangements that needed to be made.

One day Laura went to the supermarket and was standing in the produce section when she saw Tom, the man she had met at Carolyn's party, across the aisle. He was hefting a head of romaine lettuce in his hands. He examined it, put it back, selected another one. He was absorbed and did not notice Laura. She first thought she would say hello, and they could push their carts side by side down the aisle, as though they were wheeling baby carriages. Maybe they could drop off their groceries at their respective apartments and reconvene for supper. They could talk about the progress of Laura's divorce and the death of Tom's wife, and after a while they would feel purged. They might fall in love. Tom was handsome, with a kind face and a dark beard. He wore those round wire-rimmed eyeglasses that always made men look compassionate.

Suddenly she turned away from him, busied herself among the endive and the basil. She placed her hands against the hill of crushed ice where the vegetables were kept, and peered into the narrow mirror above it. She could see part of Tom's back across the way, and she waited until he was gone from the mirror, and then she relaxed. She didn't want to see him again, even though he was probably a lovely man. She had been planning on continuing down the aisle, heading for the meat freezer, but now she changed her mind. She could come back tomorrow. She pivoted her cart and quickly headed for the check-out counter, where she was lucky enough to be first on line.

She carried her groceries around the corner and had to shift the bags in her arms to open her front door. Just as she was coming in, the telephone rang, and she dropped everything in the hall and ran to answer it.

It was Jane. Laura recognized her voice immediately, that slightly hoarse start to her words. "Is this Laura?" Jane asked.

"Yes," she answered, and she plunked herself down into a kitchen chair and put her feet up.

"This is Jane Bloom. Your table is ready."

Laura had forgotten all about the table. "Oh, that's great," she said. "Thanks." Then she decided to risk embarrassment. "I was hoping I'd hear from you sooner," she said.

"I'm sorry," said Jane. "It's been a terrible time for me. I wanted to call you, but I just haven't been able to. I can't explain it now. I'm at work." Then she asked if Laura could possibly meet her later that week for dinner. The table would be delivered within a few days; Laura suggested that they initiate it by having dinner at her house. They decided on Saturday.

She hung up the telephone and sat in the kitchen for a while, leaving the groceries abandoned in the hall. She was soon going to see Jane Bloom again. She could envision her standing over a huge table, glazing it with a brush. She could see her arm moving back and forth, working as delicately and persistently as a lover, the pale, neutral surface being covered with light.

There was a good reason why Jane hadn't called. She had spent the past month trying to get over a profound feeling of grief. It had immobilized her, she said. She hadn't called anyone; she had simply gone to work every day and tried not to think at all. Five weeks before, right after she and Laura met, Jane had been formally disowned by her parents.

"I thought I was too old to have it really affect me," she said. "I'm twenty-five and haven't lived at home for years, but it got to me anyway. It was so definite, the real end of things. Like the death of childhood or something."

All of this was said over dinner. Ian sat next to Laura at the new table and sucked spaghetti into his mouth, strand by strand. He was with Laura for the weekend, because David was going away with his girlfriend.

"It's not the financial part that means anything," Jane said. "It's not that kind of disowning. My parents don't have much money, and I never expected anything from them that way. But

I always try to make it down to Florida for the holidays every year. My mother actually said to me, *We don't ever want to see you again.* Right over the telephone."

Laura tried to imagine what it would be like if her parents were to disown her—financially, spiritually, any way at all. How would she bear that, the implicit statement "You are no longer our child"?

"What made you want to tell them?" Laura asked.

"I just wanted to tell the truth for once," said Jane. "I hate all that lying. When they ask me about men, I always have to make things up. For years there was this man Stuart, who I invented. I thought the name sounded Jewish, and I knew they would like that. Stuart Federman. The lie got more and more elaborate. In my mind Stuart looked like James Dean, and he worked in a sporting goods store. I had a dream about him once. This handsome man came and tapped me on the shoulder, and said, 'Do you know who I am?' 'No,' I said. 'I'm Stuart,' he answered, and then we began to kiss just like in a fairy tale. When I pulled back I saw that he had turned into a woman. I think it was my friend's sister. 'There is no Stuart,' I said to my mother on the phone. 'No Stuart, ever. I made him up to please you, and I can't keep it up any longer.'" Jane paused.

"He was like one of the imaginary friends from my childhood," she said. "My parents ran a hotel, and we lived on the third floor. Sometimes I would go out onto the terrace of their room, and I would sit and have long conversations with this person I made up, Mrs. Strong. She was like a man but wore an apron. That's pretty obvious now, but back then everybody thought it was very cute. One night my mother was sick of hotel food, so we had a barbecue on the terrace. She set five paper plates out on the table, and my father said, 'Who's that for, Barbara?' 'Mrs. Strong might be stopping by,' my mother answered, and I was thrilled. She had jumped right into my fantasies, like they were real."

Ian suddenly looked up. "I don't have any imaginary friends," he said. "Some kids do. I don't."

"Well, sweetie, that's because you have real friends," Laura said. "You have fun with Joshua, don't you? And Lisanne?" He nodded solemnly, then went back to his dinner.

Laura and Jane looked at each other across the table. Jane smiled then, but with some effort. Laura wanted to say, *I will never disown you*, but it was absurd. To disown, you had to first own.

Later, after Ian was asleep and the dishwasher was going, they moved from the dining room into the kitchen and sat drinking tea. There was a sleepiness to the room. Jane held the tea egg by its chain, slowly lowering it into her cup.

"I'm glad I came over," she said. "It's very relaxing here."

"I'm glad, too," said Laura. She looked at Jane carefully for a moment, and then she calmly asked her to stay. Jane nodded. It was so much easier this time, the whole process of courtship, and there was no hurry. They finished their tea. Laura rinsed the cups and upturned them on the drainboard. The orange eye of the dishwasher was glowing like a night light.

She went in then to check on Ian. She stood in the entry of his room and watched him as he slept. He had flung his pillow to the floor, something he often did in sleep. He was curled up tightly like a shell. She remembered picking out those pale blue pajamas for him, going to the department store one day and buying a miniature approximation of what she used to buy for David.

She realized that Jane was standing behind her. She turned around; Jane was looking into the room with interest. "What a great room!" she whispered. "All these toys; it's perfect."

They walked together down the hallway and into Laura's bedroom. She had cleaned up furiously that afternoon, had nudged the vacuum cleaner into every possible crevice, sucking up dust and stray paper clips. She had smoothed the comforter more tightly than she ever had before. The bed was like an island, a sandbar in the middle of this calm, dark sea. She went and switched on the small reading lamp next to the bed. Now Laura and Jane threw long shadows on the wall.

Jane sat down on the side of the bed and pressed her hands to her eyes for a second. "I want to apologize for not being the best company tonight," she said. "Things are hard for me right now."

Laura sat next to her and put her arm around Jane's shoulder. She had never touched her before, and had no idea of what she would feel like. It was just a warm shoulder, a rounded edge underneath a maroon shirt. They kissed, and Laura thought of Stuart, and Jane's dream. Was she being transformed now, as in that dream? Was she a changeling?

They undressed and disturbed the perfectly made bed. With their clothes off they peered at each other tentatively; Jane's muscles were packed in densely against each other. The calves of her legs were hard, even at rest. They always seemed flexed. But it was her arms that Laura thought about again and again after Jane left the next morning. When Jane wrapped her in her arms she felt all the protection of a safety bar being lifted into position on a roller coaster seat. You sit down, and the man locks you in — *thunk* — the thick metal rail eases into place. You just know you won't fly out; you can take every hill and every unexpected drop.

She looked at Jane's hands in the muted light of the room, and they could have been anyone's. Did gender really matter so much? What about the singularity of a particular face, or body? There was a dark half-moon of wood stain under each of Jane's fingernails. The thumb of the left hand had a small beauty mark right over the joint. Jane still wore her bracelet, but even that no longer signified gender. Out in the street, men with hair down to their waists breezed by every day. Last week Laura had seen a man with small bells on his fingers and a sapphire studding each ear.

They had somehow slid down to the edge of the bed. Jane

pulled her back, dragged her as if from choppy water, and moved her to the middle. They were centered there once again, and Laura had to stop to draw a breath, to pull away and feel the air on her skin for a moment.

It is daylight, though, that tests everything. You look at the face close to yours and ask, *Does it hold up even in the strong light of morning? Does it bring happiness, or at least the potential for happiness?* When Jane woke up she was bewildered at first. She turned and saw Laura, and then she looked around her and saw the Degas prints on the walls, the clothing piled on the chair, and it slowly came back, like a forgotten name. Laura was still asleep, even though the room was bright.

Jane lay on her back for a while. Whenever she woke up in a new woman's bed, she liked to have a few moments to herself, a little time to look around the room. The window was pushed open, and the curtains were moving. This was a good sign. Laura was a woman who liked air, she thought. Jane had once had a lover who insisted that the windows be sealed shut all the time. Her apartment had been like a convection oven, with the smell of stale heat always there. But this apartment smelled pretty good. Jane lay under the unfamiliar blankets and ran her hand over the fabric. Something light, all cotton weave. She noticed things like this.

When Laura woke up they stayed in bed for a few more minutes, awkwardly talking, and finally they got up and ate breakfast together in the kitchen. Ian sat in the living room, cradling a cereal bowl on his lap and watching cartoons. Every few seconds they could hear dynamite explosions followed by Ian's appreciative laughter.

Laura looked embarrassed. She sat at the table in her robe, and she said, "He's such a sweet kid, but he actually likes that stuff. All that violence."

"He's normal," said Jane. "I bet that most pacifists started out in life watching cartoons. Gandhi. Joan Baez."

Laura smiled. "Did you?" she asked. "Were you a normal kid?"

Jane rested her chin in her hand and thought about it. "Not really," she said. "I was probably a lot lonelier than Ian is. Hotels aren't exactly friendly places to live. You make friends, but then they leave with their parents three days later. It's the ultimate betrayal."

She told Laura about the Mermaid Hotel in Miami Beach. The place, she explained, had already been run-down by the time she was born, and her mother and father argued about money all night. Jane could hear them shouting to each other as she tried to sleep in her adjoining room — room 3482, directly across the hall from the ice machine. Sometimes, when the arguing stopped, Jane heard someone open the sliding door of the ice machine, and then there was the sound of cubes thudding into a bucket.

"I spent most of my time playing jacks in the cocktail lounge," she said. "My brother Sam ignored me. He played with his ant farm, or else went swimming. I'm so fair that if I go out in the sun for too long, I get sun poisoning, so I stayed in all the time." Jane would walk in a big circle around the hotel, trying to find someone who would talk to her — anyone: a maid, a bellhop, a sympathetic tourist. Sometimes she stayed in the hotel bar, talking to a barmaid she was in love with. Verna had long, lacquered nails and was always tapping them restlessly on the smooth surface of the bar. Mostly, though, Jane just rode the elevators up and down or wandered through the halls. There was always a fine dusting of sand along the green carpet, and Jane would follow it as though it were a trail that might actually lead her somewhere new. After all these years, she said, her brother Sam still lived in the hotel. He sat on the beach most of the day, his nose greased white.

"I don't know how I sprang from that family," Jane said. "Sometimes I think I fell from a star."

Jane lived in Queens now because the rent was cheap. She

lived in a two-family house on a quiet street, and sometimes she would sit in the window and watch the kids play Frisbee outside. She would imagine what it was like to grow up in a normal home, where people weren't there for just a week at a time, where no one carried room keys on big red plastic disks.

"It seems pretty normal here," said Jane, looking around the kitchen. Ian's drawings were attached to the refrigerator by fruit magnets. Pots hung on hooks, and bottles of spice were lined up in a rack.

"I guess it is," Laura said. "Nothing very big has happened in my life. It's been pretty normal. Except," she said, "getting involved with a woman."

"Tell me," said Jane, and Laura took a long sip of coffee, as though buoying herself up for something difficult, and then she told Jane more about Julia Price. She described her vividly, Jane thought. She seemed to be leaving very little out. She talked about how Julia dressed, and spoke, and how Julia would bring over a pint of Swedish ice cream and they would eat it together on the couch. That was bliss, Laura said. A kind of temporary bliss, made urgent by the fact that Laura had never thought it would last. When you were with Julia, you knew that everything was ephemeral.

Jane knew a few women like that. They were cut from the same pattern. There were variations, of course; years before, there had been Sandy Falk, who had a throng of women surrounding her all the time. Sandy ran a tai chi class in Northampton, Massachusetts, where Jane was living. The class was for women only, and sometimes Jane would sit in the park and watch them going through their exquisite underwater motions in their billowing white pajamas. There was Sandy at the helm, her arms moving slowly, weaving patterns. She was very powerful, with her hands slicing up the air.

"Those women make you crazy," Jane said. "The ones you obsess about."

Laura looked down. "I obsessed about you a little," she said. "When you didn't call."

"No, it's different," said Jane. "I'm not the way you described this Julia. I couldn't pull that off if I tried. We're taught to think that *any* strong feelings we have for women are obsessive. I've spent the past few years trying to undo that."

"I don't know how to," said Laura.

She looked suddenly embarrassed, so Jane changed the subject. "What was your marriage like?" Jane asked. "You haven't said anything about it."

"I never know what to say," Laura said. "It wasn't *terrible* in that way you read about." She stood to clear the dishes. Over the running water, her back to Jane, she said, "Whenever I see David now, I think, *What a handsome man*. But it's the way I would think about an ad in a magazine, a man modeling a shirt. Handsome. Remote. And that's fine with me." She paused. "Did you ever think about getting married?" she asked.

"No," said Jane. "I was never involved with a man. I never felt that connection with any man. You know." As she said this, she wondered about Laura, and what connection there might be between them. She felt oddly comfortable in her apartment, among the accouterments of this woman's life. Laura didn't flaunt her money; she seemed to live modestly. The apartment was big, but it wasn't all cluttered with mirrors with curlicue frames, or those useless little throw pillows. The apartment looked as though someone nice lived there. And now it had Jane's table in the dining room. It was the only really good piece of furniture in the place.

She sat across from Laura and studied her. Laura was pretty, but she wore a ratty bathrobe, the kind that only mothers seemed to wear. Jane had never slept before with anyone who had kids. It was an interesting thought. She liked the idea of this woman having kids. Laura must know something about taking care of people; all mothers had to know a lot about that. She imagined

Laura helping Ian through the flu, coming into his room with a thermometer and a tray of food. Standing and shaking down the thermometer with quick, sharp movements of the wrist. Jane remembered how her own mother used to do that. Jane would lie in bed, observing the way her mother's wrist snapped down and the tip of the thermometer caught the light. Jane would open her mouth willingly to receive it.

She could see Laura fretting over Ian, sitting at the side of his bed and holding his hand. Ian came into the kitchen now, leaving the TV on in the living room.

"If you're done in there, go shut the TV off, sweetie," Laura said. He turned around and went back into the living room. He came back a second later and stood in front of her.

"Ma, I'm bored," he said. "Play Crazy Eights with me."

"In a while," she said. She gathered him up into her arms and sat with him on her knee. Jane felt jealous then, and she wasn't sure whom exactly she was jealous of. Ian was squirming but happy in his Dr. Denton pajamas. Laura planted a series of kisses on top of his head. She sat and stroked this little boy, and it was her right, her responsibility, even. Jane felt all the stroking, the waves rippling through the room. Ian had the lovely flesh of children — marzipan-smooth and touchable. Jane wanted somehow to be in this woman's life, this little boy's life. There was something so smug about families, though; they were a closed unit, an unbroken circle. Families had secrets that they never shared with anyone outside.

She didn't want to seem so needy; it wasn't a state she was used to. She had had many lovers, had visited many households, among them communal families, with somebody's kids running around shrieking and being carried to the bathroom. She had rarely felt as much at ease as right here, in the airy rooms of this apartment. The wind circulated, ruffled the blond hair of mother and son. *We all look alike*, Jane thought. *We all have the same hair. Maybe I am the long-lost member of this family, separated from them at birth.*

In the late morning, Jane knew she had to get back home. She was in the midst of re-grouting her bathroom, and weekends were the only time she had free. She and Laura stood together in the front hallway. Ian was holding on to Laura's leg, and talking to himself a little. "Rice-A-Roni," he was saying. "The San Francisco treat."

"So, will I see you soon?" Laura asked.

"Very soon," said Jane. The next day was Monday, a work day, and her thoughts would turn back to measurements, and blades, and varnish. Laura would make drawings and send Ian off to school. They would each carry on their very separate routines, as always.

"How's the middle of the week?" asked Jane. They agreed on Wednesday. It seemed like a good time — the center of activity, just when things were getting to be too much. Wednesday, the very heart of the week.

Back in Queens, a dog was barking in that Sunday afternoon way. A group of little Puerto Rican girls in white dresses were going by outside, like a throng of tiny brides. They wore white ankle socks, Mary Janes. First Communion, Jane thought, watching them skip down the street.

She opened her mailbox with the key — nothing much: a Sears catalogue, and a Xerox copy of an invitation to a dance party. "Where the Girls Are," it read, and there was a picture of Connie Francis underneath. At the bottom, in ink, was written, "Jane, try and make it. We miss you. Holly and Lynn."

In the apartment, Jane went around and opened windows. She wanted the air to blow through, as it had at Laura's. She wanted the rooms to have that same family feel to them. She went to the refrigerator and took out a Rolling Rock, then put a Bessie Smith record on the turntable and sat down in her old velvet armchair. She drank the beer, sitting there with her eyes closed, her foot tapping.

Sometimes Jane wished she were black. She felt an affinity

with black women, especially when they were singing all those wailing, downtrodden songs. At work, when she was the only one around, she could turn the radio dial away from Rock Palace and switch it to a blues show. She could usually find some plaintive female voice singing about undying love and oppression; the two were inextricable. One day at work she had heard a song by an obscure blues singer named Mamie Frye. She had put down her saw and listened closely. The old recording was thick with static, but still she could make out the lyrics:

> My man done treat his woman like a heap of dirt.
> O lord he left me broken, o lord he left me hurt.
> He never dressed me up in finery,
> or took me on an ocean liner, he
> never loved me with a kinda respect.

Sometimes she sang the song to herself, holding her hand in a fist, pretending that she was singing into a microphone. She wondered if Mamie Frye was a lesbian. If she wasn't, Jane thought, maybe she should have been.

Now she drank her beer and listened to Bessie Smith for a while. She loved to drink beer on weekends. Not to get a buzz on, but just for the taste, and the weight of the bottle in her hand. She felt happy. She kept thinking about Laura. Holly and Lynn would laugh if they saw Jane now, if they knew about her latest love interest. "Going for the femme this time?" Lynn would kid her. "Going bourgeoise?"

Jane thought of all the small objects floating around Laura's apartment: alphabet blocks, hand towels in the bathroom, napkin rings engraved with little flowers, and framed photographs all over the place. There was one picture of Laura's parents — sweet-looking people standing in front of a house. The sun had bleached out much of the color.

After all this time, Jane still needed that family connection. She thought of her own parents rattling around in their big, dying

hotel, and of all the old people coming through on vacations —
a different clientele from when Jane was a kid. Once, at age nine,
standing in the white industrial kitchen before the dinner hour,
she had looked down the steel countertop at an ocean of pineapple
juice glasses, all of them lined up and glistening. *All those mouths
to feed*, she had thought, and imagined a thousand heads tipping
back to drink from those little glasses.

Everyone sat at family tables except at dinner, when children
ate in the adjoining children's dining room. Jane — neither a
child nor a parent — had the privilege of vaulting between both
worlds. She wandered like an overseer around the big rooms with
their mealtime din, her hands behind her back. First she would
watch the parents eat — men in dinner jackets, women in white
dresses, with little purses. These were never the rich people (they
all stayed at the St. Moritz). These were earnest vacationers with
precious time off from small towns and bleak cities. On the beach
the women stuffed their teased hair into rubber caps embellished
with rubber flowers. Their bodies were cinched into bathing suits
that held their breasts up as though hands were supporting them.
Jane was also free to explore the beach, in her sunhat and T-
shirt and a coating of sunblock. She observed families at seaside,
watching as mothers smoothed Coppertone on their husbands'
and children's backs. The whole place smelled as if it were frying.
Jane's own mother was inside at the bell desk, lecturing the
bellhops about courtesy. Her father was in the office muttering
over the ledgers. Her parents were rarely available.

Sometimes Jane would join a table of children in the pink
children's dining room, but she would usually get disgusted and
leave. Vacationing children were often loud and rude or else
terrified of having to eat without their parents. Sometimes they
would sit at the table and weep.

At twelve, Jane found a best friend. His name was Clemente,
and he was a bellhop in the hotel. He was a few years older than
she, and was the only one around who would talk to her for long

stretches of time. Even Verna, the barmaid whom she loved, was always busy mixing piña coladas and consoling lost, middle-aged men in the dark bar.

Clemente was Cuban, like many of the hotel workers. He was small, with light brown skin and dark eyes, and he talked in a sweet, shy voice. He had decided that Jane was someone he could trust, and one day he took her aside and said, "I am madly in love with a boy on the beach. Don't tell your parents or I'll get fired." He told her all about Tim, a blond sun god who wore Speedo racing trunks and could swim faster and longer than anyone else. "Please," said Clemente. "I want to spend some time with him alone. Just half an hour, that's all. He lives with his parents, and I have two roommates. We don't have any place to go. Do you think you could help me?"

So one afternoon Jane stole the passkey from behind the desk and opened an empty room for Clemente and Tim. Then she stood out in the hall, keeping guard while the two boys slipped into the room and made love. It was exciting for her. Maids walked by wheeling carts, eyeing her suspiciously. Jane held her breath as they passed.

At twelve, she understood a couple of things deeply. First: Clemente felt about Tim the same way that she, Jane, felt about Verna and had always felt about certain girls in school. Second: for some reason, it was important never to talk about this love with anyone, except, perhaps, those who felt similarly. Clemente had understood something about her. He had said to her one day, "You love Verna, don't you? I've seen the way you look at her. Like you can't breathe."

"Yes," Jane had said, surprised. "That's right." He could read her mind; this amazed her.

A few years later, after Clemente had left his job to work in a better hotel down the strip, he told Jane the names of the bars in Miami that might interest her. He told her Hollywood stories about women who had been lovers with other women, men with men. He let her borrow all of his movie magazines, and she spent hours looking at Audrey Hepburn's dark mouth. Finally he left Miami and she had no idea of where he had gone. He was so small and delicate and impish that she often couldn't help but imagine a tragic end to his life: Vietnam, or a fag-bashing on the docks of some big city.

She thought of him now as she drank her beer, thought of him as an eternal teenager, lost to the world. Clemente had been an orphan — that was the thing that had seemed most impressive to her — and now she was one as well. She had a set of parents who suddenly refused to recognize her existence, who had said, dramatically, over the telephone, "You are no longer our child," and then hung up forever.

"It *doesn't* make you an orphan," her friend Danielle had insisted. "It just makes you an adult."

A lot of people had been kicked out of families for similar reasons, Jane knew. On holidays, the disowned children gathered together for their own celebration. A group of friends packed into a tiny Brooklyn kitchen, basting a turkey. Maybe this year Jane would be doing the same thing.

She kept thinking of that photograph of Laura's parents, the way they had smiled shyly at the camera, and had their arms around each other. She knew somehow that they would never disown their daughter. How could they? Laura was so acceptable, after all, with her sundresses, her sprawling apartment, her interesting job, her beautiful son. Jane wanted to find some way to tap into that world. She wanted to call Laura up immediately, to go back to that apartment, to breathe in its air.

Early that morning, when she and Laura had gotten dressed together, she had watched Laura struggling with the second button on the back of her blouse. Laura tried to reach it, an arm flapping like a bird's wing. It was an oddly delicate moment, a private one. Jane went and stood behind her. She waited a moment, herself half dressed, silent. Then she slipped the button through its loop, and turned Laura around to face her.

PART TWO

Origin of Species

Ⅰt was her theory, on good days, that everyone gravitates toward the best possible life. Couples separate, then grieve, but eventually find more appropriate lovers. Or else maybe a woman learns that what she secretly desires is to live alone forever. Imagine—a lifetime spent staying up all night reading the best library books, and being able to turn out the light when she chooses. This isn't loneliness; it's what she always dreamed of.

There were many variations on the theme, but it was all the same in the end; you had to be miserable for a while, but then one day you found the real thing. It was the way life worked.

Laura thought of this now as she and Jane lay in bed one Monday morning. They were in a tangle, both of them awake and blinking but unwilling to get up yet. Laura shifted, rearranged the sheets. They were new sheets—Jane had bought them on sale that week, and they were dotted with sunbursts. She would never have picked them out herself, but she liked them because Jane had picked them. She was touched by the brightness of the color, the aggressive repetition of orange blotches.

No matter how often she mulled over it, in the end she felt wonder at how she had gotten to this point in her life. It was like the surprise ending of a de Maupassant story she had read in college, the one in which a woman's glittering necklace proves to be a sham, and all those years of agony were pointless. It could have been so easy, one learns at the final, pivotal moment. Laura could have been living with a woman all along.

Sometimes in the evening she would look across the room and there would be Jane, her head tilted down as she read a mystery novel. Laura would suddenly feel stirred by the quiet in the room — a paradox that left her bewildered. The edge was missing, the hard, glossy edge that had been there with Julia.

Would Jane be enough? Laura had wondered at first. Jane was always puttering around the apartment, fixing things, or coming over to Laura at the drawing table for an embrace. Jane always set the table for dinner, and each night she did something different with the napkins: little origami swans, or tricorn hats. One night she wrote their names in big, looping script on the napkins. "Ian," one read; "Laura," "Jane," all of it in bleeding magic marker.

There was a calmness that Laura was aware of much of the time. Jane made love like a young girl, her head tipped up for a kiss, her shoulders back. Sometimes Laura felt as though she and Jane were in a big, safe room together. They lay around like babies, like puppies, like abandoned toys.

"I don't want to move from this bed," Laura would say. It might be three in the afternoon, a day when Ian was off with David for the weekend.

"You don't have to move," Jane would answer. "We can just stay like this forever, and die like this. We'll be found a few years later, sort of shriveled up like those dolls made of dried apples. But we'll be smiling."

"Tell me that story again," Laura said. The week they had begun living together, Jane began telling Laura a story. It was tentatively called "Two Girls in Love," and it took place in the cave era.

"This story begins before the dawn of time," Jane had said, and Laura had burst out laughing. Jane waited until she was through, and then she went on. It occurred to Laura that Jane was taking this story quite seriously.

"The earth had just been formed," Jane said, "with all of that hot lava and the ice breaking up into continents, like we learned in fourth grade. But contrary to what we were taught, the first apes who roamed the earth gradually evolved into a species of women."

"What were they called?" Laura asked.

"They were called Cro-Magwomen," said Jane. "Just listen. Men didn't exist at all. The earth was cooling off from all of its volcanoes and everything, and these baby Cro-Magwomen lived in little pockets of earth, little craters, until the atmosphere was safe for them to walk around in. Then one by one they rose up out of their craters and peered out into the world. They learned how to walk, and they roamed the earth, lonely and hungry. Once in a while two of them found each other, and immediately they felt better. Even their hunger lessened. They would sit in the crater of an abandoned volcano and look into each other's eyes.

"One day," Jane said, "a young girl was crawling along the surface of the earth, weak and hungry and all alone, when in the distance she saw another girl and began to make her way toward her. Soon the two of them were standing face to face, and they began to make little sounds. They started to communicate through these sounds. Pretty soon they had created a whole language that they could speak, and they told each other that they would stay together forever. They promised that they would keep each other warm."

"What did they eat?" Laura asked.

"They ate only one thing," said Jane. "A fruit called curasa melons. They were small and oval and a light green color. They had a strange taste."

"Describe it," said Laura.

Jane squinted. "You know the way milk tastes at the bottom of a cereal bowl?" she said. "All sweet from sugar, and warm, like a wonderful soup? It tasted sort of like that. The pulp of the curasa melon had no seeds. Anyway," she said, "these two girls had no need for anyone else. They were perfectly happy to eat curasa melons all day and just sit on the top of a hill and look up at the red sky. A few years went by, and one day, when they were nine, they began to kiss and hug and do other things."

"Other things?" said Laura. "Other things? They're only *nine*."

"It's my story!" said Jane. "If you want to tell your own story, go right ahead, but this is my story, Laura, and I'm going to tell it the way I know it."

"Sorry," said Laura. "Please go on."

"I'm just about done," said Jane. Her voice was flatter now. "So they lived like this for many, many years. Eventually they grew old and weak, and then their relationship was different. It was slower, and they spent more time inside their favorite crater, building fires, and singing old Cro-Magwoman folk songs."

"I'm sure you know a few," said Laura.

"I don't feel like singing right now," said Jane. "Anyway, they lived very quietly until one day one of them died, and the other just sat there and wept. Her tears fell into the hard, dark earth. They were planted there. This is a significant fact. Since these two women could not procreate, the only thing they could leave behind was bones and tears. Eventually the other woman died too, and there was no one around to remember either of them. But they had left little bits of themselves in the earth, and even though the era changed and men came onto the earth as well, bones and tears fed the soil, so that in another time, another place, these two women might one day live again. The end."

Laura sat up in bed and clapped. She saw years of this, years of listening to Jane's stories, and years of getting up with her in the morning. It was a staggering thought, and yet somehow it was also comforting.

As a child, Laura had flourished in the safe arms of her family. They had been isolated out there on the farm, and sometimes now the apartment had a similar atmosphere. It was possible for two women to live well together in New York City. On the street, people sometimes shouted horrible things, but in the building, nobody cared what you did. Like everyone else, you shut your apartment door and nobody knew a thing about you. You weren't friends with your neighbors; in fact, you barely knew their names. Sometimes you met in the elevator, or at the incinerator, carrying sacks of garbage, and you smiled awkwardly, but that was it.

When Jane first moved in, a year after Laura had met her, there had been no stir, no raised eyebrows. Ian had been four then, and he had taken to Jane quickly. She played her guitar and sang to him. They whispered to each other, sharing secrets that they kept from Laura. One night Laura came home from the supermarket and found the apartment empty. She soon realized that Jane and Ian were hiding; she could hear them rustling and restraining giggles behind the couch. She stood in the center of the living room, her arms full of groceries, and she was overwhelmed.

In the five years that they had lived together, it continued to work. Ian seemed happy. At nine, his blond hair had darkened a bit, but it still hung in his eyes. He was skinny, with elbows that jutted out when he walked. He was not an athlete, nor was he the last child picked for every team. His main talent, the thing he loved best, was something that perplexed Laura. It separated him from her more than anything else — more than his age or his gender. Ian was a whiz at math. He brought home equations and showed them to Laura and Jane, who were often confused. "No, look," he would say, exasperated. "I'll start all over again. You have to subtract here, instead of adding." Then later he said under his breath, "Girls are stupid at math."

"If you think that," said Laura, "then don't bother us. Nobody likes to be insulted, Ian."

And he would grudgingly apologize.

This was typical parent-child tension, Jane assured her. Ian was a level kid, and he did things quietly. He liked being with Laura and Jane; there were very few screaming matches. The only problem, back then, was David.

When Laura had first told David that she and Jane wanted to live together, he had become sarcastic and made some comment about Ian living among the Amazons. They had fought over it strenuously, and David had hinted about asking for full custody.

"Is that what you want to do?" Laura said, and her voice was panicky. "Do you really think I'm a bad mother?"

David claimed that he just wanted what was best for Ian. He wanted to give him a normal life. Laura thought about David's childhood—his screaming parents, and his sullen, overweight sister. As a boy, David had sat out on the front stoop reading *Microbe Hunters* and praying for an escape. He had had an awful childhood, one in which there was no peace. But it was, of course, a normal childhood by most standards. Nothing terrible had happened. No one had died or deserted. There were no beatings. It was comparatively average, and still it was terrible.

It would never be that way with Ian, and David knew it. "Ian and Jane get along very well," Laura said. "Please, David. I want it to work out, too." Finally they agreed that they would give it a try. David would watch Ian closely during their weekends together, and try and gauge how he was really doing.

Jane moved in early in the summer, and those first weeks were spent in a warm, domestic haze. The window fan spun slowly, pulling heat from the apartment. Jane and Laura sat together drinking iced tea in the evenings while Ian ran around naked, shrieking happily.

One day, after Jane had been living there for a week, Laura was alone in the apartment, and she opened the bureau drawers that were now reserved for Jane's things. She felt like a spy. There on the clean shelving paper of the top drawer, Jane had placed three T-shirts, some underwear, and four pairs of socks balled into small, soft fists. Laura felt a swell of feeling for her—the humbleness of her belongings, the things she needed to get by in the world. It was so minimal, so spare. Jane could pack up and feel complete in someone else's apartment. Laura tried to picture the home Jane had grown up in; she imagined the heavy, interchangeable drapery of hotel rooms, and a drinking glass wrapped in paper on the bathroom sink. It was all so sterile; she could barely imagine it.

Her own childhood was so far removed, yet at her best moments with Jane she was reminded of being a kid in Iowa. She felt a languor that extended into most parts of the day and night. It had never occurred to her that love didn't have to be fraught with tension, that it could be uncomplicated and still be profound. It wasn't just that they took such delight in each other or that their quiet moments were unbroken by a sense of temporality, as had been the case with Julia. It had more to do with the exquisite balance of temperaments, and everything else seemed like a bonus, thrown in for good measure.

She and Jane rarely went out for the evening, and when they did it was usually by themselves, or else to a big party. At first they had dinner a couple of times with Carolyn, and once with Rachel, but there was awkwardness to the evenings. Laura wasn't sure who was responsible, if anyone. Jane became very shy at these dinners, and Carolyn tried to overcompensate by asking a lot of questions.

"What sort of wood is the best to work with?" she asked, or, "Are there a lot of women woodworkers around?"

The day after that first dinner, Carolyn called and told Laura that she really liked Jane. "Come on," said Laura. "You didn't like her."

"No, I did!" said Carolyn. "I really did! It's just that she's different from you, Laura. You know what I'm talking about. I have to get used to her. It would be like that with almost anyone. It takes time."

There wasn't anything bad to say about Jane, after all; she was quiet and charming and always cordial. But she wasn't educated, she wasn't an artist; there was no commonality to be found.

"Well, I'm glad you're happy together," Carolyn said. "It's more than I can say for my own life."

Happiness had to exist for the sake of itself; you couldn't expect everyone to share in it. One afternoon that first summer, Laura took Ian to the park. The other mothers were sitting there on the bench, watching their children play on the grass. The thin woman was still among the mothers, although the elegant woman and her son had stopped coming to the park a few months before. They must have moved, Laura thought. Perhaps they had fallen on hard times and had to give up their apartment. People's lives were always shifting, even when you weren't taking notice. Trees fell silently in forests, and people left their homes in the middle of the night like refugees.

Laura sat down on the bench between the thin woman and another mother whom she had come to think of as the odd woman. Ian ran out into the grass and kicked a soccer ball around. Soon all the children had joined in.

"How are you doing?" Laura asked the thin woman.

The woman sighed, moved a strand of hair out of her face. "Oh, not too bad," she said. "How about you?"

"My life has changed," said Laura. "I'm living with someone now."

The odd woman joined in then. "It's a new age," she said. "My own husband and I have been together for fifteen years, and we couldn't be happier. We make love all day. All day. I'm not kidding. Jennifer always has the TV on, so she never hears a thing. But that's all that life is made of, don't you think? Fucking and loving and heating up dinner for your kids."

Laura and the thin woman exchanged nervous glances. "Yes, I guess I know what you mean," said Laura.

"It all goes by so fast," said the thin woman. She peered out over the grass. "I just want to slow it down sometimes." Then she turned to Laura. "So you're living with someone," she said. "That's good. It will be nice for you, and for your boy. Just to hear voices in the house means a lot."

Laura nodded. She felt oddly sanctioned by the thin woman's words. These days, she was looking for approval from everyone. When it was time to go, the mothers collected their children and began to leave the park.

"Goodbye!" they called out to each other. "Goodbye!"

"And good luck," the thin woman added, waving.

"I think," said Jane one evening that first August, "that you secretly want to tell your parents about us."

They were sitting at dinner. Ian was drinking from a Krazy Straw. Laura watched as the milk traveled through the loop. "I don't know," said Laura. "You could be right. The idea of telling them feels very *right* to me, but when I think about it hard enough, I have no idea of how I would go through with it. Or even why. It's not as if I need their permission."

"It's a strange thing," said Jane. "When I finally told my parents about myself, I guess I did it because I knew that this was the way things were and they weren't going to change. On the other hand, I felt sort of bad about not having a woman I could present to them and say, 'See. Here is the woman I adore. She's not a freak of nature, and neither am I.' You're in a much better position, Laura, because it's not a *state* you want to tell them about, not a condition. You want to tell them about me, I assume, and about your life. That's a wonderful kind of thing to tell. It's big news."

They discussed it for weeks, and finally Laura decided to go to Iowa in the fall. It had been a year since she had seen her mother and father. They were always asking her to visit, asking her to bring Ian, and now she called and told them she was coming. She would bring Ian, she decided, but not Jane. That would have to wait. Her parents knew that there was someone else living in the apartment. Occasionally they called and Jane answered the telephone. Laura had lightly explained that a friend was living there for a while, and her mother had said, "That's nice. I'm glad you have good friends and you're not alone."

Laura felt a certain measure of guilt for lying, for omitting. She still drew money from her trust fund each month, and now so did Jane. They had a joint checking account; it was frightening and yet thrilling to see their names linked together on the upper left-hand corner of each check: LAURA GIOVANNI/JANE BLOOM. 300 CENTRAL PARK WEST, NEW YORK, N.Y.

Laura and Ian flew to Iowa in late September, when it was still warm enough there to sit on the front porch every evening. On her first night, she and her mother and father sat drinking Seven-Up and looking out over the property. The yellow porch light was on, and bugs whirled around under the beam.

"So, what's the good word?" her father asked.

He always said things like that, sentences that had no particular meaning. "Oh, nothing much," she always said, and so she said it again now.

Ian was running through the grass, chasing Hector the dog. There was something about this elderly dog belonging to her elderly parents that made Laura want to cry. Hector and Ian were running in circles around the field, playing with a stick. Ian wrested the stick from Hector's jaws, then flung it across the grass.

"Uck, it's wet!" Ian yelled.

This was it, the moment of moments. Laura and her parents had already talked about her father's bad back, her aunt Maude's broken hip, how David was doing, and how Ian liked school. Conversation thinned out; they were waiting for her to talk.

"You know," she said finally, creaking forward in the rocking chair, "there are some things I've wanted to talk about with you." Neither of her parents said anything. Her father kept twisting his soda bottle around and around between his hands. "Well, I guess I've fallen in love," Laura said. "With a woman."

Her father's hands stopped moving. Everything was quiet. Only Ian and the dog still ran in hectic circles.

"I don't understand," her mother said in a tiny voice.

"I'm in love," Laura said. "With a woman named Jane Bloom. You know, my friend who's been living with us."

Her heart was rising up and pounding out the sound of her words. It was like trying to have a conversation in a steel mill. She couldn't hear herself; could they hear her? She didn't say anything more; inexplicably, she was crying. Her mother did not come over to comfort her, or stroke down her hair. She just sat in her wicker chair, unmoving, unmoved.

"Is it us?" her father finally asked, embarrassed. "Does it have something to do with the way we raised you, Laura?"

They were both staring at her, their eyes bright as the eyes of small animals in the dark. "No," she said when she could speak. "It's not you. It has nothing to do with you. Or if it does, it doesn't matter. I mean, I'm happy. I'm telling you this because I want you to know what's going on with me. You always ask things on the phone, and I always want to tell you the truth."

They were terrified, she realized. Terrified of change, of big news. Every time a telegram came to the house, they would hold each other's hands, getting ready for something terrible. It would usually turn out benign — news that one of their pigs had won some prize in a distant county fair, or that a relative was arriving. They had not been touched very often by disaster.

But this wasn't disaster, either. "Look," she tried, "I know it's hard. I know it's a shock. I don't know how to make it any easier for you."

Her mother looked out across the field. "I guess I'm old-fashioned," she said after a moment. "I don't understand a lot of things that go on in the world. Drugs. Watergate. It's very different from when I was a girl."

Laura didn't know what to say, and so they just sat together, rocking. After a while Hector clambered up the steps, Ian following. The dog put two wet paws in Laura's mother's lap, but she didn't seem to mind. "Calm down," she was saying to him. "Just calm down."

Laura stayed in Iowa for two more days, and no one mentioned the subject again. Her parents were very loving toward her, but they didn't ask any more questions. One night she eavesdropped on them. Their door was open a crack, and she was on her way to the bathroom.

"I guess she knows what she's doing," Laura heard her father say.

"Oh, I suppose so," said her mother. "Could you hand me the dental floss? Thank you."

Silence. "I just don't follow it," her father said.

"I know," said her mother.

"Maybe it's not our place to follow it," he said after a moment.

Then something was said that Laura couldn't hear. Then a thump, as though a book or shoe were dropped to the floor. And then, "Do you want to get that light?" And then darkness, and then she dared not listen. But she hoped that her parents comforted each other that night, and every night. But maybe, she thought later, it wasn't her place to know.

CHAPTER TWELVE

Even now, after all those years, she could not quite remember his telephone number. She knew it had twos in it, and a six, but she sometimes reversed the digits and ended up calling a suspicious old woman who screamed into the receiver.

Now she sat on the edge of her bed looking up his number in her pocket address book. It was four in the morning, and the night-table lamp was on. Laura flipped quickly to the page with David's number. She felt nervous, calling him in the middle of the night, yet she knew it was the right thing to do. Jane had agreed. "He'll come right over," Jane had said, and of course she was right.

David answered the phone on the first ring; it always used to seem to her that when he slept, he was never very far from the surface of consciousness. "Hello," he said, always prepared to be responsible, his voice alert.

"David, it's Laura," she said. "I'm sorry to wake you up, but it's Ian. He has a high fever and a terrible cough. I don't know how he can get through the night."

"I'll come over," said David. "It should take me about twenty minutes or so."

Laura heard someone murmur in the background; it must be Vanessa, she thought. He and Vanessa did not officially live together, although Ian said that she was always there when he went to David's for the weekend. Laura had met Vanessa on several occasions over the years, and had never managed to like her. She imagined Vanessa now, begging David not to go uptown, not to go take care of his sick child, but to stay there in bed with her. She would make it worth his while. This was an unfair image; Vanessa wasn't evil in any way, but for some reason Laura liked to think of her like this.

Down the hall, Ian was still coughing desperately; his cough had the deep, cracking resonance of an underground explosion. Jane was sitting on the edge of his bed, wetting his face with a washcloth. She was talking to him softly, telling him jokes. "This man goes to a psychiatrist," she was saying, "and he says, 'Doctor, you have to help me. Last night I had a dream that I was a teepee, and the night before that I had a dream that I was a wigwam. What do you think it means?' Then the doctor says, 'It means you're two tents.' Get it? Two tents, too tense." Ian laughed, then went into another coughing fit.

Laura stood over the bed. It was so hard to see your child be sick; you wanted to take on the fever yourself. She had seen Ian through all the usual childhood diseases—at six he had come down with the mumps, at seven the chicken pox. Now at nine he was in the throes of a bad flu, and she hoped he didn't have pneumonia. Jane sat and looked worried, but Laura wondered if Jane could possibly feel the same anxiety that she was feeling.

Ian's eyes fluttered and shut. He groaned once, then let out another deeply rooted cough. Laura held a tissue to his mouth, tipped his head up from the pillow.

"How about some tea?" Jane asked. "Maybe that would help." Without waiting for an answer, she went into the kitchen.

David showed up a few minutes later. His hair was uncombed, and he looked slightly wild. He was wearing a winter jacket with an old T-shirt and jeans underneath. Laura watched as he sat down on the bed and snapped open his black bag. He unbuttoned Ian's pajama top and pressed the flat disk of his stethoscope lightly against Ian's chest, listening closely. Laura stood aimlessly behind him during the examination. After a few minutes David motioned for her to come out into the hall with him.

"It's only a flu," he said, "with a real bad cough. His lungs don't sound that bad, but I think he should have a vaporizer. Do you still have that old hot steam one that we used to keep in the storage closet?"

How odd that he should know where things were in the recesses of the apartment. David was a trace of an earlier life, but every once in a while the worlds collided. Here he was now, standing and talking to her in the middle of the night. She and Jane were both wearing bathrobes. Laura felt suddenly embarrassed, as though they were orphans and David was the visiting physician dropping in on their orphanage.

David was certainly cordial to Jane, but it was clear that he still didn't approve of her. He always nodded hello when they met, but he could not really address her directly. He panicked if he was left alone in a room with Jane.

"I'm giving Ian a strong cough syrup, which he should take every four hours," said David. "And just some Tylenol. He should feel better in the morning."

Laura looked through the doorway at Ian lying in the bed. She wondered if he still fantasized that his mother and father would remarry. At nine, did kids still have those kinds of hopes? David was a good father, even an obsessive one. He always picked Ian up on time, and his child-support checks showed up regularly on the first of each month. He was elaborate in his love for Ian, and physical in a way that many fathers weren't. Laura still worried about Ian growing up without a male figure in the house.

She had read as many books on the subject as she could find—long texts that stressed the importance of identification with the father. She read a book called *Domestic Matriarchy and the Feminization of the Male*. She knew it was very reactionary, like the books on homosexuality that she used to read, but still she agreed that it was important for Ian to have a visible father.

At Ian's school, Laura and David came to parent-teacher night together. They sat and talked with Ian's teacher about his progress. This year, his fourth-grade teacher was a young woman named Layla who spoke in soothing tones to David and Laura as though they too were children. Laura could imagine sitting on a beanbag chair in the classroom and listening to this woman read *The Phantom Tollbooth* aloud.

"I'm glad you're both so participatory," Layla said. "It's very helpful for the kids to have both parents involved in what's going on at school. Ian is a wonderful boy. I enjoy having him in my class." And she went on to extol Ian's virtues—his excellence in math, his real sophistication at using a pocket calculator, his keen sense of logic, his hand-eye coordination. He was also good at building things, she said, and at this Laura felt a sudden rush of pride. It was Jane who had taught him this skill. When he was very small Jane would take him downtown to the shop and show him how to handle different tools.

Ian wrote essays for school about his life at home, and he often directly referred to Jane, calling her "our friend Jane, who lives with us." During one school conference years before, Laura had stammered out something to Ian's teacher about the unusual situation at home, and the teacher had responded without surprise. "Oh, we have children from all sorts of families here," she said. "We have one girl who's grown up in a collective Sullivanian apartment. Last year I had a boy who lived with his father, his mother, and his father's girlfriend. The kids do fine as long as they get enough attention. I really don't think it makes a difference whether their parents are heterosexual or homosexual."

The words *homosexual* and *heterosexual* were jarring to hear.

Laura could not think of herself in these terms; they just didn't seem to apply. Whenever she saw David, she was reminded of her earlier life, and of how it had turned on its own axis so easily.

David was happy in his new life. He looked good, too, with his hair loose and curling, and going prematurely gray around the edges. He had retained his good looks; maybe it was Vanessa who was responsible for that. Sometimes David came to the apartment with Vanessa to take Ian for the weekend. Once Vanessa walked in holding a giant bat kite. Since they were uptown, she explained, she thought they could fly kites in the park.

The bat kite seemed perfect to Laura, a wonderful symbol. She could picture Vanessa standing in the wind, unwinding the string of this giant black vampire bat, and watching as it lifted its wings and shadowed the entire sky. Children would run away in terror. Vanessa was tall, with long hair and a tense, corded neck. She kept her mouth set very tightly when she wasn't speaking.

Now she was waiting for David back at home in the middle of the night. Did she resent the fact that he had once had another life, that he had a little boy from his marriage? Laura wondered. According to Ian, Vanessa was "pretty nice." She seemed to show real interest in him. She had once told Laura that she thought Ian was extremely gifted.

"Yes, he is very bright," Laura had responded.

"He's a pleasure to be with," Vanessa had said, but her voice made everything sound inauthentic.

Later, Laura had discussed her with Jane. "Look, you don't like her either," Jane said. "Why is it so important that she like us?"

"Because I want everybody in the world to like us," Laura said. "So I know that we're okay. That we're not deviant inverts."

"You can make a joke," said Jane, "but I know that part of you is serious. Part of you disapproves of everything you do. You're sort of like your own Nazi."

It was unnerving, how much Jane knew. It was purely logic,

Jane always explained when Laura complimented her on her intuition. Since she hadn't gone to college, Jane said, she had made up for it by learning to think logically on her own, to read people's expressions, to listen carefully to inflections. And she had learned to work with her hands, too, and use her body well. She was a runner now, and woke up every morning at seven to jog in the park. She was usually in some kind of graceful motion. When she was still, as now, standing in the hallway in her bathrobe in the middle of the night, she looked out of her element.

David snapped his bag shut and kissed Ian goodbye. He gave Laura some medication and a prescription to fill, and assured her that Ian would be all right. "You're positive you still have the vaporizer?" he asked.

Jane said, "Yes, I just saw it the other day when I was cleaning out the closet."

David looked surprised. It was as though he had to remember that Jane actually lived there, that she didn't just lightly dance around the surface of the place — she also went *into* things, into drawers, under tables, deep into the backs of closets. She explored it all, because it belonged to her.

Laura walked David to the door, and Jane hung back, holding her robe tightly around her. The temperature in the apartment had dropped down low. "Goodbye," David said. "I'll call you in the morning." And again, as though she might possibly forget, he said, "Now be sure to find that vaporizer."

David drifted off in the cab going home and woke up with a start. He was so used to this by now; he couldn't really imagine what life had been like before being a doctor, before being on call. How did normal people live, and sleep? This was such an odd skill that doctors had to learn — how to think in the darkest, densest hours of the night. In the beginning, during his residency, David would stand under bright surgical lights at four in the morning, supervising the stitching of someone's head gash, and he would still be fantasizing about sleep, imagining all the deep folds of the bed waiting for him back at home. He would picture the long, white body of his wife. She would keep the bed warm — her side of the bed, anyway.

He returned now to his own apartment. As he walked in he saw that a light was burning in the living room. Vanessa was up. She was curled in the big armchair reading *Shogun*. It pleased him that she would wait up for him like this. She was wearing one of his green surgical shirts; it hung down just below her hips. She put down her book and stood up.

"Is Ian okay?" she asked.

"He's feverish and has a bad cough, but it's nothing unusual. He'll be fine," said David, as if by rote. He took off his coat and dropped down onto the couch. In a second Vanessa was sitting next to him, and her long nails were lightly raking his arm, "giving him the chills," as she called it. He loved it; a field of gooseflesh rose up. Once in a while at the hospital she stopped by his office when she was on a break, and if he was on the telephone she would stand over his desk and run her nails up his arms. In a way it was like a spell, always reminding him of the ways he could be moved.

He was greatly moved by her; he realized this more each day. Sometimes they fought, but they always ended up fatigued and acquiescent and tumbling into bed. It was a relationship powered by a strong, mixed current of feeling. He had not experienced that in years. Not since he was a teenager, actually, and those girls from St. Catherine's School would dance with him at the spring dance, their pastel dresses damp with sweat, their skin and hair smelling heavily of lilac. There was nothing subtle about those girls. David and his friends would arrive at the dances in a pack, and afterward each boy would go out in a car somewhere to make out with a dark-haired, tough Catholic school girl. Their names were Teresa, Gigi, Dee. They kissed boldly, not like the girls at his own school, and when he left, late at night, his entire body would smell just like them: unsubtle, aromatic, slightly spoiled. Somehow he thought of these images — the backs of cars, the damp, thin fabric of dresses — as representing passion, and when he and Vanessa made love now, he liked the way her nails were so long, like an animal's. This too was passion. He wanted to live with this, to marry this woman.

There were many sides to Vanessa; she was like a geodesic dome, he sometimes thought. She could be so understanding, the way she talked to her clients. Once she played back a tape of a family counseling session. Grown men and women cried on the tape, and there was Vanessa's voice coming through gently in the background, helping these people through their crisis. She would be a terrific mother. They talked a lot, these days, of having kids.

"Do you think we would be good parents?" she asked him. "I mean, the combination of us together? I already know that you're a good father, and I think I'd be a good mother, but you can't always tell how the combination is going to work."

"Yeah," said David. "I think we'd be great." Still, it scared him to think of having more kids; they weren't even married yet. Ian would always hold a special place for him — primogeniture ruled. Vanessa was good with Ian, although a little stiff.

All these *women* for Ian to be raised by; it was staggering. Sometimes he thought about Ian living in that household with Laura and Jane, and he panicked. Ian would become neurotic, would want to wear dresses, would flounce around. He would hate women. Or he would hate men. No, he would hate himself. Then David would feel embarrassed for thinking such thoughts. Ian would be fine.

David tried to monitor him carefully, asking all the right questions. At dinner one night in the Village, David said, "So do you guys have fun during dinner, you and Mom and Jane?"

"We eat, mostly," said Ian. "I guess it's fun. Sometimes we play Geography."

"That's good," said David. "If you have a friend home after school, do you introduce him to Mom and Jane?"

"Sure," said Ian, shrugging.

Vanessa looked across the table at David, signaling to him. *Enough*, she was saying. *Don't push.*

"It's not that I'm not concerned too, David," she said later, when dinner was through and Ian was off watching TV. "You just have to be more subtle about it. He'll catch on and wonder why you're asking him so many questions. He's a very bright kid; I'd love to test him sometime."

One day in the office, after the nurses had gone home and David was closing up for the afternoon, he stood in the waiting room, looking around at the sea of toys and kids' magazines and comic books, and he imagined a future in which he and Vanessa had their own children. Their life would be satisfying; they would spend their money well, and be industrious and loving with their children.

David sat down on one of the low plastic chairs. He absently picked up a magazine and leafed through it. He found himself staring at a full-page drawing of a circus crowded with clowns and tumblers and horses. It gave him a shiver of recognition; it was Laura's drawing, of course, and there were objects hidden throughout the picture. Even when he was so far removed from her, when he was not thinking about her at all, she somehow insinuated herself in the tiniest way. "FIND THE HIDDEN PICTURES, by Laura Giovanni," it read. Children loved her pictures. She understood children in the same way that he did, and Vanessa did not. When Vanessa had her own children she would loosen up and begin to understand the secret language of parents.

Vanessa's face when they made love was always released from its tight cast, and opened in surprise. She slid her whole long self into him, like sand pouring through a funnel.

Now he sat with Vanessa in the living room in the middle of the night. They would have to get up for the day soon anyway, so there was no point in going back to bed. He sat sprawled on the couch and she ran her fingers up and down his arm, and finally she stopped and encircled his wrist with her hand. There were so many private moments that went on in people's homes. This one second, in which she caught his wrist like this, like a handcuff—he would remember this second forever. It was so slight, so unimportant, and yet these were the moments that resonated.

Laura probably had times like this with Jane. He was sure of it, even though he could not quite picture it. He saw the two women sitting close together in their bathrobes. Maybe their faces touched lightly, all that soft peach-skin. *Why would a woman choose to be with another woman?* he often asked himself. It was a question that troubled him deeply because he could not answer it, and he felt left out of something. Some real female secret. Women were much more intimate with each other than men were; that was part of it. Laura looked relaxed with Jane. Their relationship was not a big challenge.

It was so late, and his thoughts were not making sense now; they followed each other without real order or reason. But he could not help thinking of Laura and Jane standing together in Ian's bedroom, two guardian angels at the foot of his bed. He hoped they remembered the vaporizer. He thought of its green glass dome, and the way the water percolated gently, making a little *blip* sound, then a snuffle as the steam was released. The atmosphere would be moist and breathable, and the two women would stand and watch until Ian fell asleep in that safe pocket of air.

CHAPTER THIRTEEN

Jane insisted that there was a moment before she was mugged when she suddenly knew it was about to happen. She didn't even see anyone in the shadows; she just felt something in her bones, something that made her stop and look around. It was, she told Laura, probably like the feeling a person gets when she is about to be struck by lightning.

It was a fluke that the station had been empty. Jane had just stepped off the train and was walking along the platform. At the other end she could see a man in a glass booth counting money. She felt it then, and she stopped and looked around her in the dark light of the subway. She heard the catch of someone else's breath, and then two men sprang out at her from nowhere. They leaped at her like cats off a wall.

"Don't move," one said.

They were practically kids, she realized in that first moment: two teenagers in T-shirts. Black kids with sharp, dark eyes. One of them had her around the waist; his arm held her fast. The other one danced around in front, and he had a small knife in his hand. Jane rolled her eyes away, so as not to watch this. She had not even remembered to scream, or try and break loose. It was all out of the question.

"Where's your purse?" the one in front asked.

She had never carried a purse, and had always gotten chastised because of it. "Where's your purse?" Jane's mother used to ask in the same accusing voice when Jane was about to go out for the evening. How bizarre, she thought now, that these muggers were demanding the same thing.

"I don't have one," she said.

"Your wallet, then," said the one who held her.

Jane fumbled in her back pocket for her wallet, and the kid in front grabbed it from her hand.

"Now just stay here, lady," he said. "Don't you move."

As if in afterthought, the other kid shoved her hard into the wall. Her shoulders smashed against it, then her chin. She let out a cry. She could hear them running away, and then the groan of turnstiles as they left the station.

Jane moved away from the wall. She cupped her chin gingerly, and then placed a hand on each shoulder. It was as though she had fallen off a bicycle and skinned herself. The pain was sharp, fresh, close to the surface. Jane took a series of deep breaths, and then she walked out of the station. The man in the booth was still counting money.

She could not stop thinking about the wallet that had been taken. She thought about all of the things she would never see again. There was a head shot of Laura. There was a photo of Laura and Ian in the living room, a series of I.D. cards, a picture of Audrey Hepburn that Laura had given her as a joke, and about ninety dollars in cash. Jane stopped at the corner of the block and cried into her hands. Then she wiped her nose and eyes on her sleeve and kept walking.

It would never have happened at all if it hadn't been for the commute. Jane was traveling each morning out to Plainview,

Long Island, and then back again to the city at night. Her furniture store had lost its lease, and the owner had decided to relocate. He had found a good, inexpensive location in Plainview, a town about fifty minutes from Manhattan. Woodworking jobs were few, and Jane liked the men she worked with, so she decided to give it a try.

In the beginning of November, she began commuting against the rush of travelers each morning. They were all headed into the city, and she was headed out. The trains leaving Pennsylvania Station were nearly empty in the morning, and she slept during the ride.

Jane came home after the first day and announced that the new store was beautiful. It was much bigger than the one in Manhattan, with large windows and better facilities. At first she was enthusiastic and thought it would work out fine. Every day Laura stayed home and worked on her drawings, and Jane went off to the suburbs. Sometimes she had to stay late and would get home after ten. Laura would leave her some dinner in the refrigerator. On those nights, Jane would be exhausted; she would eat her dinner silently in the kitchen, then go right to sleep. She was usually too tired to talk. It was not ideal, they agreed, but it was not too bad. Thousands of people commuted every day and never complained.

Then came the night that she was mugged. When she got back to the apartment, Ian ran to greet her. "What happened to your face?" he asked.

"I got mugged," said Jane. "Where's your mom?"

"Ma! Ma!" Ian called. "Jane was *mugged*!"

Laura came out of the kitchen, wiping her hands on her jeans. "What's this?" she asked. "My God, honey, you're bleeding."

In the bathroom, with a washcloth and a dropper of Merthiolate, Laura tended to Jane, cleaning and painting her chin and shoulders. "You're branded," Laura said, marking her with the bright red lotion.

"Ssss," Jane winced, turning her head to blow on a shoulder.

157

Laura sat on the edge of the bathtub, facing her. She locked Jane's knees between her own. "You want to call the police?" she asked.

"What's the point?" asked Jane. "Those kids are long gone. They've probably spent all the money on video games already."

"It's terrible," said Laura.

"I always thought I was safe from things like this," said Jane, "because I could act self-possessed, and walk like I wasn't afraid. I was always positive that it was the women in high heels and gold chains who were mugged. The women with big hair. I never figured that anyone would bother me, because I look so nonrich."

"I guess it doesn't matter how you look," said Laura. "The subways are terrible. When I think about Ian traveling alone, it makes me crazy."

"He can't ever travel alone," said Jane. "It's certainly not safe for children."

"Well, eventually he'll want to," said Laura. "And then what are we supposed to do? Keep him under lock and key?"

"We don't have to think about it yet," said Jane. "For tonight, let's just go to sleep."

Laura capped the bottle of Merthiolate and wrung out the washcloth. Together they walked down the hall and into the bedroom. Jane's face glowed as though marked with warpaint.

For the next few weeks, Jane went to work each morning, but she could not fall back easily into the routine. She was exhausted by the time she came home in the early evening. All she wanted then was a shower, a beer, a plate of food. Laura laid out thick towels in the bathroom and put a couple of bottles of Rolling Rock in the freezer. She cooked big meals in stew pots and casseroles. Nobody said much during the meal; Jane almost nodded out at dinner each night. Ian began to bring his math book to the table and would ostentatiously prop it up in front of his face.

After dinner Jane went right to bed. She was too tired to make love. She slept the way she always had — facing in — but she felt like a dead weight in Laura's arms. Laura would lie awake for hours. All of this was familiar to her: the silence, the tension of what was not being said. It was like her marriage to David.

It was Jane who was having it worse, though. It was Jane who had been mugged in the subway, Jane who had to travel out to the suburbs and back.

One evening Jane came home, sat down in the living room, drank her beer, then stepped into the shower. Laura walked into the bathroom to get a comb, and Jane heard her and called out over the water, "I've decided to quit!"

She was a moving blur behind the glass. "What do you mean?" Laura called back. "Why?"

Jane shut off the water, and the last drops spattered down the drain, then it was quiet. She slid open the door and stepped out. "Because I don't want you to leave me," Jane said quietly, wrapping a towel around herself.

They went out into the bedroom. Laura sat on the bed and watched as Jane got dressed. "Explain," Laura said.

"Well," said Jane, "I feel like shit when I come home. I realize that I'm not much fun to live with, and I don't want to do that to you. Or to Ian." She sighed. "I know a million people get mugged in New York every day, but I just don't like being one of them. I don't like traveling after dark anymore. I used to be so brave. I used to head out to my apartment in Queens sometimes at three in the morning. I would have conversations with old drunk men on the train. You've changed me, Laura," she said. "I'm more self-protective now, I guess."

"So what are you going to do?" Laura asked. "Stay home with me all day? Not that I would mind."

"Oh, I'll get something else," said Jane. "I like this job, and Bernie is a sweetie to work for, but you can't have everything." She slipped a white T-shirt over her head and put on a pair of drawstring pants. She was dressed and about to leave the room, as though the conversation were over and everything resolved.

"Wait," Laura said. "You can't just decide something like that. You're happy at the store. That means a lot."

"Happiness isn't given out in great quantities," Jane said. "I have enough good things. I'll survive."

"I know you'll *survive*," said Laura. "That's not the point."

But Jane was tired and just wanted to eat dinner. She would not talk any more that night.

After they went to bed, Laura stayed awake and imagined living in Plainview. She had gone out there with Jane once to see the new store. The town was ordinary — a suburb with tract houses and neat lawns. She pictured herself living in one of those houses. It would be the sort of house that she had once drawn for her hidden pictures page. In the summers, Ian could run through lawn sprinklers, or play Freeze Tag and Spud with his friends. Laura would go out and call him in to supper every evening, just as the sky was dimming down. The suburbs had always appealed to her in some way. They seemed to be such neutral territory. She was impressed by the still, shaded streets. She also liked the idea of a real neighborhood; she imagined backyard barbecues on summer nights, block parties, pool parties, a chorus of lawnmowers revving up on Sunday mornings.

It was David who had wanted to move to New York in the first place, David who had had a job waiting for him there. Laura had never questioned the move. All along, she had always assumed that the city was the best place for anyone to live. Now she tried to think of reasons that she needed to stay there. All she could come up with were ridiculous ones: Because of the park. Because of Zabar's. Because of the museums.

She grew excited as she thought about it, and she woke Jane up, something she rarely did. "I'm sorry," Laura whispered, lightly shaking Jane, "but I need to talk to you."

Jane slowly surfaced, put her hands over her face. In a few

moments she was awake. Laura turned on the bedside lamp. It was three in the morning.

"I've been thinking about the suburbs," she said. "About us moving there."

"Oh?" said Jane. "When did this occur to you?"

"Tonight," said Laura. "I used to think about it all the time, but there was never a reason to move. Now we have a perfect excuse. We could have a backyard," she said. "We could have a hammock."

"Oh, well, a *hammock*," said Jane. "In that case, we should definitely move."

"Come on," said Laura, drawing closer so their foreheads touched. "Be serious."

"I'm always serious," said Jane. "It's three in the morning; can't I make a joke?"

"Yes, but would you really consider moving?" asked Laura. "You know I'm not spontaneous. You know I have to think about things forever before I do them. This time the idea really interests me. Just think about it. The schools out there are good, and free, and Ian could actually ride a bicycle. You could drive five minutes to work. I could have a nice study. I'm sure we could get a mortgage on a decent house."

Jane didn't say anything for a long time. Laura wondered if she had fallen asleep again. But finally Jane said, "I'll think about it, okay? But now you have to let me sleep."

"I'm wide awake now," said Laura. "What should I do?"

Jane sighed heavily. "Okay," she said. "I'll tell you a story." Then she launched into "Two Girls in Love." This time the story had shifted to another era.

"Centuries passed," said Jane, "and the world became a very different sort of place. Men roamed the earth, often starting wars. Women hid out in caves, building fires. The Middle Ages came, and many people were wiped out from the plague. Life was a constant series of funerals. In a small town, I guess you could call it a hamlet, there lived two girls. They had been infants together because their mothers were friends. When they were eleven years old, they decided that their life was very oppressive and they would run away. They gathered food from the larder —a whole basket filled with smoked hams, and cheeses bound up with string, and a gourd full of fresh goat's milk. Anyway, as soon as they had everything they needed, they set off to find happiness. They did not know where they were going; all they knew was that they wanted to be together."

"I'm a little confused," said Laura. "Were they lovers?"

"They loved each other," said Jane. "That's all we know. You can interpret that any way you like. So," she said, "they set off together down the road in the middle of the night. They walked and walked, holding hands, until sunrise. They were very tired, so they decided to find a place to sleep a while. There in the distance was a beautiful farm, sort of like the place where you grew up, I guess. They snuck into the barn and fell asleep in each other's arms in a haystack. It was barely an hour later when they felt a pitchfork poking them awake.

" 'Hey, you two girls!' said a farmer. 'What are you doing here? You are going to be arrested and burned at the stake for being unaccompanied by a man!' The two girls raced out of the barn, their clothes and hair covered with straw, and they ran down the road and away from the farm. They realized that they couldn't continue to travel like this. They would have to disguise themselves. So they cut their long, flowing hair into short, Dutch-boy haircuts."

"Sort of like yours," said Laura.

"Similar," said Jane. "Similar. Anyway, they looked like beautiful young boys, since they hadn't reached puberty yet. They continued to roam the countryside for weeks, stopping every night to sleep and eat a little. Occasionally they helped out at a farm. Everyone loved them now that they were thought to be boys. Girls fell in love with them. 'You're not like other boys,' said one girl. 'Other boys are so tough and mean, and always picking fights. But your skin is just as soft as a girl's, and your temperament is fine and peaceful and loving. Please let me live with you both forever!'

"The girl's name was Lucinda, and even though she was beautiful herself, with a long black mane of hair, the two girls said they must leave her, for they were happier on their own. Years went by," said Jane, "and it became harder to disguise themselves as boys. But luckily, knighthood became the latest fashion for young men, and so the two girls dressed themselves in heavy armor, and no one ever guessed they were female. In fact, it was these two girls who originated the term 'breastplate' on a suit of armor."

"They became knights?" said Laura. "I thought you said they were nonviolent."

"They were special knights," said Jane. "They became famous because they always traveled as a pair and they always averted violence rather than caused it. They would lure their enemies toward them, and then they would quickly dash to the side, so their enemies were confused. They would do this again and again until finally the opposing knight would say, 'Prithee, what in the world are you trying to do?' At which point our girls would reply that they were trying to make him see how ridiculous all this running around and fighting wars on horses was. Eventually they would dismount and shake hands. The opposing knight, after being given a good lesson in nonviolence, would then beg them to lift their iron masks so he could see their faces, but of course they refused. The two girls simply said farewell, and then raced away on their horses once again. They lived like this until they became too old for knighthood, and then they spent the rest of their lives quietly. When they were old and frail, they decided to let their hair grow long again. Instead of growing in gray, as they assumed it would, it grew in the most wonderful assortment of reds and browns and blonds. They lived in an abandoned, burned-out castle by the sea, and when they died, their ashes blew out over the water. The end."

Laura's eyes were closed. "That was wonderful," she said. "It worked. I'm falling asleep."

"Good," said Jane.

They arranged themselves, shifting blankets and pillows in the bed. "I'm serious about wanting to move," Laura whispered. "I hope you know that."

"Yes, I know," said Jane.

Laura dropped off easily to sleep then, but Jane lay awake for a while longer. She too had an image in her mind that she did not want to let go of for the night; it was a small, white house, on a block lined with trees. It was a house right out of a Dick-and-Jane reader. It was nothing like the Mermaid Hotel. This was a real house, with a fence outside, and a front porch. Around the back there would be a small, neat yard with a swing attached to a big tree. Laura and Jane would stand at the back door, looking out through the screen. Ian would be riding that swing, pumping his legs so hard that he soared over the identical roofs of all the houses in the neighborhood.

CHAPTER FOURTEEN

One night David came over to discuss the move. It wasn't even close to a reality yet — they had no house, no details planned — but he sensed that they were serious. He brought Vanessa with him. They sat together on the couch, and Laura stared at the skim-milk transparency of Vanessa's skin. Jane hovered in the background, pouring coffee.

Ian walked into the living room then, already in his pajamas for the night. "Hi," he said. He knew that a big discussion was about to take place, and that it concerned him, but he clearly wanted no part of it. "I'm going to my room to do fractions," he announced, and everybody said goodnight in unison, as though it had been rehearsed.

The idea of moving was always hardest for children. Ian claimed that he wasn't upset, but Laura was sure it would hit him eventually. She still remembered the hostage face of Annie Carrington as she sat in the back seat of her parents' car, heading for Idaho. Children who were moved ended up being swallowed by some sort of Bermuda Triangle. Who knew what had happened to Annie? For a few months there had been letters, but after a while they stopped, and years later, when Laura tried to contact her again, her letter had been returned, with a stamp on it informing her that there was no one by that name at that address. She imagined Annie and her family traveling around in a caravan for the rest of their lives, a Gypsy troupe, lost to the world.

Laura watched Ian walk down the hall to his bedroom, hiking his pajamas up in back. "Well, I guess we should get started," David said. "Why don't you tell me what you had in mind, Laura."

"Okay," she said, and she spoke loosely about the proposed move. She talked about the safety of the suburbs, how good the public schools in Plainview were supposed to be. They would try it out for one year, just to see how it worked, she said. It would not be forever.

"I just want to ask you something," David said. "Why are you thinking about doing this?" He laughed. "I mean, the *suburbs*! You have a choice apartment in a great building, Laura. Yeah, I know all about the store moving and all, and Jane getting mugged, but why would you want to actually leave the city? You have enough money, between child support and your trust and *Jumping Bean*. I'm not trying to give you a hard time. Don't misunderstand. I'm just truly curious, Laura. It all seems so *impulsive*."

He addressed everything solely to Laura, but Jane cut in and spoke to him, unaddressed. "Because it's hard sometimes," Jane said. "And because we want a change. We both like trees, and having a backyard. And neighbors. We want to give Ian some of that." She paused. "We don't experience the city the same way you do," she said. "It's very different for us. It's a whole different place."

For David, the city was a social center; he and Vanessa went everywhere together with ease: to doctors' conventions, big dinner parties. They took long, close walks along the river. It had been the same way when he and Laura were married. They would walk through the park on weekends in the beginning, arms locked around each other. People smiled at them, beamed indulgently at these two people who were so clearly, so completely in love. In the evenings, during the first weeks of marriage, David and Laura rarely cooked dinner. Instead they went to their favorite Szechuan restaurant and always ordered the Happy Family vegetable plate.

Once Laura and Jane were walking along Amsterdam Avenue, lightly holding hands, when a man came right up to them, blocking their path, and started shouting in their faces. "You fucking dykes!" he shouted. "You make me sick! Why don't you go somewhere where people can't see you? You're disgusting, you know that?"

He was wearing a business suit and a tie, and behind him stood his wife, clutching her purse and looking mortified. Finally she pulled him away. Laura and Jane were so shocked by the encounter that they stood there, silent for a minute. For the rest of the day, Jane kept berating herself.

"I should have screamed back at him," she said. "I should have done *something*. When I was younger I was so much quicker to react."

There were other incidents: once in the supermarket on Broadway, and once in a movie theater, and finally Laura refused to be physical in public with Jane unless they were below Fourteenth Street. The Village somehow felt like a safety zone. Occasionally they saw other women with their arms around each other, and they would smile, establishing a tacit connection.

Vanessa and David could float through Manhattan, oblivious and in love. David was easing into his new life, settling in for the duration. Laura studied him as he sat on the couch, and she listened as he made vague objections about taking Ian out of the city, but she realized that his objections had the sound of formality to them. He had made the same fuss when Jane first moved in, and after a while he had calmed down. He really couldn't sustain an objection now, either.

Laura also knew that he wanted to be with Vanessa, to be young and unencumbered. He didn't want a custody battle on his hands, a major war between the sexes. He asked a battery of questions about the intended move, but after a while the questions thinned out and he relaxed.

He sipped his coffee, stretched out his legs. "I'm not here to make judgments about your lifestyle," he said. "I just want what's best for Ian. I hope you both know that. I don't want there to be any hostility here."

"I know," said Laura.

"If Ian wasn't involved in this, I wouldn't dare question a thing," said David. "You've made your choices, Laura."

"So have you," she said.

Nobody spoke for a moment. Vanessa looked down. She had barely said a word all evening. Laura felt sorry for her; Vanessa's function here seemed unclear. She was like David's muse: silent, inspiring, but never called on for an opinion. She sat next to him and held on to his sleeve.

The house, when they found it two months later, was pink, not white. The backyard was a small, square plot of grass. It did not look the way Laura had pictured the place they would live, but still the air had a lovely cool smell to it, like crushed leaves and fertilizer. The house was on a quiet street named Leona Drive. The real estate agent explained that all the streets in the neighborhood were named for the women in the builder's family. Around the corner was Janet Road, and two blocks away was Carla Drive, and nearby, Marsha Road.

"It's really a women's community," Jane whispered to Laura.

The real estate agent, Mrs. Farber, walked ahead of them up the front path, fumbling with a big keyring.

Inside the house, faded brown carpet covered most of the floor. There were little indentations where the furniture had been. The house was a split-level, like all the other houses on the block. They followed Mrs. Farber up the carpeted steps and into the master bedroom. She flung open the closet doors and Laura and Jane dutifully peered inside, nodding. This was only out of politeness, though; the size of the closets would not sway them either way.

"Do you have any children?" Mrs. Farber asked, closing the doors.

"Yes," said Laura, startled. Were there rules here — no pets, no children?

"The elementary school is around the corner, on Janet Road," the woman said. "Walking distance." Then she paused. "You're sisters?" she asked. "You look so much alike."

Laura just stood there, not knowing what to say. No one had ever asked them this question before.

"Yes," Laura said quickly. "We are."

Jane shot her a look. The woman only smiled. "How nice," she said. "Now let me show you the bathroom."

They followed her down the hall, and tested out the faucets and glanced into the shower. Jane kept looking at Laura and shaking her head, but Laura looked away each time.

It was the toolshed out back that sealed their decision. There it was, an empty metal structure just taking up space. "I could use it as a workroom," Jane said. "I've always wanted a workroom."

They walked out into the middle of the yard. The property was banked by high bushes. Through a thin place among the branches Laura could see into a neighboring yard. She stood close, looking in. She could see a few lounge chairs framing a big, shimmering built-in pool that took up most of the property. A teenage boy stood at the side of the pool, skimming leaves off the surface with a net.

Later that afternoon, as they rode back to the city on the Long Island Railroad, Jane and Laura sat looking out the window at the sparse scenery: yards of telephone wire, abandoned warehouses with the windows punched out, and station after station that looked exactly alike. Men and women smiled down from billboards, their teeth blackened, mustaches drawn in. Jane and Laura sat with their shoulders touching.

"Why did you tell her that?" Jane finally asked.

Laura looked out the window as long as she could. "I got scared," she said. "That's all. I didn't want her to know anything about us."

"Well," Jane said, "I don't want to move out here with you if that's your attitude about it."

"It's none of her business if we're sisters or lovers," Laura said.

"But you don't need to lie," Jane said. "I'm too old for that, Laura. We've been living together too long to start lying. Why the sudden change?"

"I never felt questioned," said Laura. "As soon as I told my parents, everything else seemed easy. I felt like I could tell anyone and it would be all right. I just had a setback out there."

Jane looped her arm around Laura's shoulder. "People watch you more carefully in the suburbs," she said. "It's not like the city. It's family territory. Everybody knows who lives where."

"Why do we have to tell them anything?" asked Laura. "I don't see why anyone needs to know. Nobody asks *them* about their sex lives."

Jane looked at her. "We're not talking about a sex life," she said. "If that's what you think this relationship is based on, maybe we'd better have a talk."

"Stop being mean," said Laura.

"I'm not," said Jane. "But you've got to wake up, Laura. If you want to live with me and Ian out there in a sweet little house, then you've got to face facts. We are lovers. And we're raising a son. And I'm not about to start pretending otherwise, so you'd better think really hard about it before signing anything."

The woman across the aisle looked up from her crossword puzzle and stared. Laura was embarrassed. "We're being listened to," she hissed.

"So what?" said Jane. "This is much more important. Everything can't go exactly the way you'd like it all the time. This isn't your childhood, with happy farm animals running around and everything being taken care of. You may have money, Laura, but it's not enough now. You've got to decide how you want to live. And you've got to let me know."

"I'm sorry," said Laura, and she looked down. "You're right, you're right," she said. "It's just hard for me sometimes. I do want to move out there. I know it might be difficult, but I think I want to try it, at least."

"You're sure?" asked Jane, her voice softer now.

"Yes," said Laura. They sat close together again, and began to conspire about life in the suburbs. Neither of them had any idea of what they might actually be getting into if they took the house. They were trusting only their shared instinct, and the way the rooms had smelled so pleasingly of camphor, the echoes of some earlier life.

When they got home, they sat in the living room and discussed everything exhaustively. This was only the fifth house they had seen; perhaps they were being too quick about it. Carolyn had recommended Mrs. Farber to them. She was somewhat officious but also extremely reliable. She would call up and say things like, "I've found something, and it's a steal." Laura had had no idea that real estate agents actually spoke like that.

That night a couple of Jane's old friends came over, and all they talked about was the move.

"Well," said Holly, raising a wine glass, "I want to propose a toast to our home-owning homosexual friends."

"We haven't even made an offer yet," said Jane. "And you're just jealous."

"What do you mean?" said Holly. "Jane, I grew up in *Woodmere*. The Five Towns! Do you know what that was like for me?

I lived in one of those houses, just like the one you've described, only richer, and I went to the same kind of school that your kid is going to go to. I was desperate to get out. On weekends my friends and I would go to the mall to shoplift. There was nothing else to do. Absolutely nothing. Long Island is a giant mall."

"Oh, calm down," said Lynn. She turned to Laura. "Do you know how many times I've heard this song and dance?" she asked. "We all had our miserable childhoods. But now they're over. We all crawled out of the suburbs, or the city, or wherever. So what if we disgraced ourselves? I can never go back to Tenafly. I'm sure the whole town is still talking about how I seduced Michelle Torres. We were in home ec together; we used to make out behind the sewing machines."

Holly and Lynn had been living together in Brooklyn for years and years. Now they both worked in a print shop. They had steady jobs, ordinary lives. They had never wanted to have children. There was nothing particularly radical about the way they lived, and it upset Laura that they would make fun of the intended move to Plainview.

"We have a child to raise," Laura finally said. "It's different."

"We're just kidding you," Lynn said. "Holly gets vitriolic sometimes about her horrible past. Don't get upset."

The next day Lynn stopped by the apartment with a going-away present, even though nothing was definite yet. The present was a tiny orange kitten who she insisted was called Elizabeth Cady Stanton, Lizzie for short. Laura deposited the kitten in Ian's arms, and he cradled it tenderly.

"Can I really keep her?" he asked. "No kidding?"

"She's got to be your responsibility totally," Laura said. "Feeding and litterbox." In the past Ian had kept only tropical fish, which he usually ignored. Once in a while a decomposing fish would float to the surface of the tank and have to be scooped out with a teaspoon.

But now she knew the move would be difficult for him, and

she thought a kitten might help. Over the next few weeks, Ian went everywhere with Lizzie, and he slept with her at night. Laura and Jane went to look at the house in Plainview one more time and decided to make an offer. If everything went as planned, they could move by August.

At night in bed, she and Jane went over the same material again and again. "You can have your own workroom," Laura would say. "That's a plus."

"And you can turn the den into a study," said Jane.

"Ian can walk to school by himself every day," Laura said.

"It's very safe," murmured Jane.

Then they would panic and not be able to sleep for the rest of the night. They would sit in the kitchen and scramble up some eggs, or stare at David Susskind on TV.

"I feel so *responsible*, all of a sudden," Laura said. "Buying a house seems so much more traumatic than having a baby, for instance."

She knew that it had something to do with the fact that no one approved of the move. Everyone had applauded Ian's birth, had cooed and sent things, but now friends treated the move with disbelief.

"I feel like I'm staying in one place," Carolyn had said, "and you're just whizzing ahead. All I can do is watch. You never cease to amaze me, Laura. I just can't picture this—lesbians in suburbia. I didn't think there *were* any there."

"It's just a trial move," Laura said. The word "trial" struck her as funny; she and David had gone through a "trial" separation once, and later Jane had moved in on a "trial" basis. It was a safe word for unsure people. You could test things out without having to commit yourself for life. The only time Laura had made a firm commitment was when she married David. Maybe if they had called it a trial marriage, it would have lasted.

Nothing is permanent, she reminded herself as she showed Carolyn's friends Dan and Marie Brazer around the apartment.

They wanted to sublet for at least one year. They were stylish art directors, and they walked through the rooms already discussing the details they wanted to change. They planned where bookshelves could go, where track lighting might be installed. They drew up an unofficial lease for one year and celebrated the deal over dinner. Halfway through the meal, Laura began to feel terrified. If she and Jane hated the suburbs, they would now have to tolerate it for at least a year.

On moving day, the first week of August, Carry Nation Movers took everything safely from the city to the suburbs. Jane had found the movers through Holly; they were all women, and their slogan, WE CARRY THE NATION, was painted shakily on the side of their van.

"Careful now," Laura said, hovering over them in the living room.

"Don't worry," one said. "We never bang anything up."

Laura had to leave the room. She walked down the hall and into the kitchen, where Ian was sitting on one of the two remaining chairs, swiveling slowly in a circle, the cat in his lap.

"You okay?" she asked, and he nodded, but looked doomed.

They had borrowed Carolyn's Volkswagen, and they rode out to Plainview behind the moving van. They followed over highways, past tall buildings and a long stretch of water. Jane drove, and Ian sat strapped into the back seat. Laura had brought along some apple juice for him. He sat glumly by the window, holding his thermos cup steady.

That night, their first one in Plainview, Long Island, in their new split-level house on Leona Drive, Laura took a tour of the rooms by herself. They had been unpacking all afternoon, and now that evening had come there was a lull in the house. The rooms had a brash, electric-light look about them; there still weren't enough lampshades to cover all the naked bulbs. The living room was as bright as a supermarket.

Outside the front window, she could hear a few random neighborhood sounds: a dog barking, a door slamming, and then a car whooshing by. The headlights of the car made a slat pattern edge along the wall. This was so different from the city; in the city, you usually weren't aware of distinct sounds. Instead, it was an alloy of noise you heard, a blend of cars and cries and some unidentifiable overlay—white noise, it was called.

She walked down the hall. Ian was sitting in his new bedroom, cross-legged on the bed in bright lamplight, reading a book called *Chisenbop: Fun with Finger Math.* He was surrounded by a sea of boxes.

"Goodnight, sweetie," she said. "Do you have everything you need?" He looked up at her and she could see that he was counting; his mouth moved silently, and his fingers went up and down as though playing a piano in the air.

Back in the master bedroom, Jane was getting ready for bed. Laura walked in and watched as Jane pulled a T-shirt over her head. She could see the dark shadow of an underarm for a moment, and the fine down in that perfect, scooped-out place. Jane was often aware that Laura watched her like this, but she did not see herself as a piece of statuary. Sometimes she seemed self-conscious when Laura watched her. Now she was plain and candid, getting ready for bed in this unfamiliar place. She smelled like turpentine, no matter how much she bathed. Laura was accustomed to it; it made her think of planks of wood, and of Jane hard at work the first day they met, all friction and noise. Jane made wonderful sounds when she was working—little releases, syllables of air.

"We can leave if we don't like it here," Laura said as they stood in the bare bedroom. "Nothing is irreversible, right?"

She realized then that the windows were all uncovered, and the people next door could see right in. *This is suburbia*, she thought, and she stepped out of view.

CHAPTER FIFTEEN

Whis first moved to Plainview, all she could think about was space. The division of property, the closeness of her life to someone else's. There were bushes all around the yard, but still she could hear everything that went on next door. The neighbors, a family named Frankel, gave pool parties nearly every day. Laura sat in the yard and listened to the water being dived into. There would be the hollow slap of a body into the pool, and then shouts, and laughter. "Watch me, I'm Esther Williams!" she heard someone call.

One day Elaine Frankel showed up on their doorstep. She was a small woman with red hair and a tight, tennis-playing body. She was a Girl Scout leader, and could often be seen leaving her house with her thirteen-year-old daughter, Sybil, both of them wearing matching green uniforms.

"I'd love it if you would come to dinner," she said. "How about tonight, at eight?"

Laura told Elaine that they would be delighted. That evening she and Jane were ushered into the Frankels' front hall. The house had a compact elegance to it. There was thick gray carpeting on the living room floor, and the coffee table was a slab of glass. There were three expensive art books lying on top of it. Jane and Laura sat at the dining room table with Elaine and her silent husband, Larry, who retreated to the bedroom right after dessert.

Elaine continued to chatter on about the neighborhood. She told them that she was very involved with the PTA. "We're trying to be alert to our children's needs," she said. This year, they were concerned with the playground at the elementary school. Children had been splitting open their heads on the blacktop. The committee was trying to get the school board to lay down some rubber panels underneath the swings and the jungle gym.

"I'm sure you'll want to get involved," said Elaine, "since you have a little boy. He's *your* son, right, Laura?"

"Yes," said Laura stiffly.

"Look," said Elaine, "there's something that's been on my mind all week, and I just thought I would come right out front and say it, if I may." She paused, and cocked her head to the side. "You're a couple, right?" she asked.

Laura put her coffee cup down. She could feel Jane looking at her in that moment. Jane was not going to say a word, Laura knew. She was just going to sit there.

"Yes," Laura said. "We are."

"I thought so," said Elaine. "You'll forgive me, but I haven't known any women like that before. I've known several men, of course. I used to work as a costume assistant in the theater. I helped out on *The Fantasticks*. There were always homosexual men running around," she said. "I realized that it was their right to live like that if they wanted to. Who was I to judge?" She stopped talking for a few seconds, and stirred her coffee. "It's a different story," she said, "living here in Plainview. It's not a cosmopolitan place. Frankly," she said, "I think you're asking for trouble. Remember, I personally see nothing wrong with how you live, but others will. And, of course, there's your son. That's where I start to say, 'Maybe it isn't fair, bringing an innocent child into the middle of this.' As long as it's just two adults, it's your right to do what you want, but when you add a kid into the equation, then I say, 'Uh-oh.' My immediate reaction is to think that you ought to give this a lot of thought before school starts next week. Maybe you'd want to get separate homes for the time being — there are some nice garden apartments nearby in Syosset. It would probably be a lot easier."

"Elaine," said Jane, "we've thought a lot about it."

"I'm just trying to help," said Elaine.

"We're doing fine," Jane said, and she suddenly sounded very tired, as though she had been repeating this for years.

"Please don't be offended," said Elaine. "I only meant this as a tip."

"A tip!" said Jane. "It's more than that."

"I don't wish you unhappiness," said Elaine. "I'm just telling you what I see down the road. I'm pretty perceptive."

There was an extended silence. Laura couldn't think of a thing to say.

Sybil came into the room then. Her Girl Scout uniform hung lankly on her thin frame. "Mother," she said, "you said you'd help." Her voice was plaintive. She held a pair of scissors in one hand, the blades open.

"It's her James Taylor scrapbook," Elaine explained. "And I did say I would help." She turned to her daughter. "I'll be right in," she said. "A promise is a promise."

Outside the house again, walking the few steps home, Jane and Laura were silent. "You okay?" Laura finally asked.

They stood on the sidewalk. Across the street a lawn sprinkler magically turned on. Water stuttered out. "Yes," Jane said, "I'm fine. So she's sort of a jerk. We'll live."

"She's not a bad person," said Laura. "I don't think she's malicious or anything."

"The problem is," said Jane, "that she means what she says. She thinks she's being wonderful to us. It's the best advice she knows how to give us — better than telling us what butcher to go to, or what dry cleaner."

They went inside. Ian was lying on the living room couch, reading a book. He had been reading all day, had taken twelve books out of the public library with his new card.

"Anybody call?" Jane asked. "I want to make sure the phone actually works."

"No," said Ian. He didn't look up.

Laura stood by the door and listened to the sounds that came in through the screen. This was her latest obsession. Tonight there was almost nothing out there — just some trees rustling together, and the same barking dog she heard every night. She imagined this poor dog chained in a yard forever, like Prometheus.

"It's because of summer," said Jane. "Everyone is away. Most of the kids are at sleepaway camp. That's what Elaine Frankel said."

Elaine knew her facts. One morning during the last week of August, big silver tour buses started showing up in the parking lot of the school around the corner. The buses had signs in the windows, with names like Camp Arrowwood, Camp Del-Mar. Children poured out when the accordion doors opened. They collided with waiting parents; they flooded the neighborhood. Laura could hear their shouts in the street. Ian met a few of them; Elaine Frankel had made a list of the nearby children who were his age. Her own children were too old — Sybil was a haughty thirteen, and Jack was sixteen. Around the corner was a boy of ten who desperately needed friends, Elaine said. His name was Todd Berger, and his mother had died. It was a suicide, she said, lowering her voice.

School was to begin on September 7. The week before, Laura took Ian in to be officially registered. Jane wanted to go too, but Laura said no, it wasn't necessary, she could manage it herself.

When they walked into the empty school they heard the sound of a typewriter somewhere down the hall. A janitor rumbled a trash barrel along the shining corridor. Ian walked next to his mother, taking everything in.

"The hall is wider here," he commented. "At the Calder School it was skinny."

She didn't know whether this was a criticism or not. He seemed impartial, just looking around and peering into classrooms. At the principal's office Ian sat idly in a chair while Laura filled out several forms. The principal was a big, slow-moving woman named Mrs. Hoffman, who actually said, "Welcome," and bent down slightly to shake Ian's hand.

"You will be in Miss Brenner's class," she said. "I'm sure you will like it there."

As they left the building, Laura conjured up images of Miss Brenner. She might be a young, gentle woman, like Ian's teachers at Calder. She would bring her dulcimer into school sometimes and teach the children to sing "Kumbaya."

Laura and Ian walked across the deserted athletic field, out past the jungle gym and the swings, which looked forlorn to her in their stillness. The seesaws were tipped up—the first one with its right end in the air, the second one with its left, the third one again with its right. They were like a free-form piece of modern sculpture. At Calder, of course, there had been no playground; the kids had to run around a tiny all-purpose room during gym class and struggle with a gigantic bladder-ball. At Ian's new school, gym was held in a big room with latexed floors. Basketball hoops hung perilously high. Laura imagined Ian jumping up and sinking a few baskets, just palming the ball and letting it whisper easily through the net. But Ian had very little interest in basketball. It wasn't that he was awkward; mostly, he preferred to be still.

She went with him again on his first day of school. This time, Jane did not even ask to go. Laura and Ian walked together down the street, and she was conscious of the distance Ian kept between them. Children were springing up out of nowhere, walking in clusters of twos and threes. There was Sybil Frankel in her Girl Scout uniform, flanked by two familiar girls. They were light years away from Ian, and would never have anything to do with him.

All the children came wearing their best clothes — red shirts and green dresses, big plaid patterns, polka dots. Everything looked painstakingly pressed. Laura watched Ian in his blue Windbreaker and hightop Keds, his schoolbag slapping against him as he walked. He looked like one of them, she was relieved to see.

When the principal showed them to Ian's classroom, Laura was surprised to learn that Miss Brenner was old. She had her hair drawn tightly off her face, and she greeted Ian solemnly, placing both hands on his shoulders and steering him toward a desk in the back. A bell shrieked, and for a moment Laura was confused; then she remembered that this was the sort of school where bells signaled the beginning of the day, and the end. She thought of Pavlov and a pack of waiting dogs.

Taking one fleeting look back through the glass, Laura saw Ian easing into his seat. He was so far in the rear of the room; what if he couldn't see the board? He would get lost in those rows of desks, the way Laura used to get lost in the field behind her parents' house. She walked back down the street. There was not a single child in sight now.

Back at home, Jane was hanging paintings. She was kneeling on the living room couch with a few nails in her mouth, centering a framed painting on the wall. She was going to resume her job at the store the next morning. She had asked for four weeks off to move, and she and Laura had used that time well. They had bought a Dodge Dart at the dealership in town that Elaine Frankel had recommended. They had stood out in the sun looking down rows and rows of shining cars.

The last time Laura had driven a car, she was in college, and

181

she and David had taken his blue, finned Plymouth out into the Connecticut woods for the day with a bottle of wine. David had gotten lightheaded and asked Laura to drive home. He lay sleeping in her lap as she drove, and she had experienced an uneasy power then, thinking, *I could drive us anywhere now, or I could kill us both*. It wasn't that she wanted to kill them; it was just the first time she had been in any sort of command with David. While he slept, his breath sweet with Rhine wine, Laura drove down the long, dark road humming to herself.

Now she was driving again after ten years' reprieve. She would have to get a new license. She took the Dart out onto the Long Island Expressway and entered and exited, feeling as though she were part of a complicated square dance. The drivers tacitly acknowledged each other as they glanced sideways, changing lanes.

Life on Long Island required a good deal of driving. She would have to take Ian to the dentist, to the shopping mall, into the city to stay with David. She was glad that Jane loved to drive; Laura felt very safe with her at the wheel.

It was a safety that extended itself in many ways. When Laura came home from Ian's school that first day and saw Jane hanging paintings in the living room, she felt it again: a relief that Jane was actually there, taking this new life seriously, hammering her convictions deeply into the wall.

They worked on the house all morning, and then every weekend after that. Laura liked it when she and Jane had two days alone together. They puttered around and rearranged furniture. Two days away from Ian was a perfect amount; any more than that made her feel bereft. When he returned on Sunday nights, they would eat a big, festive dinner. The kitchen was almost finished; baskets of utensils hung from the ceiling, and braids of garlic were tacked to a wall. It was a great room, and the window looked out into the backyard. They could see trees and Jane's toolshed. Occasionally a stray child would run through the yard, taking a short cut home.

Each morning Jane and Laura and Ian converged in the kitchen. On the day that Jane went back to work, everyone was silent at breakfast. They all had their heads bent over their plates as they ate their eggs. Jane and Ian were both washed and dressed for their day. Laura still sat in her bathrobe, feeling the loose material against her skin and knowing that there was nowhere she needed to go.

When Jane and Ian had both left, Laura went into her study. She took out her Rapidograph and put in a new fine point. Bottles of ink were lined up on the desk in a row, ranging from the palest rose to the purest black. She sat down and began to draw an underwater scene, with starfish and divers and a giant clam. Laura drew her pictures as if on automatic pilot these days. She had long ago gotten the formula down pat. She simply sent in her illustrations, and they were approved by the new editor, and published as usual. The magazine was doing poorly these days; it was too expensive to produce. Children were buying comic books and playing video games instead. She still received fan mail once in a while, letters from children that were always gratifying. They came from different places across the country, from children who signed them with phrases like, "Sincerely, your friend Alissa Krakow, Willamette Central School." Laura tried to imagine these faceless children sitting at sweet little desks at home and writing her letters. These children responded to her drawings more than Ian ever did. He never seemed too impressed.

Sometimes she felt inadequate, but she had no scale to test adequacy. Whom could you compare yourself with? She knew other mothers, of course, but all families were different. She remembered sitting for hours with the other young mothers in Central Park, watching the children play in the sandbox. She had understood the *guesswork* of motherhood then — how all of those women dealt with their kids by pure estimation. The bottom line was that you had to protect your kids in whatever ways you could.

It was perilous everywhere. Even in the suburbs, Elaine Frankel warned of playground dangers, poisoned Halloween candy. And there were more subtle invasions. People watched you so carefully here; it was part of living in a neighborhood. Elaine Frankel had probably called up every member of the PTA and told them about the lesbians on the block. They would have figured it out sooner or later, anyway. Two women in their thirties did not live together. It was just not done. Or if it was done, the women were usually widowed, lonely, seeking a quiet backgammon companion. They carefully labeled items in the refrigerator so there was never a mix-up over whose cottage cheese belonged to whom. They lived civil, quiet, respectful lives, and kept an equally respectful distance. At night they tucked themselves into their twin beds.

But two women and a child was a difficult combination to figure out. It wasn't questioned during daylight hours; it was assumed that two female friends might take one child to a shopping mall, or out for a walk. At night, the absence of a father was noticed more strongly. Where was the car pulling into the driveway, the man coming up the walk with a folded newspaper under his arm? The tired father lowering himself into an easy chair, his child begging him to listen to a riddle, to watch a cartwheel demonstration?

One night Laura, Jane, and Ian went out to the local Chinese restaurant for dinner. At the next table a family sat in uncomfortable silence. The mother looked as though she had been crying. Laura watched as the daughter quietly played with her chopsticks. All around the restaurant, families were seated at tables. The suburbs were geared to children. Everywhere you went, you felt it. Every menu in restaurants had a child's section, with dinners called the Zebra, the Bashful, the Moose.

Even in Ian's school there was an annual Family Spaghetti Dinner. It was the social event of the season, according to Elaine Frankel, and everybody went. Jane stared at the flyer that had come in the mail. "I'd like to go," she said. "It would mean a lot."

"I don't know," Laura said. "Maybe it's not such a good idea. It's only the beginning of school and all. Ian's just starting to make friends."

Jane looked down at the flyer again. " 'All family members welcome,' " she read. " 'All you can eat for five dollars. Benefits go to the PTA.' "

"Stop," said Laura. "If you really want to go, then I won't stop you, Jane. I just want to be sure that it's the best thing to do."

In the end, Jane stayed home. She sat in front of the television set while Laura walked around looking for the keys. "They've got to be somewhere," she said. "I just had them."

"Ma, I found them!" Ian called from the bedroom.

"We're ready to go," Laura said, but Jane didn't look up. She continued to watch her show. "Please don't be angry," Laura said quietly. She put her arms around Jane's neck and kissed the side of her face. "Please."

Ian came into the room then, anxious to leave. "Ma," he said. "We've got to go." He looked at Jane. "I guess you're not coming, right?" he said.

"No," said Jane. "I thought it would be better if you guys went alone."

Laura gave her a look and then walked out the door, Ian behind her. It was unclear to her how much Ian understood. He didn't seem to want Jane to come, she thought. On some level he understood that it was difficult. He loved Jane, she knew. They were very playful together, like siblings who were born years and years apart but who happened to get along well. He listened to Jane when she told him to clean his room, or feed the cat, but she never had quite the same authority that Laura had.

When they walked into the school, the gymnasium was over-heated and smelled strongly of Italian food. Teachers dressed as chefs stood behind long steam tables of spaghetti.

"There's Miss Brenner," Ian whispered, with the embarrassed reverence that all children had when they saw their teachers outside the classroom. Miss Brenner was ladling out tomato sauce and occasionally waving to her students.

The lunch tables were outfitted with red-and-white-checkered tablecloths. Laura and Ian sat down at a table by themselves. In a while another family came over and sat down with them.

"Hello," said the father. "I'm Louis Gelb, and this is my wife, Sheila, and our daughter, Beth."

Laura shook hands and introduced herself and Ian. The Gelbs were most definitely a unit; they consulted each other throughout the meal on every small thing.

"Should I get one meatball or two?" Beth Gelb asked her mother in a whisper.

"I would think one would be enough for you, miss," said her mother. The daughter leaped up to the steam table, clutching her plate.

Sometime during the middle of the meal, Elaine Frankel made her way across the gym to say hello. "You two doing okay over here?" she asked.

"Fine," said Laura. "We're having a good time."

Actually, the lights of the room were bright and hot, and she wished that she could run away. But Ian was enjoying himself. He was talking to Beth Gelb about fractions.

"Well, why don't you come over to my table for spumoni?" asked Elaine. "I'll introduce you to some of my friends."

Laura felt bullied by Elaine but she agreed to switch tables for dessert. She apologized to the Gelbs, and took Ian's hand and followed Elaine across the shining floor.

Elaine introduced them to a large, boisterous table of people, all of whom seemed to know each other intimately.

"This is Laura Giovanni and her son, Ian," Elaine said. "They've just moved in next door to us."

Everyone besieged Laura with questions. She found herself sitting in the middle of the group, talking on and on about *Jumping Bean*. At least two of the mothers and several of the children were familiar with her hidden picture drawings. Laura wasn't used to the attention, but after a while she found herself talking naturally, even enjoying it.

"Are you divorced?" a woman asked, and the question was not meant in a gossipy way. The woman had desperate eyes, and seemed to be looking for a comrade.

"Yes," said Laura.

"Me too," the woman said. "We should have lunch sometime. It gets hard."

It was a moment in which Laura might have said, "Thank you, I'd love to, but I think you should know that I'm not lonely anymore. I live with someone." But the room was noisy and Laura's spirits were high, so she just eased out of it by saying, "That would be nice." As she spoke, she could see that Elaine was listening.

At the end of the evening, Laura and Ian walked home with the Frankels. Laura and Elaine walked a little bit ahead of everyone else.

"I'm glad you came," said Elaine. "And you handled yourself very well, very discreetly."

Laura said nothing. She pushed her hands deep into her pockets, feeling like a traitor, wanting only to be with Jane. When they reached the house, Laura barely said goodnight. She just whisked Ian inside and softly closed the door.

CHAPTER SIXTEEN

He married her in secret. They both took the morning off and went downtown to City Hall, where Vanessa's best friend, Ilene, was waiting on the steps, a large bouquet in her arms. "I'm freezing," Ilene said. "Let's go inside."

In the warm recesses of the massive stone building, they waited on an endless line, and two hours later they were married. Afterward the three of them had lunch together at a Blimpie's restaurant. David liked the idea of that lunch; he knew that years later he would be telling the story of the day he and Vanessa had gotten married, and people would laugh. "Then we had lunch at a Blimpie's," he would say. "It was the only place we could find nearby, and we were both very hungry."

Sitting with her in the neon brightness of the restaurant, he felt assured that this had been a good move. She was wearing a simple white dress with small violets stitched across the front. She didn't mind sitting there with him, all dressed up. Her wedding band shone on her finger. He sat next to her on an orange plastic seat, and he wished he could slide closer, but the chairs were bolted to the floor.

"You guys are incredible," Ilene said, shaking her head and smiling. She was another social worker at the hospital. It seemed that all of their friends worked at the hospital. Everyone knew that he and Vanessa lived together, and they were just waiting for them to marry. Vanessa had originally wanted a real church wedding, but he had convinced her that this was much better, much easier. The idea of a real wedding made him nervous. When he had married Laura, he was able to go through with the whole formal ceremony because he was very young then, and wanted a taste of adult life, of the way he understood that adults lived. Now that he knew, he didn't want to go through it again. He loved Vanessa, and she loved him. He would marry her in private.

She looked happy with the choice as she sipped her Tab and held his hand. It was not even noon, and there were very few people in the restaurant. David felt triumphant. Vanessa had moved into his apartment a few months earlier. At first she had changed things around — had taken down his framed prints of Holland and replaced them with a poster of a seashell by Georgia O'Keeffe and a photograph of Baryshnikov in flight. David didn't complain; he hung the Dutch prints in the bathroom. Mostly he was delighted to live with her. She cried easily, but could also be consoled just as easily. They spent a good deal of time sprawled on the couch, or on the thick white rug in the hallway. Sometimes he felt as though they were locked into permanent adolescence together. Occasionally she would even talk baby-talk to him, and he wouldn't mind. He often had the sense that their love involved the act of spoiling each other. Marriage just meant that the indulgence would last forever, like some thick, sweet cream that never turns.

There was no time for a honeymoon now. They would take one later, in the summer perhaps. The first order of business was to have a baby. This was understood; as soon as they got married, they would try to conceive. Vanessa was thirty-five. One afternoon she had her IUD removed. She brought it home in a small plastic bag as a souvenir. It was a Dalkon Shield, and it looked to David like a fishing lure. Now they relegated it to Vanessa's night-table drawer, with the emery boards.

"Do you feel strange without it?" he asked her in the afternoon light of the bedroom, slipping himself easily into her. He paused then, held still.

"No," she said. "Not really." They stayed like that, tantric, and then they were laughing and couldn't make love at all. In a few minutes they were serious again, and their lovemaking became equally serious. He felt industrious; he burrowed in as deeply as he could until she cried out and held his head in both hands.

David told Laura and Ian about the marriage a few days after it took place. Jane answered the phone, and he had to be patient for a moment, saying, "How's the house coming along? How's the job?"

"Fine, fine," she said, and he knew that she had no interest in talking to him either.

She put Laura on in a minute, and they talked for a little while about the usual matters: child-support payments, Ian's school. Finally Ian himself got on, and he told David about what had happened that day during math hour. He seemed okay; it really was working out. There was something, David supposed, about the combination of Laura and Jane that was peaceful for a child. Dull, almost. But children responded to things like that; wasn't "Mr. Rogers' Neighborhood" a big hit, after all? Laura and Jane were both low-key and attentive. No one could accuse them of negligence. Whenever he really thought about it, though, really stopped to imagine Ian being raised by lesbians, he became unnerved.

Vanessa knew more about this sort of thing than David did,

and she assured him that it seemed to be okay, that there were no statistics to prove that Ian would end up homosexual himself. "I can't go so far as to say that I think it's natural, David," she would say. "But certainly, if we're talking about the amount of love and attention that a child might receive in such a situation, there doesn't seem to be a problem here. If anything, the problem lies in finding healthy role models. And you're around him a lot, so I think that takes care of it."

But he would lean close to her and say, "Are you sure?" And she would have to concede that no, she wasn't really sure; it was all a question of guesswork.

He kept in constant contact with Laura and Ian, and he heard every small detail that went on in his son's life. He wanted to have a complete picture of the things Ian was going through. *Describe your new bedroom,* he said to Ian once over the phone; another time, *What is your social studies homework for tomorrow?*

The night he told Ian that he had gotten married, Ian responded with silence. What had David expected? There was a long pause, and then Ian said, "Oh."

"I wanted you to be the first to know, kiddo," David said. "Now I want to tell your mom. Could you put her back on?"

Laura got back on the phone, and David told her the news. She too was silent. "I don't know what to say," she finally said. "I guess it was expected. I'm glad you're happy, David. I just wish you had let me know in advance. Why did you wait until after the fact?"

The truth was, he hadn't really thought about it. He had wanted to do this whole thing privately, without any input from other people. This was his new life, and he felt very protective of it. Still, he wasn't sure why he hadn't told her; maybe it had been irresponsible.

"It's a big thing for Ian to hear," said Laura. "I can't talk, because he's in earshot, but didn't you give any thought to the fact that he might feel upset? I mean, it's not every day that his father gets married."

"Well," David said, floundering, "it's not every day that his mother moves in with her lesbian lover, either."

"At least I was up front about it," said Laura. "Ian was aware of what was going on."

"Maybe that's not so healthy for him," said David. "Or are you suddenly so progressive?"

"I don't want to continue this right now," said Laura. "I think I should go."

"I'm sorry," David said. "I did what I thought was best. I'm sorry you think I acted badly."

But Ian seemed unaffected by the marriage. It didn't change the state of things; marriage was a formality. Vanessa had been in David's life for years, and Ian had long ago accepted her. What else could he do, actually? You didn't question your parents' choices.

David remembered how, as a kid, he had never noticed the decor in his parents' apartment. He had just inhabited the place blindly, putting his feet up on the couch, eating each night at the dining room table. It was only years later, when he was at Yale and came home for vacations, that he noticed how the apartment looked, and was horrified. He had never thought of the flocked wallpaper in the dining room as being in either good or bad taste. And the paintings, heavy oil landscapes with gold frames and little lights above them — they now looked to him like the kind of art that was sometimes sold in the lobbies of movie theaters. He sat in his parents' apartment as though he were an uncomfortable guest. He hated himself for his sudden disdain, but what could he do? Something in him had changed.

But Ian wouldn't be that way for years. Until he grew up, he would think it was fine that his father lived with Vanessa and his mother lived with Jane. He would be more open-minded than most kids. At ten, Ian seemed pretty tolerant. He wasn't a whiny kid. Instead, he sulked. He would turn around and leave a room if he was upset. Then he would go play with his pocket calculator for a while, and it seemed to make him feel better. Everyone needed an outlet like that. For David, it was making love with Vanessa, or lifting weights. When he made love, he felt all of his body pushing outward as far as possible. He would make his skin become so alert to touch that physical sensation became much more important than whatever argument he had been having or whatever kind of frustration he had felt at work. The same was true with lifting weights, although the pleasure was different. When David lifted weights at the Yale Club gym, he always wore white. He felt exceptionally clean in this endeavor, and his sweat soaked him to the skin, so that when he stripped afterward for a shower, he felt as though he were peeling off a layer of his own skin, and a new self was emerging underneath. He would dump his drenched clothes in his gym bag and head home, feeling triumphant as he dodged the traffic.

It had occurred to David, somewhere along the line, that it was important to feel things constantly. Whether examining a patient, or playing squash, or watching a movie, or being with Vanessa or with Ian, he wanted to be aware of sensation. It was odd, but he felt things most acutely when he was with Ian. He still thought of Ian as his little boy. It was a phrase that had lodged in his mind, even now, when Ian was a gangly ten-year-old with such a serious, responsible air to him. He wasn't particularly playful, at least not in the typical ways. He and David liked to play number games together. They went over math problems, and tried things out on Ian's calculator. David and Vanessa had given Ian that calculator for his eighth birthday. He was the first kid in his class to own one. He stayed up late at night doing problems in bed. "Don't ruin your eyes," David said lightly, because he felt that he should, but he was smiling. His kid was a math whiz.

One weekend Vanessa tested Ian. She had gotten hold of a

copy of the Wechsler-Bellevue Intelligence Test, and she sat Ian down at the kitchen table with some paper and No. 2 pencils.

"I just want to see how bright he is," she said. "I bet he'll have one of the highest scores I've seen." So David left them alone in the kitchen, and sat in the living room with a book on the endocrine system. Every once in a while their voices wafted out into the living room. "Which one of these things," he heard Vanessa say, "does not belong with the others?"

There was a pause, and then Ian said, "The pair of dice."

"Very good," said Vanessa. David went back to his book.

Later that night, Vanessa sat by herself at the table, tallying up Ian's score. "It's just as I thought," she said when she was through, "he's in the most superior range. The one-sixty to one-seventy range. It's really impressive. He's a genius. Extremely gifted. He can do anything he wants."

David wondered about the logic of this. Did being a genius mean you could do anything you wanted? Did it unleash you, set you apart from everyone else? People had always told David that he was extraordinarily gifted. To get into his high school, he had had to take all sorts of admission tests, but still he had been locked into his old life for so long. Still he had his ungiving parents with their ugly wallpaper, and then his rigid wife Laura, who slept with her back toward him. There was no real freedom; it was all a tradeoff. You had to put in years of service before you could do what you wanted. Even now, he supposed that he ought to feel free finally, but he didn't. He felt locked into place, fastened by his love for Vanessa and Ian. That was the function of love; it was a harness, protecting you from yourself.

Strangely, he didn't even want to feel free anymore. He preferred the anchor of a home and a family; he was too old to wander around Europe with a backpack. He would leave that for Ian to do in about ten years.

All he and Vanessa talked about now was having a baby. She wanted it more than he did. Her periods were irregular, but still they sluggishly arrived. She kept in such good health, with her calisthenics and her high-fiber diet. Several months passed, and still she could not conceive. Some people waited years, he knew, but Vanessa was thirty-five; she ought to have a baby soon.

"What if I'm infertile?" she said. "Then what?"

"I'm sure you're not," he said. "We'll give it a while, and then you can go see Ed Sussman."

But he began to wonder if something was seriously wrong. It certainly wasn't him — he had gotten Laura pregnant, and years before that, one of the St. Catherine girls had insisted she was pregnant with his child. She had had an illegal abortion in Sheepshead Bay and the whole thing was moot.

When he thought of Ian's birth, he wanted to relive the experience. He wondered if you could feel the same thrill the second time. Mostly, what he remembered from Ian's birth was the heat in the room, and Laura's guttural cries, and then the wet, glowing head of Ian coming through. David had wanted to sink to his knees then in the delivery room, but he had steadied himself, grabbing onto the stirrups, and thinking, *I am a doctor. I am a father. I will not faint.* Then it was over, and everyone was congratulating them, and he looked into Laura's eyes and saw that she was fine, actually smiling, and asking for a sip of water.

He did not talk about any of this with Vanessa, because he knew she would become upset. She didn't like to hear about that earlier part of his life; she had had no claim over him then, no point of entry. But she loved Ian. She admired him more than she actually loved him. "I know he's so fair," she said once, as they watched Ian sleep, "but I still think he looks a lot like you, David. It's the mouth. He has the same mouth."

David squinted at Ian, and after a while conceded that there were real similarities. But he had to squint for a long time, as though looking at an optical illusion.

Sometimes, when Ian came for the weekend, they would walk together arm in arm down Horatio Street. David would reach out and rough up Ian's hair; it was a spontaneous impulse, almost involuntary. He wanted to touch his son all the time, to make contact. Vanessa would watch this, and she would smile, but he thought she felt left out. *We will have our own children, you and I,* he would silently tell her. *They will have my dark hair and long fingers, and your sculptured features and delicate bones.*

One Saturday in the early spring, David borrowed Ed Sussman's Saab, and he and Vanessa drove out to Long Island to pick up Ian. Although Laura and Jane and Ian had been living in the house for eight months, Vanessa had never been there. Today they planned to take Ian to Bridgehampton to spend a weekend at the beach.

Jane was out front when they arrived, kneeling on the lawn and planting seeds in a flowerbed. She raised up her spade in salute. "Go on in," she said. "Laura's getting Ian ready."

Inside the house, Vanessa stood and looked around as much as she could. She went into the living room and just stood in the center. She too had grown up in the suburbs — a small town outside of Chicago. As she looked around the house, David wondered if she was thinking of her parents' house. He had met her mother and father a few times. They were elderly and dull, although Vanessa claimed that her mother had always been very supportive of her. Once, when Vanessa was twenty-five and had just come out of a bad relationship with a man, she went back to Chicago for a rest. Every night she sat between her parents on the couch in the dark living room, watching "The Tonight Show."

"There are no good men out there," she would say, and her mother would assure her that one day she would meet the right man and everything would resolve itself. Vanessa's two sisters were both married. One had gone north, one south. Vanessa was the only one left to worry about. Her mother spoke to her in gentle, calming tones, and her father continued to watch TV. "Look at that guy," he said once in a while, pointing to the set.

Flip Wilson was dressed as a woman. "What a clown." Both her parents laughed easily. They were comfortable in their life.

Vanessa didn't want a suburban life for herself. She would never want to leave the city. She called herself a dyed-in-the-wool Manhattanite, and as David watched her sometimes on the streets of the city, he understood what she meant. She could always hail a cab more quickly than he could. She would just stand out in the street in a coat and scarf, her long hair blowing, her arm raised straight up, and cabs would vie for her fare.

She seemed out of her element whenever they left the city. Once, when they were on vacation in Curaçao, she had convinced him to spend time in the town nearby rather than on the beach. Surprisingly, he had liked it. He had dreamed of lying on the white sand with her, with a jar of cocoa butter and a good paperback novel, but all she wanted to do was go exploring different shops and restaurants. Vanessa couldn't stay on the beach; her skin was fair and she needed to wear sunblock. Laura had been the same way. Why were women so sensitive? he wondered. He and Vanessa sat on their shaded terrace, sipping sugary drinks from coconut shells, and then at night they hit the night life. He did not rest on this vacation, but he was never bored, either.

In Bridgehampton, he would take Vanessa and Ian out for a wonderful seafood dinner, and then afterward they would sit in their borrowed house and play number games. Vanessa always joined in; it was a way of getting closer to Ian. She was a good sport about it.

Now Ian came out of his bedroom holding his weekend bag. "I'm ready, Dad," he said.

Laura came up behind him. "Hi, David," she said. "Hi, Vanessa. Sorry for the delay. We've been cleaning out Ian's closet, trying to find something decent for him to wear. He outgrows everything by the minute."

"He looks fine," said Vanessa. "This is a very casual weekend."

She paused. "I like your home," she said. "I like what you've done with it. It looks very comfortable."

Laura offered to make some coffee, but David said no, they needed to be on their way. "We'll be back Sunday evening at around seven," he said. "Here's the number out at the beach."

He watched as she kissed Ian good-bye. She put her arms around him and he responded warmly. Ian was becoming a little more physical lately. It was a tender moment, and David didn't want to break in. Parents had such distinctly individual relationships with their children; he saw this all the time at work. Sometimes, when a child was critically ill, one parent would be very demonstrative, while the other one would stay away, would barely touch the child.

Most fathers stayed away, no matter what. They were afraid to touch even their healthy children. David was determined never to be that way. He wanted to embrace Ian as Laura just had, and have it be natural. It was hard to change patterns, though. Usually he and Ian embraced in a solid, clubby way. Sometimes David welled up with emotion and he had to pull away, or else tickle Ian's stomach and make him shriek, or lightly cuff him under the chin.

In the car on the way out to Bridgehampton, Ian sat up front with David while Vanessa stretched out in the back with a file she was working on. "How's Todd?" David asked Ian. Todd was Ian's new best friend. They had met that fall in school and sat next to each other in class. David had once taken both boys out to a Mets game for the day. Todd was shy, like Ian, but he had a troubled look. It was Cap Day at Shea Stadium, and Todd wore his plastic cap low on his forehead all day, hiding his eyes. He was an artist, Ian had said earlier. He spoke of Todd worshipfully, and David worried for a moment that there was some sexual tension between the boys, but then he let it go. At age ten, it was natural. David remembered the way he himself used to enjoy wrestling with his friends at that age. There was such a wonderful sensation: that desire for the imprint of hard arms and legs against your own, that slow, grating, competitive pressure.

He wondered if that was the way women felt when they went to bed together. He asked Vanessa once if she had ever felt attracted to another woman. She gave the question some serious thought. "Well, if you mean a crush, like at summer camp, I suppose I felt that sort of thing once, for Stacey Meltzer. But I never consciously wanted to do anything with another girl. The thought of it is unimaginable," she said.

He wondered, then, if the thought was imaginable for Ian. Did Ian even think about these things yet? Laura and Jane had explained a few things to him, and later David had added his own words. He heard his own voice as he spoke, and was aware of sounding artificial. He sounded like a public service filmstrip about lesbianism.

"I'm very impressed with the way you've been handling things, kiddo," he had said. "I know it's an unusual situation, you living with your mom and Jane like that." He looked away. "There is nothing wrong with being a lesbian," he said. "I can't say that I understand it, but I have to be tolerant of it. It's just another way for somebody to live. God knows there are enough choices now to drive anybody crazy. I still have a lot of faith in the traditional family. Vanessa and I hope to give you a little brother or sister soon. I think you'll probably want your own family when you grow up, too. It will be your decision, of course. I do think it's possible for people of the same sex to love one another. I guess your mother loves Jane very much. As long as there's love involved, you can't go too wrong, can you?"

He realized that he was saying this last part as though it was a real question that Ian might actually be able to answer. He was looking for reassurance from a ten-year-old boy. He was constantly looking for it. As they drove out to the beach, Ian riding next to him, David looked for it still in small ways.

"This is a pretty amazing car," David said. "Don't you think so?"

He was trying to impress his son with a car that didn't even belong to him. "Yeah," Ian said. "It looks expensive."

"It is," said David. "And wait till you see the house where we're staying."

He tried to stop himself from talking like this, from placing the emphasis on possessions. But he so much wanted to win Ian over; seeing him embraced by Laura had been unsettling. He didn't want her to have a monopoly on Ian's love. Ian had also been kissed goodbye by Jane; David wondered how she thought of Ian — as a son, maybe, or a stepson, or perhaps just as a little boy who happened to belong to her lover. He didn't know. Just because Laura was living with a woman didn't mean that he had to be deeply involved with specifics.

There is nothing wrong with being a lesbian, he had told Ian, and now, as he drove, he wasn't even sure that was true. Sometimes he went into a panic like this for no reason at all.

Ian was playing with the automatic sunroof of the Saab, making it slide open and shut with a little mechanical purr. On the radio, which was tuned to an oldies station, the Beatles were singing "Norwegian Wood." It was amazing to realize that that song was considered an oldie. Things became old so quickly. David had used up his boyhood, and his adolescence, and one family, and now he was trying to create another family. Sometimes the passage of time was astonishing. A physician friend of his had once figured out how many hours a doctor spends at work during the first year of a residency; it was some staggering figure.

David didn't want to burn himself up with work. That was why he had his wife with him now, and his son. He wanted to be held in place, fastened to this life. Ian continued to play with the button that controlled the sunroof. The smoked glass slid back and forth, bringing shade, then light. Vanessa leaned forward and gave David the chills along his arms. She smiled at him, and he swerved a little before smiling back.

CHAPTER SEVENTEEN

A child was missing. Her name was Bernadette Beshar, and she lived in Syosset, the next town. Photographs were circulating; they showed a twelve-year-old girl wearing braces and a Snoopy T-shirt. Signs were posted in neighborhood stores, and bulletins were read over the local news.

"That poor little girl," Jane said one night. They were watching the news during dinner. There was an interview with Mrs. Beshar; she was a heavy woman who cried into her hands as she spoke. "I just sent her off to school, as usual," she said, "and then the school called later and asked was she sick. Because she hadn't been sick once in two years, and always won the attendance medal. And that was the last time we saw her." Then she began to weep harder, and the camera cut away again to the photograph of Bernadette, with a caption underneath that read, HAVE YOU SEEN THIS CHILD? A toll-free number was provided, in case anyone had information to give.

"I can't watch," said Jane. "It's too upsetting."

"What do you think happened to her?" Ian asked. "Did she get lost?"

"No, I doubt it," said Laura. "I think somebody kidnapped her, sweetie. It's just such a shock to imagine that happening out here. I mean, the neighborhoods are good, and things seem so safe."

That afternoon she sat down to work, but the drawings seemed to her absurd. She was doing a beach scene, with small children playing in the sand. She hid objects among the waves and in umbrellas. She thought of this missing child, hidden somewhere, and she had to put down her pen.

The next day Elaine Frankel came by to invite Laura to an emergency PTA meeting. They were going to be discussing the kidnapping, she explained, and possibly taking some preventive measures. This was a good opportunity for concerned parents to get involved, she said. They were hoping to start a Childwatch program in the community.

Laura had managed to put off attending a single PTA meeting all year. She had wanted to remain somewhere in the background, to give Ian a chance to settle in, feel a part of his school. But now Elaine was encouraging her harder than usual. "Please consider it seriously," said Elaine. "Think of that girl Bernadette."

It felt like a command, and all that night, Laura could think of little else but Bernadette Beshar smiling at the camera. She thought of Bernadette's mother and father sitting in their own split-level house, unable to sleep. She saw the mother wandering into the kitchen in the middle of the night, sitting at the table and lighting a cigarette. She might sit there smoking, looking out into the peaceful night, wondering how so much quiet, so much darkness, could conceal so much.

The PTA meeting was held the following Wednesday, and Jane wanted to go, which surprised Laura. Sybil Frankel agreed to stay with Ian for a couple of hours. She came into the house wearing her green uniform.

"Hi, Mrs. Giovanni," she said. "Hi, Mrs. Bloom."

This made Laura want to laugh. Sybil immediately found her way into the living room and turned on the television. Ian came in and sat down next to her. He did not like to be left with a sitter, but he silently tolerated it. His method was just to ignore Sybil and focus on the TV.

"Well, Ian," said Laura, "Jane and I will be back in about two hours. Please go to sleep on time, sweetie. If there are any problems, you can call Sybil's dad. We'll be right down the block at your school."

"Bye," said Ian, glancing up.

Jane and Laura walked down the street together. They dropped arms as they approached the lights of the school.

Inside the gymnasium, rows of folding chairs had been set up. Parents were milling around — mostly women, but a few men as well. Most of the men seemed to be with their wives. There was only one man who stood alone, drinking coffee. He was tall, with dark hair and an ill-fitting suit. Laura felt as though she and Jane should go stand by him, whispering, *It's okay. We don't belong here either.*

Elaine Frankel was tapping on the microphone. After everybody was seated, she stood there and welcomed the parents. "This is a very important meeting," she said. "Before we get started, I'd like to introduce a few unfamiliar faces to you. First off, we have with us Mike Berger. Most of you knew Annette Berger, who is sorely missed." There was a pause, and a murmur among the audience. Everyone was looking sympathetically in the direction of the big, dark man. He looked embarrassed. "We're very glad that Mike has decided to join us tonight," said Elaine. There was spontaneous applause. "And also," she said, "I'm equally delighted to see my friend and neighbor, Laura Giovanni, here with us tonight. She is an extremely talented artist who for the past several years has been drawing wonderful pictures for *Jumping Bean* magazine, which I know many of your children read. Perhaps we can draft Laura to do some artwork for the carnival next year," she said.

Laura looked down in her lap, smiling. There was no mention of Jane, who just sat quietly next to her, still wearing her Windbreaker. By the end of the meeting, Laura had volunteered to be one of three women to run discussion groups in the fall about child abduction. She would have to attend several training sessions first.

"Are you sure you want to take on the responsibility?" Elaine asked, coming up to her at the reception.

"I'm not too busy," said Laura. "I work on my drawings in the morning, and then I have the rest of the day free until Ian comes home. I want to do something else. This interests me."

"Well," said Elaine, "do you think your living room is big enough to hold the meetings in? Maybe you'd want to hold them at my house."

"Elaine," said Laura, "your house is exactly the same size as mine."

Elaine shook her head slowly. "Could I talk to you a minute?" she asked. "Alone?"

Laura left Jane and followed Elaine Frankel over to the other side of the gymnasium, underneath the basketball hoop. "What is it?" Laura asked.

"Well," said Elaine, "I'll just be up front about it. Do you really think it's a good idea to have all these families into your house? They're not going to be people you know well, and you're leaving yourself open to talk. As I've said, this can be a pretty small-minded community. I'm just not sure it's the best idea, Laura. You know," she added, "I was frankly surprised that Jane came tonight."

"Elaine," said Laura, "you are the only person who makes me feel nervous. Everyone else just leaves us alone. I get upset only after I talk to you. The rest of the time, I'm just living my life."

"Come on," said Elaine. "You're cautious, I know you are. You bring Jane out, but just a little. You're still the visible one."

"You mean the presentable one," said Laura.

Elaine ignored this. "I like you both," she said, "but I also believe in the protection of children. That's what this whole meeting is about, after all. That's what you've signed up for."

"I'm aware of it," said Laura. "But I don't want to talk about it anymore. I've told you what I think."

"I'm sorry," said Elaine. "I won't mention it again. And I'll certainly come to your discussion group in the fall. But still," she said, "there's bound to be *some* talk."

They walked back across the gym. Jane was leaning against a wall, drinking coffee. The crowd was thinning out. Laura looked for Michael Berger, the man who had been introduced at the meeting. She had figured out that he was the father of Ian's new friend, Todd. Michael Berger had already gone home for the night; she would have to meet him some other time.

As they walked home, Jane said, "What did Elaine want?"

"Oh, the usual warnings," said Laura. "She doesn't think it's a good idea for us to bring anybody into our house." Laura expected Jane to make some snide comment, but she didn't.

Finally Jane said, "You know, I feel slightly invisible."

"I'm sorry," said Laura quickly. "I told Elaine that she was being ridiculous."

"I don't mean with Elaine," said Jane. "I mean this whole thing. I feel like I'm your slightly embarrassing date. As though you had to have your brother accompany you to the prom."

"What do you expect me to do differently?" Laura asked. "We went over this before we moved here. Did you want me to stand up in front of those people and say, 'Don't forget about Jane. She's new in the community, too'?"

"Oh, forget it," said Jane. "It's not worth fighting about."

"No, really," said Laura. "I mean, what could I say to them: 'This is my parenting partner, Jane Bloom'?"

"I guess not," said Jane. "I just get depressed. I want it both ways. I want to make life easy, but I also want to be acknowledged."

"As what?" Laura asked.

They stopped on the sidewalk. A car went past, and they watched it roll slowly down the street. "I'm not sure," said Jane. "As your lover, I suppose, but also as part of your household. As someone in Ian's life. I keep thinking about Bernadette Beshar. It upsets me just as much as it does you, even though I'm not a mother. I worry about things, the way you do."

"I'm sorry," Laura said again. She thought of Jane in the house with Ian, singing to him, packing his lunch.

"Oh, let's go home," Jane said. "I didn't mean to get you upset. We're doing okay, I think." Then they embraced under the streetlight.

Back at the house, Sybil was quietly picking out a song on Jane's guitar. "Oh, I've seen fire and I've seen rain," she sang, her voice splitting delicately on the high notes.

Ian was fast asleep, the covers already kicked to the floor. Every night he slid down under the blankets, and every night he kicked them off in his sleep.

"Everything fine here?" Jane asked, and Sybil said yes, there had been no problems, and no phone calls.

Laura went into the front hall where they kept a crock with petty cash in it, and she extracted three dollars to give to Sybil. She watched from the door as the girl galloped across the lawn to her own house. *You never knew.* That was what Elaine was always saying. You never knew. You had to be careful. Children were breakable.

One afternoon the week before, they were driving past the local shopping mall and they saw that a small traveling carnival had been set up in the parking lot. There was a concession stand, a spookhouse on wheels, and a few try-your-luck booths. There was also one ride. It was called the Spider, and Ian asked if he could go on it. Jane gave him some money, and he went and bought a ticket, then joined the line.

A teenage boy stood at the entrance to the ride, tearing tickets.

He looked stoned, or half asleep, and Laura suddenly felt extremely nervous. She remembered reading accounts of children being killed on makeshift rides — horrible stories about the bobsled ride flying off its track and soaring through the air, the children still shrieking.

Laura looked around. The whole place seemed threatening. Children drifted past, eating blue ices. Their lips were blue, and they looked as though they had been dragged from a lake. Laura wanted to run up to the ride and yank Ian back down. Instead she just stood at the rail next to Jane, watching. The children were being directed into small black cars. The attendant wandered around lifting the safety bars. When everyone was in, he went over and pulled the lever back. All the cars began to move. They rose hesitantly, bouncing along on the air. There were eight Spider arms, and each arm held a child. The attendant was sitting slumped in a folding chair at the foot of the ride, reading a magazine. He wasn't paying the least attention to the children.

Laura stood and watched, holding her breath. The ride picked up speed, and Laura panicked. What if an arm of the Spider broke off, flinging Ian across the parking lot? What if the whole ride collapsed, smashing its arms down onto the pavement? What if, what if? There were so many variables at work, and you didn't know which ones to focus on.

As she watched Ian growing up daily, becoming too big for his clothes, she wanted to stop time, to freeze-frame this year with him, when he was still a sweet, skinny boy. That would all change soon, Elaine Frankel insisted. Her own son, Jack, was sixteen now, and all he did was play air guitar with his friends. He stood in the Frankels' living room, an old Jimi Hendrix record blasting on the stereo, and he pretended to be playing along with Jimi. He sank to his knees and gyrated. He contorted his face, as though he were in extreme pain.

When he wasn't doing that, Elaine explained, Jack was smoking pot in the garage. She was always finding the charred ends of joints on the garage floor, like mouse droppings. Danger was everywhere, Elaine said. It was in angel dust, and in the cars of men who waited in parking lots after school let out. It was in the streets, in zones where the traffic was heavy, and in the candy dropped into the bottoms of Halloween bags.

Why did Laura think Ian was immune to all this? She had always believed him to be blessed, to walk around with a divine light that saved him from danger. He was so good, so balanced. All he did was work on math problems, or see his friend Todd after school. He was a wonderful student, and Miss Brenner did not ignore him at the back of the class as Laura had feared she might.

Now the ride was spinning crazily, and the arms of the Spider lifted and lowered. Children screamed at synchronized intervals. The joy-scream of children was exactly the same as the terror-scream; there was no discernible difference in modulation. When parents heard a scream, they raced to the window, the door, out into the street.

Every night on the news, Bernadette Beshar's mother kept appearing. Each evening she seemed to fall apart a little more. Her hair was disheveled. One button earring was loose. Her husband accompanied her sometimes, but he would not look into the camera. He muttered something about how he missed his little girl, and how unbearable her absence was. There was a tiny microphone clipped to his tie. He coughed, his head down, and it came out like thunder. *It's just not knowing*, he said, *that makes it worse. We want God to give us a sign.*

In a world where God gave signs, Laura thought, then people might also be told how to live. If you did something right, you would be rewarded with a moment of God's presence; perhaps your house would suddenly be flooded with light. The carpeting would ripple; dishes would tremble in the cabinets. You would understand then that your life was on the right track. Your choices had been good ones; all was sanctioned.

"Trust yourself," Jane was always saying, but she couldn't possibly be objective. There were moments when trust was irrelevant and you had to act on dumb instinct only.

Laura had felt that way the night she had stood in the doorway of Ian's bedroom and tried to talk to him about herself and Jane. They had been living in the house for several weeks. Ian was standing at the mirror in his room. He was in pajamas, fresh from a bath, and his skin had a fever-sheen to it. His hair was dark with water. He stood and combed it carefully, exacting a part down the left side.

"You know," Laura said, "if you ever want to ask questions about things you don't understand, feel free."

"Like sex?" he asked, looking at her in the mirror.

"Anything," she said. "Like me and Jane, for instance. Anything you want."

"I think I know most things," Ian said.

Laura stopped, then went on. "Do you know that Jane and I are lesbians? Have you heard that word?"

"Yes," he said, impatient. "I know what it is."

"And you know that it's okay?" Laura said. "That it just means that we love each other?"

"Yeah, yeah," said Ian.

He didn't want to go any further with it; he never did. She had expected to have some kind of dialogue about ways of loving, about varieties of human experience. But Ian was already on his own, cut loose when she hadn't been looking.

On the Spider ride, the children were still screaming into the wind. Laura looked around her; other parents waited at the rail. They all looked uneasy. In a few minutes the ride started to slow, and the arms of the Spider skimmed the ground, bumping along in a final crawl, bringing all of the screaming children back down to earth.

The Slumber Party

When he went to visit his father one time, they walked on the moon. There was a special exhibit at a museum, and you went into a dark room where the floor looked like the surface of the moon. There were strange lights turning on the ceiling, and everybody walked around very slowly. You had to be careful that you didn't trip and fall into a crater. There was a man dressed in a space suit, waving at everyone. Ian and his father held hands and walked across the moon. Afterward they ate lunch downstairs.

It was so bright in the cafeteria that Ian had to squint. "That was a pretty neat exhibit," his father said. "Don't you think so?"

"Yeah," said Ian. "I guess."

They sat with plastic trays in front of them. The table had just been sponged down. Ian rested his arms on it, even though it was still wet. He ordered a plate of Jell-O. It was in different colored cubes, like a plate of big jewels. He wasn't really hungry; he just liked to look at it.

"You know," said his father, "sometimes I miss you so much.

I wish that we could see each other every day of the week. I try and picture you in school, maybe doing a math problem, or else having lunch with a couple of your friends. I try and imagine what you're eating for lunch."

They talked about school a lot when they were together. His father wanted to hear about school all the time; he wanted to know every little detail.

Ian had told him about the latest project they had done that week: baked records. You took an old LP record, he explained, something you hated, and you put it in the oven. The teacher did it for you. After a while, the edges curled up like a shell, and then you took it out and used it as a candy dish.

Ian had stood in the kitchen of the teachers' lounge, thinking, *This is so dumb.* All the kids had piled in. The librarian, Mrs. Bunch, sat at a table smoking, watching them. This was where the teachers went during lunch. They sat and smoked; the ashtrays were filled.

The whole thing was pretty stupid, and Ian made a face at his friend Todd. Todd made a face back. They didn't even have to say anything; it was like that most of the time. After school, Todd usually went home with Ian, or else Ian went over to Todd's house. Sometimes he stayed for dinner. The Berger family ate TV dinners almost every night. That was what Ian got served every time he went over there. They weren't poor or anything, but you would sit at their dining room table and fold back the tinfoil cover on your little dinner tray. Steam would float up in your face. After dinner, Todd's father would get up really slowly, as though he were old, and go in to watch television for the rest of the night. Todd and his brothers and Ian would light matches for a few hours. There were never any dishes to wash.

One night, right after Todd and Ian had started to become friends, Ian said, "I just realized something."

They were upstairs in Todd's room. "What?" Todd asked. He hardly even looked at Ian. Sometimes he got sleepy in school and put his face down on the desktop. Miss Brenner was always sending him down to the nurse's office so he could take a nap.

"You have only boys in your family, and I have only girls," Ian said. Todd didn't answer. "Maybe we should have your father go out on a date with my mother," Ian tried.

They spent a lot of afternoons at Todd's house, but everything was depressing. They fooled around with Matchbox cars until it was time for Ian to go home. Todd's father would be sitting in the living room watching "The Honeymooners," but not really watching. At five o'clock Ian would walk out of that depressing place, leaving Todd there with his father, a sad man with big hands. The TV dinners would be heating up already; Ian could smell them all the way down the hall.

Ian thought his life was fairly average. He went to school, and the library, and the movies, and over to Todd's house, and every weekend he went to stay with his father in New York. It was only Vanessa who was always telling him that his life was extraordinary.

"You've had quite a few adventures for a ten-year-old," she would say.

Once when Ian was eight and was spending the day with Vanessa, she had tried to get on his good side. She took him shopping at a department store and paid for everything with a credit card. Later that day, when he and Vanessa got back to the apartment, she wanted him to try on all the clothes she had bought him. He didn't want to, but he figured he'd better not complain. He went into the bathroom and took off his shirt and pants, and in the meantime Vanessa got a telephone call. He opened the door a crack to listen.

"Hi, Bev," she said. "Yes, he's here with me for the day. David's at work until late. Tomorrow we'll all do something together." Then her voice got low. "Well," she said, "I don't think it's morally wrong—only violence is immoral—but when I really stop to think about it, I guess I'm just very conventional at heart. David worries all the time, and I never know what to say. I mean, she's the mother. They're grown women, after all."

Ian didn't understand any of this when he heard it. But he stored it away in the back of his mind, and suddenly it made sense. Vanessa had been talking about Jane and his mother. *Of course,* he said to himself, because by then he knew the whole story. He knew what went on.

His mother had explained it to him one night; she had come into his room and told him about being a lesbian, which he already knew. After he told Todd, Todd kept asking questions. He pretended not to be shocked at first, but he kept bringing the subject up again and again. There was one time when Ian and Todd smoked pot together, and Todd started talking about it.

School had ended for the day, and Todd asked him if he wanted to hang around the playground for a while. It was March and there was still some snow on the ground, but Ian figured something was up, so he said yes. They walked out past the swing set. It was just standing there in the snow, like deserted dinosaur bones. Todd looked around to make sure nobody was looking; then he pulled a joint from his pocket. "Look," he said, "I got it from a sixth grader."

They lit the joint and inhaled, and passed it back and forth, choking at first until they got it right. After a while the sky looked brighter, and Ian began to feel cold.

"I need a blanket to get under," he said. They walked out into the middle of the empty field, and plunked down in the snow. They just sat there for a while, not saying anything.

"Do you think it's okay that your mother's a lesbian?" Todd finally asked.

Ian thought a minute. "Yeah," he said. "I guess. I already told you a hundred times."

"It's a stupid word, anyway," Todd said. "Lesbian. *Zzzzzz.* It has a buzz sound to it."

"*Zzzzzz,*" Ian repeated, and then they were both saying it

together. They got up and shook off the snow, and then they began to run around like airplanes, making buzzing noises. They did that kind of thing a lot.

Sometimes, though, Ian needed to be away from Todd. He would go find the cat, and he would take her underneath the porch. There was a secret narrow place where you could crawl in. He would go into the darkness and stroke her as he lay on his back. She didn't like it at first, but then after a while she fell asleep on his chest. He could feel her breathing there. When she slept she sounded like a lawnmower far away. Nobody ever knew where Ian went. Sometimes they would call him, but he wouldn't answer. And then they would just stop calling.

One time his mother and Jane stood right over his head. "Ian! Ian!" his mother shouted.

"He'll come back," said Jane. "He's probably off with Todd, being boys together."

"Do I hear an edge of irony in your voice?" said his mother.

"Yes," said Jane. "Because I know you like it when I get ironic. I remind you of your old days with Julia."

"Don't," said his mother.

"Come inside," said Jane. "Just for a little."

"No," said his mother. "I want to find Ian."

"He'll come home," said Jane. "Come."

Ian listened. The cat vibrated on his rib cage. "Oh, God," his mother said in a real soft voice. Then she laughed, and there were footsteps, and then the screen door banged shut. Ian fell asleep under the porch and didn't wake up until it was really dark. He was freezing. Lizzie the cat was clawing at him; her nails were pulling up threads.

He thought of that day a lot afterward. Todd was good in art, and once Ian asked him if he would draw a picture of his mother and Jane, so he would know what it looked like. Todd knew exactly what he meant. The next day Todd handed him what he had done. There were two women lying in a bed without any clothes on. He had used pastels, and their skin was a very bright pink. The room was white, and curtains blew in the window. It was very peaceful. He hadn't outlined the pink skin, so you couldn't tell where one woman's body ended and the other's began.

"Where are their tits?" Ian asked. "You didn't draw them."

"Well," said Todd, "you can't see them from this angle."

Ian kept the drawing in his room for a long time, under his bed. He would be lying on the bed sometimes, doing his math homework, and then he would just pull out the drawing and look at it for a while, then put it back. He worked on his homework every night from seven to eight. When he couldn't figure a difficult problem out, his mother and Jane weren't too much help. His mother said to him, "Oh, Ian, I'm so *bad* at math. Do you want to call up your father?"

But he always felt weird calling all the way to New York just to say, "Dad, say a car leaves New York at four P.M., traveling sixty mph." So he went into his room and did his homework on his own.

He spent a lot of time in his room, which was a lot bigger than his old one in the city. "It's time to redecorate," his mother said one day in the spring. "It's your room. You can do what you want with it."

"Okay," he said. "I want to paint the walls black and put up glow-in-the-dark paint and black-light posters."

"Fine," said his mother, and so the next day they went out and bought two cans of Midnight Sheen black paint. They were going to start painting on the weekend, but that night in bed, Ian had a terrible dream. He dreamed that the walls of his room were the walls of a cave, and that all the things on them came to life: giant hamsters, eels, a pumpkin head. He woke up and said to himself, *Forget it*. They returned the paint and got Eggshell White instead. Ian put up the same old posters and some of Todd's drawings. Not the naked women, of course.

There was a time when he actually saw it happen, his mother and Jane. It was very different from Todd's drawing. One night he was lying in bed, wide awake, thinking about a math question and trying to figure out a new way to do it. He liked to play with his pocket calculator in bed, because the numbers shone bright red. He was doing that for a while, and then suddenly he got thirsty, and he thought, *Maybe I'll get a glass of milk.* So he went downstairs and into the kitchen. It was the middle of the night, about three in the morning, and he assumed that his mother and Jane were fast asleep. He stood in the little square of light from the refrigerator and poured a glass of milk from a bottle in the door.

He was about to go back upstairs, and was holding the cold glass in his hand, when he heard something from the living room. He stood in the hall and looked in, not making a noise. If it was a burglar, he would be able to sneak over to the telephone and dial 911.

But then he heard a voice, and he knew it was his mother. She sounded different; her voice was quieter. Sometimes when she was nervous she would talk really fast and her voice would shoot up to the top of the scale. But now it was low, as though she were telling a bedtime story, as though she were saying, *Goodnight, moon.* So he slid against the wall and edged over to the doorway so he could look. That was when he saw it.

His eyes had just gotten used to the dark. He saw the couch across the room, and the afghan, which had been thrown to the ground, and the cushions from the back. The wooden floor glowed; it was like a pond with all this stuff floating on the surface. A mill pond, like in that song. There was light from the moon — just a little bit, squeezing in, but enough.

His mother was on the couch with Jane. They were kneeling and facing each other, really close. They were kissing and their bodies were tight, like machines. Their hands touched each other, very slow. Every once in a while they would pull away, and his mother would say another couple of words, like, "What? Tell me, what?"

He couldn't move. He couldn't drink his glass of milk. He was pressed against the wall forever, watching. And then they just collapsed on the couch; they sank right into it. There was no more talking, and no rustling sounds or anything, because those sounds came from clothing, he thought, like when material rubs against material. The sound of a little kid in bed at night having a nightmare.

They still hadn't noticed him, and now he knew they never would. He was safe. He jumped away from the wall and made his way back upstairs. The milk sloshed against his glass with every step he took. He went and sat on the edge of his bed, and he drank the milk real quick. It left a mustache. He kept it there for a minute, a little cold swipe over his lip. He felt very peculiar: cold and warm at the same time. He put the glass down on the floor by his bed. In the morning the cat would come in and put her tongue in the bottom of the glass. Then Ian would pick her up and hold her against him, listening to her breathe, until it was time to get up for school.

But now he just lay there, and he felt his body go tense. His pajamas had tiny pictures of airplanes on them, and every airplane was exactly the same. They were flying up into the sky in neat rows. It was a yellow sky filled with red airplanes. Ian suddenly felt that he was too old for pajamas like that. He pulled the top over his head and left it by the bed, next to the glass. And then he pulled off the bottoms, too. It was as though he were getting ready for Thursday night bath. He just lay there in bed with no clothes on, and then he hugged himself as if he were very cold, but he wasn't really cold anymore. He ran his hands across his chest. He pretended he was blind; he pretended he was Helen Keller, learning.

When he used to play with Matchbox cars, sometimes he would run them across his body as if it were an intricate highway.

He liked the way the little hard wheels felt going across him like that. Now he pretended he was a road again. There weren't any thoughts in his head, just pictures—Jane and his mother, then his father and Vanessa. Everyone came in twos.

It was dark, it was late, and his pajamas were in a heap on the floor. His walls had all the safe posters on them, and Todd's drawing of a horse, and another one he had done, of Neil Armstrong landing on the moon. Ian opened his eyes and could see outside to where the branches of a tree collided into each other. He was glad he hadn't painted the walls black. He was glad that the walls were Eggshell White and smooth, and that the man in the store had let him return the cans of Midnight Sheen.

In the morning, when his mother came in to wake Ian up for school, she found him naked, and he was embarrassed and leaped under the covers. "Don't look!" he said.

"Did you get a fever in the middle of the night?" she asked him.

"No," he said, but she didn't listen. She put the back of her hand against his forehead and left it there for a little longer than usual. He thought she knew something, but he didn't know what. He turned his head to the wall. She dropped her hand.

CHAPTER NINETEEN

They were taking Vanessa's temperature all the time now, and then leaping into bed. She kept a log book of her potentially fertile times, as Ed Sussman had suggested. She made a graph with different-colored magic markers; it looked like a project that Ian might have done for school. Still she did not conceive, and they grew exhausted from making love incessantly.

One night at two in the morning, they sat propped against the big pillows in bed, watching the late show. There was an unbearable sadness in the room. Ed Sussman had told them that Vanessa's IUD might have left her infertile. He suggested that they keep trying to conceive, but also consider "other options," as he phrased it.

David cupped his hand over Vanessa's shoulder. She was crying silently in bed. He said a few things, tried to comfort her, but it did no good. He was stunned into thinking about a childless life with her. She would grow bitter without children. She was obsessed with the idea of giving birth, and he knew that this would never change.

On Saturday morning, when Ian came to the apartment for the weekend, David expected Vanessa to be withdrawn and close herself in the bedroom. She had stayed up crying all night, and now her eyes were swollen, but she insisted that she wanted to go out somewhere. David suggested a movie, and so they all went to see *Fantasia*, which had been David's favorite as a boy.

He sat between his wife and son, an arm around each of them. Mickey Mouse was trying to stop a flood, and an army of brooms was coming alive. Ian had never seen the movie, and his eyes widened at every trick of animation. Vanessa and David smiled at each other. Ian was young enough to be doing most things in his life for the first time. This was his first *Fantasia*, David thought. The first time David had seen the movie, he had been dropped off at a theater in the Bronx with his sister, Celeste, thirty years before. The stern usher had walked up and down the aisles, swinging her flashlight and making idle threats.

When *Fantasia* ended, David, Vanessa, and Ian went around the corner for some falafel. Ian had never eaten falafel before. "The only time we get to eat out in Plainview is if we go to Chan Luck restaurant," Ian said. "The rest of the time we stay in."

"Who's a better cook," Vanessa asked, "your mother or Jane?"

"My mother," Ian said simply. "Jane always makes the same thing: eggplant."

The afternoon was free of tension. David wondered if Vanessa would insist on making love when they got home. They had been finding ways to make love surreptitiously even when Ian was in the apartment. They would make sure that he was firmly planted in front of the TV set in his room, and then they would tell him they were going to take a nap. Silently they would make love — gritting their teeth, pressing thumbs into flesh, uttering nothing.

But when they got home from *Fantasia*, they all sat around and played number games. Then Vanessa cooked dinner, and they stayed up late, watching sitcoms. Finally Ian was sleepy, so they sent him off to bed. He came in to ask one last question, and he was in his pajamas. They were too small for him—his ankles stuck out below the thin blue material.

"I want to make sure that we're going to buy that new calculator tomorrow," Ian said. "We are, right, Dad?"

"Of course we are," said David.

"Well, goodnight again," Ian said, and he returned to bed.

They listened as his door shut, and they sat quietly for a few moments in the living room. "I love him," Vanessa finally said.

David was surprised. "Do you?" he asked.

"I thought you knew that," she said.

"So then why did you say it?" he asked. "You must have meant something more than just that."

Vanessa looked at David fully; she took his hands. "Because I really want you to know it," she said. "I've been so absorbed in the idea of having a baby that I haven't thought about anything else. I get worried when you're with Ian. Because it still keeps you involved with Laura," she said. "And I can't think about that."

"We could adopt," he said in a whisper, and it was immediately the wrong thing to have said.

"Great," said Vanessa. "We can get ourselves a Vietnamese baby and name it Wendy. Is that what you want?" She looked at him fiercely. "I want *your* baby, David," she said. "That's the only one I want."

As the weeks passed, they made love less obsessively, and only when they felt like it. They tacitly ended their temperature-taking rituals, and David saw that Vanessa's log book lay untouched under a pile of magazines on the bureau. They distracted themselves with movies and good food. On the weekends, when Ian was with them, they took day trips out to Westchester or the beach. There was nothing David could do for Vanessa except be with her, fortify her in whatever ways he could. One Saturday David had to work all day, and Ian stayed with Vanessa. When David got home, he found the two of them sitting in the living room, and Ian was showing Vanessa all the things his calculator could do.

"It has a memory," Ian was saying.

"Hi," said David, coming into the room. "What have you guys been up to?"

"We made dinner from scratch," Vanessa said. "Ian is a very good apprentice."

Dinner was quiche and salad. David imagined Ian standing in the kitchen next to Vanessa, both of them wearing matching aprons. "Now you wash the lettuce," she would say, handing him a big white head of iceberg.

Vanessa and Ian looked conspiratorial. David exclaimed over the dinner, said it was the best he'd eaten in a long time. "We should have you around more often, Ian," he said, and Vanessa quickly looked away, smiling strangely.

That night in bed, as they slipped between the sheets, he said to her, "What was that funny face you made at dinner?"

"When?" she asked.

"When I said something about having Ian around, I think," said David.

Vanessa took a novel off her night table and opened it to the silk bookmark inside. "I just felt happy," she said. "It seemed like a good idea, having Ian around more." She paused. "I love having him with us," she said. "He's so easy. I mean, he's not like most children. When he's cranky, he doesn't inflict it on everyone. And he's so incredibly smart. I think he's going to do big things."

It was Vanessa who initially proposed spending July with Ian. "We could get a house at the beach," she said. "We have the money now."

"I don't know if Laura would allow it," he said. "Maybe she wants him to hang around the neighborhood or something, since it's his first full summer there."

"I thought she said everybody goes off to camp," Vanessa said.

"And he can hang around the neighborhood all year. Don't you want to spend more time with him? You said you did."

"Of course I do," said David, "but it's complicated."

She didn't understand the subtleties of this; he couldn't just whisk his son off somewhere on the spur of the moment. Divorced parents had to agree mutually on every point. Laura was usually accommodating, but David always had to bring everything up to her each time, have it turned into a big issue. There was very little room for spontaneity.

He mentioned the idea to Laura the next weekend, when she drove Ian into the city and dropped him off. She thought about it for a few days, discussed it with Jane, and finally she agreed that Ian could stay with them for July.

It amazed David how easily the month went. They had found a house through their friend Ed Sussman. It was in Bridge-hampton, just down the street from the beach. They spent most of the time swimming in the warm water of the bay. Ian was becoming a good swimmer, less fearful. "Watch me, Dad!" he would say, and he would dive down under and pop up again in a totally unexpected location. Once he climbed onto David's shoulders, and David walked, wobbling a little, out toward the sandbar.

"Let me get the camera!" Vanessa said, and she raced out of the water and back to the house. She returned a few minutes later with the Polaroid, and she took several shots, one after the other, of David and Ian clowning around. In one photograph, Ian was spraying David with water, and all you could see was a pale green wave like a curtain, with two faces faintly visible behind it, looking through.

On the last night of their vacation, Vanessa spread all of the photographs out on the kitchen table.

"I want to get a scrapbook for these," she said. "I'll write on the cover 'What We Did on our Summer Vacation,' like an essay for school."

They were sitting around and packing that night, and there was a leisurely feel to the evening. David and Vanessa were drinking Cinzano from the tall frosted glasses that belonged to the owners of the house. It was a very calm night, with occasional breezes filtering in through the screened windows. If David listened hard, he could hear the roll of the water down the street. They were all settling in for the night, but he suddenly had the urge to go for one final walk along the beach with Vanessa.

"Will you be okay if we take a little stroll for a few minutes, kiddo?" he asked Ian.

"Yeah," said Ian.

So they left him in the house and went down to the end of the street, where the beach started. It was very dark, but still David could make out the horizon line. Everything was deep blue, all the edges washing over. "It's beautiful here now," he said, and he felt the need to whisper, as though they were in church.

They walked to the edge of the water, and watched a small wave approach, then stop, just inches from their feet. "Let's go in," David said. "I've always wanted to go swimming at night."

Surprisingly, Vanessa agreed to go in. She peered around her, then lifted her blouse over her head and stepped out of her shorts. When David had stripped, too, they folded their clothes over a rock. There wasn't a single light or voice along the stretch of beach.

The water was cold, and they eased in slowly, blind to everything. It was only when they were up to their necks that David began to make out the many green, glowing patches of water all around them.

"Look!" he said. The water had become phosphorescent in places. He remembered reading a biography of Madame Curie once, when he was in high school and loved science more than anything. His favorite scene in the book was where Madame Curie went to the laboratory late at night, and inside the dark room, things were glowing green under Petri dishes. Madame Curie stood inside this ring of green lights and knew that she was involved in something momentous. She had isolated radium for the first time.

David bobbed next to Vanessa in the water, and they were surrounded by this strange, prophetic glow. It did not altogether surprise him, then, when Vanessa suddenly grasped his arm with her wet hand and said, "David, I have to tell you something. I want Ian to come stay with us more. I mean, to live with us."

"Vanessa," he said, "are you serious?"

"Yes," she said.

He tried not to think about what an impossible idea this was, how Laura would never allow it. He felt elated, for some reason, and he hugged Vanessa as she shivered in the dark water. Finally it was time to get back to the house. Reluctantly they left the water and put their clothing back on. They walked along the road, holding their shoes in their hands, stepping carefully over pebbles and chips of glass.

"I feel terrific," Vanessa said. "Freezing, but terrific."

They could see a light inside the living room as they approached the house. Ian was a silhouette in the window, leaning over the table. They let themselves in and sat with him for a while, and finally he went to bed. Vanessa and David stayed up very late, finishing their packing. They would leave shortly after dawn the next morning. First they would drop Ian off at Laura's, and then continue on into Manhattan.

They got into bed that night, and for the first time all month it was chilly, and David had to get an extra blanket down from the linen closet. They lay under the weight of two blankets, already reminiscing about the summer. David plucked grains of sand from Vanessa's fine hair.

In the morning he got up and walked down to the beach one final time. He looked into the water, and he could see a swarm of jellyfish right near the shore. It occurred to him with a start that this was the reason the water had lit up like that the night before. It had been so beautiful, such a striking image, and it turned out to be nothing more than a school of disgusting, stinging jellyfish. He could not get over it.

They dropped Ian off early in the morning. Jane was awake and about to leave for work when the car pulled up. She went out front to greet them. "Hey!" she called out to Ian, and he came out of the car and ran across the lawn to hug her.

"Hi, Jane," he said. She saw that he looked rosy from the sun. His nose was peeling, and his hair was almost white.

"You look great," she said. "Sorry to be home?"

"No," he said. He was smiling. "Is Ma awake?" he asked.

"She's just getting up," said Jane. "She'll be thrilled to see you." Ian trotted inside.

David and Vanessa were standing by the car. "Can I give you some coffee?" Jane asked.

"No thanks," said David. "We need to get back to the city. I'd like to say hi to Laura, though."

"Come on in," said Jane. She walked ahead of them up the front path. She felt self-conscious, even now, unsure of what they were thinking as they followed her inside.

Laura came out of the bedroom in her bathrobe, and they all watched as she and Ian were reunited. "Sweetie pie," said Laura, and she wrapped her arms around him. "You're sunburned," she said, "and I think you got even blonder. You look albino."

They had talked to Ian on the telephone every night. He had said he was having a good time at the beach, and he told them about the horseshoe crabs he had found along the shore, and about the small sailboat he and David had ridden in once. Ian had been gone for only one month, but it was the longest time he had ever been away from Laura and Jane.

"What are we going to do all summer?" Laura had asked Jane when Ian first left. The neighborhood was drained of children. Sybil Frankel was shunted off on a teen tour this summer, and Jack Frankel was on an Outward Bound trip. Todd Berger was off on scholarship to an arts camp in the Poconos. There were very few kids around.

"We could go away for a weekend," said Jane. One Saturday they went up to New Hampshire to visit some of Jane's old friends. Danielle was a friend whom she hadn't seen in a long time, and now she was running a collective house for women near Peterborough. The women there were still caught up in the dreamy web of the collective life; it felt familiar to Jane, but at the same time she was far removed from it. She was the suburban one; that was how she had been branded.

Everybody shared things in the house. Cats walked over all the surfaces, delicately dipping into bowls of food on tabletops. Laura and Jane slept in a dusty, unused room for the weekend. At one A.M. they lay close and listened to the sounds of voices above and below. Every once in a while they could hear water running through the pipes, and the closing of doors.

"You've spoiled me," said Jane.

"How?" asked Laura. "How have I spoiled you?"

"I never used to be rich," said Jane. "You've been so privileged your whole life. Do you realize how lucky you are? I mean, I'm lucky now too; it's such a novelty for me. I used to eat yogurt every night for dinner, and paint houses in my spare time. But it was okay; I didn't complain. Every night we would sit around listening to Holly Near records. There was a whole bunch of us living in this one apartment in Northampton. We were poor, and we all had jobs in stores in town, but we weren't starving or anything. In the evenings we used to come home and be poor together. I always knew that my life wasn't going anywhere big, but it didn't really matter. Now I'm so far away from all that. Coming here reminds me of it."

"Here's your last chance to go back to that life," said Laura. "You could move in here and leave me stranded in the suburbs."

"Never," said Jane. This was a game they played once in a while. They acted out small psychodramas of different possibilities, some real, some unreal: What if I left you. What if we were blind. What if we were French. What if one of us was a man.

Laura smiled, and bent down and kissed her. They could kiss in any strange room and feel at ease. That was what was so lovely about sleeping with the same woman for years. You knew what to expect; you could conjure up the feeling anytime. There was something extraordinary about the *known*, especially after so many years of different women. Jane used to feel disoriented when she first got involved with a woman. She had to figure it all out quickly, make assumptions much too early. Sometimes she just wanted it to be over, and she wanted to be left alone. It wasn't worth it. There had been Sally, who did nothing but smoke dope the entire time she stayed with Jane. She just sat on the bed with a record album in her lap, lovingly rolling joints. She was stoned all the time; her conversations were silly, rambling, noncommittal. Her favorite phrase was *"You* decide."

And there had been the woman Lisa, who wore all of Jane's clothing and never gave it back. Jane had run into her in town months after they had stopped being lovers. The woman was wearing Jane's favorite scarf knotted around her throat, and her favorite pair of bright wool mittens from Peru.

There was such an incestuousness to the women in the Northampton community. It was the first women's community Jane had ever known. It astounded her; these women didn't have to go to dark bars at night to be themselves. They lived together, ran food co-ops, worked in a feminist bookstore. Jane thought she would stay there forever, working as a stained-glass maker at a crafts shop on Main Street. At first she lived in an apartment with three other women, all of whom had been lovers with each other at one time or another. Jane began sleeping with one of the women, Margie, sneaking into her room late at night. Finally everyone knew, and then Cass, who had the bedroom across the hall, approached Jane and asked her to move out.

"Margie and I were very much in love last December," said

Cass. "It's painful for me to watch this going on in my own apartment."

Then why do you still live with her? Jane wished she had said. *Why do you stay so close, so involved in each other's lives?* But instead she said nothing. Jane moved out finally, into another group apartment a few blocks away.

She stayed in Northampton for three years. In certain ways it was idyllic; there were many trees, and a beautiful pond. Smith College sat smack in the middle of everything, and Jane would watch as young women walked to class carrying books. Sometimes they would be dressed to go horseback riding. They all looked very rich to her. She hated them, and yet she couldn't stop staring. She was just their age; she could have been sitting in classes with them, discussing the meaning of life, or sipping tea with them at four o'clock in the afternoon, instead of sitting in this peeling apartment with a group of women who lived on the fringe. She imagined sharing a room with a Smith girl, climbing the stairs of one of those white, gabled houses where the students lived. Inside the room there would be two beds with patchwork quilts, a few stuffed animals, and piles of thick, impressive books. This was how Jane imagined it, anyway. She never did get to see the inside of a dormitory. She would approach a building, but could never bear to knock.

Laura had been like those girls. In Connecticut Laura had walked through colorful leaves in autumn, and stood in an art studio, painting still lifes. She had bought clothing at a store in town called The Campus Cat. She had attended vespers on Sunday, had sat at a carrel in the library every evening. It wasn't fair, but nothing was.

"You got your own education," Danielle always told Jane, but in some basic way Jane still felt cheated. By the time she was seventeen, her parents hadn't known what to do with her. She had a "bad attitude," they said. She was antisocial; she didn't dress properly. Jane left home that year, soon after the night a bar she was in was raided. She wasn't hurt in the raid, but she had been shaken up, had felt the animosity of Miami, felt it directed right at her, and knew she could not stay.

The bar was called Doubles, and it was a mixed gay bar — men on one side of the room, women on the other, and the dance floor crowded with couples. Some men were dressed as women, and a few women wore tuxedos and talked in tough voices. The music had a strong bass to it, pounding under the surface.

It was 1966. Jane had told her parents that she was going to the movies that night. She stood against a wall in the bar, drinking beer and looking around in wonder. She had been there a couple of times before, but she still marveled at the way the women touched each other. She had always kept her desires to herself, or moped around the hotel, inarticulately in love with Verna the barmaid.

Suddenly a Cuban woman came over and started to talk to her in a smooth voice. "Are you a girl or a boy?" the woman asked.

"A girl," Jane said.

"I know," said the woman. "I was just teasing. Do you want to dance with me?"

Jane nodded, and they began to dance, the way people did in the ballroom of the Mermaid Hotel, when Tommy Slate and his orchestra played. Jane was afraid to touch the woman; her fingers were like ice. She was terrified, way out of her league. But then she realized that she didn't even *have* a league; she was nothing, just a lonely, boyish blond girl who lived in a hotel room and was filled with thoughts she could never talk about.

The woman enclosed Jane in her dark arms, and that one gesture, that encircling, changed everything. Soon the two of them were necking in a corner. "Necking" was the word Jane always used when she told the story. It was such a dated word, so much a part of that era. In dark corners, illicit lovers necked rather than kissed.

Jane was caught up in this woman's arms, lost in the kiss,

when all of a sudden there was a commotion up front, and then a fleet of policemen burst into the bar and everyone started shrieking. The woman slipped away from Jane. A chair was hurled across the room; a man in drag was being punched in the face, over and over. Jane managed to make her way to the back, figuring that there had to be an exit somewhere. Soon she was pitched out onto the dark street, and it was very late, and she burst into tears.

Walking home, she went down to the beach, hoping the water would calm her. The night was warm and smelled of hibiscus blossoms, but in the distance she could still hear sirens, and could still remember the way that woman had asked her, *Are you a girl or a boy?*

She had realized then that she was part of a certain breed, a kind of girl who would always be mistaken for something else. Nobody could quite pin you down; you would spend the rest of your life being able to slip through the cracks, if you wanted to.

There had always been women like that, Jane knew. *Before the dawn of time,* she once said to Laura, as she began telling her one of her stories of two girls in love. The girls in the stories were ageless; they were time-travelers. They had gone from the cave era to medieval times, and then to the pioneer days.

"In a covered wagon on the old pioneer trail," began Jane one night, "two girls were traveling for months and months, following the other covered wagons to make a new home out on the prairie. These two girls wore bonnets and frocks when they were in public, but when they drove their wagon, they dressed in jeans and flannel, because it was most comfortable. One of the girls liked to wear a bandanna around her neck; it made her feel rakish. Anyway," said Jane, "at night they would sit deep inside the wagon, smelling the wonderful smells of wet canvas and salt pork and soap. They lay together in the darkest part of the wagon, and nobody ever disturbed them. At night sometimes they could hear the rain spattering on the canvas roof, but it never leaked in. They lay listening to the rain, and to the sounds of their horses munching hay out front. They were deeply in love, these girls, and as the years passed their bond grew unbreakable. Finally they reached a good place to settle forever, but there was some friction from the other pioneers. Nobody had ever heard of two girls living together."

"Sounds oddly familiar," said Laura. "Have I read this somewhere before?" ·

"Without even blinking," said Jane, ignoring her, "the girl in the bandanna announced that there was nothing wrong with two women living together. After all, she said, it was cheaper this way, and the house was bound to remain clean and nice. After a while the other pioneers began to accept the presence of these two women. They called them the Pioneer Sisters. Everyone liked to come over and have a campfire at the Sisters' cabin. It was always very festive there. Even though the world was filled with commotion, the two women kept their home peaceful, and nobody objected. Of course," she added, "it helped that nobody had any idea of what these two did when they were alone. Everyone sort of thought they spent their entire time making shoo-fly pie and patchwork quilts. The myth of women's folksiness protected them, and allowed them to be privately passionate for the rest of their lives. When they died, many, many years later, they were buried side by side, and their tombstone read: THE PIONEER SISTERS: LOVING FRIENDS AND GOOD HOMEMAKERS IN LIFE, BEAUTIFUL SPIRITS IN HEAVEN."

When Jane was through, she and Laura lay looking at each other for a while in the gray light. "I forgot something," Jane said, and then she added, as she always did, "The End."

CHAPTER TWENTY

I an was reading Vanessa's files. It was his favorite thing to do
these days, and it was pretty easy, too, because in the fall she
started storing them in his bedroom in the apartment. When no
one was around, he would close the door and pull out a few at
random.

"Summary," they always said at the beginning, and then they
would tell the details of someone's life. The first one was all about
a man named Gonzalez, Manuel D.

"Manuel Gonzalez is a forty-one-year-old Hispanic male who
has been employed for ten years by Grumman Aerospace In-
dustries," it read. "In the spring of last year, Mr. Gonzalez's wife
Alma came to Family Services because her home life was becoming 'unbearable.' After one session with a screener, she re-
vealed that her husband had been beating her regularly. Mr.
Gonzalez agreed to come in for therapy the following week, and
he has been in therapy with me ever since. Couple therapy will
begin as soon as we can arrange an acceptable schedule. In our

sessions I have been focusing on Mr. Gonzalez's ego strengths rather than his weaknesses, and have been helping to give him a new sense of self-worth. He has been performing well at his job, and there have been no further violent episodes with his wife."

Ian closed the folder and opened another one. "Summary," it read. "Karen Bregman is a nineteen-year-old Caucasian female who is currently a sophomore at NYU. For the past six months, Ms. Bregman has suffered from serious eating disorders. She finds herself obsessed with losing weight, and admits to inducing herself to vomit after meals."

Ian quickly closed the folder and opened one more. "Summary," it read. "John Hyam is a thirty-year-old Caucasian male who works as a drug counselor at Rainbow House. He has found himself becoming clinically depressed over the past few months. Sometimes he has trouble waking up in the morning and going to work. He claims to have become too involved in the lives and problems of his clients, who are mostly young, male drug abusers. He is in danger of losing his job due to lateness."

Ian closed this folder as well, and then dropped all three onto the bed. These were people's real lives—they had to live them every day. Some people had terrible lives, like his friend Todd. Once Ian and Todd were sitting in the playground after school. This was becoming their regular meeting place. They were sitting underneath the jungle gym. It was getting dark outside, and the ground was laced with shadows from the bars of the jungle gym. Ian and Todd sat in the middle, and Todd was drawing in the earth with a twig. He always looked very serious when he was drawing. Today he was talking about his mother, who had killed herself. Usually he didn't like to talk about it, but for some reason he wanted to talk about it now.

"My mother died in the garage," he said. "She sat in the car with the motor going and got carbon monoxide poisoning."

"Why did she do it?" Ian asked.

Todd shrugged. "I don't know," he said.

"Do you think you would ever kill yourself?" asked Ian.

"I don't think so," said Todd. He drew a picture of a man in the dirt, then erased it with his foot. "Life isn't too bad or anything," he said. "I think maybe if I had a fatal disease, or if I thought the world was going to come to an end, or like if it was Hiroshima and your skin started to peel off your body, then I would do it."

They had just finished the Hiroshima unit in school. They had looked at full-page photographs of women running through the streets, holding babies in their arms. The captions explained that people's skin just burned right up, that their hair crackled into flame.

Ian looked around the playground. There was no one else there; it was as though he and Todd were the last people left in the universe.

"We might not live to be our parents' age," said Todd. "The whole world might explode."

"What do you mean?" Ian asked, but he knew.

"The whole world might end in a mushroom cloud," said Todd. "Every single house would be blown away."

If it was true, Ian began to think, then what was the point of going to school every day? What was the point of cleaning up your room, or setting the table? You could just say no when your parents asked you to do a chore. You could say, "There is no point in doing anything. We're all going to be wiped out."

Usually Ian did everything he was supposed to do. He fed the cat every day and took out the garbage. He made his bed and used Endust on his furniture. He was actually much neater than his mother and Jane. Their room was often crowded with clothing and books and broken things that Jane was planning to fix. They also usually messed up the bathroom much worse than he did. Sometimes Jane and his mother took baths together, and when they left, the room was sopping wet. Damp towels were strewn all over the place, and there was a sprinkling of baby powder on the tile floor. The mirror was usually all steamed up, and you could write things on it. Once Ian wrote "Shit" and "Fuck" and "Cock," and then immediately erased them with his hand. But the next day the words returned, very faintly, like ghosts.

His father and Vanessa, on the other hand, were extremely neat. Once Ian was eating an apple and he left the core in an ashtray in the living room. Vanessa picked it up and said, "Ian, what's this?" as though she were new to this planet. What she really meant, of course, was, *What is this doing here?* She held the core delicately by its stem. "Please dispose of it properly," she said.

Everybody's parents were slightly embarrassing. Even his father agreed with this. "It's very hard for me to go back to the place where I grew up," his father once told him. "It's difficult for me to see my parents."

Ian had gone there with his father a few times in his life. His father's aunt Luisa was always visiting; she was fat and religious, and sat with a string of rosary beads in her hand, praying to herself. She moved her lips like a little kid learning to read.

Once Ian went there with his father for the afternoon. His grandparents began to fight over what to serve for dinner. They started to speak in Italian, and their voices grew very loud. They had a little Chihuahua named Peppy; he was like an insect, and he began to jump up and down in the air, almost flying. Ian sat on a hard chair and listened to the dog yip.

"Come here, Ian," his aunt Luisa said, beckoning to him. Ian got up and went over to her chair. She put her arm around him and brought him in close. "Did you know that your mother lives in sin?" she said, very casually.

Ian just shook his head and stood there. He looked at his aunt Luisa. She was staring at him and playing with those black beads. There was a big cross on the wall over her head. If you looked closely, you could see that it was also a clock. It was four in the afternoon, still light out. Ian could hear some kids playing in the street. He wanted to join them, to go kick a playground ball down the entire block.

"I have to go outside!" he said, and then he ran out the door and buzzed for the elevator. It came right away, and he went down to the first floor before anybody could stop him. When he got to the bottom he raced outside and just swallowed down the air. He couldn't breathe. His heart was pounding, and he held on to his chest with both arms, doubling over. A couple of kids stood and watched. "You okay, little boy?" an older girl asked, but he didn't answer.

In a minute his father came out. He saw Ian and rushed over. "What is it, kiddo?" he asked. "What's wrong?" He put his hands on the sides of Ian's face.

"I don't know," said Ian, when he could talk again. "I can't breathe. I think I have emphysema."

Then his father reached out and pulled Ian right down into his arms, and held him there. Ian's chest was going in and out, very fast, like a baby bird's.

"You'll be all right," his father said. "It's just an anxiety attack. We'll just sit here until it goes away. We have all the time in the world. I used to get them a lot when I was a boy. I survived it, and so will you." He continued to hold Ian like that for a while. They didn't say anything for a long time, and finally Ian's heart began to slow down, and he forgot about not being able to breathe.

"You feel better now?" his father asked.

"Yeah," said Ian.

It was almost dark, and they heard a voice. "Davy," it said. They turned around, and Ian's grandmother was standing in the doorway of the building, wearing a bathrobe and slippers. She said something in Italian. Ian's father answered her, and then said in English, "Everything's okay. He was just feeling a little restless, Mom."

They went back into the dark lobby. An old woman sat in a wheelchair, facing the wall. Ian's father pulled back the gate of the elevator, and they all got in. There was a sign on the wall that said No Spitting. Ian tried to imagine his grandmother wanting to spit but then seeing the sign and waiting until she got upstairs to spit.

They went up to the sixth floor, all of them facing forward, as if there was an interesting movie being shown on the door. They all stood so they didn't have to touch each other. When the elevator stopped, they got out single file and walked back to the apartment.

Everything was very calm now. There was a light wind blowing in the open window, and the Venetian blinds were clanking. Ian's grandfather was standing at the window with a little radio earphone in his ear, listening to a game. Ian passed by the kitchen and saw his aunt Luisa inside, stooping down over the floor, spooning dog food out of a can and into a little orange bowl. Peppy was jumping into the air like a marionette.

They left soon after that. In the subway station, waiting for a train, Ian and his father played number games.

"I'm thinking of a number," his father said.

"Is it a prime number?" asked Ian. He was very good at this particular game.

"Yes," said his father.

They stood and looked down the tunnel in the direction the train was supposed to come. The tracks curved around, and they were wet, as though it had rained in the subway.

"It wasn't too terrible a day, was it?" his father asked. "I know families are difficult, ours in particular. But you feel okay now, don't you?"

"Yeah," said Ian.

The tunnel was suddenly cloudy with light, and the train arrived. The ride was very long; his father read the newspaper while Ian leaned against his shoulder. The car was empty except for a young black girl and a very old man. The lights kept blinking on and off.

"You want to take a little nap, kiddo?" his father asked. "Don't worry, I'll wake you up when we get to our stop."

Ian nodded, and was suddenly very tired. But right before he fell asleep he realized that he hadn't guessed his father's number.

That fall, Ian was elected a member of the math club. Three new members were asked to join every year, and this term Ian was one of them. Andrea Flood and Kevin Marder were the others. The club met once a week after school. The members all sat around a table with the teacher, Mrs. Roseman, talking only about complicated math problems.

The first meeting of the club was going to be held on Wednesday. On Tuesday, Ian went home with Todd after school. They played Trouble for a while, and then Sorry, and then Clue, and finally it was time for him to leave. His mother and Jane were supposed to pick him up, and they were all going out to dinner at Chan Luck.

At six o'clock the doorbell rang. Ian was surprised; he expected them to honk, the way they usually did. Todd's brother Dean answered the door. "Dad!" Dean yelled. "There's two ladies here!"

Todd and Ian came halfway downstairs and stood looking through the railing. There were Ian's mother and Jane, talking to Mr. Berger. Immediately Ian was embarrassed. He and Todd looked at each other.

"I thought it might be nice for us to say hello," Ian's mother was saying, "since our boys are such good friends. I saw you once at a PTA meeting but never got a chance to say hi, and then you didn't come back."

"Yes," said Mr. Berger. "Would you like to come in?" He was holding a drink in one hand and a copy of *Newsday* in the other.

"That would be nice," said Jane.

Todd and Ian stood on the steps watching as they all sat down in the living room. All of a sudden Ian's mother said, "Oh, hi, boys. I didn't see you hiding back there."

"We weren't hiding," said Ian.

"How are you, Todd?" she asked, and then Ian knew that they were supposed to go into the living room, too. They were going to be included in the conversation.

"I'm okay," said Todd. He threw a leg over the banister and jumped down into the room, Ian following. Dean and Jeffrey were down in the rec room watching TV. Ian could hear the theme song from "The Brady Bunch" starting up.

"Can I get either of you a drink?" Mr. Berger asked.

"Yeah, I want a Scotch," said Todd.

"Very funny," said his father. "I meant either of the ladies, so watch your mouth, Todd."

Mr. Berger went over to the counter where there was a whole line-up of bottles and glasses, and he poured out some wine. Ian sat on the rug next to Todd and looked around. His mother and Jane were sitting next to each other on the brown couch. All the furniture in the living room was very dark, and the walls were paneled, so it looked as if you were inside a cabin. There was thick carpeting on the floor that was sort of a burned color. Even Mr. Berger looked dark. He sat in his big recliner chair and leaned back a little.

Ian's mother and Jane looked so different from Mr. Berger. They were both golden-colored, Ian thought. They sat there very politely, holding glasses of wine in their hands. Nobody seemed to have too much to say; they all just sat there drinking.

Finally Mr. Berger said, "You're divorced, Mrs. Giovanni?"

"For quite a few years," she answered. "And please call me Laura."

"I guess you know that I'm a widower myself," said Mr. Berger. "My wife, Annette, died a couple of years ago."

"Yes," she said. "I know. I was very sorry to hear it."

"We all do what we can," said Mr. Berger. "I work at Prudential, and I keep long hours. I have three boys to raise. It isn't easy."

"I can imagine," said Laura.

"How do *you* manage?" Mr. Berger asked. "Do you have a housekeeper or something?"

"Oh, no," she said. "But it's easier because there are two of us running the house, not just one."

"Do you live there too?" Mr. Berger asked Jane.

"Yes," she said, and she took a sip of wine.

Mr. Berger leaned back in his recliner. "Todd mentioned something like that, but you know kids. They never get their facts right. He seemed to think there was something funny going on. I told him he had a vivid imagination. It really cracked me up."

"I don't think it should be important what we are," said Laura.

"What?" asked Mr. Berger. There was a long pause. "Look," he said, "I know it's none of my business."

"You're right," she said. "It's not."

Ian started to get nervous. Todd whispered that they should go upstairs. They crept out of the living room, and no one seemed to notice. "I guess you're not interested in my opinion on the matter," they could hear Mr. Berger say, "so I'll just quit while I'm ahead."

Jane started to say something, but Todd and Ian were already climbing the stairs and didn't hear.

In the car on the way to Chan Luck, Ian sat in the back and pretended to be looking over an algebra problem.

"Relax," Jane was saying. "He wasn't *that* bad."

"Yes he was," said Laura. "Just the way he was looking at us."

"I think he was a little drunk," said Jane.

"He should talk about raising children," said Laura. "Did you see that house? It was like a mausoleum. No wonder his wife killed herself."

"Hey, calm down," Jane said.

"I know, I know," said Laura. "I'm very sensitive to these things."

Ian wanted to be elsewhere, to forget it all. But all that night he kept thinking about his mother and Jane sitting in the Bergers' dark living room. He and Todd didn't talk about it, but they both knew how uncomfortable it had been. They acknowledged it silently. The next day was Wednesday, and Ian didn't get to talk to Todd very much because he had to go to math club after school. He sat between Andrea Flood and Kevin Marder and had a decent time. They started discussing probability, which was very interesting.

On Thursday Ian asked Todd if he wanted to come over after school, but Todd said he was busy. Then there was Friday, and Ian went into the city to stay with his father and Vanessa. By the time he got home on Sunday night, it was too late to call up Todd. They hadn't spent any time together since that afternoon at Todd's house. It felt very strange to be apart for so long; Ian felt uneasy about it.

In school on Monday, Todd spent a long time at the pencil sharpener before the bell rang, so there was no time to talk. Even at lunchtime he didn't feel like socializing. They sat next to each other at a table crowded with kids. Adam Bracken was shooting milk through a straw. A couple of girls were shrieking and threatening to tell the cafeteria monitor. Ian just sat there with his tray in front of him. He looked down at his lunch; there was a plate of macaroni and cheese on the tray, and a little red carton of milk, an apple that was dented, and a dry brownie. He wished he were at home having dinner with his family.

When the bell rang at the end of the day, Todd quickly left the classroom and walked outside. "Hey, wait up!" Ian called, following behind.

Todd turned around. "I can't," he said. "I have to go to the orthodontist today."

"So I'll walk with you," said Ian.

Todd just stood there. "Can't you take a hint?" he asked.

"What are you talking about?" said Ian.

Todd made a loud clucking sound with his mouth. "I don't feel like being your best friend anymore," he said. "Okay?"

"Why not?" said Ian. His heart was racing. "Just tell me why not."

"Just because," said Todd.

"Is it because I made math club and you didn't?" asked Ian.

"No," said Todd.

"Then *why?*" Ian asked.

"You figure it out," said Todd.

Ian thought hard. Something struck him. "Is it because of my mother?" he asked. Todd didn't say anything. "*Is* it?" Ian asked.

Todd said, "You're brilliant, Giovanni. You figured it out."

Ian just stood there clutching his books to his chest. "I don't get it," he said. "What's the big deal?"

"Leave me alone," said Todd. "I don't want to talk about it anymore." Then he turned around and began to jog away across the field. Ian watched him go. He kept watching as Todd got smaller and smaller and disappeared into the trees at the edge of the property.

Ian went and sat underneath the jungle gym. He crawled in as though it were a cave. He thought back to what his father had said, about how there was nothing wrong with being a lesbian, and how his mother had said the same thing. She and Jane loved each other, and that was all there was to it. They lay in bed at night and touched each other all over.

His father had said that when you were ready for sex, you'd know, because it would feel right, and everything would happen without instructions. When you were in love, then you slept in the same bed every night. Ian couldn't imagine what it would be like to share a bed. He liked to talk to himself a little bit at night, and if he were sharing the bed with someone, the other person might think he was insane. He never said crazy things, though, like a bum on the street. He just sort of went over what had happened during the day. He pretended he was being interviewed.

How was school? he usually asked. Okay. *Did you do anything interesting?* Well, we learned about probability. We also had bomb drill, and had to crouch away from the windows with our hands covering our eyes.

If you slept in a bed with someone, you would probably have conversations like that in the middle of the night. Ian thought about his mother and his father, back before he was born, lying in bed in New York City. His mother was pregnant in this scene. Ian was curled up inside her, still an unborn baby, suspended in warm water.

—What do you want to name the baby, darling? his father would ask his mother.

—I don't know, David. What do you want to name it?

—Hmmmmm. If it's a girl, let's name it Sarabeth. That's a pretty name. But if it's a boy, let's name it . . . Jimmy?

—No.

—Tommy?

—No.

—How about Ian? his father would ask, and his mother would say that she thought Ian was a great name, a wonderful name. And then they would both start to picture Ian, what he might look like. They would think about how they would all live together for a long time. They had no way of knowing it wouldn't be like that. Ian's mother said that she used to think they would be together forever.

Ian felt like crying as he thought about all this. It had been a terrible day. He knew that he would never be friends with Todd again, even if Todd apologized forever. As Ian sat there, he began to feel as if he couldn't breathe. This was exactly the way he had felt in front of his grandparents' apartment building the day that his father had come outside and held him. Now he sat underneath the jungle gym, and he held himself in his own arms until he could breathe again.

247

When *Jumping Bean* published its last issue, the editors threw a party in the office, and supplies were handed out like favors. Laura took home a whole wheel of magic markers. The magazine could no longer afford to publish, which was no surprise to anyone.

Laura felt some nostalgia, but mostly she was relieved. In the next few weeks she would have to start looking for other freelance work. Carolyn knew of something at *Highlights* and thought there might be some graphics at "Sesame Street." In the meantime Laura was very involved in Childwatch. The first discussion group was to be held the following Thursday night in her living room. She had been preparing throughout the summer and had attended a seminar taught by a local police officer. Her head was filled with statistics about missing children.

Bernadette Beshar still hadn't been found. Laura thought about her often; they all did. She pictured Bernadette at the bottom of a sandpile in a construction site, or behind the bushes in the yard of an abandoned house. Sometimes, in a moment of hopeful fantasy, Laura imagined that Bernadette was still alive. She had been kidnapped by a kindly but misdirected woman and was now living in some other suburb. She was told that her name was Cynthia now, and every day her former life unwound itself a little bit more from her thoughts, becoming as loose and nebulous as a dream one has dreamt under ether.

On Thursday night at eight, families started arriving at Laura and Jane's house. They were young and nice, and all she wanted to do was let them in, give them soda and Planter's mixed nuts, and then become friends with them. She did not want to have to be so grim.

She would have to get used to this; every Thursday night for the next ten weeks, different groups of parents and children would be sitting in her living room and listening to her speak. By eight-fifteen, everyone was assembled and waiting for her to begin. She was very nervous, but Jane kept smiling at her.

"Ever since Bernadette Beshar disappeared last spring," said Laura, "we have felt that it was important to take some action. I'm a mother myself," she said. "I'm not an expert on this. I'm just another concerned parent like yourselves."

Her voice sounded so awkward to her, so unconvincing, but she kept going. It was all well rehearsed; she spoke about Bernadette Beshar, and some other cases that had taken place on Long Island in the past few years—children who had been abducted from playgrounds, or shopping malls, or while walking to school. She urged parents to have their children fingerprinted, to teach their children to memorize their address and telephone number, and to know how to dial the operator. She talked to the children about the importance of traveling in groups.

Finally she had them act out a psychodrama. Sybil Frankel played the role of a little girl on her way to school. A father named Lloyd Herron played a child molester. "Come into my car, little girl," he said. "I have some Jujubes to give you."

Everyone laughed nervously. "What do you say, Sybil?" Elaine Frankel prompted.

"I say, 'Okay, I love candy!' " said Sybil, and a couple of the other children laughed.

"No," said Laura, cutting in, "that's not right. Let's be serious." She thought about Ian walking to and from school every day. He had been going by himself lately; for some reason Todd wasn't around. She would watch Ian shuffle down the block like a lone pilgrim.

"Sorry," said. Sybil. "How's this? I'd say, 'I don't want your candy!' And then I'd run home as fast as I could."

"That's good," said Laura. "That's exactly right."

She spoke all her prepared lines to them. She looked around the living room at these attentive faces, some of which she recognized from the PTA or Ian's class. Parents sat close to their children. Laura began to feel less self-conscious. Nobody asked her where her husband was; it was an irrelevant detail. She sat next to Jane on the floor, their legs lightly touching. At the end of the psychodrama, she set up the movie projector and showed *Can I Go Home Now?*, the movie that was on loan from the school. The movie was very simple; it depicted a young girl saying goodbye to her parents and going for a walk in the woods, and then being lured into a car by a strange man. Then it cut to the girl's parents back at home, anxiously waiting for her return. At the end of the film, all you saw was a child's pair of red sneakers floating down a stream. There was no music.

The movie lasted twenty minutes. When Laura turned the lights back on, she saw that the children looked stricken. They were sitting even closer to their parents. Sybil Frankel had her arms around her mother and father.

"I know it's upsetting," said Laura, "but it's supposed to be. I hope you remember it for a long time."

She thought about all the missing children who would never be found. When you were a parent, you tried to keep your child as close to you as possible. Sometimes Laura would watch Ian play in the backyard. She would just sit by the window and look out, knowing how ephemeral the moment was — his lean, boyish presence on the lawn, the fact that he belonged to her. Now he was in his room doing homework, and all she could see, as she peered down the hall, was the light under his door. She wished that he were sitting there between her and Jane. She looked around at the other kids who sat wedged between mothers and fathers.

At the end of the evening, Laura and Jane stood around talking to Rob and Ellen Baskin. They lived nearby, on Sheri Street, and they said they would invite Laura, Jane, and Ian to dinner very soon.

Laura missed having friends nearby. She and Carolyn spoke to each other once in a while on the telephone, and they occasionally met for lunch when Laura came into the city, but their friendship had lapsed. Their lives didn't intersect in too many places, and this saddened her. It struck her that she didn't like anyone as much as she liked Ian and Jane. Were all families that way? she wondered. She thought there must be a shared sensibility in most families.

She looked forward now to having dinner with the Baskins. They were the same age as Laura and Jane, and they both worked for a textiles firm nearby. There was something sympathetic about their faces. Laura kept thinking about them for the rest of the evening. After everyone had gone home, she and Jane cleaned up quickly, walking around and gathering cups, emptying ashtrays.

"You were really impressive," said Jane. "I could never get up and speak to a group of people like that. You're so articulate."

"It's easy after you get started," said Laura. "You look at their faces and know that they're listening."

After they were through cleaning up and had folded the movie screen and put the projector away, they sat for a little while longer in the living room. Jane leaned her head against Laura's shoulder. "I'm sleepy," she said. "I lugged an oak table out to the van today, because one of the movers was home with a cold."

Laura massaged Jane's shoulders, pressed her fingers down

hard, leaving impressions. "That feels wonderful," said Jane. "A wonderful kind of pain. Don't stop."

Finally Laura glanced at her watch. "It's almost eleven," she said. "Ian ought to be in bed."

She called out to him. "Sweetie," she said, "are you in your pajamas yet? It's way past your bedtime."

There was no answer. She called again, and still no answer, so she got up from the couch and knocked on his door.

"Come in," he finally said.

He was sitting cross-legged on the bed, his pocket calculator in his hand. "What is it?" he asked.

"Didn't you hear me call?" said Laura.

"Yeah," said Ian. "So? There's no law that says I have to answer."

"Why are you being nasty?" Laura asked.

"Why don't you just leave me alone," said Ian. He began to press buttons on his calculator.

"Ian, I am talking to you," said Laura. She walked over to the bed and yanked the calculator from his hand. "I want you to listen to me!"

"Oh, why should I?" said Ian. "What's the point?"

Laura stared at him. "You are going to be denied television privileges for a week," she said.

"Whoopee," said Ian.

"Would you please tell me what's wrong?" Laura asked, and now she was getting worried. He had rarely spoken to her like this.

"Nothing," said Ian.

"Talk to me," she said, and she felt the helplessness of centuries of mothers, all of them bribing their children for answers, for some sign of life.

"Did something happen in school?" she asked.

"No," he said quickly. "I want to get into my pajamas, please."

"It can wait a few seconds," said Laura. "I'm your mother," she tried, and was embarrassed at the impotence of these words.

So what if she was his mother? Mothers couldn't protect their children, not really. The mother in *Can I Go Home Now?* had just stood by the telephone waiting for some word from her daughter. Mothers waited their whole lives, taking cues from the world.

Ian would not give. He continued to sit there on his bed, and he looked sleepy, distracted. She was surrounded by sleepy people, her lover and son nodding off before her eyes, and yet she was wide awake. She wanted to make Ian stay up and tell her what was wrong.

But all she said was, "Okay, Ian. I'm not going to squeeze it out of you. I guess you should get ready for bed."

Back in the living room, Jane was fast asleep on the couch. Laura stood in the hall, not knowing what to do. She could sneak off and watch television all night, she supposed. She kept thinking about the child in that movie, and about the girl who was missing from Syosset. Parents pretended authority, made up rules as they went along. Her own parents hadn't known much more. They probably hadn't agonized over it, though. Laura sometimes asked them questions about her childhood, trying to reconstruct as much as she could.

"Did I talk to myself when I was a kid?" she had once asked her mother on the telephone.

"I don't remember," her mother said, and this startled Laura. How could she not remember? Why hadn't the information stayed lodged in her mind forever, bronzed in her memory like a pair of baby shoes? And then Laura felt embarrassed for caring so much, for needing to know.

But her mother had said she didn't remember. There was a distance between them; it had to be there. Her parents telephoned twice a month, and sometimes Jane would answer. They were polite and asked how she was, and told her they hoped they would meet her someday, but it was always an awkward exchange. They would not come East; they were just not up to it.

When Laura married David, she and her mother were confidantes. And when she became pregnant, her mother always had good advice on maternity clothes, morning sickness. Her parents came to New York when Ian was born. David brought the baby in for them to see, and the whole hospital room was charged with family warmth, the continuum of love and faith. It was unshakable; it was the strongest thing anyone could know. Laura had imagined a lifetime of dinners with Ian and David. Thanksgiving day, a table set with linen and crystal. Candles burning, flowers floating in water in a bowl. And then more children — a fleet of them, perhaps.

Giving birth to Ian was like giving her parents a present. When David handed the baby to Laura's mother for the first time, she had said, "Thank you," as though Ian were really meant especially for her. Laura had done her job. Ian was curled up in soft cotton; he was in one perfect piece.

Laura had traded it all in for this life with Jane. Sometimes, when she was alone and began to think about the circumstances, she was horrified. *Oh no,* she would think, *I have made a series of bad and irreversible choices in my life.* There was Jane, sleeping face up on the couch. Uncomplicated Jane, who was happiest when left alone with some wood and tools and a good blues station on the radio.

There was no way to understand why certain people complemented each other. Sometimes Laura felt as though they had been thrown together by default, by some accident. Their household was built of spare parts — women and children only, the survivors of a sunken boat, the only ones allowed onto the life raft.

She stood in the hallway and continued to watch Jane sleep. She knew she should wake her, lead her into bed, as she would a child. Jane always slept heavily. Sometimes at night Laura would grow lonely, and she would turn Jane toward her just to feel her breathe, to be reminded of what was constant.

She thought about all the married couples in the living room that night. She thought of Rob and Ellen Baskin, and how they had held hands as they left. She was sure that she and Jane would become friends with the Baskins; she had seen something in their marriage that she liked. Something that she recognized from her own life.

She and Jane did it all so quietly. They wore no rings; they had no certificates of fidelity. No one thought of them as married; two women could not marry. But then she recalled the lesbian wedding she and Jane had attended in New Hampshire the summer before. It was held at Danielle's farm, and there were one hundred guests, all of them women.

"I cannot take this seriously," she had told Jane as they drove up the highway.

"Oh, I've been to one of these before," Jane said. "In Northampton. It's no big deal."

This was a Jewish lesbian wedding. The women to be married were named Susan and Amy. They had been living together for six years and had decided they wanted some sort of official union. A rabbi had been selected, a recently ordained gay woman who was summering in Provincetown.

On Saturday morning Susan and Amy walked out onto the lawn, dressed similarly in long, diaphanous dresses. They had sprigs of flowers in their hair. Amy's family lived in California and knew nothing about the wedding or even the relationship, but Susan's mother rode a Greyhound bus up for the weekend from Brooklyn. She had long ago accepted her daughter's life. "What can I do?" Laura overheard her saying to another guest. "Fish got to swim. Birds got to fly. Susan's got to live the way she wants."

A hundred folding chairs were set up on the grass, and at one o'clock, everyone took her seat. An airplane hummed overhead, then disappeared into the clouds.

"Women," the rabbi said. "Welcome."

Laura glanced at Jane out of the side of her vision, but Jane's expression gave away nothing. She looked placid, without even the hint of a smile. Laura felt like standing and giggling. Everyone else was stony-faced.

Now the rabbi was reading an Adrienne Rich poem. In a minute Susan and Amy were reciting the vows they had written. Then a wineglass was wrapped in linen and placed on the grass. Laura wondered who would break it. Who would be the man? The rabbi said a prayer in Hebrew, her voice very clear. The women repeated it after her. When the prayer was through there was silence, a moment of suspense. Amy and Susan looked at each other, and then both of them stepped forward to break the glass together. Both were the man, or neither.

"I now declare your marriage official," said the rabbi. "You may embrace."

And with that, the two women leaned in and kissed for a long moment. The wind lifted the sprig of flowers right off Susan's hair. They drew back, and the guests applauded grandly. Laura found, to her real surprise, that she was moved.

Amy and Susan were ethereal; they floated around the lawn for the rest of the afternoon. Danielle had placed the stereo speakers out on the porch, and everyone danced on the grass. First there was a traditional hora, then the Supremes, and then finally, when a lot of champagne had been drunk and the lawn was littered with corks, the party quieted down and Danielle put on some bland feminist folk music. A woman with a reedy voice sang about wanting to go down to the river with Persephone in her arms.

Laura realized that she felt moved in a way she had not felt at her own wedding. As she and David drove away from the church after their ceremony, she had leaned against his shoulder and felt the brush of unfamiliar material against her face. They were both done up like packages. She couldn't wait to take off her wedding gown, to unwrap the stiff crinoline and hang it up in a closet.

She had been displaced that day, lost somewhere in the billows of material. During the wedding ceremony, her father had stood and given her away. It was such a peculiar phrase, *being given away*; it had a double meaning. She thought of Jane now, who had been given away by both her father and her mother, abandoned forever.

Maybe all parents felt it was their responsibility to give their children away — releasing them into appropriate marriages, or dropping them on the doorstep of aberrance. *We never want to see you again*, Jane's mother had said, and even now, after over seven years of silence, it still chilled Laura that they had done this to their own child.

The things parents did to their children were unspeakable. You could lecture parents and children about the dangers of men in cars offering candy, but what about the things that went on within the house? In the suburbs, all the houses looked alike, with their yellow porch lights and basketball hoops over the garages, but such divergent lives went on inside. Laura and Jane were the only lesbians in the neighborhood, as far as she knew. Next door, Elaine Frankel planned Girl Scout badge projects with her daughter. Down the street, an old couple knelt on their front lawn, planting zinnias. And in the next town, a mother and father wept over the disappearance of their daughter. Everyone had a private grief or joy.

Laura saw that Ian's light had finally been turned off for the night. He was falling into sleep, as he did every night, as all children did, and their parents had to let them go, hoping there wouldn't be nightmares or sudden fever.

Ian seemed unhappy these days, but Laura did not know why. He would have to tell her himself; she couldn't coax it out of him.

The truth came out at dinner two days after the meeting. Jane innocently asked him, "What's new in school? Anything big happen this week?"

Ian burst into tears and stood up, knocking his chair back into the wall.

"Hey, hey, calm down," said Laura, and she reached across the table and held his wrists.

Ian was sobbing. He sat back down and wept for a minute while Laura and Jane asked questions, trying to see if they were hot or cold. Was it about school? they asked. Was it about the math club? Was it about Ian's father? What? they asked. *Please*, they said, *tell us.*

"Okay," Ian finally said, when he had calmed down a little. "Todd dropped me." He recounted the story of what had happened with Todd in the playground. Then he fled from the table and went into his room. They could hear him crying behind the door.

Laura and Jane sat across from each other, stunned. It was as though a delicately constructed machine had collapsed — all of their good intentions, all of their speeches about different kinds of love.

"God damn that man, that Michael Berger," said Laura. "He had to go and ruin Ian's one good friendship."

"So what do you want to do?" asked Jane.

"I don't know anymore," said Laura. "I can't stand seeing him like this. It breaks my heart." She paused. "Maybe he shouldn't be here," she said. "Maybe it's only going to make him neurotic. One of those kids who are always on edge. Getting an ulcer before they're twelve."

"What do you mean he shouldn't be here?" asked Jane.

"He could go to David's," Laura said. "He could go live there and have a normal family, with two parents everyone would approve of. Parents he could bring to the Family Spaghetti Dinner."

"I can't believe you're saying this," said Jane.

"Well, do you have any better ideas?" asked Laura. "I just want him to be happy, Jane. Not traumatized."

"Well," Jane said quietly, "I'm sure David would love it. He and Vanessa are always acting like they'd jump at the chance. Vanessa thinks Ian is an angel."

"I don't know what's best anymore," Laura said. "I don't want him fighting our battles. I couldn't bear it if Ian went to David's, but maybe that's selfish."

"In any case," said Jane, "he'd have to decide this for himself. He's old enough. He knows how to make decisions."

"Do you think I'm overreacting?" Laura asked.

Jane shook her head. "No," she said. "But I don't have any more experience with this than you do. Talk to David if you want. Talk to Ian. I really don't know what to tell you, Laura. This one isn't easy. In the meantime," she said, "he's still in his room now. Just sitting there."

"So what are we supposed to do?" Laura asked. "Go in there and tell him that everything will resolve itself, that life works that way?"

Jane shook her head. They sat there for a long time, just staring at the line of light under Ian's door.

CHAPTER TWENTY-TWO

One morning David found Vanessa tilted over the toilet, sweeping her hair out of her face, preparing to be sick. He poked his head in the bathroom doorway. "You okay, honey?" he asked. Ian peeked into the room over David's shoulder, then shrank back.

"I'm a little queasy," she said. "Close the door, okay?"

"You sure?" David asked.

"Please!" she said, heaving, and David shut the door so she could be sick in private.

"Come on, kiddo," he said to Ian. "We'll go into the kitchen." He scrambled some eggs for the two of them, and Ian worked the electric juicer.

"What's wrong with Vanessa?" Ian asked over the hum of the motor.

"I don't know," said David. "A little stomach flu, maybe. It's going around. I'll take a look when she comes out."

He and Ian sat down at the table and ate a good breakfast. He was concerned about Vanessa, but he also wanted time alone with Ian. Laura had called him before the weekend and told him what had happened at school, how Todd had turned against Ian. David remembered a similar incident from his own childhood, when Scott Finelli had suddenly refused to play stickball with him. They always used to play together, and then one day Scott said he didn't want to, and that was that. David never learned the reason, and it had haunted him since. He imagined running into Scott on the subway now, and chasing him through the cars, yelling, "Why, Scott, why?"

David wanted Ian to be the most popular kid around, yet that was clearly not to be. But this was terrible — Ian was being ostracized because of Laura and Jane. He felt like beating up that Todd Berger and his father, and then he felt like beating himself. Maybe he had misjudged; maybe the situation wasn't working. Lately he had been wondering.

Weekends with Ian had been deliriously good. He felt as though they were a real family when the three of them were together. Watching Ian across a table in a restaurant, and then watching Vanessa's smile, David could lean back in his chair and feel contented. They had established a true equilibrium. One night as he and Vanessa lay in bed, they both fantasized about having Ian live with them, and about what school he would attend.

"He used to go to Calder," David said. "He could go back there if he wanted, but maybe we could send him to Fieldston instead, or the Friends School."

"Ilene's niece goes to Friends," said Vanessa.

They each had pictures in their heads of Ian in school, Ian coming home with a couple of classmates. The appeal of this fantasy was stronger than ever. Ian could come live with them on a trial basis, as with everything else they did. David would mention the idea to Laura gently, saying he wanted to test it out, have Ian live with them just for the next school year. Ian could spend weekends in Plainview.

"It's only fair," David would say, and Laura would have to admit that he was right.

David felt elated as he finished up his breakfast. He nearly forgot about Vanessa, who was still in the bathroom. "Why don't you stack the dishes," David told Ian, "and I'll check on Vanessa. Go see what's on cable; I'll be right in."

He knocked on the bathroom door, and Vanessa weakly told him to come in. She was sitting on the closed toilet, leaning back with her eyes shut.

"You okay?" he asked, feeling her forehead.

"I think so," she said.

"You don't feel warm," he said. "But let's get you lying down. You look pale."

As he straightened the blankets around her, he thought for a moment that she might be pregnant, but he ruled it out at once. They had barely been making love these days; they had stopped their routine of temperature-taking months ago. Now they had settled tacitly into childlessness. They would try for a baby in another few months; in the meantime they talked a lot about work, and Ian, and where they would spend Christmas vacation. They had to make plans soon.

"Spain and Portugal," Vanessa had suggested, but David dreamed of the Middle East. He imagined Ian returning with all sorts of photographs he could bring to school. Pictures of sphinxes and camels and ruins. Everyone would crowd around to look; kids loved things like that.

"Are you too sick to go to the planetarium today?" David asked her, sitting down on the edge of the bed.

"I'll be okay," she said. "I just want to lie here."

"Are you thinking the same thing that I am, possibly?" David asked. He didn't even want to say it, to jinx the minuscule chance of its being true.

"I think so," she said, "but I doubt very much that we're right, David, so I don't want to be let down. Please talk to Laura soon about letting Ian live with us for a while. That would make me happy. I can't keep hoping that I'm going to have my own baby. Ed Sussman said my chances were diminishing."

But the pregnancy test was positive; David performed it himself at the lab on Monday. He and Vanessa went careening down the hallway, banging into walls. David couldn't concentrate for the rest of the day. He took a break in the afternoon and went downstairs to the hospital cafeteria. He sat there as if in a trance, and watched as orangeade and grapeade churned in twin vats, side by side. He thought about names for the baby. Dustin if it was a boy; Alexandra if it was a girl. The baby would have Vanessa's light, wavy hair and David's dark skin. Or else it would have David's thick, dark hair and Vanessa's light skin. That would be even more interesting and exotic. He thought about having a little girl. He liked the sound of that — *my little girl* — just as he had liked the sound of *my little boy*.

Ian was back in Plainview, and that night they called him up to tell him the news. Each of them got on an extension. "Well, you'll never guess what," David said.

"What?" asked Ian.

"You're going to have a little sister or brother," said David. "Vanessa's pregnant."

There was silence, and they held their breath. Finally Ian said, "Wow, that's great. Congratulations."

David thought how sophisticated his son was; he felt altogether filled with proud father feelings. He and Vanessa were going to have a late dinner that night at the Odeon. When they got home they would make love for hours. They would never have to take Vanessa's temperature again, or record their lovemaking in jumpy red and green lines.

"Let me talk to your ma," David said to Ian, and Vanessa discreetly hung up her extension. David told Laura the news, and she congratulated him without reserve. In that moment he realized how long it had been since he and Laura were married.

There was no animosity left; it had all diluted over the years, been replaced by distractions, by lovers, by the sum total of their new lives. He felt as though they had come very far.

"I'm very happy for you," Laura said. "I know that's what you've wanted."

"Thanks, Laura," he said, and he was moved. "It's nice to hear you say that."

He and Vanessa canceled the Christmas trip and decided to hang on to the money because now they would be needing it for other things. "We'll all go somewhere soon," David told Ian. "Right after the baby is born."

Winter was quickly approaching. One night it snowed lightly, and in the morning the streets were dusted white for the first time that year. He and Vanessa went out for a croissant and coffee before work, and she slipped on the pavement and David grabbed her elbow, held her fast.

"Watch it," he said, imagining the loss of a tiny tadpole life in that one instant. There could be no slipping, no falling.

The apartment was just big enough for three; Ian would have to share his room with the new baby. Eventually they would find a bigger place; there was plenty of time to think about all that. One afternoon David went out on impulse to a store called The Baby Boom. It was filled with objects in pastel tones. Gentle bell music played in the background. The whole store had a soft, nursery-colored light to it. The women who worked there were porcelain-fragile and slender, and looked as though they might be the type to die in childbirth.

David walked up to the counter. "Excuse me," he said. "I want to buy a crib for our baby, even though it's not due for a long time."

"Oh, is it your first?" the woman asked.

"Yes," David said, on instinct, and immediately felt bad. But it *was* his first, his and Vanessa's. It was their first, together. He ordered a crib, which would be delivered in a week. He wanted

264

to bring something home that day, so he impulsively bought a mobile made up of different shapes. Airplanes and sailboats and pelicans bobbed on delicate wires. He carried the mobile back home, unwrapped, holding his arm carefully outstretched.

Ian was coming into the city on Saturday. He was taking the train out by himself, and David would meet him at Penn Station. Ian was still depressed these days, Laura had said. He and Todd remained enemies.

At eleven-twenty on Saturday morning, there was Ian, waiting patiently against the round information booth at the Long Island Railroad. They went home and drank the hot chocolate that Vanessa had made. Ian was quiet, and David had to keep plying him with questions to get him to speak. School was okay, Ian said. The only thing new in his life was that he had been to the dentist and found out he needed a retainer. He would be going to see an orthodontist soon.

"Oh, it's not so bad," David said. "A lot of my patients have braces or retainers. Just be careful if you kiss a girl who also wears one. You might lock."

He didn't often imagine Ian with girls, or Ian having a sex drive at all. It was as though he had forgotten about the phenomenon of adolescence. In a couple of years Ian would sprout fur. He would burst into puberty, with voice changes, wet dreams, the works. David remembered lying in bed as a child and carefully examining every inch of his own body. The new dark hairs had horrified him at first, but after a while there were just so many that it was all blurred for him; it became who he was. He was a body covered with a field of hair now; there was nothing to be done about it. He had gone out and bought his first wallet that week — it had seemed the right thing to do. He wore a keychain on his belt, like his father. He studied batting averages, had an amazing memory for them.

Boys were different these days. It was because parents were raising their children more progressively and letting them listen to that Marlo Thomas record, the one about being free. Many of the old anxieties just didn't apply anymore. If David's new child was a boy and he wanted a doll, that would be fine. Anything would. David only wanted the baby to turn out okay, to have ten fingers and ten toes and a steady, pumping heart.

David and Vanessa talked about the baby with Ian. "So, how do you really feel about our news?" David asked. "Has it sunk in yet?"

"Yeah," said Ian. "It's great. I told you that."

Vanessa had thought that Ian might be upset and had wanted to buy him a book she had seen in a store, called *But I Don't Want a Baby Brother!* David flipped through it and saw that the book was much too unsophisticated for Ian; it would be an insult. Ian was eleven; he could read Jack London if he wanted to. All he seemed to enjoy reading, though, were math books and biographies. He knew about people whom David barely knew about—obscure childhood facts from the lives of Chaim Weizmann, Harriet Tubman, J. Robert Oppenheimer. He loved to read about other lives, to figure out what went on elsewhere, way before he was born.

"The world was better then," David always said, talking of the forties and fifties. He had told Ian many stories about how the world was safer back then, and things had cost less, and everyone was more hopeful. Nobody thought the world was going to end in nuclear holocaust, the way they did today. Everybody thought the United States would triumph over disaster. These days children lived in fear of the bomb. Even Ian talked about it sometimes. He spoke about it with genuine interest.

One night Ian came into the living room where David was reading, and said, "Dad, what do you think our chances are of getting killed by the Russians?"

David looked up, startled. "It's not that simple," he said. "I don't think it will come to that. But I can't give you percentages."

Ian *needed* percentages; he needed the whole thing turned into figures, in order to understand. He felt safest among lines of numbers; his pocket calculator was like a masturbation device, David sometimes thought. Ian ran his fingers across it and it calmed him down as nothing else could.

At night David came in to make sure that Ian had enough blankets. Ian was sitting up in bed in the dark, playing with his calculator. The new mobile hung right above the bed. It danced slightly on an invisible current.

"You sleepy?" David asked from the door.

"Sort of," said Ian. "I'm just thinking about things."

David took this as a cue to come in. He walked into the room and sat down at the foot of the bed. "Like what?" he asked.

"Todd," said Ian, and his voice had a melancholy ring. This was what the loss of a best friend had done to him.

Men had a secret code among themselves; it was felt in quiet moments of sharing something: communing at a lakefront perhaps, or on a long drive cross-country. David had never had too many friends, but he was always very close with the ones he did have. In medical school he had been intimate with Hal Thomas. They worked so hard together, staying all night in the emergency room, and then later they would go home, back to their squalid student apartments on Dwight Street. They drove together through New Haven as the city was just waking up. Sometimes they stopped for coffee and doughnuts at a roadside diner. Most of the patrons were truckers — ruddy men bursting out of flannel shirts. Big, silent men with unmoving faces. David and Hal sat among these men, and they felt a part of them. They were all guys who had to be up at this same ungodly hour, whether it was to drive a meat truck to Indiana or just to be a medical student at Yale. They all thought about their lovely sleeping wives or girlfriends. David and Hal sat at the counter and hunched over their coffee cups. They didn't even have to speak in order to understand.

Now Hal was a neurologist in Los Angeles, but he and David

still sent Christmas cards to each other. They loved each other in a way that David knew could never be expressed. He would never want to, actually. It was the kind of thing that, if said, would be ruined. You could spend just a few hours with a man, traipsing around a city in the early, industrial light of morning, and you would feel it. You would both be breathing in the same air, and also taking in the same impressions of the day: how the sky had looked, and the row of factories on the side of the highway. You never had to talk about it; that was the thing about these friendships. You didn't have to be like women, reporting everything.

Once when David was walking past the bedroom, he heard Vanessa talking to her best friend, Ilene. She was saying something about orgasms. He couldn't believe it. It was something specifically involving her sex life with David, not just some statistic. Something like: "Well, first *I* had an orgasm, which is unusual, because David can come in like two seconds." Then she laughed and said, "Sometimes he's like a microwave, if you know what I mean."

David walked around hurt for days, wanting to say to her, "Tell me what you meant by that comment about the microwave," but of course he couldn't, because then she would know he had been listening. But they all listened to each other; you had to in such close quarters.

In this apartment he and Vanessa and Unnamed Baby would be a perfect triumvirate. Then there was Ian, who made four. What was the word — quadumvirate? Now David sat at the foot of Ian's bed, just looking at his son.

"Do you think you'll try calling Todd?" he asked.

Ian shook his head. "No way," he said.

"You guys had a lot of fun together," said David. "But it's his loss, you know, kiddo. I think you're a wonderful friend to have."

Ian rolled over on his side, facing David. "We used to do things all the time," he said. "I showed him math problems, and he showed me drawing technique, not that I'm any good. But he taught me things like shading. I don't understand why he won't be my friend anymore. What's Ma got anything to do with it?"

"I think you'd better ask Todd," said David.

"I can't," said Ian. "Whenever I see him, he just turns around. I stopped him on the corner of Linda Place the other day, and he called me by my last name. 'Giovanni,' he said, 'just leave me alone.' And he has a new best friend, Richard Springer. I think he's told Richard about Ma. Richard gives me mean looks, and I've never done anything to him in my life!"

"Well," David said helplessly, "when you see Todd next, maybe you'd better call *him* by his last name. You'd better call him Berger. You've got to get angry now."

"That would be funny," said Ian. "Calling him Berger. Like hamburger. I could just say to him, 'Hey there, hamburger.' He would be really surprised." Ian chuckled to himself; David was glad to see the small comfort that children took in such things.

"I know you're unhappy," said David, "but you'll make other friends. You two have spent so much time together that I'll bet you didn't have time for anyone else. You probably never got a chance to met some of the kids in your class. Aren't there any you like? What about Kevin Marder?"

David had studied Ian's class roster once. He had wanted to know all the names, to ask Ian about each one. Ian had gone down the list telling David who was good in math, who was a diabetic, who was picked last in gym class. Kevin Marder was one of the other math whizzes. David liked the idea of a new math friend for Ian — someone gentle and untroubled. Todd was a boy with too many problems.

If Ian lived in the city, he could go to school with little artsy kids from interesting families. Kids whose parents were both soloists with the New York Philharmonic. David imagined picking Ian up at school on an occasional afternoon, waiting on the front steps with other fathers and mothers. Children would come streaming out of the doors, carrying finger paintings and notebooks that contained the beginnings of novels.

"What do you think it would be like to live here in the city?" David asked lightly. "And go to school here and everything."

Ian looked at him. "I don't know," he said. "I used to do it, but I don't remember. I guess it would be okay."

"Vanessa and I have been talking about it a lot," said David. "Thinking about having you come and live with us during the school year full-time, starting in the fall. You could visit your ma and Jane on weekends. You wouldn't have to see Todd. Does that sound like something that would interest you?"

Ian looked alarmed. "When do I have to decide?" he said.

"Oh, it's just an idea," David said. "You have plenty of time to think about it. I just wanted to throw it out at you, see what you thought."

Ian relaxed. "It might be fun," he said. "I saw an afterschool special once, called 'City Boy, Country Boy,' about two friends who change places. The kid in the city gets lost on the subway at first."

"Well, you're already an old hand at city life," said David, "because you've been coming here on weekends. You know your way around pretty well. It wouldn't be very scary for you."

Ian yawned and looked about to drop off; David didn't want to push. He straightened the covers around Ian, even though he knew they would be kicked off in the middle of the night. He leaned over the bed and kissed Ian's forehead, as he did every night Ian stayed there.

"Goodnight, kiddo," he said in a whisper, encouraging sleep. As he stood up, he knocked into the mobile, and all the sailboats and pelicans and horses were shaken into a small fury and had to be untangled.

CHAPTER TWENTY-THREE

In every photograph of Bernadette Beshar, she was wearing a T-shirt with a picture of Snoopy on it. Whenever Ian saw a girl with a T-shirt like that, he became excited. *I've found her!* he would think, and he would approach the girl and see that she looked nothing like Bernadette Beshar. Girls wore Snoopy shirts everywhere you went. At the Walt Whitman Mall, there were lots of them. Ian would go there with his mother and Jane, and they would stroll around among the other shoppers. He thought a lot about Bernadette Beshar these days, ever since he had been going to his mother's classes.

The first time he went, it was on a night when he was in his room doing a few math problems for extra credit. He got bored after a while, and went out into the living room, where his mother was speaking to a group of people. He knew a couple of the kids from school, and they were all sitting with their parents. Ian went and sat in a corner of the room, behind a plant.

His mother was saying, "This could happen to our children,

and we want to do whatever we can to prevent it. I'm going to show a movie now, which dramatizes the problem pretty effectively."

Then Jane shut off the lights, and Ian's mother pulled up the white screen that the school had lent her. Ian watched the movie attentively. The last shot was of a pair of red sneakers floating down a stream. That meant that the girl was dead, or else it meant that she was walking around in the woods forever, barefoot.

When the meeting was over and everyone had gone home, Ian helped clean up. His mother seemed very happy that he had sat in on the meeting. "It made me feel good to have you here," she said. "Next week I'd love to introduce you to everyone, to tell them you're my son."

Ian stacked the used Dixie cups and threw them in the garbage in the kitchen. He picked Lizzie up by the scruff of her neck, and slung her over his shoulder. Then he went back into the living room, where his mother and Jane were just finishing up. His mother was about to rewind the film.

"Can we see it backwards?" Ian asked. It was something that his teacher had allowed them to do in school once, and it had been hilarious. Everybody had to get a signed permission slip, and they had seen a movie about how life begins. At the end of the movie, when the teacher let them see it backwards, they watched as the red, screaming baby got sucked right back in. Ian had laughed along with everyone else.

Now his mother looked doubtful, but then she said, "Oh, what the hell. It won't break the film or anything." So she showed the movie backwards, and the sneakers went floating the other way, and everyone walked backwards, and finally the little girl was reunited with her parents.

When it was over, his mother and Jane just sat there looking at the screen and letting the projector cool down. "That's it," Jane said softly. "Ian, do you want to get ready for bed?"

Maybe, he thought, Bernadette Beshar would be reunited with

her parents too. Sometimes Ian thought about Bernadette, and he imagined her throwing pebbles at his bedroom window at night. He would wake up and look outside, and there she would be, down below, wearing her Snoopy shirt, and smiling at him just like in the photograph. "Let's go play," she would say. "I'm not really missing. I just ran away to have some fun for a while." So then he would creep downstairs and they would watch a little television, or maybe they would go outside and take an illegal swim in the Frankels' pool, where Ian had never been. Finally they would be tired, and they would sleep together under the trees. In the early morning, he would convince Bernadette to go back home because her parents missed her very much.

In all the newspaper stories, Bernadette's mother had said that she wasn't going to change her daughter's room around, that she was going to leave it exactly as it was, because she hoped that Bernadette would be home soon. But it had already been seven months, and there were still no clues.

Ian liked the fact that his own room never changed, except when he wanted it to. His mother and Jane just left things alone, unlike some mothers, who went into their kids' rooms to vacuum and ruined elaborate science experiments and Lego fortresses.

In the city, his bedroom was growing more crowded every time he went there. Just last weekend he found a big blue crib in the middle of the room, and there was barely any space to walk.

"Sorry about that," said his father. "I wanted to set it up to see how it looked, and now I have to figure out how to dismantle it. It's more complicated than I thought."

Ian had to squeeze past it to get to his dresser. He stood and looked into the empty crib. In a few months there would be a baby lying there, curling its fat hands around the slats. A baby looking right back at him; they could have staring contests. When there was a baby around, it was all that people talked about. He knew that the baby would take over.

Ian got undressed in the cramped room. He looked past the

273

crib and out the window. It was snowing hard, and a few people were hurrying along the street.

He thought about what it would be like to live in the city full-time. It didn't really make a difference whether you lived in the city or the suburbs; the only thing that really mattered was what it was like inside the place you lived. At Todd's house, for instance, everything was relentlessly depressing.

Whenever he thought about Todd, Ian felt terrible. He used to cry about it, but only when he was alone in bed at night. He would think about Todd and his drawings, and the way Todd used to concentrate so hard, squinting at a piece of paper. He and Todd always had a good time together. He thought about what his father had said, about having Ian come live in the city in the fall. It was the latest topic of conversation here and in Plainview.

One afternoon his mother and Jane drove Ian into the city, and they stayed for a while in the apartment, discussing the situation. Ian hung around outside the living room, unsure of what to do with himself.

"We don't want to turn this into a custody case," he heard his mother say.

"Neither do we," said Vanessa. "I think we all want what's best. We all have Ian in mind."

"Wait," said his father. "Let's take this from the top, okay?"

Ian had heard enough. He went into his room and squeezed past the crib, which his father still hadn't bothered to dismantle. He turned on the tiny portable TV, and he watched "The Brady Bunch." He knew that Todd would probably be watching it too. He thought about how he and Todd used to lie in front of the large-screen color TV in Todd's basement. They would turn the volume up very loud and watch for hours. No one would ever disturb them.

Now Ian was spending time with Kevin Marder. The first time Kevin came over after school, Ian's mother had said, "What a lovely boy. So poised."

Ian had told Kevin right away about his mother and Jane being lesbians. Actually, he had used the word "gay," which his mother said was just as good. He had said it lightly, that first afternoon, wanting to get it over with. He and Kevin were sitting on the floor of Ian's room, working on problems, and Ian said, "My mother and Jane are gay, you know."

Kevin looked at him and said, "Really?" Ian nodded. "I saw an episode of a TV show about that once," Kevin said. "I forgot which show it was. This girl says she's gay, right? At first her parents get upset, but then they get used to it." He paused. "How did she have *you*?" he asked.

Ian said, "She used to be married to my father. Every weekend I go stay with him in New York."

"Oh," said Kevin. "Is he gay too?"

This made Ian want to laugh. He thought about his father lying in bed with another father — both of them wearing big suits and ties and saying, "I love you" in deep voices. The only other father he could think of was Mr. Berger. He thought of the two of them kissing, and the picture was pretty funny.

"No," Ian said. "He's married to a woman."

"I have a cousin who's gay," said Kevin. "He's my first cousin Neil, and he's seventeen. He lives in Merrick, and he comes to dinner once in a while. My parents are really nice to him. Once he came with his boyfriend."

Ian laughed nervously. "Is he fruity?" he asked.

"No," said Kevin. "Does your mother have a mustache?"

This made Ian laugh again, and soon he and Kevin were laughing hysterically. Finally Ian's mother came into the doorway and said, "What's so funny, boys? I figured this had to be something really good." This only made them laugh harder, and his mother finally just shook her head and left the room.

But Ian still kept thinking about Todd. Once he dialed Todd's number, and Dean answered. Ian held the receiver in his hand for a moment, and then hung up. His heart was pounding. He didn't know what he had hoped for; did he wish that Todd had answered? Todd would just have said, "Giovanni, I know it's you. Leave me alone already."

They still saw each other in school every day, but school was neutral territory. It was only after school, in different places, that Ian was afraid of seeing Todd. There was one awful time when they ran into each other at the orthodontist's office. Ian and his mother were sitting and waiting when suddenly Todd walked in with his father. Nobody said a word. Todd and his father were frozen for a second in the middle of the waiting room. Finally Mr. Berger sat down in a chair across the room, and Todd went up to the receptionist's window and knocked on the glass. The woman behind it slid it open. "Hi, Todd," she said. "We're running a little late. Just have a seat."

There was an agonizing twenty minutes during which nobody said a word. They all sat there with magazines in front of their faces. "Tie a Yellow Ribbon 'Round the Old Oak Tree" was being piped in through the ceiling. Ian was reading an article in *Reader's Digest* about a boy who came back from a fifty-six-day coma. Everybody in the article said it was a miracle. Ian's father had once said that there was no such thing as a miracle.

"It's a word that people use a little too loosely for my taste," his father had said. "When a patient of mine gets well, I think it always has more to do with modern medicine and correct diagnosis than anything else."

But everybody said it would be a miracle if Bernadette Beshar were still alive. And now, Ian thought, it would be a miracle if he and Todd were ever friends again. He sneaked a glance over the top of his magazine and saw that Todd looked deeply involved in whatever he was reading. Finally the receptionist called Ian in, and he was happy to go.

At home that night Ian tried to eat dinner with his new retainer in. It was difficult, and finally he just took it out and placed it on a napkin, which he had been specifically told not to do.

"Make sure you don't accidentally throw that out," Jane warned.

There was something slightly disgusting about the retainer sitting there, pink and wet. He avoided looking at it as he ate his dinner.

During dessert, his mother put her spoon down and said, "I think we should all talk."

Ian looked at her. "Yeah?" he said.

"You know," said his mother, "we've all been discussing what you should do next year, sweetie. I know that you've heard bits and pieces of different conversations, and that your father has talked to you some." She paused. "Jane and I have wanted to find a good moment to bring it up with you," she said, "because it involves you most of all."

She looked very distressed as she spoke, as though she might even cry, and he hated that more than anything else.

"What are your feelings about it?" Jane asked.

Ian shrugged. "I don't know," he said. "How am I supposed to know what to do?" He looked back and forth at his mother and Jane, but neither of them said anything. "What do *you* think I should do?" he finally asked.

His mother took a long time to answer. "Honey," she said, "I know you're only eleven, and in a lot of ways that's very young, but in another way, it's *your* life, and you've got to decide where you want to live it. Where you're happiest. I wouldn't have given this too much thought if it hadn't been for how depressed you've been lately. The whole thing with Todd. I know this isn't the most tolerant place on earth. As you get older, people are going to ask even more questions. They're going to wonder about being raised by two women, and they're going to say things you may not like. There's nothing either Jane or I can do about that. We can't protect you from it."

She finished talking, and then she really began to cry. Jane handed her a clean napkin to use as a tissue.

"I'm sorry, Ian," his mother said. "I don't mean to scare you. But the idea of not having you live with us just makes me un-happy. I can't even imagine it."

Jane interrupted her then. "When you're away at your father's for the weekend," she said, "we get very lonely. We sort of mope around the house. I can't understand why Elaine Frankel sends her kids off for the summer. When you were out at the beach last July, you should have seen us."

"But it's your choice," said his mother. "We'll live with whatever you decide to do. We just want you to be happy."

This was what all parents said, Ian knew. It was what mothers and fathers said on television. He thought about all the families he had ever known: his own, and Todd's, and the family of that girl in the movie. The Beshars. All the television families, like the Bradys, with their six symmetrical kids and Alice the maid. Everyone worked their problems out, managed to live together. He didn't know anyone with the same situation as his. But Kevin hadn't freaked out when Ian told him about his mother and Jane. Kevin had thought it was slightly strange, but still interesting. Todd was the only one who couldn't handle it. Todd was definitely fucked up.

When they finished dessert that night and his mother had stopped crying, Ian went into his room and closed the door behind him. He had been excused from helping with the dishes. Even with the door closed he could hear the sound of the kitchen faucet, and then the chugging of the dishwasher. Jane put a blues record on. Ian listened to the faint, sad music. He stood in the middle of his room and looked around him. There were all of Todd's drawings, still tacked to the walls. Some of them had curled with age. There was the drawing of Neil Armstrong landing on the moon, and a drawing of a horse, and one of a bright orange mushroom cloud. There was a drawing of Ian at his desk, playing with his calculator. There were at least fifteen drawings tacked up all over the room. Ian stood there and thought about Todd, and he went up to the picture of Neil Armstrong and pulled it off the wall. It ripped right out, and the tack stayed in. He went around to every single drawing, ripping them out, really hard. Some of the tacks came out with the drawings and fell with a little *ping* to the floor, but most of them stayed in, and when Ian was through, he was left with four white walls studded with thumbtacks.

Ian held all of Todd's drawings in his hands, and then he ripped them in half, into two even pieces. He stood there, looking at what he had done, astonished. He went and put on his ski parka, and told his mother and Jane that he was going for a walk.

"But it's too cold," said Jane. "And it's late. Where are you going, Ian?"

"Out," he said. "I'll be right back." They didn't try to stop him. They just stood in the kitchen holding dishtowels and looking worried as he left the house.

It was freezing outside, and really dark now. Ian quickly walked around the corner to Linda Place. A woman was standing on the street, walking a dog. Everyone else was inside; Ian could see smoke rising from several different chimneys along the block. The lights in Todd's house were on, and the car was parked in the driveway. Ian stood on the sidewalk out front for a minute, the drawings in his hands. In a quiet voice he said, "Fuck you, Berger," the way his father had wanted him to.

His father still asked occasional questions about Todd, but lately he was preoccupied with Vanessa. At the apartment, all he and Vanessa did were breathing exercises. In and out, in and out, they breathed together, partners in everything. Once they wanted Ian to lie down on the rug and do the exercises with them, but he was embarrassed and said no.

He still thought about Todd all the time, and even had dreams about him, but the situation was hopeless. Todd was a jerk, but it was his problem. There were other things to think about. Next year was the seventh-grade math fair, and Ian was planning on doing a project with Kevin. They were both getting interested in probability theory.

If Ian lived with his father and Vanessa, he would have to

sleep in the tiny bedroom, and it would smell of milk, and worse. All night the baby would cry. This baby was what his father and Vanessa wanted more than anything in the world; he had heard Vanessa say that once. Now they would get their wish. Tomorrow Ian would tell them that he had decided to keep living with his mother and Jane, and he wondered if they would be surprised.

Now he walked up to the front porch of Todd's house. Even though the door was closed, Ian could almost smell TV dinners coming from inside, just the slightest edge of a metallic food smell. He thought about ringing the bell, but then decided not to. He dropped the ripped drawings onto the porch, and the pieces scattered like leaves.

CHAPTER TWENTY-FOUR

H e was going to stay. Laura had spent the past few weeks in a quiet panic, envisioning Ian's empty room, the books lined up on the shelves, the cat asleep on the unused bed. She imagined waking up and eating breakfast alone with Jane every day. No homework to look at, no report cards to sign. Mothers eventually had to give up their children, but by that time they were usually ready. When children were eighteen and college-bound, they barely looked like children anymore; they were tall and strapping, with deep, adult voices and licenses to drink, and drive, and even marry, if they wanted.

But for now, the thought of relinquishing her eleven-year-old son was unbearable. She still liked to help him part his hair, to stand over him and draw a comb along his scalp as he tilted his head down obediently. She always had to refrain from kissing his head.

David was openly disappointed by Ian's choice. "Maybe someday he'll want to spend a year here," David said. "When the baby is older and we have things settled. I know I haven't been the best father lately." His voice sounded very wistful to her.

Ian came home each Sunday with stories of how David and Vanessa had taken him shopping at baby stores, or brought him along to a Lamaze class. Children were always put aside when a new baby was about to be born; it was an inevitable deposition, a real betrayal. Perhaps Ian had felt betrayed when Laura first fell in love with Jane. Had he felt neglected then, and just not shown it? And had he also felt pushed aside when David married Vanessa? Laura didn't know, and now she realized that she had never asked.

One Saturday morning, Laura woke up before Jane, and she crept from the room to heat up some coffee. As she poured it from the pot, she saw that Ian had accidentally left his bite plate at home that weekend; it was there in a saucer on the counter. She picked it up and held it in the palm of her hand. Ian's *retainer*. How poignant the word seemed now; she wanted so much to retain him, to keep him close. He had left a small piece of himself behind.

It wasn't just his bite plate, it was everything. Everywhere she looked in the house, Ian was in evidence. On the refrigerator were two math tests that he had gotten 100%'s on, and his teacher had affixed gold stars to the top. His books were everywhere, those biographies that he read like an addict. And even the smell of him was there, that boy-smell of dirt and pencil shavings, and something excessively sweet, like sugar burning. This wasn't evident in any one particular room of the house, but it was deeply coded into her perception of him.

That was a function of the passage of time, she supposed: the locking-in of perceptions so they became immutable. She felt that way with Jane as well. The night before, she and Jane found themselves alone in the house, and they closed the blinds in the living room in case Elaine Frankel was out salting the icy sidewalk. Laura leaned forward, kissed Jane's neck, the rim of her collarbone, and Jane dropped her head back. It happened every time like clockwork. Laura wondered about that motion, the head dropping back—was it done for effect? Did Jane drop her head back because she knew it looked dramatic? Or was it something else—looking upward for some quick rush of stars, some meteoric pour while she was being touched, covered, brought to life? There was Jane with her head tipped back, watching the ceiling. Her eyes had taken on a blankness, the eyes of a blind woman. How often blind people appeared to be smiling, Laura thought. Jane had that same look, that cloudy-eyed half-smile. It was a smile of someone temporarily released from thoughts. A baby smiles at the simplest things: a penny, a color. Laura used to hold a prism in front of Ian when he was an infant, and he would clap his hands as the beam jumped to the ceiling, was refracted there. Jane smiled when Laura kissed her collarbone, and Laura thought to herself: *Why is she smiling? What is going on here that codes into happiness?*

It was a pattern that had been formed so long ago, when they first fell in love. It was unbreakable. When patterns were broken against people's will, Laura thought, how terrible that must be. To walk around still with the coding for sensation, and still feel it all, even in the absence of the love object. Bernadette Beshar's parents still kept their little girl's room neat, still kept the stuffed animals lined up on her bed, the bottle of Flintstones vitamins in the kitchen cabinet. There were signs everywhere, little indicators of presence or absence.

She remembered this even back to her marriage, and how when David moved out there were still small traces of him in the apartment. The day he left, he unscrewed the tie rack from the inside of the closet door, but three tiny holes remained where the screws had been. Every time Laura opened that door for the next five years, she would think of David, imagine him holding a paisley tie against his shirt, saying, "Laura, does this match?"

When Jane woke up, Laura brought in some coffee, and they drank it in bed. The telephone rang as they were drinking and

Laura answered it. The voice on the line was unfamiliar; it was a man, asking tentatively if Jane Bloom lived there. He sounded apologetic. "Yes," said Laura. "Who's calling, please?"

There was a long pause, and then the man said, "This is her brother."

Her brother. Every story that Laura had ever heard now ran through her; she thought of Sam on the beach in Florida, Sam in his hotel room playing with his ant farm. Sam and Jane leaning their heads back and eating powdered candy from Pixie Straws. She saw Sam, yet in every image he was still a child. He was the brother from Jane's childhood, stunted there forever.

"Just a minute," Laura said. She held the phone muffled against her bathrobe, and she said to Jane, *"It's your brother."*

Jane quickly looked up. She put her coffee cup down on the night table, rattling it in its saucer. "You're kidding," she said. She gestured in the air. "What should I do?" she whispered. Laura shrugged. Finally Jane leaned across the bed and took the phone.

"Hello?" she said suspiciously. In a moment her voice was more normal. "Yes, hi," she said. "Well, *obviously* I'm surprised." She talked stiffly for about five minutes, and finally she began making plans to see him.

When Jane hung up, she just sat in bed for a minute, shaking her head back and forth. "God," she said. "It really was him."

Sam was in New York for one week. He had never been there before, and had decided to take a package tour of the city, and then return to Miami and the Mermaid Hotel, where he still lived. He had gotten Jane's telephone number from her friend Danielle. He had to coax it out of her, he said.

"He's very anxious to see me," said Jane, lying down on her back. She closed her eyes, stretched out her arms. "I said I would," she said. "Tomorrow. Don't ask me why. I just agreed to meet him. He sounded desperate. What could I do?" She paused, still lying there with her eyes closed. "Would you come?" she asked.

Laura didn't know what to say. "Do you think it would help?" she asked.

"I'm not sure," Jane said. "I'm not even sure why I'm going. We have to be in the city anyway, to get Ian."

"What will you say to him?" Laura asked.

"I don't know," Jane said. "I guess I'll tell him off," she said. "Say something like: 'Where the hell were you when I got disowned? Still sitting on the beach all day?' He was always so *quiet* when we were kids; it's no surprise that he didn't stick up for me, but *still*. He was my brother. I just feel like sticking it in his face, showing him my real family, letting him have a look at a real life. Maybe it would make him wake up; I don't know."

Laura thought about Sam and wondered if he might have done something once, made some heroic gesture. Couldn't he have told his parents that if they stopped having anything to do with Jane then they would lose him as well? The loss of two children would be too great, and the parents would have begged forgiveness, would have invited Jane to come down to Miami to talk it all out with them. Eventually she might have brought Laura down with her. They would sleep in the exact room that Jane had grown up in. Laura would lie in Jane's arms, pinned under taut hotel sheets. The dark room would no longer be sterile, or sad. They would make love in it, and later bathe together in the special whirlpool bath, drying themselves off on thin, stubbly hotel towels, then standing under the infrared light together, glowing like coals.

There had been times, over the years, when Jane would need to be alone, and she would go for a long run through the neighborhood, or escape to her toolshed to work for a few hours. Laura could always hear music coming from her transistor radio, and the drone of a saw, and she knew that Jane didn't want to be interrupted. Maybe Jane was back in some labyrinth of childhood sadness at those times; maybe she was remembering what had happened, and what her mother had said on the telephone, and was still grieving. She would never tell.

285

On Sunday morning they rode into the city. Jane drove, and Laura sat as close to her as she could get while still wearing a safety belt. The traffic was light. They drove along Thirty-fourth Street a few times, and finally found a spot near Madison Square Garden. Jane was such a good parallel parker; she eased neatly into the space. They buttoned up their heavy coats and got out of the car.

Jane looked anxious, and Laura held her hand as they walked to the corner. It was very windy, and the street was almost empty; pieces of garbage cartwheeled along the sidewalk. As they turned the corner, Jane said, "There he is," and she didn't have to point. Sam was the only person leaning against the front window of the coffeeshop. His hair was blond, like his sister's. He was of medium build; in fact, everything about him looked medium. He was a man on a street, nothing more, and yet Jane had some real connection to him, a whole shared history with him. He saw Jane from a few yards away, and shyly lifted up a hand in salute.

Laura stood slightly back, watching as Sam and Jane approached each other uneasily. Sam was wearing a heavy, dark coat. There was a big camera slung around his neck; it looked oddly out of season. Finally he reached out his hand, and he grasped Jane's wrist. It was something like a handshake, something like an embrace. He held her whole arm, as though escorting her onto a dance floor.

She introduced him to Laura then, and Laura got a close look at him in that moment. He was a plain man, she saw, middle-aged at thirty, with baby skin and Jane's pale blue eyes. His face was soft and pink, with the kind of bland neutrality that Laura had seen years before among the Amanas. Sister and brother shared basic physical traits — the same kind of skin, and eyes, and hair — but it seemed as though those elements were shaped over entirely different matter. Sam looked malleable; his features seemed recently formed, and still in the cooling stage, not yet hard.

286

"Well," said Jane, "let's go in here. I'm freezing to death."

They ducked into the steamy coffeeshop. None of the tables had been cleared, so they sat down at a cluttered table in a booth, Jane and Laura on one side, facing Sam. A waitress came over and removed the dishes, then wiped a sponge across the surface. The smell of ammonia hit them all at once, and they drew back in unison. Then the waitress handed out three shiny red menus and left them alone.

They studied the menus for as long as seemed reasonable, and finally Sam closed his and said, "I guess you're surprised to see me."

"Yes," said Jane. "To say the least."

"Well, I was coming through New York anyway," he said, "so I tracked you down. I had to tell Danielle that it was an emergency before she would give me your number. I mean, you're my sister and all — why shouldn't I be able to call you?"

Jane put her menu down. "Look," she said, "I thought I was going to give you a hard time today, Sam. I had it all worked out in my head. But now I just don't feel like it. It doesn't seem worth it."

"But you're angry?" he asked.

"I try not to think about it," said Jane. "But when I do, I tend to feel angry, or else depressed. But it's ancient history already. I feel a little ridiculous even discussing it."

Sam looked down, embarrassed. "There was nothing I could have done," he said. "I was caught in the middle with you and Mom and Dad. I didn't want to get all involved. I didn't think they acted great, but it was what they felt, right? What could I have done?"

Laura knew that he wanted to disappear, to be whisked back to Florida and away from all this. His life there was small and unsurprising. He was bookkeeper for the Mermaid. Once in a while he went to hotel management conventions in Orlando or Sarasota. She imagined him on his tour bus in New York, peering through the green glass at this alien city.

"Do you want me to leave?" Laura asked. "Do you two want to be alone? I could go to Macy's or something."

"No," said Jane. "Stay." She put her hand over Laura's. The waitress returned to the table, and they ordered. When she was gone, Jane said, "So tell me things, Sam. Tell me about your life."

Sam cleared his throat. "Well," he said, "things aren't so great. I thought of writing you. Dad had triple-bypass surgery last month, and he's not doing that well. He's sixty-nine, after all. I thought you'd want to be told," he said. "Maybe you could call him or something."

Jane shook her head. "No," she said. "I don't think so."

"Well, it's your choice," said Sam. "They're too embarrassed to call you at this point; I just thought you might like to get in touch with them. They wouldn't give you a hard time or anything."

"I know that," said Jane. "But it's ancient history, Sam, I told you."

"Okay," he said. "I just thought I'd mention it."

Jane nodded, and Laura looked back and forth between brother and sister. Their orders came then, and they ate in silence. Finally Jane said, "How's the hotel doing?"

Sam looked up, relieved. He buttered his toast, ate it quickly, then wiped his mouth. "Well," he said, "we've been losing money, but that's nothing new. Dad's still thinking about selling the place, which I think would be a good idea. He just can't compete with some of these other places — they have headliner acts down the strip: Alan King, Dionne Warwick. And frankly, Mom and Dad just don't have the energy to run a hotel anymore; I don't even mean physical energy. They're kind of distracted by everything. It happens." He paused. "I think about leaving Miami," he said, "but I'm not like you, Jane. I can't just pick up and leave. And it's really not so bad. I have friends. I date."

His voice trailed off. There were a few awkward minutes, and finally the meal was through and they all stood up to leave.

When they got back outside, Sam said that he wanted to go to the top of the Empire State Building. His tour group had gone there yesterday morning, but he had accidentally slept through his clock alarm in the hotel room.

"We'll walk you there," said Jane, and the three of them walked along the sidewalk, Jane in the middle. When they arrived at the Empire State Building, Sam said, "I don't suppose you have any interest in coming up? I'll pay," he added.

Laura realized that she had never been. "Want to?" she asked Jane, and Jane shrugged, and they went up.

Sam paid the fee, and they rode the elevator with a Chinese family. Sam stood with his feet slightly apart, like a man staking out a place for himself. Laura looked down at his shoes and felt so sorry for him in that moment. His shoes were highly polished, with big, thick buckles. She imagined him sitting in a shoestore in Miami, trying to find a good pair of "walking shoes" that would be suitable for New York pavement.

When the ride ended, they went out onto the deck and stood with the few other tourists who had braved the cold. A lone woman in fur stood on tiptoe, peering through a viewer, putting in coins and turning it slowly on its axis. Laura wondered idly if the wind was strong enough to blow them all off the roof. But Jane and Sam were holding on to the guardrail with their gloved hands. They all looked down over the edge at the dotted line of cars. It was so cold today that most people were indoors, probably sitting in front of fireplaces, or television sets. Laura still liked to think about people's lives in panoramic terms.

She thought about herself this way, too — imagined peering through a viewer into the window of her own house and watching the domestic scene inside, making assumptions about it. Two women and a young boy are sitting at a kitchen table eating dinner. Everyone is animated. The boy is trying to explain a math problem, but the women are confused, and the boy grows exasperated. His hands fly up, and he describes geometric circles in the air. A cat jumps onto the table, is immediately brushed off. After dinner, dishes are washed, nighttime rituals begun. Anyone peering through the viewer would agree: years and years have gone into this life.

Now Jane was posing for a photograph, standing at the rail with her hair whipping up, and Sam took an especially long time setting the focus on his camera. Finally he was satisfied, and the print wheezed out, turned from blank to a color image of Jane standing at the rail, holding on.

"We've got to get Ian, Jane," Laura said, looking at her watch. "I told David we'd be there by three."

They were silent during the ride down. The elevator was like a shrine. "Can you find your way back to your hotel?" Jane asked her brother when the doors opened.

"It's just around the block," he said. "I can find it. I wanted to go see Pennsylvania Station first. I hear it's gigantic."

So they said goodbye to him at the corner, and he held Jane in a loose embrace, his arms caging her lightly. When he left, they watched as he walked away, his hands pushed deep into his pockets.

"Are you okay?" Laura asked.

"Yeah," Jane said.

"You sure?"

"Absolutely," said Jane. But she looked as though she might cry, and they stood on the street and Laura kissed Jane's hands, her face, her eyes. They were standing very close, but their bulky down coats kept them slightly apart, made a buffer between them.

When they got back to the car, this time Laura drove. Jane played with the radio dial. She couldn't find anything decent, so she snapped it off and leaned back in her bucket seat. Finally she said, "I'm glad I saw him. Really. It's a relief."

"In what way?" Laura asked. They were stopped at a traffic light on Seventh Avenue.

"Because now I really know," said Jane. "I mean, I always thought it was all resolved for me, all this family drama. But then I see Sam again, and I just feel *sad*. Not doomed or anything, or orphaned. I can't believe that I don't feel something stronger, but I don't. Just a twinge." She shook her head. "And this whole thing with Ian," she said, "it makes me want to focus on it, and figure it out. I don't want this family to fall apart because of this. I know Ian's going to have a hard time, but I'm so *relieved* that he's going to be with us. I feel like throwing myself into everything. I feel like becoming Ms. PTA with you. Not that we have to stay in the suburbs forever," she said.

The light switched to green, and Laura had to face forward and drive, but she felt moved by this sudden, disjointed eloquence. Jane turned the radio back on, settling now for some terrible Muzak, heavy on the strings.

David and Vanessa's apartment was still draped with Christmas lights, long past their season. "We're feeling festive these days," Vanessa said, "and we couldn't bear to take them down."

Laura stood and looked around the room. Then she did what all those women on the street had always done when she herself was pregnant: she placed her hands lightly across Vanessa's belly, uninvited.

In a moment Ian came into the room. Laura and Jane kissed him hello, and then he sat down on the floor to lace up his sneakers. He seemed to enjoy having all these adults towering over him. David walked in with a tray of tea and cookies. He looked very tired, Laura thought. She remembered that look from the time she was pregnant. He had been so tense, always ready to spring for the door. One hand was always on the telephone, prepared to summon the obstetrician from a dinner party, or from sleep.

"Things are pretty hectic around here," David said. "I already feel the *presence* of this baby. It's so real to me even now. You were the same way, Ian," he said. "I was so excited before you were born. You weighed seven pounds, ten ounces. That's big."

"And you kicked the hell out of me," said Laura, and everyone laughed a little.

Ian slid over to the couch and leaned back in the space between Laura and Jane. "Sleepy, sweetie?" Laura asked, and he nodded. She put her hands flat against his shoulders. "We ought to be heading out soon," she said. "There's school tomorrow, and he looks exhausted."

Vanessa nodded. "He did a lot of walking," she said. "We went uptown to look for baby clothes. Ian helped me pick out a few outfits. He has terrific taste."

Suddenly the new clothing was brought in, and Vanessa was taking items out of tissue paper: tiny unisex jumpsuits in terry-cloth, white shoes that were made of butter-soft, crushable leather, a bonnet the color of the sky.

"David's already putting all the poisons on the top shelves," said Vanessa. "Can you believe it? And today he even went to look for those safety plugs for electrical outlets." She laughed. "It will be a long time before we get to that point," she said. "I can't even imagine what giving birth is like."

David put an arm around Vanessa and kissed her cheek. Expectant parents looked so intimate, no matter what they did. You just knew that all they thought about was their baby, and each other. It wasn't unusual for men to grab their pregnant wives and kiss them, or for tears to spring to their eyes for no reason at all.

Laura felt as though she were eavesdropping on something deeply private. She wanted to gather up her own family and leave. There was a long ride ahead, and a pot roast defrosting on the counter at home.

"We've got to be off," Jane said. "But we'll see you next Friday."

They all stood up at once, and David put his arm around Vanessa, who was swaying slightly.

Out on the street, the wind had died down. They had parked

the car on Bank Street, and decided to walk for a little while before heading home.

"Did you have fun this weekend?" Laura asked Ian.

"Yeah," he said, "but I wanted to see Kevin, because we have to get started on our probability project for next year. We have to flip a coin at least a thousand times, Ma."

"That's a lot," she said, stupidly — it was one of those pro-grammed *mother* responses that she tried to stay away from.

She thought about next year, and about Ian starting seventh grade. They would take him shopping right before school started, and buy him spiral notebooks, hard pink erasers. She wanted to fill their house with Ian's things.

As they walked down Horatio Street, Ian began to explain his probability theory to Jane, who listened attentively, or pretended to. Laura walked slightly ahead of them. They passed the open door of a laundromat, and she felt a warm blast of sweet-smelling air, clean air.

On the next street she noticed a poster in the window of a crafts shop, and something made her stop and look. She was startled; it was an advertisement for a show that was opening at the Euphrates Gallery in SoHo.

"Julia Price: A Retrospective," it read. She looked closely at the photograph of Julia's face, so much older than when she had last seen it. *I used to touch that face,* Laura thought, but it was all so many years ago. *I used to look at Julia for hours, centering her in my vision, imagining her to be a single frame, a still.*

She almost pointed it out to Jane, but decided against it. Laura turned away from the window, kept on walking. Behind her she could hear Ian and Jane's voices, but she couldn't make out what they were saying anymore. She was starting to feel tired now, and wanted to head for the car.

It was only later, when they were back at home, that she felt the weight of the day, some alloy of feeling that she couldn't name. Dinner was through and she and Jane were cleaning up for the night, collecting the scattered droppings of family life: tennis shoes, the *TV Guide*, Ian's abandoned coins of chance. They walked around the house, extinguishing lights, and Laura was reminded of the slumber parties of her childhood. She thought of how she used to drift off easily on someone's floor, lying close to another girl.

It was always a perfect sleep, with just their elbows touching. The contact was so light, so nearly weightless, that it was like an imagined touch. Throughout the night there would be intermittent whispers, and even an occasional shriek. Finally the mother would appear as a shadow on the carpeted steps, uttering that one weary, resonant syllable: *Girls*.

It was always outrageously late then, but time meant nothing. Timeless, weightless, formless, even; it was like being an astronaut, she thought. But even so, she wanted some contact. She wanted it, and she didn't know why. It wasn't that she was scared of the dark; that had stopped years before. Laura and another girl lay next to each other in their matching sleeping bags, thin arms colliding.

Now she followed Jane down the hall to bed. As they walked past Ian's room, she could hear him breathe and turn in his sleep. Everything in the house was quiet, rustling. She thought then how wonderful it was that nobody would have to go home, that everyone could spend the night.

ABOUT THE AUTHOR

Meg Wolitzer was born in 1959. She attended Smith College and was graduated from Brown University in 1981. Her first novel, *Sleepwalking*, was published a year later. She lives in New York City.